FILTHY SECRET

THE FIVE POINTS' MOB COLLECTION: SIX

SERENA AKEROYD

DEDICATION

TO YOU, darling reader.
    For loving this universe.
    For letting me write this.
    For accepting me.
    For falling for the O'Donnellys.

FOREWORD

HELLO DARLINGS,

Please keep in mind that throughout this universe, suicide, graphic scenes of violence, child abuse, parental grief, miscarriage/non-viable pregnancy, sex trafficking, and abortion/therapeutic termination are ongoing themes.

I'm fortunate because I can write this book as this universe is complex and beloved.

This is not your standard romance novel, though you will get your happily-ever-after.

This is about YOUR love affair with all things O'Donnelly. Finn and Aoife's secrets are the main crux of the novel; however, it is centered around FAMILY secrets too. Expect to see all your beloved faves and to experience the gamut of emotions.

It is **INTEGRAL** to read *FILTHY SECRET* because in this book, **I CLEAN HOUSE**. It is the only novel in the Five Points' Mob Collection that cannot be enjoyed as a standalone.

Remember:

Aoife = Ee-fah

Eoghan = O-wen

Aela = Eh-la

Now, grab tissues, a wine bottle, and chocolate, and I will see you on the other side.

Much love,
Serena
xoxo

PS.

The second FILTHY SECRET hits 200 reviews, I'll be dropping a bonus scene in my Diva reader group!

You can join here to read it when it happens: www.facebook.com/groups/SerenaAkeroydsDivas

There's also a release week giveaway going on here: https://kingsumo.com/g/teo2w4/filthy-secret-release-day-event

Triggers:

- Miscarriage,
- Domestic violence,
- Assisted suicide,
- Gun violence,
- PTSD,
- Torture,
- References to child sexual assault,
- General violence,
- Series character death

PLAYLIST

If you'd like to hear a curated soundtrack, with songs that are featured in the book, as well as songs that inspired it, then here's the link:

https://open.spotify.com/playlist/2DNmXILFJVCzRVbon7moWg

THE CROSSOVER READING ORDER
WITH THE SINNERS & VALENTINIS

FILTHY
FILTHY SINNER
NYX
LINK
FILTHY RICH
SIN
STEEL
FILTHY DARK
CRUZ
MAVERICK
FILTHY SEX
HAWK
FILTHY HOT
STORM
THE DON
THE LADY
FILTHY SECRET
REX
RACHEL
FILTHY KING
FILTHY DISCIPLE
THE CONSIGLIERE

<u>THE ORACLE</u>
<u>LODESTAR</u>
<u>SILENCED</u>
<u>END GAME</u>
<u>FILTHY RICHER</u>

PART 1

ONE

PAST

AIDAN JR.

"BLESS ME, Father, for I have sinned. My last confession was two weeks ago."

"That's a long time for you, Aidan," Father Doyle rumbled.

My mouth pinched at the corners, his disapproval getting my back up like nothing else could.

Da made me come here today.

Da.

No one else.

And seeing as I didn't feel like getting my ass kicked, I'd come.

When I peered around the small box where my brother had been raped, I felt my skin start to crawl.

Uncle Paddy had fixed all my problems.

He'd made Father McKenna's corpse disappear.

But that didn't clean my soul.

That didn't help me sit in this fucking box without wanting to wreck it.

That didn't make the aftermath of knowing I was just as capable of violence as my father any better.

"Aidan?" Father Doyle prompted.

I should want to confess my sins.

I should want to share the burden, begin the journey toward forgiveness, but I didn't want to atone.

Murder was a sin, but what that bastard had done was far worse. I felt no guilt, no shame—

"Aidan? It's time to confess, boy."

My nostrils flared at his demand.

That was how McKenna had reeled Conor in—priests had power over us. They were the only people who could make my da tremble at the knees. The police and the IRS didn't do that, just the priests.

"I had dirty thoughts about Kitty Greaves," I lied eventually.

Father Doyle grunted under his breath. "Is that all?"

I murdered one of your brethren and I wish I could do it again.

As he gave me my penance, I clenched my fists, and in God's soapbox, I made a vow.

When my time came, when I sat in the seat of power, and reigned over the Five Points, this bullshit would come to an end.

We'd answer to no one.

Not even God himself.

TWO

AOIFE

PRESENT - CHRISTMAS DAY

"DO you know how much I love you?"

A smile danced on my lips. "I mean, I could guess. But are we talking metric or imperial here? You know I'm a baker, Finn. Be specific."

Before I could tease him much more, he rocked his hips, thrusting harder into me until my eyes fluttered to a close.

No longer was I thinking about inches or centimeters, just that my husband filled me so full that I wasn't sure where he ended and I started.

A groan escaped me as he thrust back inside me, doing this thing with his hips that had my G-spot screeching to life in a wonderfully rude awakening.

My hands dug into his shoulders and I moaned out a promise, "No more teasing, no more teasing."

"Definitely no teasing the father-to-be," he growled in my ear, sucking on my earlobe in a way that tickled rather than sent shivers down my spine.

My moan morphed into a laugh. "What about the mother-to-be? She deserves an orgasm," I retorted, my words broken as he lived up to the task and moved a little harder, a lot faster.

"You deserve something, that's for sure," he rumbled, dropping his mouth now so that it was hovering over my lips.

I fought fire with fire because with a kiss, that was the only place

Finn let me attempt to conquer him. As I explored him, savored him, reveled in him, I felt the second something switched on.

Gone were the teasing strokes, and in their place, I felt his tension start to brew as he tugged on my bottom lip.

"Mine," he ground out.

My pussy clenched around his dick at the declaration, a declaration that always had me squirming and celebrating.

This hard man, this mobster, this brilliant mind, this beautifully scarred soul—he called me his.

I'd never imagined that belonging to someone could feel like this. Had never imagined I'd want to.

Who wanted to be owned by another person?

But if Finn owned me, I owned him.

It was a mutual possession, and that was what made it so perfect—

"Say it," he rumbled, breaking into my thoughts.

"Yours," I breathed.

"Who do you belong to, baby?"

"Y-You." I ran my hands over the length of his spine, rubbing the taut muscles with my fingers before I dug my nails into the firm curves of his ass cheeks.

A hiss escaped him. "You will always be mine, Aoife. You know that, don't you?"

I blinked bleary eyes at him. "I k-know that," I whimpered as my toes curled into his calves, digging into them as much as he was digging into *me*.

"Good." He crooned, "You take me so well, baby. So fucking well. So perfect for me. Mine," he ended, sealing it with a kiss he pressed to my lips, before he speared his tongue into my mouth, telling me silently that the time for words had long since gone.

As he rocked into me, his tongue slid against mine, fucking me there as fast as he fucked my pussy. He reared up slightly, grabbing my legs and repositioning me so they were spread wider apart, absorbing my gargled scream with his kiss as he pounded my G-spot.

Again, and again, and again.

He angled my legs so the front of my thighs were against my chest, and he seemed to sink deeper into me as he joined our mouths once more.

I sobbed into his kiss, broke down into it, then was reborn in it as I came.

I came so damn hard and for so damn long that I was literally crying as the pleasure pummeled me.

Pleasure so fierce, so riotous, that it was painful.

It hurt so good.

So good.

Heart racing, lungs burning, I dragged my mouth from his before I passed out from the lack of oxygen and screamed with the ferocity of my unending orgasm.

It went on for what felt like an eternity.

Ceaseless.

Endless.

The darkness was there... beckoning me, enticing me with its comforting embrace, then he nipped my bottom lip and he brought me back to him.

"No passing out," he chided gruffly, but I heard the relief in his voice.

A relief that was undoubtedly founded in the fact that I *hadn't* passed out—he didn't like it when I did that.

We all had our quirks. Mine was that I didn't like waking up to find my pussy empty. I loved the feeling of him deep inside me because I felt that connection to my soul. It bound us together, made us a force to be reckoned with, and in the months and weeks ahead, I'd need that.

Carrying Jacob hadn't been easy.

Finn knew that too.

I also knew he'd never wanted me to get pregnant in the first place, but he'd let me try because I told him I didn't want Jake to be like him or me—only children.

The next eight months were going to be rocky, but we'd get through them.

Together.

"Love you, baby," he rasped, his mouth caressing mine, not letting me answer him just yet.

The holiday season had been particularly stressful this year, and I could hear the release in his tone and knew that he'd found some peace in our joining.

Dazed and punch drunk, still full of him, I broke our kiss, reached up and nuzzled my nose against his jawline, then mumbled, "Love you too."

He tilted his head down so that he could press a softer kiss to my lips. "Need you, Aoife. Need your love so fucking much."

His words had me blinking back the fog from an orgasm that was like an atomic bomb.

I squeezed him in a hug but he was pulling back. At first, I frowned, because Finn didn't do that, he didn't pull away, then as he slipped out of me, I watched him watch us together.

He sighed at the sight of cum slipping out of my pussy, and I, in return, sighed at the sight of him kneeling between my legs.

Four years we'd been together, and I never grew tired of looking at him.

I'd gotten to this weird phase in my mind where I was starting to forget the moments when I hadn't been with him. He seemed to drown everything else out, and I knew that was a coping mechanism as well as that old adage of time healing all wounds.

We'd met when I was still grieving my mom, and now, my recent memories were tied up in him. Not all of them were joyous—this Christmas included—but he was like a black hole.

He absorbed everything.

Snatched it away, stealing it from me so that I was entrenched in him.

Some might consider that unhealthy, but I was happy with my life so what was the harm?

Groaning when he rubbed his fingers along my slit, the digits gathering our wetness, he muttered, "I never get tired of looking at this."

"Good," was my stout reply.

His smile made the tiniest of appearances. "Good? Nothing else?"

"What do you want me to say?" I tacked on drowsily, slurring the words again as he sparked remnants of pleasure and turned them into glowing embers. "You fucked me mindless."

Finn chuckled softly. "I want to look at this pussy forever."

"You can," I said sleepily. "It's not going anywhere."

He made me jerk when his fingers slid into me, and my legs snapped together in reaction.

I hissed when, his eyes on mine, he repeated, "I love you." His voice was insistent this time.

Like he was demanding I *knew* that he loved me.

My head fell back against the pillows as he slid his cum-slick fingers along my sensitive flesh.

"I love you too," I breathed, uncertain of why he was tormenting me with pleasure, uncertain of why his insecurities were rearing their head now. "But baby, I can't take anymore."

His lips quirked into a cocky smile. "Is that a challenge?"

"No, I just know you don't like it if I pass out."

Had he forgotten already?

If his repeated vows of love weren't clue enough, here I had proof that my husband's headspace was not where it needed to be.

He groused under his breath as he stopped petting me, but then I whimpered as he pressed a kiss to my mound.

Before he could climb away, I snagged his hand in mine and whispered, "Finn? What's going on?"

My charming, debonair husband was a mobster, sure, but to look at, you'd never know it.

He wore expensive suits and costly watches, his shirts were hand stitched and his shoes were made by some monks in Tuscany or some such BS.

Beneath that surface veneer of a businessman who pioneered a corporation that was on track to break a billion in turnover this year, however, there was Finn.

The boy I'd known when I was a toddler.

A teen whose abusive father had seen him running away to the streets.

A man who'd been reared in violence and had adapted to it, joining the Irish Mob and becoming a Five Pointer...

He was multi-faceted, just like anyone, but Finn was different.

It was only after we'd married that I realized something had broken him along the way.

I tugged on his hand, knowing full well he'd come if I pressed, and he did. He slipped onto me then twisted us both over, tangling our legs in the wet spot and making us one big knot on the sheets.

With my breath brushing his lips and his mine, our eyes on each other, the faint light from the bathroom the only illumination in our bedroom at the O'Donnelly compound in upstate New York, I whispered, "Talk to me."

Telling me he loved me twice in a handful of minutes?

A nightmare last night?

His being forgetful when my man's memory was razor sharp?

Something was going on, and I wanted to know. How could I help fix things if I was kept in the dark?

He was silent for so long that I didn't think he'd speak, then he broke my heart by admitting, "You know my stepfather abused me?"

My heart stuttered, rage and compassion warring inside me as I retorted, "I'd poison his bread if I could."

I knew something was wrong, but I hadn't thought it was to do with his stepfather.

Finn blinked at that, but he smiled. "Only you could make me smile at a moment like this."

"You know if you crush up apple seeds, you can make cyanide?" I mean, you needed a hell of a lot of apple seeds, but that was how they'd done it in the old days. "I go through thousands of apples in the bakery. I know where to get a source of untraceable cyanide."

"Let me guess, Jen told you that one," he drawled with a chuckle. "She's more into the vengeance shit than you."

"I watch documentaries too," I said in a scurry. "Plus, I learned all kinds of crap at culinary school."

"'How To Poison People 101?' Isn't the objective not to poison people when you're learning to be a chef?"

I shoved his shoulder slightly. "Don't be dense."

"I'm pretty sure this life is poisonous in and of itself. A few years ago, you wouldn't have told someone you'd lace their Danish with cyanide."

Tipping my head to the side, I murmured, "That's where you're wrong. I wasn't an angel, Finn."

"No?" He smiled. "Actually, you're right. Not past tense. Present. You *are* my angel."

"Even angels can have dirty faces when they shove it in a bowl of cookie dough."

That had him snorting out a laugh. "Like Jake did last week?"

I nodded. "You're surrounded by angels with dirty faces."

I didn't tell him that I thought he belonged in the same category.

Maybe 'the life' *had* changed me. Maybe I was more risk cautious, danger aware, than before, and maybe I knew there were some things that had to be done to keep the world spinning—

I sighed.

He wasn't wrong.

Men had died on the O'Donnelly compound over the holidays.

My husband had returned to me from only God knew where the night before Christmas Eve, stinking of smoke, and wouldn't you know it? There'd been a terror attack against the cathedral in New York...

It wasn't hard to put two and two together.

Wasn't hard to think that maybe he'd been a part of that whole thing that had New York on a red alert the likes of which we hadn't seen since that horrendous September back in 'o1.

I reached over and cupped his chin. "Do you judge me for letting my morals slip?"

"Are you kidding me? I thank Christ every fucking day for that. There'd be no you and me if you couldn't deal with..." His words waned, but I heard them anyway.

If you couldn't deal with the things I have to do to put bread on the table.

"Then what's the problem?"

His hand moved over to press against my stomach. "Another soul is coming into the world. My child is coming into the life. I can't control that or stop it or change it."

Ah.

Shit.

I should have thought about that.

I was still in the happy phase. Still wondering if it would be a boy or a girl and hoping I'd get through the pregnancy without too many health issues. Unlike last time.

Finn, though I'd only told him I was pregnant this morning, was thinking about when Jake and this baby—if it were a boy—were approaching fourteen.

Fourteen... When the Irish Mob had their version of a Bar Mitzvah and introduced their teenagers to the lifestyle.

My heart shriveled at the thought of arming Jake with a gun in thirteen years' time... Would that happen? Would Aidan Sr. still be alive so Finn couldn't break the cycle?

"My stepdad raped me, Eef."

"I know he did, baby."

My thumb traced over the line of his cheekbone. Little spiderwebs of wrinkles had appeared at the corners of his eyes this past year, and I was pretty sure that had everything to do with stress and not being almost forty-two.

"It isn't my secret to tell, and I've kept this locked up inside for decades... I'd never have said a word either. Never, but—" He released a breath. "Let me start at the beginning. Conor was raped by a priest, Eef."

For a second, I thought he was joking, but then my brain just whirred to a halt because this wasn't funny in the least.

This wasn't a joking matter.

And somehow, even though it was the opposite of a punchline, I knew my husband had more to tell me than that.

So, like anyone facing a hurricane armed with nothing more than a dollar-store umbrella, I braced myself.

Knowing that even that wouldn't be enough.

Because for the Irish Mob, nothing ever was.

THREE

FINN

AOIFE KNEW I WAS A SINNER.

She'd seen that firsthand.

I'd long since passed the point of worrying about my eternal soul, but hers gave me cause for concern.

Seeing what I'd seen these last couple days, hearing what I'd heard, doing what I'd done...

I tipped my forehead forward and pressed it against hers.

"Junior and I, we found them together in the confessional. Aidan lost it. I just protected Conor. Aidan was the one who killed him." To this day, I was still ashamed that I'd stalled. That I hadn't helped punish that bastard. "All I could remember was how I'd felt after what had happened to me, and he was younger..." I shook my head, dragging my forehead against hers.

"You caught it happening?" she asked quietly, her voice calm. Soothing.

Judgment-free.

It unlocked something in my memory banks.

Let the words form.

"We did. The second I saw *that,* I knew the bastard wasn't going to make it out alive..." I released a breath and tried not to be a pussy.

Tried when just thinking back to that day was enough to trigger me.

I'd killed.

I'd tortured.

I'd maimed.

But if anything fucked with my head, it was thoughts of my stepfather and what he'd done to me.

And that day.

Witnessing Conor's abuse with my own eyes.

A visual reminder of what had been done to me in the flesh combined with knowing the kid I'd loved, part of the family who'd taken me in and who'd loved me in return, had endured what I had.

There was no peace of mind when the worst had been done to you. There was no rest, no salvation when you couldn't let go of your trauma.

I could remember the first time I'd sliced a man's collateral ligaments; only, the details were getting hazy. I couldn't remember the guy's name or why I'd punished him that way. But the feel of my stepfather's—

Exhaling, I told myself it was better now that I knew he wasn't my biological dad, but it didn't take away from the feeling of being raped.

Couldn't.

I thought of the pain of being violated. The internal scream that never abated, that clouded the soundtrack of my life.

"Finn? Baby? Talk to me."

Aoife's soft voice was like the shock of the defibrillator against my chest, restarting my heart, making me suck down a breath.

Her smell—lavender and cotton—invaded my senses, overtaking my olfactory system.

She was here with me.

She wasn't going anywhere.

Tonight was *not* that night.

She wasn't my mom.

She'd kill anyone who harmed our kids. Not with cyanide she made in our kitchen, but with a cleaver she'd learned how to wield in culinary school.

"Junior just kept on hitting the guy," I rasped. "Over and over until he was mulch. We'd sneaked into the church looking for Conor, and there was this moan..." I could still hear it. "We armed ourselves with a candlestick from the altar and a plate. That was what Aidan used on the priest.

"I remember standing by the pews, blood spattering onto me,

wishing that he'd been there when my stepfather had done that to me. Of course, I thought he was my dad back then…"

Her hand cupped my cheek. "Aidan Sr. took care of things, didn't he?"

"He killed him," I confirmed, remembering the little Senior had told me. *I took pleasure in cutting that bastard to shreds* was all he'd said. "I don't know how. Maybe I should ask for details. Maybe that would feel good, knowing how it happened? I mean, I just know he's at the bottom of the Hudson."

"He's fish food, baby."

"He is," I said simply. "So's the priest who hurt Conor." The memory replayed before I had the chance to shut it down. "The other night, Junior told Senior about Kid's abuse, about what we did that day, and he completely lost his shit."

"Didn't take much to figure out that something was wrong with him, sweetheart. He's been edgier than usual all day. Actually, Lena has been weird too."

I thought about how Aidan Sr. had tortured the Archbishop of New York.

I thought about how he'd set fire to the cathedral after dumping him at the altar so he could feel the flicker of the flames eating him alive.

But more than that, more than any of that, I thought about how he and Lena had tried to kill themselves.

Guilt, they said they couldn't live with knowing they'd let Conor down…

"My mom had to know, didn't she?" I blurted out.

She tensed up at the question, and I didn't blame her. She'd known my mom. Hers had been best friends with mine, and she'd been practically raised by Fiona too.

"You know I don't have the answer to that, sweetheart. I just know that she grieved you until the day she died."

"Good," I said simply. "Aidan and Lena destroyed a centuries-old cathedral for Conor. They tortured and burned the archbishop alive and almost killed themselves…

"My mom should have carried the burden of grief for my abuse for the rest of her life too."

I braced myself for her judgment, for her telling me that was out of line, but she didn't do that.

She didn't even tense up. If anything, she relaxed.

She softened.

Sliding up against me, she settled all her curves against my hard lines until we were cleaved together, skin to skin.

"If anyone hurt Jacob," Aoife ground out, "we'd do the same to them, wouldn't we?"

My heart didn't know what to do.

At first, it slowed down as my body was incapable of processing the idea that my son could go through what I had.

Then it raced with the need to avenge my kid, a kid who was so protected and cosseted that he'd never know what an empty stomach felt like, that he'd never be without a roof over his head.

"We would," I agreed, and that her words reflected my thoughts soothed something inside me that I didn't know was an open wound.

She nodded. "It isn't the life that changed me, Finn. Being a mom did that.

"I don't know why your mother failed you, but I knew she mourned you for the rest of her days, and I also know you're right—that did nothing for you. That didn't take away from what she let happen to you."

I squeezed her, shoving my face against her shoulder so that I could hug her harder.

"Would you feel better knowing she did something to hurt your stepfather? Even though he was already dead?"

"Maybe. I don't know. It doesn't matter." My tone wooden, I closed my eyes. "I need you to promise me something, Aoife."

Her hand slipped around me and cupped the back of my neck. "What, baby?"

"To always put our children first."

She shuddered. "Oh, sweetheart." I heard the tears in her voice, didn't need to move to see them in her eyes. "I promise," she said thickly.

I nodded.

That had to be enough.

For tonight, that had to be enough.

"Who knows about Conor?" she questioned.

"Brennan, Declan, and Eoghan don't know. Conor doesn't know that his parents are in the loop now."

"I won't say anything."

"I know you won't." I hesitated a second before grating out, "Junior and I, we burned down St. Patrick's Church."

"That means we don't have to go to *any* services now? Yay!" she cheered.

"Well, that's a novel way of looking at arson."

Her laughter bubbled free. "I'm not the Catholic here."

"Didn't you wonder why we didn't go to church last night?"

"Since when do I look gift horses in the mouth? I was just glad I didn't have to go out into the cold."

Aoife made me look devout so I wasn't totally surprised by her reaction, even if it was further proof of the life changing her.

My lips curved. "Big baby."

She shoved me in the side before she released a soft whistle. "Father Doyle is probably rolling around in his grave even though he isn't dead."

"He called Senior today. Demanding the villains suffer."

"I'll bet he did. Look at him turning the other cheek," she sneered. "Does Aidan Sr. know you and Junior were behind it?"

"Don't know, don't care." I pulled back to look into her eyes. "I watched it burn, and it was like the ties that bound Junior and me to that place burned with them."

"Do you feel lighter?"

"I do."

"Who knew arson was good for the soul? Not sure Father Doyle would like that news to spread."

At her jovial response, all I could think to say was, "I changed you."

"I grew up. I know the world is mean and nasty, and I know that we can't do anything to change that.

"I know pedophiles walk the streets every day, and they get away with it. Hurting more kids, destroying more lives.

"I know that being bad doesn't mean you'll be punished." Her fingers raked through my hair. "I told you, you didn't change me. Being a mom did that. It made me see the predators out there who could hurt my children. And not just how you were hurt either." She pressed a kiss to my lips. "We'll keep our family safe, Finn. We'll do that together." She hugged me. "Now, let's get some sleep. You need it, Smokey Bear."

She smushed my face into her tits, and her hands continued smoothing through my hair as if she could soothe me as easily as she soothed Jake.

If only that were possible.

As I lay there, I recognized there was a certain irony to the situation.

She hadn't thrown me out. Cast me from heaven for confessing my sins to her... a confession that felt more cleansing than anything I'd ever admitted to Father Doyle in the confessional where my baby brother had been fucking raped by a clergyman.

And as liberating as that was, it was also cataclysmic.

Because if it felt this good to get the truth off my back, how many of my filthy secrets could she handle without turning me away...?

FINN: *What's going on out there?*

Brennan: *Bunch of fuckers whining about being cooped up in here.*

Brennan: *It's not exactly a party, that's for fucking sure. They've all been shitting themselves since Da made his grand speech.*

Finn: *They're asking when they can leave?*

Brennan: *Yup. Not the men. Their wives. Why Da insisted on inviting them is beyond me.*

Finn: *Power move.*

Brennan: *Scare the women, scare the men? Most of these fuckers hate each other. They're not love matches.*

Finn: *It's the kids.*

Brennan: *I'd like to think Da wouldn't get us butchering kids, but with how his mind is at the moment, I don't fucking know.*

Finn: *Me either.*

Brennan: *You think it's a possibility?*

Finn: *Not today.*

Brennan: *If Da finds out someone's a Sparrow and they didn't come to him today?*

Finn: *Yes.*

Brennan: *I'll do a lot of shit for the family, Finn, but killing kids ain't one of them.*

Finn: *Aidan and I will figure out a way to stop that from happening.*

Brennan: *If he even suggests it, he's off his rocker more than we thought.*

Finn: *Agreed. We'll handle it.*

Brennan: *See that you do.*

Finn: *Bossy motherfucker.*

Brennan: *Stop your grumbling and get on with it.*

FOUR

BRENNAN

DECEMBER 26TH

I STARED at the door to my da's office.

Granted, this wasn't the same study door that I'd stared at as a kid, just waiting to get my ass hauled in and my ear clipped for whatever shit I'd done.

This was a different house, a different study, fuck, a different Brennan.

I rubbed my chin as I continued staring at the eighty by thirty-six-inch plank of wood and tried to reason out my options.

Da had just declared to his top men that today was an amnesty of sorts.

A freebie.

If the Sparrows had fucked around with you, now was the moment to come forward. If that group of self-serving, secret boys' club mother-fuckers had gotten to you, turned your head, then now was the moment to confess, and if you did, there'd be no payback.

The trouble was, I didn't know if I believed that, and after that text chat with Finn, I didn't think he believed it either.

When Da told his captains that he'd murder anyone who didn't confess today, their families too, I knew there'd be no greater incentive for the truth to set our men free.

And with my own truths to spill and a wife to protect, a wife I fucking loved, I needed this amnesty not to be bullshit.

I trusted Finn when he said he thought Da was being honest with his intentions, but this was Da.

More volatile than butane, more flammable than gas.

A squeaking sound drew my attention away from my phone. As Conor strode down the hall in a pair of bright blue high-tops that he'd combined with a D&G suit, I watched him as he slumped into the seat beside me.

I slipped my cell into my pocket as he asked, "Wassup?"

"You been watching *Scary Movie* again?" I questioned, peering at him as he peered at me.

"Maybe. Can I help that I like parodies?"

I snorted. "You like a lot of weird shit, bro."

"Not that weird. There's a porn parody of that too, but I didn't watch that."

"Should I applaud you?"

"I mean, you could." He grinned at me. "I'd take the applause. I'm sure I deserve it for something or other."

"*Tsatsa.*"

He squinted at me. "Since when did you start speaking Russian?"

"Since Camille—" I broke off before I could finish. The last thing I wanted was him knowing that Camille reverted to Russian during sex.

I took that for the compliment it was.

Especially when French came out.

I didn't have a goddamn clue what she was saying, but when she got that wild look in her eyes, my ice princess wasn't so fucking icy.

"Since Camille?" His brow furrowed. "You've been together a minute."

"So? I'm not a dumbass," I retorted. "I can pick up a fucking language book and learn it."

He squinted at me then rumbled something in Russian.

"I'm not fluent, and you're a fucking show off as well as a *tsatsa.*" A bighead.

He shoved me in the side. "Why didn't you come to me? I'd have taught you."

A man could get a complex around baby brothers like mine.

Conor was a genius. Computers, code, languages, the fucker could do it all.

Declan had it too, just in a different way. He was good at art, which was akin to admitting to being a nonce in our household, and had a gift he'd never been allowed to develop.

Then there was Eoghan. The sleeper. He had an eidetic memory, so that meant being around him was like living with an encyclopedia sometimes because he knew a lot of random shit.

Even Aidan Jr. had been granted a gift.

He had this ability to render men mute when he gave a speech.

It happened rarely, but when Da finally died and gave us some peace and quiet, the inner general in my eldest brother would stir to life.

He was going to make a fucking awesome leader.

As for myself, I was probably the dunce of the family.

Hence the complex.

What use was I other than as my father's and, eventually, my brother's muscle?

I pursed my lips at the thought then replied to Conor; "I'd prefer to be taught by Master Splinter than you."

"What do the *Teenage Mutant Ninja Turtles* have to do with anything?"

"A lot," I grumbled.

"I should be offended."

"No, you should be grateful. If you taught me, I'd have to stab you every time you fucked me off."

"You'd never stab me," was his confident retort.

"Says who?" I drawled.

Conor sniffed. "You wouldn't stab me. You lurrve me."

I rolled my eyes before I stunned the hell out of him by grabbing him in a headlock, shoving his head down, and giving him a noogie. "Who says I lurrve you?"

"Uncle Brennan?"

I paused in the act of giving the noogie, well aware that I'd been caught red handed as I turned to find my nephew Shay watching us, his head tipped down as he stared at Conor and me.

"Yeah, big guy?" I slapped my hand over Kid's hair to straighten it out some, unsurprised when he shoved me away with a glower.

"Why are you giving Uncle Conor a noogie?"

"Because he deserved it?" I arched a brow at him. "Did you need something?"

"No. Just thought I'd save you from Grandma. She's looking for you."

I blinked. "Owe you one, Shay."

He grinned at me before he hurried down the hallway and away from us both, clearly avoiding Ma.

She had a tendency to pinch his cheek whenever he was near, so I wasn't altogether surprised he was getting the fuck out of Dodge.

"Scared of a clipped ear?" Conor taunted, smoothing his fingers over his hair.

"You fucking know it." Ma's fingers were like pincers.

"Bren?" Ma demanded as she made an appearance around the corner—Shay really had spared my ass. Well, my ears.

"What, Ma?"

"Have you seen Mary Catherine?"

"Why would I?" I grumbled with a frown.

"Didn't she leave a few hours ago?" Conor replied.

Ma did the weirdest thing.

She didn't look at him.

Or answer him.

She stared straight at me.

Conor noticed as well. He straightened up, not accustomed to being ignored by our folks.

For some reason, though he was the middle child, he was treated like he was the baby of the family.

We had a peculiar dynamic, that was for sure. Eoghan, while the youngest, wasn't nicknamed 'Kid.' That moniker belonged to Con.

"You should know where she is," Ma groused. "Aren't you on security today?"

I frowned at her. "Conor just said he thought she left."

"Well, where is she? Where did she go? Her mother's worried."

Turning to Con, I shot him a look, wondering what the fuck was going on even as I asked, "You see where she went?" *Had I asked a more stupid fucking question in my life?*

Was this Telephone and we were in third grade?

"No," he said slowly, his gaze never once meeting mine, just focused on Ma. "I saw her get into a taxi. Savannah was talking to her so I didn't think anything was wrong. Plus, the kid was crying. I thought she was taking her home."

"Ain't the kid a boy?"

Con shrugged. "All I know is the little bastard cried a lot. With pipes like that, I wasn't about to get closer to the noise to find out whether it was a dude or not."

Chuckling, I said, "There you go, Ma. You have your answer. She got in a taxi and went home."

She huffed. "Aren't you going to look into it?"

"No?" I countered, even more perplexed. "Why would I?"

A harrumph escaped her, and she swarmed by, muttering under her breath, "If you want something done properly, do it yourself."

"Whoa. What the fuck did you do?"

He'd turned to watch her go. "No idea."

I shoved him in the side. "'Fess up."

"No, seriously. I've no idea."

"Michael's back in the hospital," I told him when I saw he wasn't bull-shitting me. "You know how close she gets to her guards. Maybe it's that?"

Though she hadn't been weird with me...

Still, Ma was used to me being her problem solver, but I had troubles of my own to shoot today.

Con finally looked away and turned to face me. "Da's been weird as well so I don't think it's that."

"Da's always fucking weird."

"Weirder than usual," he corrected thoughtfully, his brow puckered with a mixture of surprise, concern, and confusion.

I didn't blame him—he was Boy Wonder.

Boy Wonder was never toppled from his perch.

If he fucked up, he didn't pay for it with a busted fist or a beating, not like me. He just got fined. Heavily fined, his pay docked enough that it'd piss anyone off, but that was it.

Me? I had a fucked-up wrist because Da broke it every time I 'displeased' him. Not anymore. That had long since goddamn stopped, but it didn't take away from the fact I had a wrist that could scout out a storm better than The Weather Channel.

"Well, he ain't fined you so whatever it is you've done, it can't be that bad."

Conor's nod was slow. "True."

As far as I could remember, he'd only been beaten twice in his life.

Twice.

I was jealous.

Da celebrated Conor's quirks; he didn't punish them.

"When was the last time he gave you a beating?"

Kid admitted, "A long time ago. Remember when Mary Ellen told me I'd knocked her up?"

I clicked my fingers. "Yeah, I remember that now. She was lying, right?"

"Well, you don't see anyone calling me 'Dad,' do you?" he retorted.

"Got a point. Or 'husband' for that matter," I tacked on. "What was the second beating for?"

"You keeping count?"

"One and two ain't calculus."

His lips twitched. "Second time was bad."

"*That* I remember. You had bruises for weeks. I don't remember what you did though."

"Reappropriated funds Da sent to the IRA."

I whistled under my breath. "Jesus, I remember now. When was that? Ninety-nine?"

"Yeah." He grunted. "I haven't done anything like that for a while though. I'm not sure why Ma's pissed at me."

"Maybe she didn't like your gift."

"It was a Fabergé egg!" Conor grumbled. "How couldn't she like it?"

"Well, you did something," I reasoned.

"Yeah, I know." He scrubbed his chin, and though I sensed his confusion hadn't abated, his curious nature had him asking, "Anyway, why you sitting outside Da's office?"

"Got a confession to make."

"You a Sparrow as well?" Kid taunted.

"Yeah, I'm a fucking Sparrow. 'Course." I pushed his shoulder. "Prick."

He grinned at me, his confusion fading some. "Well? What is it?"

On any other occasion, I'd have told him it had nothing to do with him. Only this time, it did.

"I don't wanna tell this story twice."

"Then don't. Get your ass in there. It looks fucking weird, you sitting out here like this, so you need to make a move."

I'd gotten a few looks, so I knew he wasn't wrong. Normally, I'd have nothing to hide, but I had kept something from Da... something bad.

"Think he meant what he said?"

"About the armistice?" Conor shrugged. "For today. Maybe not tomorrow. You know his moods are like the weather."

That was exactly what I feared, but the truth was, I was running out of time.

Callum O'Reilly's disappearance was starting to make waves.

Da had already asked me three times about him, mostly because his best bud, Mark, was Callum's dad.

Priestley, the lying fucker's wife, had come to my place sobbing four nights ago, begging me for information about the bastard's whereabouts.

It was either have my ass handed to me or come clean.

On Armistice Day.

I knew how he worked. Had seen it in action after he'd made Eoghan toe the line before his wedding.

But I wasn't Eoghan. I was integral to command and the men held me in too high a regard for them to hold me down while he beat me. That meant he'd go after Camille because our men weren't as loyal to a new Russian bride as they were to me.

If he did that, I'd be forced to kill him.

That in mind, I got to my feet and muttered, "You need to hear this too, Kid."

He arched a brow but shuffled after me, then bumped into me when I just stared at the door, my hand balled into a fist and raised, ready to knock.

"What the hell have you done?" Conor questioned as he backed off. "I ain't seen you scared of Da in years."

He wasn't wrong, but I'd never killed a Five Pointer before.

FIVE

FINN

WHEN BRENNAN'S head popped around the door, I wasn't sure who froze the most.

Junior gaped, and I definitely stared, everything inside me rejecting what his presence in the doorway might mean, but it was Senior who rasped, "Brennan, boy, if you've come to tell me you're a fucking Sparrow—"

Bren stormed in, Conor at his back, and his immediate scowl had me relaxing some. "Do I have a label on my forehead or something? Jesus Christ."

"No blaspheming," Senior wheezed, but it lacked the usual ire that came with that chastisement. He sounded more breathless than furious. "What is it then?"

Brennan straightened his shoulders, wriggling them some as he moved toward the desk. "I got something I need to tell you."

"Not the Sparrows?" Senior almost pleaded this time.

"Not the fucking Sparrows," Brennan snapped before he blew out a breath. "Something else... something about the Sparrows but not to do with me."

"What?" Aidan Sr. demanded.

"Callum O'Reilly—" Brennan hesitated.

Callum O'Reilly had gone missing just before Thanksgiving, so, interested, I asked, "What about him?"

Senior had been driving us all crazy about him. Making us put feelers out, but there'd been no bites as far as I knew.

Brennan shot me a look. "He was working with the Sparrows."

Aidan Sr. tensed up. "*Was?*"

He dipped his chin. "Was."

Conor shoved Brennan in the back. "Callum wasn't a fucking Sparrow. I've been on the hunt for him since his disappearance, and I've found no links between him and those asswipes."

Bren twisted around. "Kid, I'm telling you the truth. He was. He just hid it well."

"How do you know?" Senior demanded, sitting straighter in his chair at Conor's defense of Callum.

"I lied to you about those men behind the jewelry break-ins at Hummels. I didn't kill them before they could talk. They talked first but I knew you weren't ready to hear what they had to say, so I dealt with it."

"You dealt with *him?*" Tension gripped Senior in a chokehold.

"I did. Remember what I told you before? That some Five Pointer informed the brains of the operation that Hummel's wasn't protected by the Points anymore?"

"I remember."

"That was Callum."

"No way was Callum a Sparrow," Conor snapped again, getting in Bren's face.

Junior hobbled over to them both so I didn't bother getting involved, just watched as he shoved one hand on each brother's chest, and in a move that I'd seen too often because he was their fucking referee with decades of experience, he pressed them apart.

"Break it up, fuckwits," he snarled. "Getting into a fight isn't going to change the truth."

"What truth?" Conor hissed. "What happened to 'innocent until proven guilty,' huh?"

"You want goddamn proof?" Brennan shoved Junior's hand aside as he reached into his jacket pocket and pulled out his cellphone.

As he did, he swiped a couple times, then, there was the unmistakable sound of someone sobbing and of fists meeting flesh.

I didn't wince—I'd heard that too often in my life, been a party to that kind of violence too much for it to disturb me.

My eyes closed of their own volition though.

Another child of mine was going to have to get used to seeing shit no one should ever have to see.

"*I-I was s-scared,*" Callum sobbed.

In the background, I heard some of Brennan's crew muttering before Callum had his ass handed to him.

"*Tell me what the NWS wanted you to do.*"

"*Let me down, Bren, please?*" Callum pleaded.

"*Tell me what they wanted.*"

"*Just to mess with commands, cause dissent.*"

"One of my circle," Senior muttered under his breath. "A fucking Sparrow."

"Where is he?" Conor grated out, his gaze on the cellphone on the desk.

I saw the devastation etched into his expression, and I sighed at the sight. "Con, he doesn't deserve for you to mourn him."

"Not deserve? He's had my back for years—"

"While selling you out to the fucking New World Sparrows," Junior rumbled, his hand moving to grip his shoulder. "That ain't no friend, Kid."

He gulped. "He was the only one I trusted."

His admission had me wincing.

Conor had a serious blind spot for those he loved. That was probably how Callum had managed to pull the wool over his eyes.

"The only people we can trust are in this room," Senior rumbled.

"Not true. Declan and Eoghan are out there," Junior argued, twisting back to glare at his father.

"Our women can be trusted," I chided as well. "Fuck if they haven't proven themselves time and time again."

He rubbed his chin, rocking back in his seat, but he didn't confirm or deny our assertions. "Mark's going to be a problem."

Mark was Callum's father.

"Ain't no body to be a problem over," Brennan disregarded. "He went to the pig farm."

Senior's fingers drummed against the desk. "You know when we don't feed them bodies, they're eating all the shitty junk food our great nation doesn't want?"

"Good thing we keep them plenty busy then," I retorted, studying Senior as he twisted away from his sons. He cupped his hand, gently tweaking his wrist while he stared out the window.

Junior cast Brennan a look. "We just have to maintain that Callum went missing?"

"Mark's not going to be pacified for long," Senior answered. "We're best friends. If a best friend ain't going to deep dive when your son's gone missing, that doesn't make him much of an ally, does it?"

"Then dive deep. You don't have to find answers that reveal the truth," I pointed out.

I saw Senior's disapproval in his profile, but he merely said, "Don't think we have much choice."

"Finn, brother," Bren rasped, turning to me. "I'm sorry."

Frowning, I asked, "What about?"

He shook his head as he turned on his phone, and the recording played once more.

"What else did they ask you?"

"If a rumor was true," he said with a groan of pain that almost had me wincing—I'd seen Bren in action. He made a Spanish Inquisitor look friendly.

"What rumor?"

"That Finn and Aoife were going to get married at St. Patrick's. I mean, they asked, but it was public knowledge. Father Doyle would have published the banns—"

For a second, it was like time froze. The words seemed to penetrate my ear drums in slow motion.

"There wasn't time for the banns to be published." Brennan's voice was like ice. *"They either told the Colombians, or they triggered that drive-by shooting, Callum. On your word.*

"That rumor they wanted clarifying was their way of scheduling what could have been a massacre."

"No! Fuck no," Callum growled, terror making the words quiver. *"That ain't got nothing to do with me. I would never have—"*

The next sound he made was a scream of pain as Brennan's fists did the talking.

I was sightless.

Deaf.

My heart pounding.

My blood like ice.

"Finn?"

Aidan Jr. was there, his hand on my shoulder. He squeezed. Hard. Enough to jolt me.

"Callum was behind the drive-by?" I ground out, my eyes wide as I tried to process that one of our own had triggered that blood bath.

A blood bath that saw my wife almost dying on the church steps.

A blood bath that had seen her miscarry twice thanks to her injuries.

That meant when she'd carried Jake, she was high-risk, and which meant this pregnancy was going to be high-risk too.

"He was," Brennan confirmed.

I stared up at Junior, seeing the rage etched into his features, a rage that was just and true because that drive-by was the reason he had gotten hooked on opiates. The reason he walked with a limp and suffered with chronic, excruciating pain.

"I can't believe he was a Sparrow," Conor rasped, shuffling over to the seat Aidan Jr. had left vacant. As he slumped into it, he scrubbed a hand over his face.

My mouth twisted as the pain cut me in two. "Brennan?"

"Yeah, *deartháir*?" he asked as he tucked his phone away in his pocket again.

Damn, I knew shit was bad if Brennan was butchering Gaelic. "Tell me you made him pay."

He cracked his knuckles. "I made him fucking pay. Don't you goddamn worry."

My fingers dug into the palms of my hands as I balled them into fists. "You should have told me. I should have been there—"

"Wasn't any time for that, Finn. I had to act fast. It was dicey enough as it was, but trust me, I made him pay. I made him *hurt* for you and for Aoife and for Aidan."

Before I could utter another word, Conor whispered, "This makes no fucking sense."

"It's what they do. Take good men and turn them with the prospect of jail time." Senior hacked out a laugh. "If I didn't hate the fuckers, I'd congratulate them on a smart system."

I shared a look with my brothers, stunned by his admission. "This isn't goddamn funny, Senior."

"Nothing about this situation is funny, Finn," he snapped.

"Then why are you laughing?"

"Because the world's caving in and there's fuck all I can do to stop it."

I surged onto my feet, but Junior blocked me and muttered, "Calm down, Finn."

Brennan shuffled behind me. "Trust me, I made him wish he'd never been born, brother. I swear to you. I fucking swear on Ma's life."

Sagging against Junior, I rumbled, "Aoife's in danger to this day because of that bastard."

"I know." Junior squeezed my shoulder again. "I know."

I closed my eyes as I dropped back into my seat. Elbows on my knees, I stared at the ground, aware that the world hadn't stopped turning—it just felt like it had.

"How many have come forward today?" Brennan asked, breaking into my thoughts.

"Two," Junior replied, his hand squeezing my shoulder once more before he hobbled off and took a seat on the edge of his da's desk.

"Who?"

"Sullivan and Walsh." He grunted. "They're no longer with the Points and are under the warning that if they so much as sniff around the Sparrows *or* Points' business, we'll have their balls."

Bren's eyes flared in surprise. Not at the threat, I figured, just the names. I couldn't blame him. I'd been shocked too.

"Walsh?" Bren demanded. "He's a fucking lifer."

Senior explained, "Said they threatened to have his daughter arrested."

Shoulders relaxing, he whistled. "Makes sense. He's already served, what? Twenty years off and on for the family. Not like more time would disturb him."

"Our kids are our weaknesses," Senior rumbled, and I turned to look at him and saw that his gaze was on the window and the yard beyond.

Blanketed with snow, it wasn't like he could see much aside from Declan who, for some fucking reason, was standing out there while taking a call, but it was clear to me that Senior had been keeping his shit together all day and was on the verge of explosion.

I just wasn't sure what that explosion would look like now, and to be frank, I got it. Explosion felt imminent for me as well.

For the first time in my life, I understood what twisted him, what riled him up and made him do the sick shit he was capable of.

I'd watched him crucify men; I'd stood back and watched him torture them. I'd even let him watch me pull those moves because that was how a man became a Five Pointer.

He was my father.

Somehow, he was all our father, and he'd let us become this. Had let us do these things and expected it of us.

Maybe I'd always resented him for that.

Maybe I'd never understood it.

Until now.

Until this moment.

As skilled as Bren was, as *infamous* at torture as he was, no one could serve that fucker justice like I could have.

"Our kids are supposed to be our weaknesses. Our women too," I ground out.

Senior swiveled in his seat, circling so that we were looking at each other. "You're not wrong," he said eventually.

"What if you don't have either yet?" Conor grated out.

"Then you don't see the forest for the trees," I told him, my gaze on Senior's all the while. "Mark won't take bullshit where Callum's concerned. He wants answers. You need to make sure he gets them, and they need to be good enough to pass muster because, bet your ass, he'll double check the information you get to him."

Senior nodded slowly, his gaze on mine as I got to my feet. "I'll see that it's done."

"I've spent St. Stephen's Day listening to Walsh and Sullivan snivel to you, Aidan, but that's not how I'm going to spend the rest of it."

I dragged off my suit jacket, hooked two fingers into the collar then draped it over my shoulder all while I worked at the knot on my tie with the other. I tugged so hard I almost choked myself, but the truth was, the only way I was going to calm the fuck down was to go and be with Aoife and Jake.

And even that might not be enough this time.

PART 2

SIX

PAST

PADRAIG

SENATOR ALAN DAVIDSON had a belly the size of the USS Missouri, an ego as large as the States, and a reputation as infamous in the Kremlin as it was in the Senate.

The Kennedys, the Bushes, and the Davidsons were all of the same ilk, but the Davidsons were a lot more crooked.

Thank fuck for small mercies.

"Padraig, such a pleasure to see you," Alan intoned as he got to his feet to shake my hand.

He grabbed one of mine with both of his in a political handshake that I thought his grandfather had taught him.

Just firm enough, not too much of a power play.

A hundred years of political inbreeding had crafted that handshake, making it balanced to perfection. But then, it was the only thing balanced about him.

Something he confirmed when he held out a box of illegal Cubans and said, "So glad you could make it."

Bullshit. A man like him was used to answering to no one, but I'd admit he'd come to heel relatively easily over the last couple years or so.

I snagged one of the Behikes and raised it to my nose. "Damn, that smells good."

Alan beamed at me. "Want some whiskey?"

"I'll never say no."

I took a seat in front of his desk, well aware that as he played bartender with me, I was one of the few he'd ever do shit like this for.

There were some perks to being Aidan O'Donnelly's younger brother.

As I reached for the cutter, I cut off the tip of the cigar, took another sniff of the fine tobacco leaf, then snagged a match from the sterling silver humidor with its cedar interior and struck it against the vesta case.

With the flickering flame in hand, I held it to the cigar tip and gave it a few puffs, sighing as I savored not just the taste, but the experience.

These old families did shit the right way.

Alan set a whiskey tumbler loaded down with amber nectar in front of me before he returned to his seat behind the desk which creaked with his weight.

As he stopped waddling about his luxuriously appointed office, I found myself wondering how in fuck he'd managed to sell himself as a man of the people when this office looked like it belonged in a stately home from the old country, but the man definitely had the gift of gab.

He might not have made it to the White House, but he was a career Senator. So someone in New York bought what he was peddling.

"Beautiful ceremony," I commented as I reached forward and picked up the glass.

"It was. Father Doyle definitely did us proud." Davidson went through the process of lighting his own cigar. "Wasn't sure if Alan Jr. would go through with it in the end."

I arched a brow. "Really?"

Alan's gaze held firm on mine. "He likes a girl he met at West Point. A fucking waitress in a diner. Can you imagine? The boy's a fool."

Love had a habit of doing that to a man. I didn't say that, however, just queried, "Want me to speak with Aidan Sr. about her?"

Alan understood what I was saying without me needing to clarify it.

He didn't even blanch at the idea of the girl being killed—*if only his constituents could see him now.*

"And make a martyr out of her?" he groused at the same time as he puffed away on his cigar. "No. Alan went through with the wedding because his mother started sobbing whenever he talked about backing out of it."

"Momma's boy," I commented with a laugh, shaking my head.

"In this instance, that works in our favor. Elizabeth's a good girl. Will make a fine First Lady someday."

If that was supposed to be a smooth segue, it failed. I knew Elizabeth was a good girl. She was of Irish stock.

Preferring to deal with the bullshit now, I told him, "Aidan was disappointed you didn't win the primaries."

Alan tensed. "No more than me."

I wafted a hand. "You're in no danger. Our friendship isn't terminated with your inability to get elected into the Oval Office."

Twice he'd tried, twice he'd failed.

The 'man of the people' act worked for a Senator but didn't seem to pass the sniff test when it came down to a presidential election.

"That's good to know." His shoulders dropped, and the mask of false joviality he'd been wearing wobbled as relief hit him.

Making the Five Points a promise and then failing to fulfill that promise was how you found yourself in an early grave.

It was good he remembered that.

These men, so influential but so forgetful that the Five Points held more power than they ever could.

I smiled at the thought and took a deeper puff on the cigar.

"Elizabeth's one of yours?"

His wary question had me eying my cigar. A Five Pointer? No. But he didn't need to know that. Not if his investigations into the girl hadn't told him as much.

"Irish?" I puffed on the Cuban, purposely misunderstanding him. "I know. As you said, she'll make a fine First Lady." I angled my head to the side as I took a deep gulp of whiskey. "Are you going to retire from office?"

He pursed his lips. "I was thinking about it. Alan Jr. needs a lot of work if he's going to be cultivated into presidential material."

"It's definitely a task worthy of your time. You promised the Five Points a president, Alan."

"I remember." He shot me a wary smile. "A Davidson never forgets his dues."

"Good to know."

"It's a shame your brother couldn't attend the wedding."

Well, that was a fucking lie if I ever heard one.

"Business always gets in the way," I dismissed, impressed by his ability to bullshit—*nobody* wanted my older brother around.

"Doesn't it, though?" he consoled.

Sinking back the whiskey, I sighed with repletion as the heat from its burn licked at my insides. Then, still smoking the cigar, I got to my feet and held out my spare hand.

"Don't let us down, Alan, and we won't let you down."

This time, his palm was clammy as it enfolded mine in a gentleman's handshake. Alan had a good poker face, I had to give him that, but controlling his expression was one thing, his sweat glands another.

"I appreciate your patience. Enjoy the party. It'll be going on all night."

I hummed as I wandered out of the office, closing the door with a snick behind me.

The Davidsons' house in the Hamptons had been one of the properties under the threat of foreclosure when he'd come to us with a proposition nine years ago. The fourteen-bedroom colonial mansion belonged to my family, not his, but it was on loan to him for the foreseeable future.

Unless he reneged, of course. But he'd lose more than just his fucking house if he did that.

As I wandered around the halls, I heard the music from the wedding party in the ballroom, but it held no interest to me.

Alan Davidson Jr. had been strong-armed into this marriage, and it was clear for all to see.

He'd barely looked at his bride once, hadn't touched her, and when it had come time to kiss her, he'd placed a peck on her cheek... They might have gotten him down the aisle, but that wouldn't continue their political dynasty if he couldn't touch her without cringing.

As I entered the wintergarten—I'd seen the deeds so I knew that was the official name of the fancy greenhouse—where daffodils grew in November thanks to Victorian heating pipes that ran under the flower beds in there—I heard the softest of moans.

My lips quirked up at the corners as I snuffed out the cigar in one of the soil beds and craned my neck to investigate exactly where the sound had come from.

In the distance, over the private beach, a flurry of fireworks lit up the sky and provided some relief from the gloom in here.

My eyes caught a couple in full embrace: her skirts up, his pants down.

I'd have laughed if that skirt wasn't part of a wedding dress.

Not much surprised me, not in my line of work, but when the lights flashed again, the sky blowing up with reds and blues and whites—ever the patriots—there was no mistaking the man who was fucking the newest member of the Davidson household.

Michael Byrne.

Jesus Christ.

There were few men whom I feared. In my position, not only was fear a weakness I couldn't afford, but the Five Points *were* the monster under the bed.

We were the ones to be frightened of.

Unless you were a *cheile*, of course.

Those fucking ECD zealots from the motherland were more insane than my elder brother, and that was really saying something.

Defrosting, I backed away, but of course, as luck would fucking have it, I walked into a goddamn planter.

With a crash, it soared onto the Victorian-era tiles, and Elizabeth Davidson née Ó Cléirigh gasped and started tugging her skirts down.

Not Byrne though.

With his gaze on mine, he pinned her to him. One arm banding around her waist, his other hand coming to her throat to hold her as he carried on fucking her while she struggled to cover up.

As I stared into the gaze of a *cheile* with the blood of thousands on his hands, who felt righteous in his actions and not like the worst kind of sinner, I knew that for catching them in the act, I was a dead man walking.

SEVEN

AOIFE

PRESENT - NEW YEAR'S DAY

WHEN MY PHONE rang and I glanced at the 'private number' on the Caller ID, I ignored it the first time.

But when it kept on ringing, and because I'd just put Jake down for a nap, I hit the connect button and snapped, "Who is it?"

There was silence on the end of the line, and for a second, I waited for the spiel for travel insurance or faster internet—not even the mob could avoid telemarketers forever—but then came a voice I hadn't heard in years.

Not outside of the TV screen, at any rate.

"Aoife."

Not a question, not even a statement. Just a soft exhalation, as if he savored my name.

"What do you want?"

If that sounded grim, then so be it.

My father had dumped me like I was trash just so that he could hop, skip, and jump his way into the White House.

When the last President had been impeached, there'd been a power vacuum at the top of his party, and Dad had managed to score himself a ride to the most famous house in the world.

"I need to speak with you."

"Then speak."

"Not over the phone. Anyone could be listening in."

I shuffled away from the kitchen and headed toward the other end that was loaded with Jake's toys now. It meant I was as far away from Finn as was manageable, because if he knew I was talking to my father, he'd be furious.

Not at me, but at Dad.

Finn knew how much it had hurt for me to be cut out and cast away like I meant nothing. If he learned I was giving my father the time of day, I knew he'd be outraged.

"You mean the Sparrows could be listening in?" I countered, not letting him throw me any BS.

"Yes," he admitted.

"I told you before, you don't have to worry about me..." If he really thought the Sparrows were listening in, then I was careful with what I said next, "I'm a woman of my word. Unlike some people."

I'd gone above and beyond to protect him and his reputation. His loyalty wasn't as strong as mine.

Dad hissed under his breath then took a second before muttering, "I deserved that."

"Yes. You did." My voice was without rancor. "I don't have time for this. I have a friend coming over for dinner, and I don't think this is a phone call where you wish me a 'Happy New Year.' So what do you want?"

"I'm sorry, Aoife."

"Sorry? What are you sorry for?" I rasped when he stayed quiet, to the point where I actually thought he'd cut the line.

It was hard not tacking on 'Dad,' but I'd never wanted to hurt him. Even after he'd hurt me.

"For everything," he said on a sigh.

My eyes narrowed, and with my toe, I kicked a soft plushie to the side where Jake had a small gathering of them. "Nice and specific."

"You know I have to watch my words."

I grunted. "Well, I don't need your apologies. Actions speak louder than words, and I know the Resolute desk is exactly where you want to be, not here visiting with me.

"So, I repeat, what do you want?"

He hesitated a second before explaining, "My approval rating has never been higher."

"You've been focused on taking down the Sparrows," I inserted.

"People are outraged by the corruption and you're taking a hard-line stance. It makes sense that you'd be popular with the masses."

"Yes, it does... but that comes with problems of its own."

"Meaning the Sparrows are out to get you?" Why did that sound as childish as me catcalling, 'The boogeyman is out to get you?'

Truth was, though, that the Sparrows *were* like boogeymen.

If they could pull the wool over the eyes of Five Pointers, then I didn't think the government had a chance at staying out of things.

"Yes, it means my family and I are targets," he said carefully. Carefully enough that I knew he was including me in that sentence.

That was probably the first time he'd ever been so inclusive, and it was because I was potentially in danger.

He should totally win the 'Dad of the Year' award.

"I'm safe. I have guards of my own," I told him stonily.

A sudden ache inside me bloomed to life.

God, I missed my mom so bad.

Why had she been taken from me when I'd been granted not one, but *two* deadbeat dads?

"You need to check their affiliations."

"I think Finn's seen to that," I drawled. "He's more concerned about my safety than you ever were."

"That's not fair," he spat.

"Isn't it? Seems pretty accurate to me. Look, if you're calling to give me a heads up, I appreciate it. I'll tell Finn—" Even if I really didn't want to have to. "—and he can up my security."

"My hands are tied here, Aoife, but I'll gladly pay for extra men to come and protect you while these active threats are ongoing."

My brows rose. "That would lead to a paper trail."

"That's how sure I am that there is a plot to hurt my family," he murmured.

I sat there, surrounded by luxury and kids' toys, and found myself accepting a simple truth—from birth, I'd been borrowing trouble. Just by having his DNA, I'd been waiting for the other shoe to drop without even knowing it.

Rubbing my eyes, I replied, "When?"

"I don't know. There's no real way of guesstimating, and trust me, I have the best analysts in the land trying to pin down dates.

"What I do know is that the chatter's been high since before Christmas. I'll message you a number that you can use to contact me in case of an emergency."

"You don't need to do that. I'll tell Finn. He'll handle everything."

"I know he's richer than me so he doesn't need the extra help financially, but I want to—"

"You don't have to," I told him coldly. "I appreciate the warning. Happy New Year."

I didn't wait for him to cut the call; I did it for him. A second later, I received a phone number via message.

For a second, I stared blankly at a train set that Jen, my best friend and tonight's guest at dinner, had bought Jake. It was expensive enough that I knew she must have done without Starbucks for a while, and gratitude filled me for her.

It filled me for Finn, and the O'Donnellys, and the family I'd made thanks to our marriage. Family that didn't sell me out so they could sit in the Oval Office.

"What's wrong, my love?" Finn's voice was soft, but I heard the tension in it. I knew him too well, as much as he knew me.

"That was my father." I peered at him over my shoulder. "He says the Sparrows are threatening his family."

Finn arched a brow. "He called to tell you that?"

I nodded. "Must be dire, right?"

He stepped over to me, sank onto the seat by my side, and curled an arm around my shoulders. "I'll fix things."

"If the President of the United States can't fix things, then I'm not sure you can."

Finn brushed his lips against my temple. "Oh, honey, don't you know the Five Points have more power than him?"

I snorted. "Your head gets any bigger, it'll explode."

He squeezed me as he chuckled. "His hands are tied. He has the biggest army in the world but he can't deploy them without Congress and Senate's approval. He can't do dick without bipartisan support.

"You think Aidan Sr. waits on things like that?"

I had to admit, "No."

"Well, then. You don't have to worry. I'll fix this."

Looking up at him, I saw the fierce resolve etched into his expression and reached up to press a kiss to his lips.

"Got news about Mary Catherine by the way."

"Oh, good!" Relief filled me. "I know Lena was worried."

"And that bitch mom of hers." He shuddered. "She went down to Ohio."

"Why?" I blinked. "That's a random state to go to."

"There's a sister chapter of the MC her man's loyal to."

"So, she's safe?"

He hummed. "She is." His mouth found mine again, and after he left me breathless, he whispered, "Does Jen have to come for dinner?"

I smiled at his complaint, then smiled wider when his tongue traced the curve of my mouth, tasting my amusement.

"She does. She's..."

I thought about the conversation we'd had earlier. A conversation where she'd told me that Aidan Jr.'s woman, Savannah, had forced a meeting between them years earlier so that she could snatch a DNA sample...

If that wasn't crazy enough, the DNA test Savannah had arranged proved that Jen, my girl from the block, a 57 varieties' kind of chick, was actually an O'Donnelly.

Padraig O'Donnelly's daughter, to be precise.

I'd promised I wouldn't say anything to Finn, that I'd keep my mouth shut, so I merely told him, "She really needs the company today."

Though he sighed, he kissed me again and asked, "Want me to call in Martha to set up the spare room?"

While he didn't like her, and put up with her for me, gratitude swelled inside me at his offer to let her spend the night.

"I'm a lucky woman," I told him huskily as I reached for his hand.

He raised the tangle of our fingers to his lips and brushed them over my knuckles. "Oh, sweetheart, I'm the lucky one, not you."

EIGHT

FINN

I WAS EXHAUSTED.

Combined with the clusterfuck that was Christmas, the past week had been hellishly long thanks to the funerals of the men who'd died in the Sparrow attack and was only exacerbated by a major fuck up with the architectural firm we used.

Well, no longer.

The last time they'd screwed up, Aidan Sr. had dealt with them, but this time, it was on me.

I wasn't about to shoot out anyone's kneecaps over business.

I'd fired them.

And I'd spread the news that they were a piece of shit firm so that no other company in the tri-state area would be using them until the current CEO's grandson was crapping into a bag in an old folks' home.

Acuig Corp. mattered.

But my name? My word? My signature?

Capable of making or breaking anyone in this fucking city.

I dropped my briefcase on the floor and stretched after I hung my coat on the rack.

All was quiet—it was two AM, so of course it was. It was unreasonable to think she'd have waited up for me—as I headed down the hallway toward our bedroom.

That was when I saw her.

In the living room.

I gritted my teeth at the way her neck was folded over, and I knew she'd have a crick in it because she *had* waited up for me.

This was my Aoife.

Of course she had. I should have had faith.

I walked into the cozy living room that was illuminated only by candles, and I sighed at the sight of her.

My angel.

I cast a glance at the hand she rested on her stomach and pressed mine to it as well after I crouched down in front of her.

"Baby," I rumbled when that didn't make her stir.

Her eyelashes fluttered. "Finn?" she asked drowsily.

"It had better be me."

Her lips twitched before she yawned. "What time is it?"

"Two AM."

Her eyes popped open. "Really?"

I winced. "It's late."

"Couldn't be later," she muttered with narrowed eyes. "Thought we agreed you'd be home for dinner?"

I heaved a sigh as I grabbed her hand, raised it to my lips and with my eyes on hers, kissed her palm. "Do I get points for calling to tell you I'd be late?"

"Points?" she asked huskily. "No. Appreciation? Yes. I'd have worried otherwise."

My throat choked and I put it down to fatigue. I wasn't sure if she knew what she did to me when she said shit like that.

No one had ever worried over me like she did.

No one had made me low sodium meals or insisted I take a thousand multi-vitamins in the morning. It was marriage. I knew that. But even having lived it for four years, it still came as a surprise.

"I never want you to worry," I grated out.

Her smile was sly. "Do you worry about me?"

"Of course," was my instant response, and I saw that I'd walked into her trap. I wagged a finger at her. "I'm supposed to worry about you."

She sniffed her disgruntlement, then let out a shriek as I jumped to my feet and hauled her into my arms a second later.

As she jolted against my chest, I peered down at her. "You should have gone to bed," I told her, even though I was damn glad she hadn't.

"I wait up for you. That's the deal," she said stubbornly, even as she pushed her face against my throat and kissed me there.

I was fucking exhausted, but that tiny goddamn kiss had my dick reacting like I'd slept for fourteen hours.

It also derailed me.

Instead of walking her to the bedroom, I diverted course to the baby grand in the corner.

As I propped her ass on the back end of it, then twirled her around so that I was between her legs, she peered up at me as a slow-growing smirk curved her lips. She rested back on her elbows and tightened her thighs around my hips.

"Think we'd slide off it?" I growled under my breath as I stared at the cami she wore that shaped her braless tits to perfection.

"Off the piano? I doubt it. It isn't a 'Slip N' Slide,'" she teased, but there was a breathy hint to her tone.

Any lingering exhaustion I felt drifted away at that, and I pressed my cock against the crotch of her short-shorts before looming over her, saying, "You want to go to bed?"

She arched a brow. "Does it look like I want to go to bed?"

"Giving you an out. Gotta look after my baby momma, don't I?" Her bottom lip was sucked between her teeth as she nipped it. I tugged it back out with my thumb, muttering, "No one bites that but me. You know the rules."

She swallowed. "I *do* know the rules."

Smirking, I bowed my head and dotted kisses along the neckline of her cami. On the return journey, I trailed my tongue across it then rumbled, "If I touch your pussy, how wet will it be?"

"On a scale of what?" she whispered.

"One to five. Five being wet as fuck."

"Two."

I smirked. "Can't have that, can we?"

"N-No," she mewled as I detached her legs from around my hips.

Sliding my hands down them, I tugged on her waistband, drew her panties off her before I placed her heels on the edge of the piano.

"Spread them, Aoife." A shaky breath escaped her as she complied, but I tutted. "Wider." She obeyed. "Wider." The move pulled her pussy lips apart, revealing her slit, and I rumbled, "Prettiest cunt in the world."

She gasped as I rubbed my thumb over her clit, watching her sex contract afterward. I teased her, monitoring every move she made, and when she rocked her hips up, I ordered, "Stay still, Aoife."

Her brow furrowed. "But I can't."

"You can if you want more."

She grunted. "Control freak."

I didn't argue, just thrust my thumb into her slit and pressed it up against the front wall of her pussy.

"You saying you don't like the control freak in me?" I taunted as she groaned, her back arching as her head fell back, exposing her throat.

I was going to bite that pale cream silk later on. Mark it so that when she looked in the mirror tomorrow, she'd remember this moment.

Clenching my jaw, I dipped down and pressed an open kiss to her clit. Sucking on it, I speared my thumb upward again, just waiting for her hips to rock. The second they did, I pulled back.

"Stay still, Aoife," I commanded.

A hiss escaped her. "Then stop doing that!"

I rubbed my thumb inside her. "You really mean that?"

"N-No," she whimpered, and that noise sank into my fucking bones.

"Eyes on me, baby," I demanded next, watching as she carefully lowered herself to the piano—I bet it hurt her elbows—and then raised her head by hooking one arm behind it.

With her head angled down now, she gave me her attention.

"You look away, I stop. You move, I stop. You tell me when you're about to come. Agreed?"

She nodded, and even in the candlelight, I saw her pupils dilate.

"Words, Aoife."

"Yes, Finn," she whispered, licking her lips.

Eyes locked on hers, I lowered my head and sucked on her clit as I rubbed her G-spot. I watched her gaze turn blurry, watched the muscles in her throat work, saw the tension in her body as she remained as still as could be.

One particularly hard suck had her legs jerking upward to clap around my ears.

I pulled back.

"No!" she cried. "I'm sorry! I'm sorry!"

"You broke the rules," I chided, removing my thumb from her slit.

"No! It hurt too good," she mewled nonsensically. "Please, I'll be better. I'll be better!"

I arched a brow at her and ordered, "Take off your cami."

Her hands snapped to the waistline and she eased herself upright then dragged it off. When her tits were exposed, I saw her puckered nipples and teased one with my wet thumb.

"How wet are you now?"

"Five," was her immediate answer.

I grunted as I dipped down to suckle on her nipple. As I pinched the tip between my teeth, her hands came up to hold me in place even as she yelped with pain. I soothed the discomfort with my tongue then moved up and over.

Nails digging into my scalp, she snapped her legs around my waist again as I began to kiss her throat. I raked the skin with my teeth then palpated the flesh with my tongue.

Only when she was arching into me did I bite her. Hard enough to leave the mark I wanted, hard enough for her to hiss in my ear. She didn't pull away though.

Aoife never did.

Rewarding her, I thrust my hand between us and played with her clit as I sucked and soothed the bite. Teasing the hypersensitive flesh had her shuddering against me, and I felt the rush of juices against my hand as she creamed at my touch.

With a final nip, I ground out, "How wet are you now?"

"*Nine*," she moaned.

Out of five? That was definitely what I was aiming for.

"Who does this pretty pussy belong to?"

My growl had her crying out.

"Words, Aoife! Who does it belong to?"

"You," she moaned.

"Aoife—" I started, an impatient growl in my voice.

She sobbed. "My pretty pussy belongs to you, Finn!"

A victorious snarl escaped me.

Angling back, I dragged down my zipper and grabbed a hold of my cock. With it in my fist, I rubbed it along her slit then rested the tip right where I wanted to thrust in deep.

"You want my dick, baby?" I whispered, letting my lips tug on her earlobe.

"Please, my love, please," she begged, her ankles crossing at my ass so her heels could dig into me.

"How about the next time you wait up for me, you sleep on the sofa, hmm?" I bartered, pulling back to look at her, seeing her brow furrow.

"I was comfortable."

"Your neck was cricked," I chided.

She huffed then rocked against me.

"You had no blanket on you."

"It's warm!"

"On the sofa, it's more comfortable *and* warmer," I said sternly.

She huffed again. "Okay, I'll wait on the damn sofa."

Now I'd gotten what I wanted, I thrust into her.

She cried out.

I returned to the scene of my earlier bite and sucked on the mark as I plowed her pussy. Hands moving to her ass, I fucked her hard and fast, giving her what we both needed.

Exhilaration rushed through me, something I could only ever feel when I was deep inside her, and I growled against her throat as her cunt clamped down and she sobbed, "Finn, I'm going to come—"

"Not yet," I grated out. "Hold it."

She let loose a mewl, and her body tensed up. More. More. *More.* She wailed. "N-Now?"

"Not yet," I snarled, feeling my own orgasm hitting me right between the eyes.

As her pussy did the fucking tango around my cock, I bit down on her throat again, aiming for the same spot as earlier, and around her flesh, I hissed, "Now."

We came together.

The explosion hit us both, forcing us closer, not further apart.

She clung to me as I clung to her. Her moans and whimpers matched my growls and groans. The symphony that was us filled the space, making better music than this fifty-thousand-dollar instrument ever could.

United against the world, we soared together, and as the inevitable fall to earth hit us, we did that as a pair as well.

NINE

FINN

"WHAT'S THIS?"

I shrugged as I spooned up the pappardelle that she'd called a simple dinner and which was better than a restaurant quality dish. "For you."

"You want to go on a cruise?" she questioned.

My lips twitched at her disbelief. "Not particularly. But we should take a break before the baby comes, and we wouldn't have to worry about flights."

Or snipers.

I didn't tell her that.

Or, Christ, they could be a part of the crew.

As I determined that I'd take a dozen guards with us if she agreed to go, she mused, "What if I get seasick?"

I blinked. "Do you suffer with that?"

"I've never been on a boat," she said with a laugh, and even though my idea might suck, the sparkle in her eyes made it worthwhile.

"Well, there's a first time for everything."

"How are you going to cope being away from the office?" She tilted her head to the side. "Let me guess. You wouldn't be? You'd bring the work with you?"

"Well, the negotiations with Hanover are still ongoing," I said uneasily.

Aoife shook her head. "You're nuts. Two hundred thousand on a cruise for you to stay inside the stateroom the entire trip?"

"I'd come out for food," I argued.

"Oh, great," she mocked, but I could tell she wasn't angry, more amused with me.

I swore, I wasn't sure what I'd done to earn such an understanding wife, but I was fucking lucky.

"It's not a good time, sweetheart," she was saying now. "I'm working on my brownies and cake pops. I think they'd make a great loss leader. The cake pops, I mean, but I need to perfect them. The ratio of frosting to cake is too much." Her gaze turned distant, and I knew she was in the land of lbs. and oz.

I grinned down at my plate. "Bakeaholic, that's you."

"Yep," she mumbled, blinking as she came back to me. "Can't bake on board a ship."

"You can if I get them to let you use their kitchens."

She snorted. "You'd do that too, wouldn't you?"

I arched a brow at her as I finished off my dinner.

"Of course you would," she said as she rolled her eyes.

With my dish in my hand, I got to my feet. Snagging hers off the table after she took her last bite, I headed over to the dishwasher.

With them tucked away, I returned to her side and pressed a kiss to her forehead. "Thank you for dinner, baby."

She smiled up at me. "You're welcome. Did you like it?"

"It was delicious." I pressed my hand to the back of her neck. "You spoil me."

"I like feeding you."

"I know. I'm thinking about getting one of those walking desks so I can walk and work at the same time."

Her eyes gleamed. "I prefer it when you do weights."

"Then you're in for a treat tomorrow."

"I know. It's arm day."

Laughing, I told her, "Yeah, of course you know my schedule."

"Like you don't know when I do yoga."

"Watching you turn into a pretzel is better than that pasta."

"I'm glad I'm sexier than carbs."

"No carb even compares to your butt." I kissed my fingers. "Perfection."

"Mostly because it's made of the aforementioned carbs," she teased.

I tutted under my breath and rumbled, "I told you not to do that."

Her nose crinkled. "Do what?"

"Talk smack about yourself."

"My butt's—"

"Beautiful." I smacked my lips again. "Biteable. Sexy enough that I wanna blow my wad whenever you bend over?"

Her smile made my heart sing. "I'll bend over more when you're around."

"My dick would appreciate that; my heart might not stand it."

With a chuckle, she shoved back her chair and got to her feet. "You're nuts."

"My nuts are your nuts," I joked, hauling her against my chest. "How was your day?"

"You're supposed to ask me that over dinner."

"I prefer to ask when you're in my arms, then I can feel your tension."

"You're nuts," she repeated, but she was smirking as she said it.

I was when it came to her.

No piece of information she told me was too small or unimportant for me to know.

Some might say I was obsessed, but I wasn't. I just knew I had the best woman in the fucking world in my arms, and I wasn't about to lose her by not appreciating the joy she brought to my life.

Other shit... Well, that was out of my control.

This wasn't.

Being her husband and Jake's father was an honor, and I needed her to know that I felt that way.

"That doesn't answer my question." I touched my nose to hers and ran it along the short length. "How was your day?"

"Louise pissed me off," she said on a sigh, referring to her assistant manager.

"Why?"

"She fucked up the cash receipts. It's okay now, though. I managed to get it sorted out."

I didn't show her my tension because then it might have looked like I had a reason for saying, "She fucks up a lot."

"She's good with the customers," she defended, "and in a pinch, if someone's ill or cuts out of their shift, she can take over."

"There are other versatile employees out there," I pointed out. "Billy's the same. You haven't promoted him."

She hummed. "True."

I hated Louise. She was a fucking snake in the grass, smiling at Aoife one minute, giving me the eye the next.

Like I'd be interested in her when I had a walking, talking, breathing goddess for a wife.

"*True*," I taunted. "You're too soft. We'll have this conversation next month when she fucks up again."

She crinkled her nose. "We won't."

"We will. Louise always messes up—"

"Always is a bit harsh," she grumbled.

I curled my arm around her shoulders as I tugged her into moving forward. With each step, she shifted deeper into my hold, her arm sliding around my waist as we headed for Jake's room.

I hated that I got home after he was in bed. Hated that my wife stayed up late because I was always fucking working. But before I could get angry at how I was doing things at the moment, the silence of the nursery, apart from his gentle breaths, settled me in a way that nothing else could.

Peace.

I wanted that for him.

I wanted him to lead a different life.

I didn't want Jake to be one of those spoiled rich kids who didn't know the value of a dollar, but I wanted him to have it easier. What was the point in busting my ass if he didn't have that?

And I'd bust said ass and work myself into an early grave so he could have a better start than me.

His future was at the top of my agenda.

Aoife angled her head against mine as we stared down at him, the gentle glow from the nightlight the only illumination in the room.

As we stood there, I let the calm sink into me, watching after a couple minutes when she rearranged his blanket and moved his stuffie closer.

Taking that as a cue to leave, we headed out of the nursery and down the hall to the living room.

With the fire blazing, I dragged her with me to the sofa and didn't settle until she was draped over me.

She laughed. "You'll be more comfortable if I sit over there."

"Says who?" I countered, leaning into the cushions as I straightened out my legs.

With her on my lap, I sighed as she positioned herself so that she was half on top of me, our feet tangling, her head on my chest.

The day might have been shitty, but my nights were always fucking wonderful. Whether I deserved it or not, this was my reward. *They* were.

Stroking my hand over her hair, I told her, "Think about the cruise."

Her head rocked against my chest. "I don't think I have sea legs."

"You won't know until we go on one," I countered.

"Why would you want to sail down the Atlantic during winter?"

"You have a point," I said on a sigh, recognizing that particular flaw in my plan.

"In May? Sure. But I don't think I'll be comfortable with being away from the doctors at that point."

I tensed some. "Speaking of, baby, I wanted to talk to you about something."

"What is it?"

"I'm thinking about getting a vasectomy."

She stilled. "Because of me?"

"Well, in part. I know you want a big family, sweetheart, but your body doesn't agree." I kissed her temple. "I think two will be enough, don't you?"

She was quiet for so long that I thought she was working herself into a rage, but her voice was rougher than I liked as she whispered, "I *do* want a big family."

"I know you do, baby." It was why I hadn't gone through with the procedure just yet.

I'd known she was pregnant before she had. The dates of her period were in my calendar at work, for Christ's sake. But I knew from experience not to bring it up, so my getting the pregnancy test as a Christmas gift had come as a genuine surprise.

We'd lost two babies before Jake, and each time, she hadn't told me until the miscarriage had happened and I'd found her in tears.

I knew what she wanted, but that just wasn't in the cards for us. Biologically, anyway.

While I hated not being able to give her the world, two losses and two gains weren't odds I appreciated.

It was time to take any and all risks away.

"I don't want Jake to be like us," she whispered.

"And he won't be, will he?" I murmured, carefully stroking her shoulders as I continued, "Not only will he have us, but he'll have Buster in there."

A surprised laugh escaped her. "Buster?"

I shrugged. "What else should we call him or her?"

"Buster's a boy's name."

Snorting, I told her, "It's non-binary."

"I'll remember to tell that to Aidan Sr. at Sunday dinner," she teased.

"Please do." I chuckled. "I like watching Shay slice into him. Remember when he explained what cis-gender is?"

"I saw a couple of Senior's remaining dark hairs turn gray after that discussion. I'm still not sure why he finds it so complicated."

"Because he's a simple man. And I mean that in the broadest sense."

Her lips twitched as she peered at me. "Well, Shay will bring him into the twenty-first century."

"God help him," I drawled.

Her amusement died as she looked at me, and in the firelight, her expression was a mixture of somber and loving. I hated to see the somber, though I knew I was the reason for it.

"Thank you for letting me try, Finn," she whispered.

"I want to give you the fucking world, baby," I said gruffly. "It kills me that I can't give you the big family you want, but I need to look after you—"

"You always look after me," she retorted staunchly.

"Yeah, well, this is my way of keeping up with that." I trailed my finger along her cheekbone.

"Thank you for not going behind my back, Finn."

She wasn't to know that I did nothing behind her back. I was keeping enough from her, and the least I could do was be candid with her on everything else.

Aoife tucked her face against my side, and as we stared into the fire, I knew we were both thinking about what we should have had, but what life had taken from us.

I'd apologized a thousand times for what had happened on our wedding day, but this was my true punishment. Not giving the woman who was my life the one, simple thing her man should give her—the large family she wanted.

She suffered for my sins, and I had to live with that every goddamn day.

TEN

AOIFE

I SMILED when a hand moved around my face and settled over my eyes. Reaching up, I cupped the wrist and asked, "Who's that?"

Finn laughed. "I hope you don't mean that."

Grinning, I murmured, "Oh, it's you. Not my other husband." I popped up onto my tiptoes, snatched his wrist and lowered it so I could kiss where his pulse beat when he grumbled at my reply. "Didn't expect you home so early."

"You weren't supposed to. This is what's known as a surprise."

"A surprise?"

A ping sounded at the elevator. "Who's that?"

The doors whirred open as he answered, "Aela."

I arched a brow. "What's she doing here?"

I didn't mind, of course. I liked my sister-in-law, but the kitchen had been hit by a chocolate bomb from a day's worth of developing a new brownie recipe.

My desire for my bakery to go insta-famous had yet to be reached, but I persevered.

With the kitchen crazy, I didn't really want guests—even if they were family—seeing my process which was messy as hell.

"She's going to look after Jake for us."

"Why?" I twisted to peer up at him. "We're here," I told him, stating the obvious.

"Not for long. It's time I took you out."

"Is that wise?"

Since Dad's call, I had an extra pair of guards when I left the penthouse.

"We're going downstairs, sweetheart. It's an elevator ride away."

"*Verdi?*" I guessed.

"I know you've been itching to try their Chicken in Brioche."

Disappointment hit me. "You need to order in advance."

He winked. "I did."

"Look at you, being all organized. I'm surprised you remembered I want to visit that one." Managing my excitement, however, I said, "You're tired, though. We can stay here. You can relax."

He smiled at me. "I'll relax when I see you in what I bought you."

My eyes narrowed. "Ahh, so this is a gift for both of us?"

"Sure is. We Five Pointers never do anything without a game plan in mind, and looking at you in that dress..." He whistled. "There's no other way I'd like to spend my evening."

My cheeks heated with his words.

"Sweetheart?" he prompted, apparently wondering why I was standing there staring at him.

"Sorry, I was just thinking." I reached up and ran my fingers along his chin. "You're too gorgeous not to stare at."

I liked saying stuff like that because it always made his ears turn pink at the tips.

Not that he'd admit it.

Grinning when his ears flushed, I tweaked the lobe of one. "I love you."

The warmth in his eyes was everything. He told me he loved me there first, silently, before rasping, "I love you too, Aoife." He dropped his chin and pressed a kiss to my temple. "You're the gorgeous one."

His hands settled on my stomach, which was flat for the moment, but his gaze roamed over my face, to my wild hair, and then to the mess I'd made with the flour I could feel dusting my cheeks and the cocoa that was undoubtedly sprinkled all over my clothes. The most wicked of grins creased his lips as he took me in.

With Aela's footsteps and a hollered, "Aoife, you in the kitchen, babe?" in the background, Finn whispered in my ear, "I'd fuck you hard against that counter if I hadn't made plans, baby. Show you how tired

I'm *not* where your pussy's concerned. Lick you up like you're the cookie dough—"

My cheeks burned even though I was used to him saying stuff like that, but each noisy step Aela made as she stomped down the hall acted like a ticking clock.

"It's brownie batter."

He blinked at me. I blinked back.

"Lick you up like you're the brownie batter," I corrected, unsurprised when he burst out laughing.

"Jesus, Finn, calm the fuck down," Aela sniped as she finally made it into the kitchen, but she had a phone in her hand, and I heard the clicks as she took photos.

I twisted around to shoot her a wry grin and saw she'd brought a big bag that was covered in paint.

I arched a brow at her, and she muttered, "He's next."

"Next?"

"For Lena's portraits. I'm still working on Declan's, but I thought I could creep on your photos of him so I can choose his positioning for when I'm ready to start."

Finn's laughter quickly morphed into a groan. "If you think I have time to pose for a painting—"

"You'll make time," I informed him. "Aela, can you make two? I want one."

She peered down her nose at me. "How many brownies do I get in return?"

"An endless supply?" I swept the platter of less-than-stellar brownies off the counter and hovered it under her nose. "Starting with this batch."

Aela snagged one, took a bite, and her eyes grew big in her face as she chewed. "Oh. My. God."

"That bad?" I grimaced. "They're not right, but I thought they were edible—"

"That's the best thing I've ever put in my mouth. Seriously. Don't tell Declan that."

Finn snorted. "Bet your ass I'll tell him that if it means you make Conor sit for a portrait next and not me."

She took another bite, pointedly ignoring him. "What kind of fucking crack is this?"

I stared at the brownies. "I didn't think they were that great."

"Let me be the judge." Finn snagged a piece for himself and took a bite. His eyes did the same thing Aela's did. "Jesus, baby, she's right. Did you put coke in them?"

Snorting, I told him, "I hope not considering I run a family-friendly establishment."

He carried on chewing. "This is why I have to work out three hours a day."

"If you have time for that, you have time for me to take sketches of you so I can paint you twice," Aela groused, but she talked as she ate which made me laugh because she snagged another brownie. Finn made me laugh too—he flipped her the bird.

Still smiling, I peered down at the unassuming batch. "I thought they were bland."

Aela sniffed. "If you need an official taste tester, please, let me know because I volunteer as tribute."

Finn snagged his arm around my waist. "She's already got an official taste tester. Me."

"Now, now, there's plenty to go 'round," Aela countered. "Don't be selfish, Finn."

"She's mine," he growled under his breath, but though his lips were smiling, I saw the stamp of possession in his eyes. That stamp that was always there. That always branded me.

I pressed a hand to his abs to soothe the beast. "I'm yours. Always."

He snagged my mouth in a kiss that I felt to my bones, and just as the brownie platter started wobbling in my hold, Aela snapped, "Watch the brownies, Finn. For God's sake." I felt it being snatched out of my hand as Finn bit down on my bottom lip, hard enough to leave indentations.

"Mine," he rasped.

I smiled, but it turned smug. "Yours."

He tapped me on the nose. "Witch. You weren't going to let me try the brownies, were you?"

He knew me too well. "They're not right. I was going to wrap them up for the food bank."

"If these are wrong, Aoife, then I want to taste everything that comes out of your oven," Aela groused.

"Being pregnant is messing with your taste buds," I argued.

"Is it messing with mine too?" Finn drawled, making me laugh.

Aela sniffed as she shot me a pointed look before she headed over to the other end of the kitchen where Jake was playing.

"Hey little dude, you don't know how lucky you are to have a mom who makes magic in the kitchen."

As she ruffled his hair up, Aela switched on the TV, and after flicking through a few channels, the news came on.

My brow furrowed as I saw the screen. "That's that hockey player you like, Finn."

"I know. Haven't you heard? He was kidnapped."

"Jeez. Isn't he Canadian?"

"Yeah." He laughed. "Canadians get kidnapped too."

"Apparently."

He tugged on my hand and walked us over to the sofa where Aela was gorging on what looked to be her fourth piece.

"Babe, you eat another brownie and you'll puke."

She shrugged. "I puke all the time anyway. This one would be worth it."

"If you say so," I muttered but I was smiling. Maybe that recipe wasn't crap, after all.

Finn slung his arm over my shoulders, but even as he hauled me into his side, flour dusting and all, his focus was on the screen.

"Bastards," he mumbled under his breath.

Aela peered up at him. "You pissed because he was kidnapped, because he's a good player, because the Points didn't get to him first, or all of the above?"

I felt his tension, but he let it simmer as he told her, "The Points rarely stoop to kidnapping."

"Rarely being the operative word there, Aoife."

We shared a look. "Aela," I told her, a warning in my voice.

"Just saying. It's all in the minutiae."

"Life often is," was Finn's retort, but his smile had died.

I heaved a sigh. "It is what it is."

"You say that like it's a *fait accompli* that our dudes have to do this shit for a living." Aela sniffed. "You never heard of mature students? Career changes?"

Finn surprised me by laughing. "Aela, can you imagine Conor in school again?"

Her eyes twinkled, and that reminded me that she'd been in high school with Declan.

"You saw him?" I questioned.

Aela shrugged. "I missed out on catching Brennan in a letterman jacket, but Conor, I saw."

"He was a letterman?"

Finn snorted. "No. He couldn't run with a ball if his life depended on it."

I twisted to peer up at him. "Did you play football?"

He winked. "Maybe."

"I can't believe you've never told me that," I complained. "What position?"

"Running back."

"Lena must have pictures of him somewhere on those damn walls of shame of hers," Aela muttered, her focus split now between us, the TV, and the brownies.

"I haven't seen any, and I helped her put most of those up." I pouted. "I need to see you in compression shorts and shoulder pads."

"I won't kink shame, but really, Eef?" Aela scoffed. "Shoulder pads do it for you?"

"They do when my husband's wearing them." I grinned up at him. "You need to find me some pictures."

He rolled his eyes. "You see me work out every day."

Aela whistled under her breath. "This conversation is getting personal. I don't think I'm old enough to listen in."

"You're older than me," I derided, but my lips curved wider as I placed my hand on Finn's abs and moved into him.

As the reporter went into details of how the hockey star had been kidnapped, I tuned out when Finn's hand went down to my ass.

While he copped a feel, Aela sniffed. "What kind of mega star like that doesn't have guards?"

"Hockey players don't have guards," Finn retorted. "Anyway, he's an infamous hermit. Hates his privacy being invaded."

"Yeah, well, because of that his home got invaded. In this day and age, everyone needs guards." Aela grumbled under her breath, "Amateur."

"You're in a particularly gnarly mood, Aela. If a pound of brownies doesn't do the trick, I'll have to remind Declan that he needs to keep you sweeter," Finn retorted.

"I'm sweet enough, and I'll remember that when I'm immortalizing you for life, Finn O'Grady. Beware of the woman holding the paintbrush."

Smiling, I patted his stomach again. "Give me fifteen minutes. I'll get showered and changed." Before I left, I asked, "Aela, you sure you can manage?"

"Betting Shay was more of a nightmare than Jake. Right, little dude?" she called out at Jake who was busy trying to build a skyscraper with blocks.

He ignored her.

She smiled. "I love a quiet kid."

"Keep telling yourself he's quiet," Finn mocked, but he folded his arms across his chest as I left to kiss a grumpy Jacob goodnight—he was *not* happy about being disturbed. "Turn it up."

Aela did as he asked, and I left to the sounds of news of the Irish prime minister's upcoming arrival in the States.

A quick shower and I was no longer dusted in flour. It didn't take me long to put on some makeup and to style my hair into a bun for ease.

With that set, I drifted into the bedroom and found the gown Finn had bought me lying on top of the comforter.

At first, I was surprised because it was black. He tended to buy me things that were red or green in color, but I was more than okay with that, especially when I picked it up and took in the elegant style.

It was cut deep at the front and at the back too so both my breasts and spine would be on display, but I knew it would cup my waist and hips to perfection.

As I dressed in some of my fancier *Agent Provocateur* panties, I managed to get into the dress. It knocked my bun askew, so I had to do it again, and as I was slipping pins in, Finn appeared in the doorway.

His gaze was hot as it trailed over my length, and he murmured, "I regret making dinner reservations now."

I peeped a smile at him. "If you hadn't, I'd still be covered in flour."

"I like you covered in flour."

Need crawled through my system. "You like me all the time."

It was a cocky statement.

I didn't even realize *how* cocky until, without even a blink, he nodded. "I do." Finn stepped over to me, hand held out. "Ready, Mrs. O'Grady?"

Slipping my hand into his, I nodded and took him in, realizing that he'd switched sports coats because my floury fingerprints didn't mar the silk. With both of us wearing black, we could have looked funereal but I knew we matched.

That was his end game.

His possessive stamp was merely enhanced as he slipped me against his side.

I knew Mr. O'Grady's best moves by now. Although he *did* have it in him to surprise me regularly.

On our way out, I peeped into the kitchen, saw Aela was still eating brownies and that Jake was focused on his building blocks, and I decided not to disturb either of them.

We headed down the hall to the elevator, and the second after the doors closed and he'd pressed the button for *Verdi*, he pinned me against the wall.

I'd expected that though—my bun was high enough on my crown that the flat of my head was flush to the wall.

See? I knew his best moves and how to accommodate them.

Smiling at him and feeling smug, I rested my arms over his shoulders and asked, "Why, Mr. O'Grady, what do you think you're doing?"

"Mussing my wife up, Mrs. O'Grady. You were looking too pristine for my liking."

I mock-gasped. "You like it when I look messy?"

He ran his nose down my cheek. "Makes me think of you when we've fucked."

Sighing, I rasped, "You get to see that often enough in bed without me looking like that when we go out."

"I like you pristine, messy, floury—all the adjectives." I felt his smile against my cheek. "But if we're heading to a fancy restaurant, and we're Jake-free for the night, I want to see you mussed."

The doors opened at a very inappropriate moment, but ours was a private elevator that served the penthouse so there was no one nearby to gawk at us.

Still, I pressed my lips to his and whispered, "I'm mussed. You can finish the job later. You promised me Chicken in Brioche."

He pulled back with a grumble, "Never let it be said I don't fulfill my pregnant wife's cravings."

I laughed. "Not sure I've reached the cravings part of things yet."

Finn stunned me by dipping down to press a kiss to my still barely-there belly. "Wonder if it'll be ice cream like it was with Jake."

Warmth filled me. "You remember that?"

"Not like I could forget." His eyes twinkled as he led me into the restaurant, his hand at the small of my back.

The heat of him there set off a slow burn ache in my core that didn't dissipate when the maître d' spotted us and guided us to the bar, nervously saying, "Your table will be ready in two minutes, sir."

Reaching for his other hand, I squeezed it, knowing he wouldn't like being kept waiting, and the guy looked suitably nervous.

"Fucking nerve," he bitched under his breath when the maître d' scuttled away.

"You're too used to everyone treating you like you're a god," I chided, amused. I'd spent most of my life as a non-entity, but Finn was very much used to the perks of association with the O'Donnellys. "It's good to come down from Olympus every now and then."

"Olympus has its perks—"

Before he could continue, his phone rang. I recognized the ringtone and arched a brow. "Aidan Jr.?"

He sighed. "Yeah."

"Go and answer it. By the time you're done, we should be able to take a seat."

"Sorry, sweetheart." I saw the irritation in his expression but he pressed a kiss to my temple, muttering his thanks before he answered the phone and snarled at Aidan, "This had better be fucking good, jackass."

Before he left, though the background music drowned him out, I managed to hear him mention something about Sullivan, Lucifer and ghosts, and I turned to watch him go in surprise.

Finn wasn't exactly religious, so why the hell would he be talking about ghosts with Aidan? I knew Sullivan was one of the two Five Pointers who'd turned informant for the Sparrows... was he wishing him to hell?

Finn disappeared quickly into the crowd, and while I watched him go because my husband in a suit was a show worth watching, I turned back once I couldn't see him any longer and found a server waiting on me to order.

"I'll have a club soda, please," I requested with a smile.

In the mirrored wall that was lined with liquor bottles, I had a perfect view of the restaurant.

Verdi was one of the building's newer eateries, and I was here for it. I loved fusion cuisine, and this was on the path to getting a Michelin star —at least, according to the magazines I subscribed to.

I saw the man walking toward me in the mirror behind the shelves before he settled at my side. I didn't say anything, even though he was way too close for comfort, and as the server handed my drink to me, I picked it up with a grateful smile then shifted away, using the move to put some distance between us.

The smell of whiskey was strong on his breath but he didn't appear intoxicated, and when I looked up, I saw he'd moved even closer.

He was an older man, in his fifties, maybe sixties, and the years had worn badly on him.

He had a full head of silver hair and a beard to match. One look and you'd think Santa, but deep in his eyes, there were a lot of emotions—all of them negative.

Was it ridiculous that I sought out my guards? I hadn't seen them so far but that didn't mean they wouldn't be somewhere in the vicinity.

"Anyone ever tell you how beautiful you are?"

The words didn't match the strange tempest in his eyes, so I arched a brow at him and shut this down, "My husband does. All the time."

"You're married?" He heaved a sigh. "The pretty ones always are."

I kept my focus averted after that, but in the mirror, I monitored him. He was looking at me. Completely turned to face me.

"What is it?" I demanded after a couple minutes.

"If you were mine, I wouldn't leave you standing by a bar."

That had me rolling my eyes. "Not even to use the bathroom?"

"He didn't head toward the bathroom, though, did he?"

I tensed. "You were watching?"

"Of course. Had to know if you were a damsel in distress in need of saving or not."

"I'm married," I said firmly, turning to look at him, but as I did, maybe it was a flicker of the light, something about his expression— "Do I know you?" Whatever I'd been about to ask, it was shoved aside by that whisper of recognition I felt.

"I doubt it. I'm fresh off the boat. Been a long time since I was in the States." He sent me a look I could only describe as curious. "The name's Dagda."

"You're Irish," I said flatly, not introducing myself.

"I am." He smirked, but was it just me or did he seem disappointed? "Was it the accent that gave it away?"

"Do you have some kind of grievance against the O'Donnellys?" I demanded.

"Who are they?" He frowned as he took a sip of his drink. "I know a

Donnghal. That NHL player in Canada that just got himself kidnapped. That the one?"

He appeared sincere, but it didn't stop me repeating, "I'm married."

"You've said that already," he drawled. "I just happened to see a fine-looking woman with a head of hair as fiery as the sun, standing on her lonesome by the bar. What kind of gentleman would I be if I didn't keep her company?"

His voice felt familiar. But how could it be when I'd never met the man?

Curiosity had me twisting to face him fully. "Your accent..."

"What about it?"

Slowly, I shook my head. "I-I—"

"Aoife?"

Finn's growl was like a splash of cold water in my face, but in a good way. Not bad.

His hand moved around my waist, and like the proprietorial alpha jackass he was, he hauled my back to his front as if I were a bag of potatoes. I didn't argue though. I needed the support.

That voice... it reminded me of something. I just couldn't put my finger on it.

"Who are you?" Finn demanded when I didn't answer him.

"Just a man standing by a bar, that's all," the stranger replied with a winsome smile that fell short because, deep in his eyes, nothing had changed.

I felt as if I'd just opened Pandora's box and was staring deep into the abyss. Everything hateful was buried within those shamrock-green eyes, and yet, I sensed he didn't hate me.

How bizarre.

He walked off a second later, raising his drink to me before he faded away.

"Aoife?"

I blinked, recognizing that Finn had repeated my name a couple times. "What?"

"Are you all right?" He growled under his breath. "Your fucking guards—"

"I'm sure they were watching. He wasn't a threat."

He grunted. "If you say so. What did he want?"

"Nothing." I frowned, repeated, "Nothing." I believed that. So why did it feel like a lie? "Is everything okay with Aidan?"

"As okay as it ever is in this fucking world we live in."

A part of me wondered if Finn was depressed by his circumstances, but Finn was the kind of man who didn't particularly have time to be depressed. He'd push through it because time was money, and money was his god.

"I heard you talking about Halloween."

It was his turn to blink, then he laughed. "You wouldn't make a great spy, sweetheart. Although, I was whispering, so you'd have the ears for it." He pressed a kiss to my temple. "Ghost guns, not ghosts."

"Do I even want to know?"

"No, you don't."

Gently, I asked, "Have there been any repercussions about Sullivan and Walsh?"

He pressed a kiss to my throat, making me shiver in his hold as he answered, "Not so far."

Distracted, I still had the wherewithal to query, "You're not certain Senior will keep to his word?"

"No. I'm not." He tugged at my bun. "Why did you put your hair up?"

Because I wasn't an idiot, I knew he was trying to change the subject, and I rolled with it, seeing as this was our time together and business took up too much of that anyway.

"It was a mess." I tapped the tip of his nose. "Give me more notice in the future."

He cast me a sly glance. "How would that be a surprise?"

My lips quirked. "Well, a bun is the compromise."

I smiled at the maître d' as he approached us, and while he guided us to our table, I cast a glance around the restaurant, trying to see if I could find the stranger.

But I couldn't.

Had he left?

And why did it bother me so much that he might have?

ELEVEN

FINN

A FEW DAYS LATER

"OH, my God, Phil Bélanger is so hot."

I only heard the whisper because I was watching her and not the game on the TV.

Aoife was sitting with Inessa, drooling over one of those books they loved to read.

The words were throwaway, a simple remark.

So why did I feel them in my soul?

Why was I stupidly jealous of a guy on a book cover?

I rubbed my chin as I looked at her: my woman, my *wife*. Mine.

"What's wrong?"

I shot Eoghan a tired smile. "Nothing."

He frowned. "Not sure I believe you. You look exhausted."

"I am. Problems with the architects, with Hanover Corp. Every fucking where I turn, problems."

"That's normal." Eoghan pulled a face. "Are you... ill or something?"

I frowned back at him. "Do I look ill?"

"I don't know. Something's going on with you. Mostly you just look like you need a nap. A long one."

I had to laugh. "Yeah. I could probably go for one of those."

His head tipped to the side. "You can tell me what's going on with you, you know?"

"Nothing's going on with me."

"Thought you were happy with how the latest projections were looking?"

"I am. We're on target to make five hundred mil by the second quarter."

"So why do you look like you could put a gun to your head and pull the trigger?"

My eyes bugged. "Jesus Christ, Eoghan. I'd never do that! Fuck, I got a family. Another kid coming before the end of the year."

He shrugged. "Never said you'd do it, just said that you looked that way."

Knowing Aoife hadn't overheard when she was deep into a conversation about the book she and Inessa were buddy reading, I scrubbed a hand over my face. "You're right. Just need to sleep. That's all."

"Well, we can look after Jacob if you want."

Despite myself, I had to smile. "I'd like my kid to come back to me the next morning. Neither you nor Inessa are exactly kid friendly."

"I can keep Jake alive. He'll sleep for most of it, won't he?"

I squinted at him. "You been waiting to offer to babysit until he sleeps through the night?"

He smirked at me. "Do I look like an idiot? Of course, I waited. Ma's been bitching at me to babysit though. She thinks it'll make me want to start a family."

"Trust me, you have a kid for longer than four hours, you'll realize you don't." Then, I conceded, "Well, when they're not yours. Wouldn't give Jake up for the world. Even if he did shit up my arms a few times."

"Jesus H. Christ. He shat on your arms?"

"I don't think he did it on purpose," I said, chuckling at his expression of horror. "I mean, he didn't shout, 'Take aim and fire!'"

"Well, it sounds pretty fucking premeditated to me."

"Can you aim where you shit if you're on your back?"

"That's not one of my kinks, so the fuck if I know."

"Anyway, point is, kids are awesome when they're yours."

Eoghan shrugged. "Inessa's barely out of high school. Why the fuck would I make her be a mom when she's still a teenager?"

"Makes you sound like a pervert."

"Trust me, I fucking feel like it sometimes when she and Victoria go on about K-pop."

"What's that?"

"I listen and I still don't know. Bunch of Korean guys doing coordinated dances as far as I can tell. She wanted to go to Korea for our goddamn honeymoon, but I convinced her to go to Ireland."

"Why would you do that?"

"Because it'll rain all the time. Do I look like a dumbass?"

"Why the fuck would you want it to rain? Never heard of Aruba?"

"I don't want to leave that room for at least half the trip."

Snickering, I told him, "If you don't want kids, then go equipped."

"I'll have more condoms with me than a goddamn Trojan factory."

My lips curved but I advised, "Don't let Lena pressure you into having kids if you're not ready for them."

"Don't worry, I won't. But I can still babysit if you guys need some time together."

"To bang?"

"Well, you said it." He arched a brow. "I actually meant to sleep. Although Aoife doesn't look as rough as you. Which, considering she's percolating another human being, says a lot about how shitty you look."

I shot my beautiful wife another glance and murmured, "No. She's always gorgeous." If anything, she was more beautiful when she was pregnant.

It was a tragedy that she'd been robbed of the ability to have the large family she wanted.

All because that fucking asshole Callum O'Reilly had sold us out.

They said secrets gnawed at you, but they did more than that. They ate you alive. Ate you from the inside out. And thanks to Callum O'Reilly, I had another one weighing down my soul.

"Why do you sound so fucking sad? Jesus, Finn, what's going on with you? Don't make me bring in Aidan to torture it out of you."

"Not Brennan?"

"Well, we don't want you dead."

I shook my head and, laughing, told him, "You have a point. Although Aidan can be pretty fucking deadly when he chooses to be."

"Bren's made it an art form."

"This is true. You're also quite good at it."

Eoghan dismissed that. "It's different when you're a thousand yards away."

"Is it? Still taking a life, ain't it?"

"It's different. Trust me, the U.S. Army invested a couple million into making me not worry about my kills," he said, totally unfazed.

I fell silent at his words, but it didn't stop me from asking, "Doesn't the guilt eat away at you?"

"You wanna know if sometimes I get in the fucking shower and weep like a baby when I think about how much blood is on my soul?"

We shared a glance.

A loaded one.

"What have you done?" Eoghan grated out after a few minutes.

"Nothing."

He scowled at me. "Don't fucking bullshit me."

"I didn't do anything," I muttered, scraping a hand over my face. "That's the problem."

"Someone else did?"

"Yeah."

"What?"

"I can't say. It would change things. Change every-fucking-thing, in fact."

"I can't tell you not to worry about it because we both know that isn't always doable." He rubbed a thumb along his bottom lip. "But we can talk about it. If you want. I won't say shit to anyone. I know Junior's your man..." He heaved a sigh. "Can we cut the bullshit?"

I arched a brow. "By all means."

Eoghan hesitated a second before stating, "It has to be the worst kept secret in the family, but I know you're Da's son, Finn. I've known for a while."

For a second, I just froze. Aidan knew now. At St. Patrick's church before we'd razed the fucker to the ground, he'd asked me for confirmation, and I wasn't about to lie. Neither was I about to lie now.

"Yeah, I'm his son," I said gruffly, the words still not falling from my lips with ease. If anything, it got harder to say them out loud, not easier.

"And let's face it, Ma might not have given birth to you, but she thinks of you as her own."

Fuck, I wished that were the truth.

"When I first met Aoife, do you know I blackmailed her into sleeping with me?"

Eoghan's eyes rounded.

"Yeah. I'm a piece of shit. I know it."

"Well, you're certainly fucking something." He tugged on his collar. "I mean, she's apparently forgiven you."

God, that was the least of my sins.

So fucking many.

Was it any wonder I couldn't sleep at night?

"Do you ever get scared you'll lose her?"

I shot him a glance, well aware he wasn't just talking about me, but himself too. "You're the one who told me I need to sleep. What do you think keeps me up at night? The job?" I scoffed. "My soul is dirty enough that the shit I do for the Points doesn't give me insomnia anymore."

"We all have our secrets."

"What are yours? Her dad?"

"Inessa is way too smart not to have figured out that I was behind his kneecaps being blown out," he said dryly, rubbing his chin. "Glad that fucker's dead though, and his soul ain't on my conscience. How long has it been since you've confessed?"

That had me blinking at him. "Why?"

He shrugged. "Curious."

"About?"

"Whether or not it works. I have to say, ever since the church burned down, shit's been different." He tapped his temple. "I used to think it was bullshit, but Da hasn't been making us go to another parish, so I've been taking advantage of the change of pace.

"I kill as easily as I blink," he said, raising his hand and flicking his index finger against his thumb as if he were pulling the trigger on his sniper rifle. "That has a dramatic effect on how I view the world."

Studying him, I had to admit nothing about this conversation was going how I'd imagined. "I don't doubt that it does."

Seemed to me that the discussion on the table was our immortal souls. The Holy fucking Trinity. When all I'd expected was to watch the rerun of the Knicks' game when he came over.

He tipped his head to the side. "Tell you a secret for one of yours?"

My brow puckered at that. "We've already shared secrets, haven't we?"

His smirk made an appearance, one that made me smile because he was such a cocky piece of shit who went through life like he was fucking James Bond that, at some point, you stopped thinking of him as a man— he was a soldier.

A killing machine.

A military-trained assassin who had more kills on his hands than even his da could compete with.

Long distance or not.

"I don't consider those a secret. Not when every woman who enters the family home figures out you're an O'Donnelly faster than we can eat Ma's Sunday roast."

"What's that supposed to mean?"

"One glance at Ma's wall of fame and Inessa was getting antsy. I've heard them talking—"

"You've heard them talking? How?" He answered with a smile, and the unholy gleam in his eyes had me shaking my head at him. "What the hell have you done now?"

"Inessa's phone's bugged."

I scowled at him. "Are you shitting me?"

"Why are you so shocked?" he questioned. "That's not even my secret. It's Conor's."

"This fucking family," I growled. "Is Aoife bugged?"

"What do you think?" was his droll retort.

Yeah, Aoife was bugged.

And this was Senior's next phase in weeding out Sparrows from the Points.

Rage filled me as I grabbed my phone and sent Conor a message:

Me: *What the fuck do you think you're doing bugging my woman?*

Kid: *Now, now, Finn. Be rational.*

Me: *Did you just tell me to calm down?*

Kid: *I didn't. I told you to be rational. There's a big difference.*

Me: *Tell that to my fucking temper.*

I shot Aoife and Inessa a look, then did something I rarely did: called Conor and spoke with him in Korean.

"The hell kind of game are you playing?"

"What's wrong?"

"What's wrong?" I repeated, snarling the words at him, well aware that Aoife was watching me, Eoghan and Inessa too. "How fucking dare you?" My temper burst into a thousand shards when a realization came to me. "Are all our phones bugged?"

"Of course," Conor replied, sounding confused.

"Of course?" I felt like my brain was about to burst out of my skull.

Of fucking course?

And he was the one who sounded confused?

"Are you just going to keep repeating my replies? That's going to get boring. Why are we talking in Korean anyway?"

"Because my wife is sitting right in front of me."

"Gotcha. No names." He hummed. "Not sure why this is coming as much of a shock to you. Let's face it, you need your phones bugged with a paranoid guy like Da around."

I frowned. "Is this a new thing?"

"Yep. A belated Christmas gift," was his cheerful retort. "Trust me, I don't want to listen to your boring conversations any more than you want me to hear them."

An ache blossomed into being in my temples. "If that's supposed to be reassuring, it isn't."

I could hear the shrug in his voice. "I wouldn't worry about it. It's a precaution."

"What kind of precaution?"

"I'm not sure. Da just asked me to hook your phones up when I upgraded the security software. I figure it's a failsafe. A way of checking the people around you too."

"Not because he doesn't trust us or our wives?" I demanded.

"Nah. Prevention is better than the cure."

I thought about what he'd said. "When I asked if all our phones were bugged, you said of course."

"I did."

"Do you mean just the family circle, or...?"

"Or the whole Five Points?" he prompted.

"Yeah," I said on a rough exhalation, though I figured I had my answer from his tone alone.

"Yup." He clicked his tongue in exasperation. "And let me tell you, we're boring as fuck. You'd think with a bunch of criminals, our runners would at least have something fucking interesting to talk about but nope."

"Can he do this?" I demanded.

"This is Senior, Finn, of course he can do this. He can do whatever the fuck he wants."

I knew my brother too well though, so I muttered, "He couldn't do it without you. That means you agree with it."

"In part."

"Kid, this ain't like you."

"One of my goddamn crew wasn't a Sparrow before, Finn," he rasped. "One of the people I treated like he was blood hadn't triggered a drive-by that almost killed my sister.

"Bet your fucking ass I think we need to be on the hunt for these assholes. I'm working with Lodestar to target their bank accounts, but it's slow going. I want these sons of bitches eradicated."

My brows lifted. "You doing okay, Conor?"

"Since when do you guys speak Japanese?" Eoghan groused, breaking into our call before Conor could answer me.

"It isn't Japanese. It's Korean, dumbass," Conor corrected, clearly hearing Eoghan's grumbling though we weren't on speaker.

Because I knew he wouldn't let it drop, I told Eoghan, "It's Korean."

"I didn't know you spoke that, Finn," Aoife called out, and when I shot her a look, my temper from before faded some.

Sure, she might glance at that book cover model and get hot under the collar, but only I could make her get that heavy-lidded look. I was the guy whom she burned that energy off on.

There was no need to be jealous.

It was the guilt talking.

That motherfucking Catholic guilt that plagued me despite the fact I wasn't even really goddamn Catholic anymore.

"I speak four other languages too," I told my woman, aware I growled the words, even more aware when she bit her bottom lip.

Fuck.

Eoghan elbowed me in the side. "Someone's getting lucky tonight."

My lips twisted into a smirk. "Still feel like babysitting?"

"If it'll cheer you up, sure."

"I think he needs to have a good fuck. Finn's been miserable recently. Aoife," Conor called out, loud enough to hurt my ear, "you need to—"

Eyes wide, I didn't let him answer. I cut the call then shot her a look and saw she was frowning at me.

"He's not wrong." Her head tipped to the side as she studied me, and I knew we were going to be talking about this later.

Not about the sex. She, more than anyone, knew I was on her like white on rice. But her concern was clear because I had been more stressed than usual.

"Did you catch the Crashers' game last night?"

I jerked my gaze from hers and, after glancing at Eoghan, muttered, "There wasn't a game."

"Nah, I know, but doubt she does," he mocked. "I figured I'd stop that conversation in its tracks before you ended up having bluer balls than you do now."

I didn't correct his misinterpretation that I wasn't getting laid, mostly because it was easier for him to think that than to discuss the reality. I just snickered and told Eoghan, "My balls thank you."

I sent a message to Aidan Jr:

Me: *You need to keep an eye on Kid. He's taking this shit with Callum to heart.*

"TMI, bro." Eoghan sniffed.

We shared a look, and I laughed. "*Bro.*"

"Weird, huh?" he agreed sheepishly. "I mean, we've called you that a thousand times before, but it's different now. Different good," he clarified.

My phone buzzed.

Aidan Jr.: *How can you keep an eye on Kid? That's his job, ain't it?*

"Even though it means Senior cheated?" I grated out, trying to pick apart why Kid's tone had put me so on edge that I'd sent that text to Junior.

Eoghan snorted, and it drew my focus his way. "Da's a psychopath, Finn. They never said it outright, but I always thought his cheating was why Ma hit him on the fucking head with that goddamn rolling pin.

"I didn't think it was because he told her that her chicken was dry one Sunday," he drawled. "Plus, I think there's a reason he's gotten worse over the years."

"What do you mean?"

Me: *It IS his job, and he's excelling at it right now. More than you fucking know. But still, I just spoke with him, and he sounded edgy as fuck.*

And if Kid happened to be reading this, then he deserved the paranoia.

Jackass.

"Guilt. Does shit to us. Changes us." Eoghan scratched his chin where stubble was growing.

"I agree. It does."

"Okay, less talk about the folks. More about us. Tell me a secret, and I'll tell you one too," Eoghan prompted.

"Why? Maybe they're secrets because they need to be?" I retorted as I scanned the new text message.

Aidan Jr.: *I'll check in with him. He and Callum were tight, you're right. Not only is he grieving the bastard's death, but his friendship as well.*

Me: *I'll try to keep on top of shit with him but this new project is taking all my time.*

Aidan Jr.: *Don't worry about it. I got this.*

Tucking my phone back in my pocket after I decided Aidan could have fun finding out Conor was a peeping Tom on his father's say-so, I watched as Eoghan slouched on the double-wide armchair, slinking back so that one ankle moved to rest on his knee.

Against the white leather, in his black suit, he looked like the killer I knew he was. His fingers rapped against the armrest, triggering a rhythmic tapping sound as he rolled from pinkie to pointer.

"I think what I'm trying to say is that confession is more important than I initially realized," he muttered eventually.

Was this really for him or a desire to ease whatever he thought was going on with me?

Truthfully, there was no absolving me of what I'd done. The trust I'd broken, irreparably, between my wife and me, there was no fixing it.

I deserved for the truth to eat me alive, to keep me awake at night.

I deserved that, but I could tell something was making him itch. Something was eating at him too. I didn't think it was just a desire to help me either.

He wanted to talk.

Eoghan never wanted to talk.

He was the strong and stoic sort. The 'suffer in silence' kind of guy.

For his sake, I hoped Inessa was someone he could confide in...

"Okay, I'll bite. Aoife's dad—"

"A nobody, right? Conor had to look into her as well."

"How the fuck do you know all this shit?" I shook my head. "I guessed he would, so I'm not pissed about that... still, he ain't that fucking good because he doesn't know this." *Until now.* I leaned forward and murmured, "Her mom had an affair and Aoife was the end result."

Tension hit Eoghan, a stillness overtaking him that spoke clearly of how interested he was. "Who's her father?"

"I shouldn't be saying dick, but the idiot has painted a target on his forehead with the Sparrows and that could blow back on us."

"Still, you can't tell your da." I said that more for Kid and his recording devices.

"Your da too," he pointed out, but his head swiped to the side. "I won't tell anyone. No need to." He mouthed, "Who's her father?"

Irony of ironies, the State of the Union flashed onto the screen, President Davidson appearing front and center.

This time, the bullshit he was spouting went on in front of Congress as well as the rest of the world. SOTU was early this year because of the New World Sparrows.

Slowly, I made a gesture at the TV. Eoghan frowned. I jabbed a finger toward it.

His brows rose then lowered but I saw understanding gleam in his eyes. Of course, that was drowned out by complete and utter shock a second later.

"Jesus H. Christ."

His mouth worked, and I had the honor of seeing Eoghan, for the first time ever, look stunned. Even when his da had forced him down the goddamn aisle, he hadn't looked this shell-shocked.

"At least he isn't Hewett?" he muttered softly.

"I guess," was my wry retort, trying not to think about the bugs. "Although we'd have better tax breaks if he were."

His nose crinkled. "True."

"I shouldn't tell you. Just telling you feels like a fucking betrayal but..."

The president had a juicy secret he needed to hide, all while trying to take down the New World Sparrows... It didn't take a genius or a Quantico analyst to tell me that it wouldn't end well.

That had been gnawing at me since Christmas.

"But?"

"But the fact that Aoife is Davidson's puts her in a set of crosshairs that I can't get her out of." As he nodded his understanding, I prodded, "Your turn now. What's your secret?"

"Not as impressive as yours."

"No BS. Hit me with it."

"Not that it is your secret, of course," he carried on, ignoring me. "It's Aoife's."

I flipped him the bird.

He just smirked, but slowly, it died. "She needs extra guards."

"No. Got an extra two on her that she knows about."

"How many doesn't she know about?"

"There are four more."

He pursed his lips. "That should be enough. Eight total now with three on a constant rotation?"

At my nod, his gaze flickered away.

Eoghan was our security man, so when he pronounced, "I'll juggle shit around. Get another few men on her," gratitude filled me.

"Thanks, Eoghan."

"My pleasure."

"Your turn for confession," I drawled when he kept flicking glances between the TV and Aoife. *Like that wasn't suspicious.*

"I got a call yesterday."

Frowning, I asked, "So? Pretty sure you get a lot of fucking calls, Eoghan."

"Not like this. Someone heard I was going to Ireland... You know what dormant means?"

"I speak English, bud. I know what it means." I scowled. "Who'd care about where you're going on honeymoon?"

He cleared his throat. "Okay, you know what it means, but in relation to the MI6, do you?"

I stared at him.

Then I stared some more.

And then, as he looked back at me, I got what he was saying.

"Eoghan?"

"Yeah?"

"Are you trying to tell me and Kid that you're MI6?" I rasped.

TWELVE

EOGHAN

IRELAND

TO SAY I was pissed at having my old employers crash my honeymoon was an understatement, but geopolitics being what they were, I knew that MI6 had to be desperate to call me in.

And they were also fucking insane if they thought I could get away with this in a place like Ballymena. A town where the highest vantage point was on the roof of a multi-story parking garage that had a total of *three* stories to its name.

Ballymena had seen recent riots because of an uptick in the Troubles that had plagued this country for centuries. I had to assume the Troubles—the war between people who wanted a unified Ireland and those who didn't—were why I'd been sent here.

"Johnathan and Siobhan Lenister, what the fuck have you been doing to find yourself in my crosshairs?" I murmured to myself as I set up my kit.

It wasn't my job to question my orders, neither was it my job to care about whoever was on the end of my scope, but sometimes, I was curious.

Especially when this married couple had done something bad enough for MI6 to call in The Whistler and for them to go to the effort of sourcing me a rifle.

As I put the weapon together, I pulled a face. "Well, you're no Amber, are you?"

I should have brought her with me, but fuck, that would have keyed Inessa into the fact that I was working on our honeymoon. Wasn't like a sniper rifle would blend in with all her *Fleur du Mal* lingerie.

I didn't think I'd survive with my balls if she knew what I was really doing today.

Although, that she could see me spending the day playing golf told me we still had a lot to learn about each other.

Squinting through the scope, I scanned the campsite to find the marker I'd placed there earlier this morning.

"Who are you, hmm?" I asked myself.

The fountain of information had run dry on this couple. As far as I could see, they were just regular folks.

But therein lay the rub.

The Whistler didn't kill *regular folks*.

He was sent in to defuse political crises in the making, to assassinate troublesome generals who were looking to overthrow governments.

A couple who lived out of a camper van?

No, that wasn't The Whistler's usual target.

The top story of the parking garage was empty right now, and with two lower levels barely full and covered, I doubted I'd be disturbed, but I didn't work with doubt. I needed to know the variables, and I'd calculated that I needed to clamber up onto the small shelter that housed the door to the staircase. Which meant I'd used my Range Rover as a fucking stepladder to get up there.

As I lay flat out on the roof of the covered stairwell, I stared around the small town through my scope and found my target—a park just beyond the Braid riverbank where the couple was staying.

I'd lived in some fucked up places in my time, but I'd never understood camper vans.

Pissing and eating in the same space didn't sit right with me, and I didn't have high standards—Afghanistan burned those out of you pretty fucking fast.

The couple had small lawn chairs set out on the grass as if it weren't ten degrees out here, a wind chime fluttered in the stiff breeze, and there were some towels hanging over a makeshift drying rack.

I found the husband and saw that he was filling a canteen of water from the river.

I'd have taken him out right then and there, but the woman was nowhere to be seen. Killing her man would clue Siobhan into what was happening. The last thing I needed was for her to drive off before I could get her in my sights.

While it was about to become a crime scene, it was an oddly idyllic setup. For all that they had to be either pissing in bottles and shitting in holes in the forest, it looked simple.

Simple was good.

I tried to imagine Inessa, my Bratva princess, dropping a squat in the forest and laughed to myself at the thought. She wasn't exactly high maintenance but I figured that hit the upper echelons of her tolerance.

Grinning to myself at the thought, and curious enough that I determined to take her glamping one day, I found my markers—the little slither of fabric I'd tied around a lower tree branch...

That was when I saw it.

There was another piece on the same tree, just a few feet away.

I stilled at the sight.

Nothing unusual there, stillness was required in my job.

But that was a marker.

It was too high up for Johnathan or Siobhan to have caught their jacket on the branch, so it wasn't a scrap of torn fabric.

Someone had placed it there.

Someone being another sniper.

MI6 had sent someone else in?

Ego definitely pricked, my brow furrowed, and though I should have focused on the target, instead, I scanned the area.

I was on the outer edge of thirteen hundred yards away from my target. I could go further, but there were few as skilled as me beyond this point so I used that as a guide.

Within seconds, I located the slightest gleam of a reflection against a scope. Considering there were hardly any vantage points in the area, that wasn't as difficult to manage as might be expected.

Jesus Christ, though.

Two snipers in Ballymena.

What the fuck had this couple done?

Now I wasn't just goddamn curious, I was fucking foaming at the mouth with the need to know why this simple pair of hippies had earned themselves a death sentence.

Returning my focus to the camper van, I found Johnathan doing as anticipated—pissing up against a tree before splashing his hands with the water he'd collected from the river.

As he zipped up, I tried to locate the woman, but she must have been inside. In these temperatures, not exactly a dumb move.

I sighed at the prospect of having to wait a couple of hours for them both to leave the van at the same time.

Take Johnathan out now, and she could just hop into the driver's seat and get the hell out of town. Instinct might have her rushing outside to check on her husband, but I didn't think so.

She'd found herself in the crosshairs of two snipers—Siobhan Lenister wasn't a regular woman, regardless that she played the role of hippie to perfection.

Pressing my finger to the trigger, I ignored the bitter cold, the chill wind, the frigid block of cement beneath me that made my body numb. All of it went by the by as I did my job. As my soul took a vacation and my mind switched off. Thoughts of my beautiful wife faded, Afghanistan and the last time I'd been in a position like this over there drifted away.

I was a blank canvas.

A clean slate.

That was when I saw it.

A third piece of fabric.

A third motherfucking piece of fabric.

What the actual fucking fuck?

I zoomed in on the marker, testing to see if it was the same sniper's handiwork, but I saw two different styles of knots at play. One tight and simple, a butterfly knot, the other circling around the branch then slotted in through the loop.

With my eye glued to the scope, I tapped my finger against my earpiece. "Call Eagle Eyes."

Within seconds, the call connected to the other sniper.

"Are you in Ireland?"

There was a pause. "No."

I grunted and cut the call.

He was.

Two more calls and I cast aside the notion that Mossad, and the disbanded but totally still active KGB, were here with me.

There was a list of other agencies from all over the world that could have been involved, but they were the usual suspects.

"Call Driftwood." The line connected to my handler. "May have a problem."

"What kind of problem?"

The cut glass British accent had me rolling my eyes.

When I'd first been approached, I'd admit that I took the whole James Bond shit to heart. I'd gotten hooked on Martinis for a while, and I'd been desperate to meet a Q. But then, I recognized it was the same old bullshit as anywhere else.

Same shit, different agency.

"Two others here."

"Bollocks." My handler rarely cursed so I raised a brow. "Any idea who they might be?"

I didn't tell him that I was pretty sure Eagle Eyes was here.

"CIA and CIS. I think." I just wasn't sure which had called Eagle Eyes in. He was a gun for hire, after all.

"CIS? Ireland?"

"You don't know?" I queried.

"No."

The question was, did I believe him? Handlers weren't always honest. It didn't exactly fit the job description.

"Who the fuck are these people?"

It wasn't the first time I'd had more than one sniper tracking a target, but two? Highly irregular.

"That's classified."

"What's classified is that I'm sharing territory with two marksmen in a tiny fucking town, Driftwood. Am I about to find myself in someone's crosshairs?"

That was a possibility.

They could be there to make sure I did the job, then they could take me out if I was their target.

For a second, I let myself think that the last time I'd seen Inessa was this morning, tucked up in bed before I left for the day. Her moaning about getting up, even though I'd booked her into an overnight spa treatment.

I thought about how beautiful she'd looked last night when I dressed her in her mother's jewels.

I thought about how her features contorted as she came.

I thought about how much I fucking loved her, when I'd never thought that was in the cards for me.

And something inside me died even as another part of me blazed into being.

Today wasn't my day to die.

I had something, *someone,* to live for now, and I wasn't about to goddamn leave her.

"Is this a trap?" I snapped at Driftwood.

"No," he ground out.

"As if I can trust a word you fucking say. You draw me in after five years of inactivity and expect me to think this isn't a setup? What the hell's to stop me from rolling off my perch right this goddamn second and getting the hell out of here?"

There was dead silence on the line, and I pulled away from my scope, about to do as I'd threatened, then he admitted, "The Lenisters are... IRA."

"So?" My da wouldn't be pleased about me shooting some Republicans, but his politics and mine didn't align. "There are plenty of fucking IRA in these parts. They were rioting here just a week ago. It's what they fucking do."

Driftwood grunted, "Okay, so they're not IRA. They're with the ECD. I'm sure you know who they are considering your infamous family ties."

Intrigue had my temper cooling down. "They're with *Éire le chéile go deo?*"

Driftwood confirmed, "Yes."

"Shit," I rasped.

"Exactly."

The ECD were pricks. They'd been behind several bombings in the 90s, which had not only made them a household name but had identified them as evil fuckers.

Standard IRA protocol was to call in a bombing with plenty of time for an area to be evacuated by the authorities. They wanted economic damage. Hitting the British coffers where it hurt was how they tried to affect change.

The ECD, however, didn't care about civilian casualties. They wanted to be heard.

"What the fuck is the Lenisters' game?"

"According to our sources, they're at the top of the ECD's sniper shopping list. They've got outstanding warrants for murdering an old couple in County Louth close to ten years ago, as well as a few dissidents in Belfast. They're what we know about.

"As for the ECD, well, there's been a call to arms to take down a prominent member of the Irish government that would *not* be conducive to our agenda. Plus rumors that someone big in the US government has found themselves in the group's crosshairs, but I'm of the mind that that is definitely chatter."

Chatter was like assholes—everyone had them, and after enough butt-fucking, they all gaped.

"No idea who?"

"No."

I narrowed my eyes upon not-so-innocent Johnathan. "The Lenisters... they're not bombers?"

"No. Well, no chatter indicates *that*. Mostly we know them as hired guns."

"So Ballymena, a town with one KFC to its name, is currently home to five snipers? That's what you're telling me?"

"That's what I'm telling you. It's imperative that they be taken out today. Do you understand me?"

"I understand you." Bet his gaping ass I fucking did. "What about the others in the area? Do I need to handle those?"

"We don't care who makes the kill. Just make sure Johnathan and Siobhan Lenister die by the day's end."

When he cut the call, and Declan immediately rang, I grunted, shut off my phone, then turned my focus onto the Lenisters.

Knowing who they were, any guilt I could have felt at taking them out dispersed some. Handlers could bullshit with the best of them, but there was a logic in what he was saying.

It was one thing when the marks appeared to be peaceful hippies, but ECD foot soldiers? Those assholes had a special place in hell reserved for them.

For myself, I was honored to deliver them to the Devil's waiting room.

Suddenly, the hours-long wait I had ahead of me, all while it drizzled, wasn't that much of a chore.

FINN: *How's Ireland?*

Eoghan: *Rainy.*

Finn: *Lol. I thought that was what you wanted.*

Eoghan: *It was.*

Finn: *So the honeymoon is going well?*

Eoghan: *It is. The plan went awry. Inessa insisted on us seeing some sights, but it's all good.*

Eoghan: *Out of curiosity, do you know why Declan keeps calling me?*

Finn: *No. Maybe answer the phone and you'll find out?*

Eoghan: *If I answer the phone, then I have to deal with whatever crap he wants to offload onto my shoulders.*

Finn: *True. Want me to find out what's going on?*

Finn: *In fact, don't worry about it. Whatever he needs you for, I'll handle it.*

Eoghan: *You sure?*

Finn: *I'm sure.*

Eoghan: *He won't be calling me for anything pleasant, Finn.*

Finn: *I know. I said I'll handle it. What are brothers for?*

Eoghan: *Appreciate that.*

Finn: *No problem.*

Eoghan: *I mean it—thank you.*

Finn: *You know what we talked about before you left?*

Eoghan: *The James Bond shit?*

Finn: *Yeah.*

Eoghan: *What about it?*

Finn: *You did the job?*

Eoghan: *I did.*

Finn: *You okay?*

Eoghan: *Stopped crying after missions when I was a kid, Finn. If that's what you're asking?*

Finn: *No. Never mind. Speak later and enjoy the rest of your honeymoon.*

Eoghan: *Thanks, bro.*

THIRTEEN

FINN

"HOW MUCH OF an in do you have with Jen?"

I frowned at the question as Sam, my driver, pulled up outside Declan's warehouse. "Aidan, what do you think? No one has an in with Jen. She's about as prickly as a fucking cactus."

Until I'd met Savannah, I thought Aoife was the only person in the city to like her best friend.

Jen was definitely *not* to everyone's tastes.

"Well, I know that already, but Savannah came back home sobbing again."

"She cries a lot, doesn't she?"

"Fuck off," Aidan grumbled. "She doesn't cry a lot. You saw her after she was attacked. She didn't shed a single tear."

I had to concede that. Armed with a mop and a coffee table book, Savannah had defended herself from a home invader then, after she passed out because of a nasty fall, and had awoken surrounded by a bunch of mobsters, hadn't even begged for her life.

Not a single time.

He was right—that took guts.

"What happened between them?" I asked. "Why did they fall out? Aoife won't tell me shit."

"Surprised you let her keep things from you."

I snorted. "You've been with Savannah for about thirty seconds, so I'll forgive you for uttering bullshit like that."

He huffed. "It's crazy."

"What is?"

"The reason they fell out."

"Spill it."

"It's crazy," he repeated, but before I could grouse about him trying to up the suspense, he said, "But I had it confirmed. She wasn't lying."

"Who wasn't lying? Savannah?" I asked disinterestedly as I scanned the warehouse's yard.

Even dusted with snow, this place looked beyond industrial, and that wasn't a compliment. This wouldn't be featured in a magazine spread, that was for sure. It was grim. Grim as hell.

Sometimes, I pitied Declan and Brennan. They came face to face with the grittier side of the Five Points on a daily basis. That was a side I was glad to have left behind a long time ago.

"No, *Jen*," Aidan grumbled. "Keep up. *Jen* wasn't lying to me."

"Keep up? You're not speaking in full sentences. Say whatever you have to say, for fuck's sake. I have shit I need to do."

"Like what?"

"None of your business," I sniped.

"I confronted Jen about the situation. Had what she told me confirmed." He heaved a sigh. "She's Padraig's daughter, Finn."

Eyes rounding, I blurted out, "Padraig as in your father's brother Padraig?"

"*Our* father's brother," he corrected, and I winced.

"Our father's brother," I amended.

"AKA our uncle. Uncle Paddy."

I was a smart man, some would say I was a financial wizard, but the simplicity of that statement had me shaking my head as I tried to process what he was saying.

It was simple. So simple. But nothing about my family ties were simple.

"Our uncle," I repeated blankly. "Padraig is Jen's father?"

"Yeah. She told me that, and I thought she was insane. So I had some of her DNA snagged, shipped it off, and got the confirmation. She's an O'Donnelly."

"Jesus fuck."

"Pretty much."

I let that roll around in my head before I asked, "What does that have to do with Jen and Savannah?"

"Apparently Savannah..." He heaved another sigh. "I swear, this is starting to feel like we're back in high school."

I had to laugh. "Been a long time since we were back there, Aidan."

"True. I'm feeling every single fucking one of my years."

"Jen does that to a man." I smirked. "Actually, it's fitting that she's an O'Donnelly. Only O'Donnellys are this annoying and manage to survive past eighteen."

His tone turned dark. "Savannah was looking into the O'Donnellys a couple years back. She uncovered a link between Padraig and Jen, went after Jen to get some DNA to confirm things, and inadvertently befriended her."

"So Jen's upset about how they met?"

"Yes."

"How did she find out?"

"Savannah told her."

"Well, that was fucking dumb."

"Yeah. She ain't been around us lying fuckers for long enough to realize that you don't call your own bluff."

"Apparently," I retorted—our secrets defined us, after all.

But then I thought about the last time I'd seen Aoife and Jen after dinner on New Year's Day.

Whispers and curse words when they thought I wasn't listening.

Secrets...

I was used to the pair of them gossiping, but that had definitely felt more different than usual.

"So, do you have an in with Jen? I've tried talking to her but no dice."

"I have the biggest in. Aoife. But she's on Jen's side." Rubbing my chin at the thought, I murmured, "Leave it with me, I'll see what I can do."

"Fuck, thanks, Finn. I appreciate that. I hate seeing Savannah so hurt."

My lips curved. "That's when you know you love them."

"When their hurt is your hurt?"

I hummed. "And when the tiniest fucking problem is more complicated than trying to solve world hunger but you'll still do it if it means they'll stop being so goddamn sad."

Aidan blew out a breath. "Falling in love is complicated."

"Could have told you that."

"Why didn't you?"

I grinned. "Because there's nothing better in this shitty fucking world we live in than having a woman at your side who'll go to war *with* you and *for* you. It's a fate I'd wish on all my brothers."

"You got your wish," he drawled.

"Apart from with Conor."

"He's in love with Lodestar."

"They ever meet?"

"No."

"Trust Conor to fall in love with a handle."

Aidan snorted. "I think they're more in contact than we think."

"Should goddamn hope so if he loves her," I grumbled.

"You'll talk with Aoife?"

"I will. I make no promises though." I took a second to process what he'd told me. "Christ, Jen is really an O'Donnelly?"

"She is. I know it's crazy."

"Man, she was after you like flies around shit in the early days."

He grunted. "Trust me, my mind went there."

I laughed but said, "I'll speak to you later."

"Cheers, bro."

Cutting the call, I flipped onto my message app.

Me: *I think you deserve a spanking.*

Aoife: *Why? I haven't done anything.*

Me: *It's what you haven't told me that's the problem.*

Aoife: *It was told to me in confidence!*

Me: *That you know exactly what I'm talking about is where we have an issue.*

Aoife: *It was Jen's secret to tell. Not mine.*

Me: *It pertains to the family. You know better, Aoife.*

Aoife: *I don't deserve a spanking.*

Me: *Since when do you decide when you deserve a spanking or not?*

Aoife: *That's not fair!*

Me: *Life isn't fair.*

Aoife: *You can't tell Jen that you know.*

Me: *Why not?*

Aoife: *Because I told her I'd keep it quiet from you.*

Me: *She should never have asked you to do that.*

Aoife: *She's my friend, and she's hurting. I had to protect her privacy. She has a right to talk about these things with me in confidence, just like you have that right too.*

It wasn't like I could argue with her about that, but still...

Me: *This is family business, Aoife.*

That was when the realization struck me. Of all the goddamn hypocritical bullshit I was spouting, this took the cake.

Before I could stick my foot in my fucking mouth even more, I closed my eyes, took a moment to figure out a way to back off from this, but she texted me:

Aoife: *I know it's family business. But it's about a man who's been dead for years! I didn't see the harm in keeping things under the radar for the moment.*

Me: *You're right.*

Aoife: *I am?*

Me: *You are.*

Aoife: *Seriously?*

Me: *Seriously.*

Aoife: *Spanking averted?*

Me: *Yes. Unless you want one?*

Aoife: *Lol.*

Me: *Does that mean yes?*

Aoife: *Of course. Ha.*

Aoife: *You sure you're not mad?*

I didn't have the right to be mad.

Not when all the secrets that were piling up between us were starting to make Everest look like an ant hill.

Me: *I'm not mad.*

Aoife: *The thought of spanking me changed your mind?*

Me: *Well, you know I love it when your ass burns red.*

Aoife: ***snorts***

Me: *Can you do me a favor?*

Aoife: *I won't speak up for Savannah.*

Me: *Please?*

Aoife: *What she did was trashy AF.*

Me: *I know it is. But Savannah's hurting.*

Aoife: *So's Jen.*

Me: *Aidan's worried.*

Aoife: *So? Sometimes apologies aren't enough.*

And there was the rub.

She wasn't wrong.

Sometimes, an apology was never enough, *could never be enough* when held up against an unforgivable act.

Because this hit too close to home, I tapped out:

Me: *I gtg, sweetheart.*

Aoife: *Okay, my love. See you later.*

Scrubbing a hand over my face, I stared at her message then tucked my phone into my pocket when dread loomed inside me.

Needing to escape my thoughts, I was on the brink of getting out of my car when my phone pinged. It wasn't a message so I peered at the screen and saw that one of my alerts had flared.

Tapping onto the link, I smiled at the site and immediately sent it to Aoife.

Aoife: *What's this? Thought you had to go?*

Me: *Read it!!! You did it!!*

Aoife: *Did what?*

Me: *Your brownie is on the site of that blogger you love! That We Cream For Ice Scream blog. It's starting!*

Aoife: *What?! What's starting?*

Me: *Read it!*

Aoife: *Shit, one second. I was changing Jake's diaper. I'm doing this all by voice.*

Well, that made sense.

Me: *Jake chooses his moments to take a dump.*

Aoife: *LOL. He sure does.*

I quickly copied and pasted from the article so that Siri would read it aloud for her.

Me: *If you've ever been to Ellie's Bakery then you'll know the baker, Aoife O'Grady, is known for the best sweet treats in Hell's Kitchen.*

To be honest, I'm not sure why more people aren't raving about them. Not only are they massive, but they're like eating nectar from the gods.

I'm wondering if it's Hell's Kitchen's biggest secret, however, because I never see them raved about and I'm personally at fault there too—I just go and eat and savor and enjoy. I don't take pictures. I just stuff my face and indulge.

Today, however, I can't do that.

Today, I'd be doing a disservice to the drug that is this brownie.

Meet the best brownie you'll ever eat.

And you need to go today and buy up a dozen because, I know, by tomorrow, there'll be lines around the door for this treat and it's so well deserved.

Aoife: *OMG!!!!!!!!*

When my phone rang, I laughed and picked it up. "Well done, baby!"

"Finn. Oh, my God, she loved it!"

"She did, and she was right to." It really had been addictive. "I'm glad I get mine straight from the source because you know what else she's right about? You're going to have lines out the door and around the block."

"I can't believe this is happening when Jake just peed on me."

I burst out laughing. "He didn't!"

"He did."

"I thought he'd grown out of that."

"Me too," she drawled. "But I'll take it. Holy shit, babe. Holy shit. I can't believe *We Cream* talked about my brownies."

"I can. And guess what? Other bloggers are going to as well."

"You don't know that."

"I do," I countered. "Have you seen the comments? She's already got two hundred."

"How did you even know she'd posted?"

"I have alerts set up."

"Alerts?" A laugh escaped her. "Why am I not surprised?"

I just smiled. "I don't know why you would be either."

She cackled. "I walked into that."

"You totally did." I pursed my lips, mind racing. "You need to speak with the bakery. Make sure they're set up for what's about to hit them."

I heard her suck in a breath. "You really think so?"

"I fucking know so."

It had rattled my cage that she didn't want me to get involved with the bakery, but I got it.

She wanted her achievements to be her own. And now that she'd done it, even though it had taken fucking ages, I got it even more.

This wasn't tainted by the Five Points.

This was well-earned and well-deserved.

"Jeez," she breathed, making my smile widen.

"You're a baking rockstar, Aoife. It's time the world knew that."

"You're making me blush."

"I'll make other parts bright red later on," I promised with a laugh, "but you call the team together to prepare for what's heading your way."

"I already had three openings—"

Smirking, I murmured, "I know."

She was silent a second, then she laughed. "Finn!"

"What?!"

"You know what I mean. I needed to hire three people before this... do you think I'll need to hire more staff?"

"Definitely."

"Wow," she whispered.

"Wow," I murmured back, grinning like a fool for her. "You going to go, sweetheart?"

"Yeah. I just... I'm basking."

"Well, bask away, babe. You deserve this. I'm so fucking proud of you."

"Oh, Finn, thank you."

"I didn't do dick. You did it all. You. Well done, sweetheart. Well fucking done."

When she sniffled, I knew what was happening, and though I wanted to hug her and kiss her, I knew—even if she didn't—that she'd have to work fast. The world was instant now. Once news spread...

I checked the blogger's Instagram. "Baby, you need to get talking to the bakery. Trust me. She shared it on IG too. I just checked. It's a video and she's already had three hundred thousand views."

Aoife squeaked then squawked, "Holy shit! Okay, love you, bye, love you, speak later, love you."

She said all that in a blur and I laughed as I barely managed to return the words before she cut the line.

I let her joy filter through me, let her success wash over me, and I reveled in it for a while.

It felt good.

So good.

That was what I wanted for Jake. Success—but earnestly achieved.

I cast a glance at the warehouse that was Declan's home away from home and a lead balloon settled in the pit of my stomach.

Knowing that I couldn't hang around here all day, I climbed out of my car, feeling oddly punch drunk, enough that I didn't even mutter any orders to Sam before I slammed the door closed.

I felt the flicker of attention from the assigned guards as they took note of my passage across the forecourt, and one opened the door for me as I approached the entryway.

A couple minutes later and I was stalking into the warehouse that was Declan's piece of poisoned paradise.

I was one of the lucky ones. My slice of hell was in a skyscraper, behind a desk as I steered the legitimate front of the Five Points, Acuig Corp., into a billion-dollar business.

Declan and Brennan weren't so fortunate.

Brennan's second home was in the Hole, a place aptly named because some parts of the city in that area weren't even served with water, never mind being a part of a police beat.

Declan's was in a warehouse where we stored a lot of our guns, ammo, and some of our drug stock.

I hated coming here.

I knew what I was, never forgot where I came from, but this was just a reminder. I couldn't imagine being Declan and having to come here every fucking day, and it was one of the reasons I was determined my children would never have to do what I did for a living. My brothers' kids, either.

With Aoife's earnest joy still filling my heart, it was strange to stand here, in this grim place, where evil shit went down, and say, "Eoghan told me you've been calling him."

Though I knew he'd seen me coming, my second-youngest brother peered up at me from his laptop and dismissed me, "I called Eoghan, not you."

"I told him I'd deal with whatever problem you've got on your hands, seeing as he's on his honeymoon."

Declan arched a brow. "You don't like getting your hands dirty."

I scowled at him. "Do you like it? It's not exactly something *to* like, is it?"

"True. Not unless you're Da." He squinted at me, took in my Gucci suit and coat with a twitch of his lips. "You're not dressed for it."

"You got a problem with Gucci?" I mocked, tugging on my lapels as I straightened up.

"No, but Gucci might have a problem with you getting blood all over that." He wafted a hand up and down and asked, "How much did that cost anyway?"

"Like you don't have expensive suits," was my wry reply.

"I don't wear them in this warehouse," he retorted, getting to his booted feet and approaching me.

"I can see why." I peered around. "What did you want from Eoghan, Dec?"

"I don't think you really want to know, Finn."

"If you were talking about torture, then you'd have called Aidan or Brennan in, not Eoghan. Stop with the petty BS. I might sit behind a desk, but I started at the exact same place you did."

He folded his arms across his chest. "Do you speak fucking Russian?"

"Yes. Of course."

"Of course, he says," Dec rumbled, rolling his eyes.

"Eoghan speaks it?"

"You know what he's like. Reads the dictionary fucking once and knows what it all means."

"Knowing what it means and understanding it are two different things entirely," I retorted.

"Well, hoorah for me you can speak the fucking lingo." He grunted like he was annoyed.

"Is this about Sullivan or Walsh?" I asked warily, naming the Five Pointers who'd been Sparrow informants.

"No. They came forward on Armistice Day. Why would they be here?"

I shrugged. "Maybe Senior told you something he didn't tell me. Maybe he went back on his word."

"He didn't. For once," Declan intoned grimly. "He hasn't mentioned any measures he wants put in place to draw out any Sparrow informants who didn't come forward. At least, not to me. Maybe he's told you seeing as you're in the golden circle."

His scorn had me huffing. "I ain't in the golden circle, whatever the fuck that means."

Da had Conor spying on every Five Pointer and he hadn't informed me of that.

Some goddamn golden circle.

The day Aidan, Brennan, and Declan discovered what Kid was up to, I'd watch the beating with a bag of popcorn.

"If you say so," he grumbled. "Come with me."

There was a central office made out of fiberglass walls whose windows looked out onto every side of the warehouse, and that was where Dec worked. But as he beckoned me out of there, I followed him to the far end where there was another enclosure. This one was made of the same fiberglass, but it had no windows.

Along the way, we passed crates, the contents of which I had no desire to know.

I wasn't sure what I expected to find in the secondary shelter, but I knew it wasn't merchandise because that was stored out in the open.

Thoughts of Aoife whispered away when Dec opened the door, and I braced myself. Not because I was scared of what I was about to see, but because the stench that came from there was worse than Jake's diapers.

My nostrils flared at the smell, but as I approached the enclosure, I knew it wasn't going to be a pretty sight because it only intensified with proximity.

"Who the fuck's that?" I rumbled as I passed Dec who leaned against the door, his arms folded, legs crossed as he took in the sight of what appeared to be a man.

Except, this man had...

I sucked in a breath. "Are they maggots?" It was a rhetorical question.

Declan shrugged. "He's a traitor."

"Who the fuck is he?" I snapped.

"The fucker who's been an albatross around my neck since I was a teenager."

"And? Who's that?" I demanded when he just smirked at the bastard hanging on a cattle hook.

"Cillian Donahue."

I frowned because that was *not* a Russian name. "Who?"

Declan huffed. "This is why I wanted Eoghan. He'd know who the bastard is."

The stirrings of a headache started to form at my temples, exacerbated not only out of irritation with Dec but from the fucking stench in here.

"What did you want Eoghan to do? Give your fist a bump in congratulations?"

"This is a historic moment."

It was?

I grimaced. "I'll take your word for it." Then, a glimmer of recognition filtered into being in my memory banks. "Donahue... Deirdre's brother?" Deirdre was his ex-fiancée. She'd been murdered a long time ago.

"Yes," Declan said with a grin that was wild and wicked and too like his father's—shit, *our* father's. "That cunt's brother."

The vitriol in his voice had me rasping, "What's he done to the family, Declan?"

"Been blackmailing me all my adult life."

"Wait, I thought Cillian was dead?"

"He went into WITSEC. That's how I found him. Well, to be fair, Caro Dunbar and Conor found him for me. Caro and Cillian have been skinning me alive for decades."

Donahue groaned at that, and when Declan cackled like he was a fucking lunatic, I muttered, "I think the fumes are going to your head."

"That's the sweet smell of victory, Finn."

"There's nothing sweet about this." I frowned at the living corpse. "Why did you ask if I spoke Russian?"

"Wanted you to fuck off. Didn't work. Figured this would get you to back away. Unless... is it true what they used to say about you?"

My perusal of the many open sores on this bastard's body that were riddled with insects was ruptured by his question.

"What did they say about me?"

"That no one walked away once you got involved in making someone talk."

My mouth twisted. "It's not exactly something I advertise, but yes. They used to say that. Aidan Sr. would send me in to handle the men he didn't want dead."

"So they literally couldn't walk away?" Declan grinned. "I like the sound of that."

"There's nothing to *like*." I frowned at him. "Dec, are you okay?"

"No, Finn, I'm not." He jabbed a finger at Donahue. "But this makes me happy."

I moved over to him, grabbed his arm and hauled him out of the back room. "What's going on with you?"

He dragged his arm from mine. "Nothing's wrong with me. I'm well within my rights to do this without telling Da. Cillian turned evidence against us—not just to a cop, but to Caro fucking Dunbar.

"Not only is he a rat, he helped the Sparrows. That means I can do whatever the fuck I want to him and Da will sign off on it."

Slowly, I shook my head. There was torture, and then there was letting a man feel himself being eaten alive by insects.

"How long's he been like this?"

"I got him here a few days after Christmas. Talk about a gift that keeps on giving."

My mind veered back to St. Stephen's Day, when I'd seen him talking on the phone in the yard at his parents' place. Had that phone call been about this fucker?

Two weeks of this kind of torture, however, went beyond business.

This was personal.

"Declan, what did he do to *you?*"

My brother blinked at me. "He stole fourteen years of my son's life from me."

And that resonated.

It hit home like nothing else could.

From one father to another, I got it. I understood his rage, felt it myself on his behalf.

I didn't ask for the details, didn't need any. Declan wouldn't go through with this level of sadism if he didn't believe what he was saying was true.

Cillian Donahue might be a traitor to our family, but somehow, he'd been pivotal in keeping Aela and Declan apart, and that had robbed my brother of the early years of his son's childhood.

There was only one appropriate response to that:

"Do you have a power washer?"

Declan tipped his head to the side. "I can get one."

"I learned this trick from Junior," I informed him as I shrugged out of my coat and jacket then rolled up my sleeves.

Declan hollered, "Hutchins, where the fuck are you?"

"Here, Dec."

I cast a look at one of Dec's crew and said, "I need a power washer."

"Gimme two minutes, Finn."

By the time I was in my shirtsleeves, Hutchins had hauled in a power washer and had hooked it up to a faucet that I assumed was used when cleaning up this room.

"You want any bleach in it?" Hutchins asked as I tossed him my coat and sports jacket.

"Nah, good thinking though."

He nodded then faded away, leaving me with the power washer gun in my hand.

"It stings like a motherfucker and it might get rid of some of the goddamn stench in here," I grumbled. "I ain't about to teach you my tricks when he's covered in his own piss and shit too."

Declan snorted. "You're so fucking fancy now."

"Yeah, that's me," I retorted as I pressed the trigger and hit Cillian Donahue square in the face.

When the bastard was screaming from the pounding sting of the water against his rotting flesh, and his skin was as red as a lobster's, I stared at the pitifully withered form and took in the massive wounds that were putrefying before my eyes.

It had been a long time since I'd slashed anyone's collateral ligaments, but I guessed it was like riding a bike.

FOURTEEN

AELA

THE FOLLOWING MORNING

"I NEED you to not freak out."

Declan, in the process of shaving, turned to face me. "Freak out about what?" He smirked. "Takes a lot to freak me out, babe."

"I just got an email from the First Lady's office."

"As in the president's wife?"

"Who else would I mean?" I grumbled.

"Do you often get calls from the spouses of heads of state?"

My lips quirked. "Baby, you ain't seen nothing yet."

He narrowed his eyes at me. "What do they want?"

"Art. What else? I'm in demand, dontcha know?"

"Why?"

"Why? Because I'm a genius. At least, according to the critics."

"I know that. I mean, why did the First Lady email you?"

I watched as he smoothed the electric razor over his throat. The act was distinctly domestic. I'd never been into domestic before Declan.

The routine shit that most people took for granted wasn't exactly a turn on, but it was comforting.

It was proof this was happening.

This was real.

After nearly fifteen years apart, I needed real. I needed routine.

So watching him shave was a pleasure, not something to be taken for granted.

Eying the up and down strokes, I murmured, "She wants me to attend the state dinner tomorrow."

"You?"

This was where it got dicey—especially with the current situation.

I nodded then verbally confirmed, "Not us."

I wasn't going to beat around the bush. He'd picked up on my specific verbiage because people might mistake the man for a filthy dark Five Points' bruiser, but Declan was smart.

Wicked smart.

"You're not going without me."

My inner feminist railed at the blanket statement, but the city was going to hell in a handbasket.

I'd spent a portion of the holidays in a fucking bunker while the family compound got raided by a private militia, and the country was destabilized thanks to the vacuums of power popping up because of those pesky Sparrows.

I was pregnant with the man's baby. He'd lost fourteen years with our kid and me, and he was feeling protective—I got it. Even my inner feminist got it, that was how crazy things were in the States right now.

"Babe, you're a mobster. You can't go to the White House," I reasoned.

"You're a mobster's—"

"Not yet I'm not," I retorted before he could finish that sentence because the dude definitely hadn't put a ring on my finger yet.

"You think I'm going to let you go to D.C. without me?" he scoffed.

"I think you're going to come to D.C. with me, but you're not going to attend the function."

"I can't leave New York right now."

"It's for an evening," I growled.

"What's with the short notice? These events are arranged months in advance. Hell, maybe even a year."

I shrugged. "I don't know. I don't care."

"It's shady."

"So? Someone pulled out and maybe I'm the second choice, but I'll take it. This night could change the trajectory of my career, Dec. And that's all it is. *A night.* We can be back by the next morning. It's not like we can't afford plane tickets to fly us in and out of D.C."

"Plane tickets," he scoffed. "We have a private jet. But the answer's still no."

Eyes narrowing upon him, I stepped deeper into the bathroom and said, "Maybe I'm not asking."

"You're sure as fuck not telling," he snapped, switching off the razor as he stared me down. "You know what's going on out there, don't you?" He prodded the air with the razor. "The world's fucking crazy. Davidson is facing off against some nasty motherfuckers and you want to waltz into his house and—"

"It's the White House," I ground out. "I'm not exactly going across the neighborhood for a visit with my mom."

"That would be safer right now, and *that* isn't safe."

"You're being unreasonable. And paranoid."

"You'd still say that if I'd died on Christmas Day?"

Everything inside me froze up at his words. "Don't say that."

"I will say that," he countered. "I'll say it over and over again because maybe that will sink into that genius brain of yours.

"Babe, if anything happens to you, to Shay, to that kid in your belly, that's me done. I might as well have been shot down on Christmas Day. You think I can go another fucking year without you and our family, you're insan—"

I didn't let him finish.

My hand slipped to the back of his neck and I hauled him down until he was the same height as me so I could stare directly into his eyes. It was either that or kiss him, and for being such a *man*, I didn't want to kiss him. That'd just reward him for thinking he could tell me what to do.

"Listen to me, Declan. I'm not going anywhere. You're not going anywhere. I've got shit to do before I die, and so do you. We've got happiness to enjoy, kids to have, Shay to torment when he gets a girl-friend, and a baby to try to not turn into your father. We're. Not. Going. Anywhere."

His voice was raspy as he stated, "That's what I'm trying to make sure happens."

"We can't just be locked in here forever, Dec. I have a business to run, and this would be great for that business.

"Her message indicated she'd like me to design some glassware. She's going off brand for a First Lady—you know how they're supposed to design their own china? She wants a set of glasses apparently. Hand crafted by me.

"Do you know how many sheikhs and Saudi Arabian princes will be after my shit when that happens?"

"You don't need the money; plus you've already created art for them."

I squinted at him, wondering if he was being obtuse on purpose.

"No, I don't need the money," I said slowly, "and yes, I've already done some work for a couple of princes, but what about the king?"

"Babe, I aim high. I want the name recognition. I want the brand identity. I want to be the next Andy Warhol, and that's not going to happen if you keep me locked up in this brownstone.

"So, you do whatever you have to to make this happen. You can lock me and load me with a gazillion *non-mobster* guards—and yeah, I expect you to hire out—but I will be attending this function and no, you won't be going with me."

His gaze penetrated mine with all the precision of a laser. Then he rumbled, "Drop the robe."

I gaped at him. "Huh?"

"Drop. The. Robe."

"I have to get Shay to school—"

"Drop. The. Robe."

My heart stopped as I saw the fire and the rage and the want and the *love* etched into his expression... We didn't have time for this.

We really didn't.

I let go of his neck and tugged on the knotted belt around my waist. As it parted, he didn't take his eyes off mine until I shrugged and the silky folds drifted to the floor.

He grabbed me by the waist, turned me around, then said, "Place your hands on the counter."

I complied.

My pulse beat like a drum in my ears as I watched him move behind me, his gaze drifting over my reflection in the mirror.

I was getting bigger. The line had appeared recently, the one that bisected my belly from the navel down, and my tits and my nipples were massive, but he looked at me like I was a model on the front cover of *Sports Illustrated.*

Heat raked down my limbs, burning me up as he watched me.

Then he tugged at the towel around his waist and bared himself. Not that I could see. Not when I was covering the good stuff.

One hand went to my shoulders, and he pressed me forward so I was bending over the counter.

The other went between my legs.

I flinched when he slipped his fingers through my folds, hating that I was so wet already when all he'd done was turn caveman on me. But no one did Neanderthal like Dec. No one could piss me off and turn me on at the same time like he could.

A soft grunt escaped him, and I watched his eyes close as he explored my sex, rubbing my clit, playing with my labia. His expression reminded me of someone who'd found inner frickin' peace, but that was definitely not what my pussy was. It might be many things, but not inner peace.

I rocked my hips back, straightening and lengthening my spine to encourage him to do more than just touch, but the hard fuck I'd anticipated morphed when he thrust his thumb into my pussy as his fingers stroked my clit.

"You think I could live without this? Without you?" he rasped.

For a second, I didn't process the words, mostly because my panting breaths were all I *could* hear.

"I'm not asking you to live without me," I retorted, spreading my legs and pressing back against him. "It's one evening, Declan. One evening."

His other hand gripped my hip and steered me so that I could feel his dick rubbing up against my ass. "One evening in a political hotspot."

"It's the White House! It's the safest place on earth!" My growl turned into a yowl as he corkscrewed his thumb inside me, jerking me onto tiptoe as I squirmed against him.

"You wouldn't be taken to a fucking bunker if something went wrong, Aela," he snapped. "You'd just be—"

Dropping my hand between my legs, I grabbed his wrist and awkwardly shoved away from him. Then, I twisted around, pushed my chest against his, and spat, "You're being crazy."

"You make me crazy," he snarled. "The idea of losing you—"

"I'm not going anywhere!" I howled. "It's one evening. A fucking boring party with tedious people. It will take a couple of hours of schmoozing then I'll be back with your insane ass—"

He snagged me by the waist, hefted me onto the bathroom counter, then spread my legs and moved between them.

Before I could finish my sentence, his dick was inside me and his face was pushing up against mine. His breath was hot and heavy as he ground out, "You're never allowed to leave me—"

While I wanted to scream with how fucking fast his cock was tunneling in and out of me, I grabbed the back of his neck again and shoved our foreheads together.

"I'm not going anywhere!" I growled even as my heels dug into his ass and I used my grip on his nape to force his mouth into joining with mine.

As he nailed me against the counter, I tongue-fucked him, fighting fire with fire, refusing to back down when this was important to me.

Like a furious beast, he claimed me and re-claimed me. Over and over. Each thrust imprinting on me, taking me, binding him to me.

But that was what he didn't understand.

He'd imprinted on me almost two decades ago.

He'd taken me and bound me to him before Shay was even a twinkle in my fucking eye.

I was his.

And he was mine.

Years had been stolen from us, but nothing else would be.

I wouldn't let it.

As I fucked him back, not just with my tongue and teeth and lips but by thrusting against him, screwing him as much as he screwed me, I felt the orgasm creep up on me with all the finesse of a hammer to the temple.

This time, when I howled, it wasn't with outrage, it was with relief and release.

My pussy clamped down around his dick, demanding his seed, demanding he fill me, demanding he brand me with his heat, and when he exploded inside me, only then did I pull my mouth from his, did I let go of his nape, and did I embrace him in a fierce hug as we both flew away, broken apart by pleasure, rebuilt again by love.

And as I slumped against him, and as he sagged into me, I whispered in his ear, "You're stuck with me until the day you die."

His arms folded around me, and he hugged me tight. "Is that a promise?"

"Bet your ass it is."

FIFTEEN

DECLAN

I WAS SUPPOSED to wait for her on the jet.

Not happening.

I couldn't do it. I didn't care if it was crazy, but I needed to be close by.

I had the worst fucking feeling, and I knew I was being paranoid, but nothing about the last twelve months had been easy. The world was crumbling down around us and my woman had just waltzed into the epicenter of the crisis to shake hands on a business deal.

A fucking business deal.

First Ladies didn't invite artists to state functions the day before the event.

They didn't discuss business at said state functions.

They danced with dignitaries.

They talked bullshit with politicians from across the globe.

They ate fancy food and drank fancy champagne while plastering on a fake *fancy* smile.

They did not discuss glassware with a woman whom the Secret Service must have identified as having ties with the Five Points.

Acuig and the O'Donnellys were slowly and steadily becoming mainstream, but fooling a bunch of Manhattan socialites was one thing. The president? The Secret Service?

No.

They knew what and who we were.

But I'd let her go anyway.

"You fucking idiot," I rasped under my breath, scrubbing a hand over my face as I waited for her to come back to me. As I waited, like Chicken goddamn Little, for the sky to fall around me.

In a car a block away from Pennsylvania Avenue, contained within the limo's confines, a stranger driving us, more strangers guarding us, I felt like a pressure cooker about to go off.

After burning off some of my frustrations with Cillian Donahue, I should have been feeling triumphant. The bastard had ruined my life, and I'd ended his. But the buzz from torturing him, from working with Finn to make the fucker's final hours as excruciating as physically possible, had faded.

Instead of feeling the glory of righteous satisfaction, I was left feeling like I was going through the early stages of a heart attack.

The driver's cell buzzed. My gaze darted over to his in the rearview mirror as he answered it.

To me, he said, "She's in the limo, sir."

Nostrils flaring, I dipped my chin, refusing to feel relieved until she was in the back of the limo with me.

Keeping my expression blank was next to impossible, but I didn't need the driver knowing how whipped I was. Any more than was already clear, at any rate.

Cracking my knuckles, I waited.

And I waited.

And I goddamn waited.

Every second that passed, dread filled me.

Between the White House and here, there were guards stationed, but that didn't mean some Sparrows weren't out seeking blood tonight.

What better way to ram the message home that they weren't done fighting by using the visit of a state dignitary as a global platform?

Just as I imagined her car being torn apart by a bomb that had been set to retaliate against the president's ongoing investigations into the secret society, a set of headlights flared inside the cabin of my limo, and I heard an engine rumbling as her car pulled up behind mine.

Her driver jumped out, rounded the car, but I got out too, rushed over to the back end of the limo, and dragged the door wide open.

Her smile was wide. Shit, it beamed brighter than the headlights. In her eyes, there was glee, but for myself, I was just ecstatic that there hadn't been a terrorist attack against the White House.

I wasn't interested in politics, but when I'd found out the reason for tonight's dinner was that the Irish prime minister was visiting, more dread had filled me.

Seeing her safe and whole and hale had me almost sagging against the car door, but she was so buzzed that she didn't even notice I was a fucking wreck.

When I shuffled into the limo, I had confirmation of just how pussy-whipped I was for her because that was the first time I could breathe.

I didn't even take a second to appreciate how fine she looked in her purple dress that skimmed her waist and made her tits look banging.

That was how freaked out I was.

Her banging tits didn't so much as make my dick twitch. She looked as good now as she had earlier, when I'd tried to fuck her before she left for the dinner in an attempt to change her mind—it hadn't worked.

My woman was goddamn stubborn when she wanted to be.

"Get us the hell out of here," I rumbled the second the driver was back behind the wheel.

At my tone, Aela stopped chattering away, and I saw her attention was fixed on me.

I didn't mean to kill her buzz, so I raised the privacy screen and murmured, "You were saying about the Irish prime minister?"

There, that proved I'd been listening, didn't it?

"Are you okay?"

Curving my arm around her shoulder, I hauled her against me. "Better now that you're back."

"You were seriously worried," she whispered, peering up at me still.

"Which part of my behavior over the last twenty-four hours makes you think I wasn't?"

"I don't know. I thought you'd recognize I was going to the White House, not the Bratva's home base."

"President is just another word for Pakhan."

She scoffed. "Hardly. One's elected democratically—"

"Yeah, you tell me how democratic Super PACs are, babe. And remember, before you say a word, that Da donates to *several* Super PACs..." At her swiftly inhaled breath, I nodded. "Uh huh. Anyway, let's not talk about politics. What happened?"

"Did you know the First Lady is Irish?"

"Irish-Irish? Or like us?"

"Like us. But her grandparents were born in County Louth. Just like mine!"

I wasn't sure why she sounded so excited seeing as Shay had told me that hers had treated her like shit.

He'd also told me they'd been murdered in a burglary gone wrong which I was sure was the work of the IRA...

Not that I raised that subject. That would definitely kill her buzz.

"Second generation Americans," I remarked instead, because I *hadn't* known the First Lady was Irish. "...did you know they tend to have an identity crisis?"

"I mean, I never thought about it, but I guess it makes sense. I never had that problem because when you're a Five Pointer, it's like you're more Irish than American anyway."

I snorted because she wasn't wrong. Still, her comment pricked my curiosity. "You actually spoke with her? The First Lady, I mean?"

"I did! I danced with the prime minister too." She twisted to face me better. "She wants me to design a thousand-piece collection, Declan. *A thousand.*"

"Who the fuck is paying for that?"

She pshawed. "Like you care about where tax money goes. Do you even pay taxes?"

"I pay some."

"You should be glad it's going to the arts."

"I'd prefer to spend that kind of money on a foundation—"

"For art that will never see the light of day like in our bedroom?" Her arched brow and militant stare finally had my dick stirring to life. "Huh?"

I shrugged. "It's safer there." Not just for the art I had shielded there, but for her too.

She rolled her eyes as if she could read my mind then said, "She was talking about how Irish families played such an important role in modern America, and because of my ties to Ireland, she was excited to see what I'd come up with."

Staring at her, I asked, "You mean she wants glassware with a distinctive Irish flair to it? I thought they were supposed to be neutral?"

"I think they're allowed some free reign when it comes to the china patterns."

"This is all highly irregular."

Aela scowled at me. "Since when are you in the know about the East Wing of the White House, Declan." She tossed her hair. "Anyway, I don't give a damn if it is or not. I'll have to hire some staff for this level of work. I'll need an atelier as well—"

As we drove past the Thomas Jefferson memorial, and onto Rochambeau bridge, I raised a hand to stall her. "I'll sort that out. Make a list of what you need and I'll—"

"Declan, I don't need your help. This is my jam. I know this shit."

"You *knew* this shit, babe. New York is a crosshatch of territorial lines and disputes just waiting to happen. I need to know where you want a workshop and who you're hiring so I know you're safe."

She was silent a second, then she muttered, "Being associated with the Five Points is a massive pain in the ass."

"You only just figured that out?"

Peering up at me, Aela asked, "Is this how it's going to work forever?"

After I pressed a kiss to her temple, I said, "I wish I could say it wasn't."

"Jesus Christ."

"I'm sorry," I breathed the words into her hair, closing my eyes as I felt the resentment and anger swirling inside her.

"You are?"

I rested my chin on the top of her head. "I really am."

She released a breath. "Okay, I can deal with it then."

Surprised, I reared back and blurted out, "Huh?"

"You know there's a saying about the O'Donnellys, don't you?"

"That we're all assholes?" I mocked.

"Well, yeah... but that's only to some people," she drawled. "For some reason, most families revere the lot of you."

"That's because Da's conned them into thinking he's the second coming."

She sniggered at that. "I'm not sure that's the exact reason, but they do treat him that way."

"What's the saying?"

"An O'Donnelly apologizes to no man."

"That's bullshit," I groused.

"Is it though? When was the last time you apologized?"

"I'm not a rude prick."

"You don't have to be a rude prick to never apologize for your actions," she pointed out. "You just have to be an entitled ass."

"Isn't that synonymous with rude prick?"

"Maybe. I taught Shay the value of an apology from the start because I knew, one day, when you hauled us back and/or tore us apart, he'd forget what it meant to say sorry.

"So, you apologizing to me means a lot. More than you know. It tells me that you don't say any of this to be a dick. You're not trying to be a pain in my ass.

"Circumstances are dictating how these things have to happen. I can work within those parameters if you really mean that apology, and I know you wouldn't have said it if you didn't. So that changes everything."

I let that sink in before I took total advantage of her concession, "You won't give me crap when I pull moves to heighten your security?"

"Not if you properly explain why you're pulling those moves. *And* not if you go out of your way to make something happen when I need it —like tonight."

"Tonight went against my better judgment."

"And yet, because of tonight, you have a very happy girlfriend. Wasn't it worth it?"

Instead of answering, I just grunted.

Girlfriend.

That label did *not* reflect what she was to me.

Aela wasn't a girlfriend.

She was my fucking everything.

As my mind whirred, I listened to her talk about the state dinner. About how the First Lady's family name was Ó Cléirigh and about how she wanted some secret design on the glass with *Éire le chéile go deo* incorporated into it.

As I listened, I reached for my phone, and as always in times of crisis and cutting shit close to the wire, I texted the one person who'd be able to pull a miracle out of his hat.

Me: *Kid, I need a favor.*

SIXTEEN

LENA

"SON, I don't really have time for this."

"Why?" Declan grumbled. "This is important. Hasn't Conor told you about what's happening in a week?"

"No." My voice dropped an octave, but it couldn't be helped.

Guilt chased the denial because I'd been avoiding Conor since Christmas.

I knew that made me a horrendous mother, but I was that already. I'd been that for years.

Too many bruises, too much blood shed, all under my watch.

"No? Why not? I thought he was going to drag you in to help?"

Agitated, I scratched the side of my neck. "Things have been hectic on my end."

"Since when? You never said anything on Sunday."

"Well, I'm not one to broadcast all my ailments over dinner," I snapped, aggrieved by his persistence. "Michael's in the hospital."

"Michael? Your driver?"

"Yes." I stepped out of the elevator as it opened up onto the floor where Michael was being treated. Jamie, my new guard, fell into line behind me. "He's been told there's nothing more they can do for him."

"Shit," Declan rasped, and I didn't chide him for cursing. Instead, I closed my eyes.

Two guards of mine, two favorites, were going to be lost to me within twelve months.

Two.

Building up a rapport with men who put their lives on the line to protect you took time, and I'd lost Rogan when some Italian soldiers had killed him as he protected my grandson and Declan's girlfriend. Now, I was going to lose Michael.

"I'm sorry, Ma," Declan muttered, and I heard his genuine grief for me.

Because I needed to be strong and breaking down in a hospital corridor wasn't a sign of weakness I could allow, I moved over to a window and stared out of the glass so no one could see my expression.

"Does Da know?"

Aidan was in a world of his own right now, and I could easily understand that.

Christmas...

Conor...

It was much too much and Aidan felt things more than most.

Only Finn and Junior were privy to our private shame—that we'd tried to take our lives. That the guilt and the horror were something we were incapable of handling.

That was why I couldn't look my boy in the eye.

I'd let them all down by allowing Aidan to make men out of them by bruising them with his might, but knowing that Conor had been molested...

There were no words.

None.

Just thinking about it had my throat closing. My ears tuning out so that all I could hear was the beat of my heart and the rushing of blood in them.

I tried to focus on taking slow and steady breaths, but that wasn't easy when I felt like I was running a race all while standing still.

Tipping my head forward, I pressed my forehead against the glass and let the cool chill sink into me.

"Ma'am?" Jamie questioned, but though I heard him, I couldn't process what he was asking.

"Ma?!" Declan snapped down the line. "Listen to me, I know you can't answer, I can hear the way you're breathing, but follow my lead, okay?"

When he started inhaling and exhaling, encouraging me to mimic him, I started weeping as I listened and breathed in time to him.

Such a good, good boy.

The best.

I was blessed.

Slowly but surely, my heart stopped its fluttering, and I managed to rasp, "Thank you, son."

I didn't deserve my boys.

Every day, I received more proof of that.

"It's okay. We'll figure something out with your guards," he told me. "You like Sean, don't you? From my crew?"

"I do," I whispered.

"Then I'll redirect him to your team."

"Don't you need him?" I *did* like Sean. He was Mary Constantine's boy, and because his father had died when he was a teen, he'd been raised right.

"I can deal. There are plenty of men who can help me, but not so many that you like."

I heaved a sigh. "I appreciate that more than you know, Declan. Thank you."

"No worries. Did Conor not tell you about the wedding next week?"

I blinked. "You and Aela are getting hitched?"

"We are. I need you to coordinate with Conor otherwise shit won't get done in time. It's a surprise for her, so don't say anything, okay?"

Pulling back, I rubbed the side of my neck. "I'll call him as soon as I'm done here."

I dreaded that call.

Aidan and I had agreed that we'd never confront our boy, that he'd come to us when and *if* he was ready to talk, but knowing what I did, how was I supposed to stay silent?

How was I supposed to hold the words back in?

This wasn't my secret to tell. This was his. And he was the one who'd suffered. Not me. I was just the one who'd failed him. Over and over and over again.

God help me, but I wished Finn and Junior had let me die. Had let those flames flicker over me and had burned my shame, leaving me to rot in hell for how much I'd failed them.

My life hadn't been easy, but a mother's lot was to try to make her children's better. Brighter. Instead, I'd condemned them from the start.

"Where's here?" Declan questioned, his words breaking into my self-pity.

"I'm at Bellevue."

"The hospital? Visiting Michael?"

"Yes."

"Who's with you now?"

"Jamie."

"He's driving you?"

"No. Fenris is."

"You like him, don't you? Or do you want me to switch him out too?"

"No. He's a good boy."

"Okay, I'll leave you to it and will work on transferring Sean over to your detail. Give Michael my regards?"

"Will do, son." I cleared my throat. "Declan?"

"Yes, Ma?"

"You're a good man. I hope you know that. Aela's lucky to have you as her husband."

He was quiet a second. "I stopped being good a long time ago, but I'll do whatever I have to to make sure I'm good enough for her." Before I could answer, he mumbled, "I'll speak with you later, Ma."

And he cut the call.

Declan had always been my special boy. So unlike his father and brothers, and for Aidan, unlike meant different, and different was bad.

Declan loved the arts. Ballet. Opera. You'd think he was into sodomy the way Aidan had gone on about that when Dec was younger.

I'd fallen for Aidan years ago, but his failings were many, and as a father, he'd been a brute. I saw that now.

Back then, I'd just thought he wasn't as bad as my da, and I'd been trying to keep the family together.

Five boys, six with Finn, were a lot to corral. Especially when they were all so damn rambunctious.

Conor always hacking into NASA or causing trouble on the internet.

Eoghan forever taking potshots with that BB gun Padraig had gotten him for Christmas when he was four.

There'd never been a day where Brennan and Aidan weren't fighting, and then there was Declan, trying to hide his love for opera and the arts by getting into squabbles at school that had me in the principal's office every day.

Life had been relatively normal, then the Aryans had taken me, and I'd checked out.

Brennan and Aidan were fully grown, but the rest of my sons were still boys. Still babies. But I'd been broken. Too broken to protect them.

So many mistakes, so many forgotten promises, so much damage wrought.

Christmas wasn't the first time I'd tried to end it all.

The last attempt, Aidan had sent me to a special center. It was why I hated hospitals now. Why my visiting Michael meant more than he could possibly understand.

Straightening up, shielding my expression, I turned away from the window, ready to show the world at large that Lena O'Donnelly was not to be messed with.

If they only knew how frail that mask was.

DECLAN: *Did you hear about Michael?*

Eoghan: *The cancer?*

Declan: *What else?*

Eoghan: *Is that rhetorical?*

Declan: *Doh.*

Eoghan: *Speak in full sentences, Dec. Jesus. Yes, I knew about Michael. Yes, I set Jamie on her to make up for his loss.*

Declan: *I'm giving her Sean too.*

Eoghan: *Good thinking, she likes him.*

Declan: *She sounds down.*

Eoghan: *She's married to Da. Why wouldn't she be down?*

Declan: *You sound miserable too.*

Eoghan: *Just tired.*

Declan: *You're on your honeymoon. You're supposed to be tired.*

Eoghan: *Yeah, I guess.*

Declan: *You ready to come back?*

Eoghan: *I'm ready for my bed. And for the quiet. It's noisy here.*

Declan: *Thought you were in the middle of nowhere?*

Eoghan: *I am. It's not quiet enough.*

Declan: *LOL. You're such a fucking weirdo.*

Eoghan: *If you say so.*

Declan: *You going to be back in time for the ceremony?*

Eoghan: *Yeah. Extended the trip and we're flying straight into Boston.*

Declan: *Good thinking.*

Eoghan: *I'm capable of it sometimes.*

Declan: *No shit.*

Eoghan: *Did Finn help you with whatever had you ringing me ten times a day?*

Declan: *He did. I'll leave your miserable ass in peace.*

Eoghan: *About time.*

Declan: *Give Inessa my love.*

Eoghan: *Will do.*

SEVENTEEN

EOGHAN

JUST LAST YEAR, my penthouse was a silent, cavernous space.

Empty.

Furnished but still vacant within.

A place where I rested my head, where I ate, and where I worked out.

It had become a home in that time. A home that was still a haven just not as quiet as it had once been.

This hotel was noisy.

This hotel was *not* a haven.

I even preferred listening to Inessa and Victoria's horrendous taste in boy bands over this hotel.

Four AM every day, a delivery van came with fresh bread from only God knew where.

A half-hour later, the owner's shower kicked on and the pipes started creaking.

Fifteen minutes after that, the furnace began raging.

Another hour in, the washing machine switched on in the kitchen.

Then came the cooking.

Followed by more pipes creaking and the furnace grumbling as guests woke up.

I'd slept in quieter barracks in Afghanistan.

"Why aren't you sleeping?"

The whisper had me tilting my head on the pillow so I could see her. This creature who had come into my life and who had made a penthouse a home, and who had changed my world.

She didn't know it. Neither had I until the other day.

"Why aren't you?"

"You were huffing."

"I was not," I argued, immediately sitting up on my elbow. "I don't huff."

She sniffed. "What woke me up then?"

"Considering we're staying in a hotel that makes an orchestra look silent, take your pick of what woke you up."

"Grouch."

"You sleep like you're dead," I retorted.

"You sleep like you're a princess."

"A princess?" I snickered. "Which princess do I take after?"

"The princess and the pea." She yawned. "Go back to sleep. It's still dark out."

"It's always dark out."

"You don't like it here, do you?"

I'd liked it plenty until I'd had to kill two people in the open air in a tiny buttfuck nowhere town.

I'd liked it plenty until I'd gotten a call from contacts I didn't want to deal with, who shoved my face in my past like they were giving me a swirlie.

"It's okay," I lied.

She patted my stomach. "We can go back early."

"No," I countered. "It's fine."

"It's not if it makes you unhappy."

I shook my head and reached over to cup her cheek. "You're too good for me. Do you know that?"

"Wouldn't say that," she said sleepily. "We fit nicely together, don't we? You're the grouch and I'm cheery. Consider me your bodyguard."

My lips twitched at her logic. "Why my bodyguard?" If anything, I protected her.

"I'll save your food from being spat in by servers you're mean to." She pressed a kiss to my arm then patted my stomach again. "Bodyguard, see?"

Grinning in the dark, I flopped back on the bed. "I can see the use in having protection like that."

"Better than a condom, that's me," she slurred before she fell back asleep.

I felt her drift off, turning slack at my side. She cuddled up to me before she rolled over. I almost pulled her back, liking the feel of her so close to me, but my phone's screen flashed on from the nightstand.

Reaching for it, I hissed out a breath and carefully climbed out of bed once I saw the message.

Unknown Sender: ***This is a secure line***

Jaw clenched, I strode toward the bathroom and tapped the number. A few clicks, and I heard a soft voice greeting me:

"Whistler."

"Dead To Me," I said grimly.

"Eagle Eyes," she continued. "I've brought us onto this call to discuss what occurred the other day."

"What's to discuss?" Eagle Eyes snarked. "Two fuckers are worm food, and we all got paid for the same hit. Sounds like good business to me."

I scratched my chin as I plunked my ass on the toilet. Though the others on the line were two of the best sharpshooters on the planet, I knew I'd killed the man. They used different bullets to mine, and I'd seen the aftermath.

Having studied their kills in the past, I got the feeling Eagle Eyes had made the other hit because Dead To Me's shot had gone a little wide.

And by a little wide, I meant a half-inch.

In our business, that could have been a mile.

"You don't think it's weird that there were three snipers on two hits? This isn't *Grosse Point Blank.*"

"Shit, I need to watch that movie again. I loved it back in the day," Eagle Eyes said with a chuckle. "And no, we don't have a union of snipers. Although that wouldn't be a bad thing. Would stop us from cluttering up tiny Irish towns in the future, wouldn't it?"

"My contact told me they were ECD."

Dead To Me hummed. "Mine did as well."

"Mine too," Eagle Eyes confirmed.

"I thought you'd stopped this game," I grumbled. "Married life and all that shit." I'd attended the bastard's wedding before the holidays, after all.

"Like you can talk," he groused at me. "We're both married—"

"This isn't Jerry Springer either," Dead To Me muttered. "What are we going to do?"

"What about?" I countered. "There's nothing to do."

I knew what she meant though. It didn't sit well with me either.

Reaching up, I rubbed the back of my neck. "We need to agree to be honest here..." I paused. "None of us were told to target the other, correct?"

"No. My kills were the two ECD fuckers."

"Same," Dead To Me agreed.

"Okay, so this wasn't the 'Man' trying to wipe us out."

"Doesn't seem to be," Eagle Eyes concurred. "That's why I don't see what the problem is."

"How did you get out of the Middle East alive?" Dead To Me grumbled.

"Had Lady Luck on my side."

My lips twitched. "You mean me?"

"Well, if that's the call sign you're going by nowadays, sure."

I almost laughed at that.

Eagle Eyes continued, "Those *cheiles* must have had a high profile target in mind to garner the attention of three separate agencies.

"My handler told me it was someone in the Irish government, and a US military target, but I don't think anyone in the US is in danger from the ECD."

Not after seeing Davidson's face splashed all over the news this week because of the recent state dinner, anyway. Not with the Irish prime minister who liked the current status quo where Ireland was split into two separate countries.

Seemed like a BOGO to me.

Dead To Me asked, "Who were you with, Eagle Eyes?"

He explained, "The Israelis sent me."

My brow furrowed. "Why would they do that?"

"Because I'm better than their best agent?" He sniffed. "Why else?"

I rolled my eyes. "So, the UK, the US, and Israel were all in league over this."

"That has to mean something."

"Not our business," Eagle Eyes argued. "Why do you care now?"

Dead To Me grunted. "I don't like the ECD."

"Does anyone?" he snapped. "It's not like hotdogs—you either love them or hate them, is it?"

While I agreed, I knew what she meant. "I think we're in no position to try to figure this out."

As was the way with our line of work, we didn't see the full play until months or sometimes even years down the road.

I rubbed my forehead as I leaned over, a migraine starting to throb at my temples that was exacerbated by all the fucking noise in the background.

"Where the hell are you? What's all that noise?" Eagle Eyes muttered.

Surprise had me straightening up. "You can hear that?"

"Sure can."

"Yup," Dead To Me agreed.

"We're all on red alert," I said flatly. "Eagle Eyes, whether you like it or not, you're freaked out."

He pshawed. "Yeah, if that makes you feel better, okay."

He didn't have to tell me dick—his hearing did that for me.

Hypersensitivity was something we lived with every day, but when we were on red alert, it made things a lot harder to handle.

"You ever find it hard to sleep at night?" Dead To Me asked.

"All the time," I rasped.

"Just once, I'd like no dreams," she said wistfully.

"I don't see their faces." Eagle Eyes cleared his throat. "Mostly, I remember other stuff."

"Like what?" I questioned softly.

He sighed. "The exhilaration of it."

"Yeah."

I had to cringe because we were all anal-retentive overachievers.

Getting long distance shots was like a competition.

Didn't matter that someone was going to become a corpse because of it. It was still exciting. And I'd been on Inessa like she was in heat and I was a goddamn dog when I'd arrived back here.

"What about you?" Dead To Me asked.

I scrubbed a hand over my face. "I don't sleep at all. Or hardly anything will wake me up. Either or."

"Did you hear that Dagda was out of jail?"

My brows rose at Eagle Eyes' out of the blue statement. "He is? Jesus. He's been inside for nearly thirty years, hasn't he?"

"Yeah. They said it was because Russia and the UK brokered a deal, but I don't know if I believe that," Dead To Me murmured. "Not considering his ties."

"We'll need that sniper's union soon," Eagle Eyes predicted glumly. "You know he's got the best eye of us all."

"He did. Until he got tortured," I pointed out. "Not sure getting old in jail will have kept his skill levels up."

Eagle Eyes grunted, but it was Dead To Me who asked us both, "Are you still in the country? I'm not."

"No."

"I am," I replied. "Four more days."

Dead To Me hummed under her breath. "Is that wise?"

"Probably not," I said dryly. "But I'm in another county so I'm away from the heat. If you find anything out, put us in the loop?"

"Agreed."

"Affirmative."

I cut the call now that business was done and straightened up. Flicking on the light, I stared at myself, saw the fatigue etched into my face and sighed before I reached for my shaving kit.

As I foamed up my face, I was about to let the blade slide up over my throat to my jawline when the rattle of the oven trays being freed from the stove sounded like a ten-car pileup outside. I jerked, nicked my flesh, and as I watched the tiny wound bleed, I decided that today was not the best day for a shave.

Inessa would just have to have beard rash between her thighs.

CONOR: *Wanna talk?*

Eoghan: *No. Why?*

Conor: *Dunno. Thought you might want to talk.*

Eoghan: *What about?*

Eoghan: *Have you been listening in on my phone calls?*

Conor: *Nope. Well, aside from the usual ones.*

Eoghan: *Reassuring.*

Conor: *Here if you need me, brother.*

Eoghan: *Thanks. I think.*

EIGHTEEN

CONOR

WHEN I OPENED the door and found Ma standing there, I tipped my head to the side in surprise.

"You got over whatever it is I did?"

She pursed her lips as she shoved her way inside my apartment. "What makes you think you did anything?"

"You've been sulking with me since Christmas."

"I haven't—" She sighed then twitched her finger at me. I leaned down so she could kiss my cheek.

Watching her take off her gloves, scarf, and coat, I stayed silent, knowing that would get her to talk.

I didn't think she knew about Da asking me to bug her phone, so I wasn't sure if that was the reason for the sulking. While I saw the necessity of having the bugs, it wasn't like I *wanted* to listen in to everyone in the Points' private conversations.

Regardless, her visit was either a toss-up between that or her and Da finding out about McKenna.

I'd be more pissed about the privacy, but that was me, and I didn't want to bring up the subject of my molester because talking about that shit was pointless.

She passed me her things and looked at me expectantly. A quick scan revealed that she'd lost weight since Christmas, and that she'd started doing that scratching thing with her neck again. Without her scarf, I could see the redness there.

When she cleared her throat, I glanced down at the coat, gloves, and scarf, and tossed them on the floor.

When she frowned at me, I muttered, "I don't have anywhere to put them."

"You have a coat rack right by your side."

"I don't," I argued. "That's a tree."

She stared at it, and so did I. "It has little hooks on it, son. It's a coat rack."

"It's a tree," I said stubbornly. It had cost me a fortune, and at no point had the artist told me I could hang shit on it. "The floor's clean."

"That's not the point," she grumbled then huffed. "I'll go make coffee."

I heaved an impatient sigh and drifted back to my office.

When I'd seen her through the cameras, hovering by the door, I'd figured I'd better let her in before she talked herself out of knocking. That meant I'd left a couple things on my screen that I shouldn't have.

Hearing her footsteps, and the clank of her making coffee in the kitchen, I knew I'd have time to hibernate some programs.

Setting the volume low as I worked, I continued listening to the conversation I'd been speeding through before she arrived.

I wanted to discard it so Da would never be able to get his hands on the information.

"At least he isn't Hewett?" Eoghan muttered.

"I guess. Although we'd have better tax breaks if he were."

"True."

"I shouldn't tell you. Just telling you feels like a fucking betrayal but..." Finn sighed.

"But?"

"But the fact Aoife is Davidson's puts her in a set of crosshairs that I can't get her out of. Your turn now. What's your secret?"

"Not as impressive as yours."

"No BS. Hit me with it—"

"Have you been eavesdropping again?"

I jerked around, shoulders tense as I saw her standing there, watching me with narrowed eyes.

When she stacked her hands on her hips, looking like my mother of old and not the one who was frightened of her own shadow, I had confirmation that she'd been acting odd because of the whole pedophile thing and not that I'd been bugging her phone.

Damn.

I didn't want to talk about it. Speaking about it with Lodestar was the last time I ever wanted to talk about it again.

Heaving a sigh, I told her, "I don't eavesdrop."

"What did I tell you as a boy, Conor?"

"That eavesdroppers never hear good of themselves. I don't do it for fun," I grumbled.

"No, I'll bet your father asked you to do it for him." She huffed but her heels clacked as she walked toward me. "Replay that."

I cut her a look. "You'd be eavesdropping too."

Ma arched a brow. "Replay the recording."

I hunched my shoulders. "Da won't like it."

"Your father knows that I don't care whether he likes it or not anymore. Play the damn recording, Conor!"

Her bark had me huffing but I queued it up to where she might have listened, trying not to reveal anymore of Eoghan and Finn's conversation to her than was strictly necessary.

Her expression turned blank, but she shot me a look and asked, "Is that the State of the Union in the background?"

"Yes."

"He's talking about the president?"

"Seems like."

"Aoife's *that* Davidson's daughter?"

Spying her pinched expression, I pulled a face but didn't answer. "That seems to be the inference."

When she plunked her ass on her chair, I quit the program and shut down the computer. Macs breathed better after a shut down. I figured this would do them some good.

"What are you doing here, Ma?" I muttered. "Aside from listening to shit you shouldn't be listening to." A thought occurred to me. "Where's the coffee?"

"Coffee?" she repeated blankly.

"Coffee."

"It's percolating." She blinked at me. "Aoife's the president's love child?"

"Well, I don't have DNA proof of that—"

"Finn sounded certain."

I couldn't argue—he did.

"Did you know who her father was?"

"No." I shook my head. "Pretty annoyed that I missed that too, to be honest." When she stared at her feet for a good couple of minutes, I reached out and grabbed her hand. "What is it, Ma? Does it matter who Aoife's father is?"

Her smile was tight. "No. Of course not! It's just... well, it's big news, isn't it?"

I snorted. "You going to go to the *National Enquirer* now?"

"Don't be ridiculous," was her waspish retort.

"Well then." I hitched a shoulder. "I don't see that it matters." It mattered if we needed to blackmail the president, but that wasn't for her to know.

"No, I don't suppose it does."

Her faint words had me asking, "Ma? What is it? Why are you here?"

"Declan said you needed help with the ceremony," was her faint reply.

"Oh." I straightened up, relieved that was why she was here and not the other elephant in the room. "Sure. Yeah. You're here to help?"

"If I can," she rasped.

Doubly relieved by the reprieve, I beamed a smile at her. "Great. Just forget about that, huh? It doesn't matter in the grand scheme of things, does it?"

"No, son, it doesn't." She shot me a fake smile that was somehow worse than what she'd greeted me with at the front door. "Now, what can I do to get that brother of yours married off?"

CONOR: *May have a problem.*

Eoghan: *What kind of problem? Jesus, can't you fuckers leave me to enjoy my honeymoon in peace?*

Conor: *What bit you in the ass?*

Conor: *Wait, you're on your honeymoon. Guess that was a dumb question.*

Conor: *Didn't see you as a bottom.*

Eoghan: *Leave my ass out of this.*

Eoghan: *And Inessa.*

Eoghan: *And what we get up to in bed. Jesus, Conor.*

Conor: *You're a prude.*

Eoghan: *I'm not. I just don't want to talk about this shit, and you and Declan have been fucking messaging me nonstop.*

Conor: *What am I supposed to do with my problem?*

Eoghan: *Send it to one of the others?*

Conor: *I can't. Not really. Only you and Finn know this, and I don't want him to know that I know, even though I'm pretty sure he knows that I know.*

Eoghan: *Well, that made sense.*

Eoghan: *What don't you want Finn to know that you know?*

Conor: *Ma overheard your conversation.*

Eoghan: *Which conversation?*

Conor: *You know when you were telling Finn that you work for MI6 and that Aoife's the daughter of the president?*

Conor: *Eoghan?*

Eoghan: *I'm here. Just trying not to think of ways to kill you from across the pond.*

Conor: *I'm safe unless you have a strain of Anthrax in your luggage.*

Conor: *Do you?*

Eoghan: *Do I what?*

Conor: *Have a strain of Anthrax with you?*

Eoghan: *No, they don't let that kind of thing through TSA.*

Conor: *Life is so boring nowadays, isn't it?*

Eoghan: *Yeah, it's a real drag. So, Ma overheard the conversation? How did that happen?*

Conor: *Thought she was making coffee.*

Eoghan: *And she walked in?*

Conor: *Yeah.*

Eoghan: *What was she even doing there?*

Conor: *Wanted to talk about Dec's wedding. You're coming, right?*

Eoghan: *As if I'd miss it.*

Conor: *It's going to be cool. Never planned a wedding before.*

Eoghan: *Better than planning the downfall of the Sparrows, I guess.*

Conor: *Actually, that's easier.*

Eoghan: *Of course it is. And yes, I did just roll my eyes.*

Eoghan: *You're a dumb fuck for thinking Ma wouldn't walk in.*

Conor: *Got distracted, I guess.*

Eoghan: *Not like you.*

Conor: *Lot on my mind.*

Eoghan: *Want to talk about it?*

Conor: *No*

Eoghan: *Good*

Conor: *Lol. Anyway, you're right. I'll leave you to get on with your honeymoon.*

Eoghan: *Was that a guilt trip?*

Conor: *Don't think so.*

Eoghan: *That you're not sure is disturbing.*

Conor: *You know that's my main goal in life.*

Eoghan: *Head case. Anyway, Ma is Ma. She won't say anything aside from to Da, and if it's about that, well, what can you do?*

Eoghan: *You're supposed to report that kind of shit back to him like a good little soldier anyway, aren't you?*

Conor: *I suppose so.*

Eoghan: *Such a sneak.*

Conor: *Says the guy who shoots people from rooftops.*

Eoghan: *Jesus, you heard that?*

Conor: *Oh, brother, I see all and hear all and know all. That you haven't figured that out yet is more disturbing than anything.*

Eoghan: *I got two words for you, Conor.*

Conor: *What?*

Eoghan: *Fuck. You.*

PART 3

NINETEEN

PAST

LENA

"YOU DOING OKAY, LENA?"

From the backseat of the Jaguar, huddled in my coat, I grumbled, "What do you think, Michael? I'm casing the joint of a woman whom I think my husband had an affair with. Whom he had a child with. Do you think I'm having a great time?"

"Sorry, Lena."

I heaved a sigh as guilt hit me. It wasn't Michael's fault that we were sitting here on this miserable as hell day.

It was unseasonably cold, enough that the rain kept showering on and off, which made it even harder to keep an eye on the tearoom where Michelle Keegan worked.

My hands shook from where they were buried in my pockets. It was a combination of the tremors that struck when I was off my meds, the desire to ring Aidan's neck, and the cold that I was hypersensitive to.

Still feeling mean for snapping at him, I muttered, "It's not your fault my husband couldn't keep it in his pants."

"No," he conceded. "But I can still wish it hadn't happened on your behalf."

I heard his sincerity, and that made me feel guiltier. "Thank you, Michael."

After another five minutes of staring at the front door of the establishment, he cleared his throat. "You wanna take your meds? I got them here."

"I took them when you went to go find a restroom," I lied.

When he heaved a sigh, I knew he was going to let the matter drop even if he didn't believe me. Michael knew me well enough by now to know what I was like on and off my medication, but he also knew not to push his luck.

Back before I'd used them, I'd seen TV shows with characters who didn't take their prescription medication and I'd wondered why they did that.

But what doctors didn't tell you when they loaded you down with your own physical pharmacy, was about the side effects. Sure, they told you to read the fine print, but experiencing it was different than reading it.

When you had to take metformin because your antidepressant made you borderline diabetic, and when your anti-psychotics screwed with your thought processes, dulled them, sometimes it was better to have suicidal thoughts.

Sometimes, it was better to let the PTSD mess with you, to allow the past to swallow you whole just to be able to think without chemicals clouding your mind.

"You want anything to eat?"

"No, but thank you," I choked out.

"We should go."

"No."

"We've been here for three hours, Lena."

"So? We were here for three hours yesterday morning and another three hours yesterday evening. You got someplace else to be?"

He sighed. "No."

"Well then." I pursed my lips, uncaring that I'd been staring at the façade of the tearoom for over ten days now.

I knew he was bored. I wasn't exactly having a hoot of a time, but when I was here, I felt like I was doing something productive.

Getting the news that Aidan suspected he had testicular cancer was one thing. His confession that he'd cheated on me and a child had been born from that relationship was another.

He'd told me because he thought he was going to die. His confession appeased *his* soul but added the burden onto mine.

The unfairness of it made tears sting my eyes.

I wished he hadn't said anything.

Wished he'd kept quiet because since he'd told me, I'd been unable to stop myself from thinking about whom he'd been sleeping with behind my back. Who the child was. When it had been born. Was it a girl or a boy...

The questions were starting to drive me crazy.

"You're sure they said it was her," I grated out for the tenth time this morning.

"I'm sure," he rumbled wearily, his focus on his phone and that stupid game he was playing. The one where you matched three jelly-beans to score points. "The Old Wives' Club doesn't get shit like that wrong."

I bit my lip, wondering if those old bitches were laughing at me behind my back. Michael said he'd been discreet, but was there anything discreet when it involved Aidan and me?

We ruled the roost. We reigned over the Five Points like king and queen. Where we went, gossip followed.

I scratched at my neck as I murmured, "Have you found anything else out about her? No links between Michelle Keegan and a Five Pointer?"

"Not by blood. Her husband was a cousin of a Five Pointer, though. You knew one of them."

"I did?"

"Cillian Donahue. He died years back. Was friends with your Declan, and his sister, Deirdre, was his girlfriend at some point."

My mouth curled as I corrected, "His fiancée. I remember them both. Horrible children."

"Cillian was a trouble-maker through and through." He hummed. "When Donahue, her first husband, died, Michelle changed her and her daughter's surname back to her maiden name."

A little girl.

Aoife.

I'd been blessed with boys, but no girl, and I knew Aidan had always wanted a girl. He might say he didn't, but he did.

And she'd given him what I couldn't.

A black Lincoln pulled up outside the tearoom, rupturing my thoughts. Three women climbed out of the back. My brows rose when I recognized one of them, and my fingers stopped rubbing the side of my neck.

Elizabeth Davidson.

God, it had been years since I'd seen her, and that hadn't been long enough. I'd never liked her.

She was a supercilious bitch whom I'd had the misfortune of knowing when I was younger, before life had taken us down two paths.

My father had wanted her elder brother to marry me, and I knew that George had all been set to propose the night of my debutante ball. That was before Aidan had showed up, bringing his usual level of chaos to my family.

It was a lifetime ago since I'd first known her, but it wasn't the first time we'd met since then.

I was the wife to the leader of the Five Points.

She was a Senator's wife.

As I wondered if the rumors of Alan Davidson cheating on her were true, I watched as she and the other two women headed into the tearoom.

It was a busy place, had an affluent clientele, but Elizabeth Davidson was definitely a step up from the corporate businesswomen who usually frequented it.

Nostalgia and a strange desire to reconnect with my past had me climbing out of the car when the two women with Elizabeth left the tearoom an hour later. They both went their separate ways just as the black Lincoln pulled up.

"I won't be long," I muttered to Michael, and before he could stop me, I dashed across the road.

I heard the honking of a car horn but I ignored it as I made it to the other side of the street, just as the door to the tearoom opened and out walked Elizabeth.

The noise from the road caught her attention, but her gaze drifted a second, held, before it swiveled onto me.

As I walked over to her, she smiled. "Magdalena O'Shea, as I live and breathe."

My eyes narrowed upon that catty smile. I'd known her as an eight-year-old and she'd been as much of a bitch back then as that smile indicated she was now.

"Lizzie Ó Cléirigh, what a surprise."

The smile faded. "It's Davidson."

"It's O'Donnelly. You'd know that seeing as Aidan donates to Alan's campaign." I tipped my head to the side. "I'm surprised you're in New York. Isn't Alan in Florida? Trying to swing enough votes to get people to forget about that unfortunate news article last winter?"

She scowled at me. "That was all conjecture."

"The best type of news usually is," I drawled.

"People in glass houses shouldn't throw stones," she hissed, dipping down from her irritatingly statuesque height to loom over me.

"Meaning?"

"Meaning my husband isn't the only one who can't keep it in his pants."

I straightened up at that, her words hitting me on the raw. "Aidan's—"

She scoffed, "Aidan's, what? Faithful? Get real, darling. Mine's about as faithless as yours, but at least Alan isn't a hypocrite. And that article last year was nonsense.

"I wish he *would* sleep with staffers. At least that would be easy to cover up." A dry laugh escaped her. "I heard all about Aidan, though. Alan doesn't like having his arm pulled."

My brow furrowed. "What are you talking about?"

"What do you think I'm talking about?" She jerked her hand toward the tearoom. "I just had to check this place out when I read the report on Alan's desk."

"What report?"

"On your husband, of course." She tsked under her breath. "I assume that's why you're here? To confront her? I wish I didn't have to dash because I'd have loved to see the show."

"The show?" I asked faintly.

"I do love a catfight. Of course, she's *much* younger than you so I doubt you'd win. That would be far more entertaining." Her smile was vicious. "I never did like you, Magdalena. I was so glad when that mobster scooped you up. You weren't good enough for George then." Her gaze dripped with disdain as she looked me up and down. It fastened on my throat. "You certainly aren't now."

She stepped aside without another word and moved over to her car. She stayed there a second too long, enough for the driver to ask her something, but she didn't bother answering, just climbed into the backseat. I watched as the driver closed the door behind her then whisked her away.

As they drove off, I stood there, shivering, feeling as frail as a sapling being blown around in a hurricane.

When Michael appeared at my side a second later, he ordered, "Stop scratching your throat."

I frowned. "What?"

He retrieved a handkerchief from his pocket and pressed it to my neck. "It's bleeding, Lena. You scratched it raw."

Pulling back, I stared down at the folded fabric and saw the red staining it. Placing pressure against it, I rasped, "I'll have it laundered and get it back to you tomorrow."

He shook his head, and like I was as ancient and as frail as that bitch had made out, he helped me over to the car.

"I'll take you home."

"You damn well won't," I whispered as I sank heavily into the backseat.

"You can't stay here," he argued. "I need to get some disinfectant for your neck."

"It's a scratch."

"It needs cleaning. Plus, you're shaking. You need some coffee and a sandwich."

"Then go and get me one from the whore who fucked my husband," I snarled.

Leaning one arm on the door, he loomed over me. "If you expect me to believe that you took your meds, Lena, you have another thing coming."

As he slammed my door closed, it was only then that I saw how late it was getting.

Aidan would wonder where I was, much as he'd wondered the past week. But he could carry on fretting. He could speak with Michael. I had nothing to say to that bastard. Nothing whatsoever.

I didn't try to stop him as he crossed the street, heading into that slut's tearoom to buy me something to eat. Something I would never let cross my lips.

Tossing the handkerchief aside, I saw the door open a few minutes after Michael went in, and Michelle Keegan, the whore herself, walked out.

Transfixed, I watched as she started to stroll down the sidewalk, well aware that she'd take the same route as she usually did. A route Michael had followed every day since I'd started this little stake out.

When she began moving out of my line of sight, agitated, I climbed out of the backseat then dropped behind the wheel. I had to adjust the seat, and it took up valuable seconds, but I managed to get the engine started a minute later.

As I pulled out, a Ford truck beeped at me as I almost crashed into it, but I barely saw it as I raced down the street, trying to catch up with her.

When I found her again, I kept my eyes on her, not even taking any notice of the traffic. As the car jolted when my tires clipped the curb, I jerked back into the middle of my lane.

Frowning, I stared at the road ahead before I glanced back to find her again.

Only, she wasn't there.

Eyes darting all over in an effort to find her, I carried on driving.

When I saw the pedestrian crossing, it was too late.

I clipped her.

I felt the car knock her down, felt the bump as the wheels rode over some part of her body.

The brakes squealed as I came to a halt.

New York City was never quiet.

Ever.

There were always people around.

Always.

But at that moment, it felt like God was on my side because there was no one here.

No one.

Until I heard thudding footsteps.

A quick glance in the side mirror let me see Michael running toward me. He took the scene in, jumped into the passenger side and screamed, "DRIVE!"

I should have immediately obeyed, but I didn't.

I was frozen.

"Where's the coffee?"

A snarl escaped him. "I threw it out. Drive, Lena. For fuck's sake!"

"Is she alive?" I whispered a second, an hour, a *lifetime* later.

"Yes," he snapped. "Drive, Lena. Get us the hell out of here!"

"We should call the cops—"

"Some people are made for jail, Lena, and you're not one of them." He pointed to the end of the road where a woman was running, heading from the small park to the left of us. "She's coming our way.

She might already have seen what happened. You need to get out of here."

I saw her and recognized that God *wasn't* on my side.

She sped up like she knew I was about to take off, like I wasn't about to call 911, and I realized he was right.

I wasn't made for jail.

TWENTY

AOIFE

PRESENT

I WAS HURTING.

It was a strange hurt. Deep inside my abdomen. It had been coming on and off for a day or so.

My biggest concern was that it reminded me of how I'd felt just before Jake's due date. Only this was two trimesters too early.

Rubbing my side, I turned to my guard who doubled up as my driver and asked, "John, can we go straight to the apartment?"

He nodded. "Of course, Aoife."

He muttered something into his earpiece, so I knew the car riding behind us, one that housed my extra guards, would be following us back to my apartment building.

"Thank you," I murmured, wincing as the rubbing only made it worse.

I knew I'd eaten too much at lunch with Jen, but damn, this *hurt*.

I'd intended on running some errands, dropping in at the bakery to make sure everyone was still coping with the uptick in business, but feeling like death warmed over, I had no desire to traipse around the city or to visit with my staff.

It was with relief that we arrived at the apartment building, and I slumped into the corner of the elevator as it shuttled me to the top floor.

When the doors opened, I hobbled down the hall on the hunt for my little man and found the kitchen in a state, but Jacob was smiling, so I didn't even cringe at the sight.

Flour dusted his cheeks and what appeared to be salt dough had his fingers sticking together as he waggled them when he saw me.

"Mama!" he crowed like he hadn't seen me in days. "Mama!"

Laughing at the sight, I leaned against the door to catch my breath as Lena grinned back at me. "He loves it."

"He loves making a mess," I corrected, stepping deeper into the room so I could kiss her cheek and ruffle my son's hair before I smacked a kiss on his head too.

Taking a seat opposite Lena, I winced as my bones rattled at how heavily I'd plunked myself down and admitted, "I'm pooped."

She eyed me as she formed a shape with the salt dough. "You should take a nap."

Lena and I didn't stand on ceremony anymore. Hadn't done so for years. But still, I muttered, "I feel bad. You come to visit and I spend most of the time running errands."

"You think I'm mad about getting to spend all this lovely time with my grandson?"

My lips curved as I watched Jake chortling away as he played, somehow managing to get the dough in his hair—this kid, I swore, was a walking, talking, breathing cognitive behavioral therapy session for OCD.

Mom would have loved this.

I had no idea where the thought came from, but it winded me. I took a second to reply, to handle the slice of pain and sweet sorrow that hit me.

"No," I denied with a wobbly smile, "I know you love spending time with him, but I shouldn't just cut and run. You know I like it when you come and stay with us."

This visit was definitely impromptu, but I wasn't going to look a gift horse in the mouth.

She'd showed up a couple days ago and had told me that I could take things easy for a while.

What expectant mother with a toddler and a busy bakery would say no to that?

"I told you I came because it's easier to handle your doctor's appointments when you don't have babies clinging to your skirts." Her gaze sharpened as she watched me rub my side again.

I reached for Jake's sippy cup and snagged some of his OJ. The sugar perked me up as I asked, "Did you and Conor get everything arranged for tomorrow?"

Lena blinked at me, and I saw something peep into her eyes that had me frowning some. "Yes, everything is ready."

"The news is going to feature the art?"

Lena nodded.

"How did Declan even get that stuff?" I grumbled, but I wasn't sure why I was shocked.

The O'Donnellys were a law unto themselves.

Why shouldn't Declan have a Vermeer tucked away that he was donating in exchange for a private ceremony within the Isabella Stewart Gardner Museum?

"I have no idea, and I didn't ask," Lena drawled. "I think both you and Jake look pooped. Why don't you both settle down for a nap while I go and make sure things are full steam ahead at Declan's?"

"A nap sounds awesome," I admitted with a sigh, well aware she'd be going to hang out with Shay who was still having trouble with his bullies *and* nightmares after his and Aela's near miss in the fall. "But even if I don't sleep, you go anyway. I'd hate to hold things up after you and Con have worked so hard to arrange everything."

"Declan never did like to wait," she retorted as she got to her feet. "His impatience definitely isn't a virtue." At my snort, she smiled then motioned a hand at the kitchen. "Leave this. I'll sort it out when I get back."

"Okay," I said nonchalantly.

She narrowed her eyes at me. "Aoife."

"What?"

"Aoife," she repeated, making me laugh.

"What?"

"Don't you dare clean up. Go and get some rest!"

I huffed, but before I could argue, another twinge arrowed down my side. I thought I managed to shield my expression because Lena was like a mother hen right now, and she'd have been all over that if I hadn't masked my features.

She rounded the table, held out her hands, and said, "Up, up, up."

I let her help me, cringing as that hurt too, but I was relieved as all hell when she shuffled Jake over to the sink and said, "I'll clean him up, put him to bed, and then head out. I'll be back before dinner."

"Thanks, Lena." I surprised myself by yawning. "I really appreciate this."

"My pleasure, sweetheart. Now, go on. Shoo."

I shot her a shaky smile and half-staggered out of the kitchen, finding my bed with relief. After ten minutes, when I still couldn't get comfortable, I knew the pathetic reason why—*Finn wasn't here.*

"God, you're such a sap," I muttered to myself.

The bed was big, but I huddled in the center then grabbed his pillows, shoved them along my back, ruffled the comforter at my front, and eventually managed to find some semblance of comfort.

It worked, anyway, because I didn't even hear Lena go out, and I only awoke when I heard a soft laugh and Jake's giggles.

The pain had gone. I wasn't sure if that was because of the nap or if it was down to the heat at my side which was no longer from the pillows. Finn was there, and God, he felt so good.

I peeped out and saw Jake was sitting in front of me, Finn's hand was on my belly, the heat filling me with a warmth that I figured soothed the pain, all while he watched Jake with a new toy—a hedgehog that had soft 'spikes' he had to fit into the slots on the animal's back.

Drowsily, I moved onto my side, and was relieved to find there was still no pain, as I smiled at him. "Hey. When did you get back?"

"About an hour ago," Finn said as he pressed a kiss to my forehead. "You were sleeping deeply so I didn't see any harm in letting you rest."

I'd needed it.

"What time is it?"

"Nine."

My eyes widened. "Jeez. I slept late."

"You did. And you missed the family announcement," Finn teased.

I shifted onto my back and asked, "She said yes?"

He snorted. "As if she wouldn't."

"Aela's independent. You know she moves in her own way."

"She's Declan's. He wouldn't have let her say no."

My lips twisted at that BS. "Like you wouldn't let me say no?"

The sparkle in his eyes always made my heart rate soar. "I'd have let you say 'no' once."

"Then dragged me to bed until I said 'yes?'"

"Something like that." He reached up and cupped my chin. "Lena's back. She said you looked like you were in pain earlier."

"It's gone. Just a cramp. Jen and I ate too much," I admitted.

"No, *you* ate too much, she probably had a liquid lunch," he said wryly.

I grinned. "You know how she works."

"Cristal is her oxygen." He rolled his eyes. "You going to be okay to travel tomorrow?"

"Oh, sure! I wouldn't miss their wedding for the world."

I heard my cell ring and started to sit up until Finn urged me back down. As he clambered off the bed, his head tipped to the side.

"Is that 'The Stars and Stripes Forever?'"

Sheepishly, I nodded.

Our gazes clashed and held as a knock sounded at our bedroom door.

"Come in," I called out, my eyes still held by his.

"Aoife? Your phone's ringing." Lena sounded amused. "I didn't realize you were so patriotic."

I cleared my throat as Finn finally broke away from me, strode over to Lena, snagged my phone, then returned to my side. It had stopped ringing by that time, but a second later, it started up again.

"I'll leave you to it," Lena demurred.

Finn stared down at my cell. "He's dogged, isn't he?"

"He's the president," I retorted. "What else do you expect?" I connected the call. "What do you want?"

Finn's lips twitched, but my father answered, "I have an update."

"Finn's here. You might as well update us both."

"Alan," Finn said, and I shot him a smile.

"Finn," my father rumbled.

"Go ahead," I directed, seeing that there was some kind of silent pissing match going on even though there were several hundred miles separating the pair of them.

"The threat has been handled."

Relief hit me. "That's great news."

"I wanted to let you know... I have to go. Stay safe."

He cut the call, and Finn murmured, "I don't like that man."

"You voted for him."

"So did you. I don't have to like him to know he was the best of two evils. Fucking democracy," he grumbled. "What kind of election is it when you've got a corrupt piece of shit on one end and a corrupt piece of shit on the other?"

"You're talking to the wrong person. You know Jen's the one who digs all the conspiracy shit."

"This isn't a conspiracy!" was Finn's snippy retort. "That's what makes it worse. What kind of world is this little man going to grow up in, huh?" He sighed and reached over to run his hand over Jake's head before he pressed his other to my belly. "Sometimes, I despair for this fucking planet."

His somber tone filled me with concern. "Are you okay, sweetheart?"

He shot me a weary smile. "I'm better knowing you're safe."

"You've been down—"

"I just need a break. The holidays weren't exactly that."

"Do you want to stay a couple days in Boston? Maybe get some downtime?"

He'd mentioned the cruise, and now I realized it was as much for me to relax as it was for him. Yet the prospect of being on a ship right now didn't fill me with glee.

"I can't. The Hanover takeover just triggered an explosion of work. I'm taking more time off than I can afford tomorrow for the ceremony."

"What are you working for, Finn?" I asked, tipping my head to the side. "We have all this." I looked around the room, the *massive* room, just one of a dozen in the penthouse. "What more do we possibly need?"

"I'm not trying to get richer," he denied.

"Then what, love?" I questioned, pressing my hand above his on my belly and bridging my fingers with his.

"I'm buying respectability."

His words had me looking at Jake. "For him?"

"For him. Senior will expect him to join the ranks. I don't know—if I don't provide another path, then..." He paused a second. "They're all I had when I was growing up. You and Jake and this little one are my family; you're what matters the most, but I—"

"You need them too. I get it, sweetheart. You don't have to justify—"

"If you knew what I did for them, what I've done..." He released a shaky breath. "It keeps me awake at night, Aoife."

"Then I need to get better at helping you sleep."

"No, this isn't on you." He stared at Jake who'd grown bored with the hedgehog and was cackling as he slammed it against the comforter. "I have to provide another path just in case Aidan's figured out how to stay alive forever."

"Aidan Jr. wouldn't force the issue? Isn't that his job? He'll want to continue the line, won't he?"

"He'll have no choice," Finn confirmed.

"Unless there's another way."

Finn nodded.

"And that's why you barely rest and why you're always working?"

"Yes. So that Jake can be free of the Points. So that Shay can be, so that the kid in Aela's belly will be, and that this one won't be tangled up in this shit world." His mouth twisted. "I was a kid when I went to Aidan, Junior at my side. We were both cocky pieces of shit when we told him we were ready to enlist." He scoffed. "*Enlist*. Like it's something to be proud of. Like it's the military."

"You were raised believing it was something to be proud of." Curious, because we didn't often talk about stuff like this, I studied him.

Life got in the way.

He talked about business deals and directors who had pissed him off. I spoke about the bakery and Jake and Jen and just, well, *life* stuff.

"I was." Bitterly, he derided himself, "Proud. Can you imagine?"

"It was different when you were a kid, wasn't it?"

"It was," he agreed. "The Five Points exploded in the late eighties when Aidan started Acuig.

"Suddenly, he had legitimate means of laundering his dirty money. It's taken nearly thirty years to get to this point, but when I moved in with them, they were rich but not like this. Not like today."

"That's a big change in a generation."

"It is. I'd like to think Conor and I were pivotal to that. Aidan started Acuig, and he had some direction, but his mind isn't business-oriented. Well, not regular business, at any rate.

"We steered things down this road, and maybe, just maybe, we can make it so that—"

I squeezed his hand. "So that, what, baby?"

"I don't know." He closed his eyes, and suddenly, his fatigue leached into his expression, revealing a bone deep weariness that I knew no amount of sleep would ever ease.

"You do," I chided.

He released a soft breath. "The Five Points aren't going anywhere. It's not going to happen. Wishing otherwise is a pipe dream. But it doesn't have to work how it does now."

"Not if Junior's in charge. I can't see him letting his son pick up a gun at fourteen—"

"It isn't the gun that's the problem. I want Jake to be able to shoot, to defend himself. It's what he does with it that's the issue. Hanging around street corners like a gangbanger..." Finn sighed. "I don't want that for my boy."

"Me either." My fingers found his wedding ring, and I rubbed it. "You've got time, baby."

"Not enough of it. Twelve years? Is that enough to change things?"

"Think about twelve years ago," I suggested. "iPods were a massive deal, TikTok didn't exist, and eBay was hot shit."

"True." He grinned, and for some reason, that seemed to cheer him up. "Do you want something to eat?"

"Is that instead of talking about this? Because we can talk some more—"

He shook his head. "I'd prefer to eat with my family. What will be will be, but I'll bust my ass to make sure Jake has options."

I was choked up as I rasped, "And I love you for that."

"Sweetheart," he breathed. "You should hate me for—"

"I could never hate you. *Ever,*" I insisted. "Get that out of your head."

His lips curved, but there was a sadness to that smile that hurt my heart.

Despite having a great evening with Lena, and the following day, celebrating Declan and Aela's nuptials in the private room in the museum with a Vermeer watching over the ceremony, that sadness remained in Finn's eyes.

And it hurt my damn heart knowing there was nothing I could do to ease it. Nothing aside from the downfall of the Five Points, which meant the downfall of my family...

For the first time, I understood his sadness.

TWENTY-ONE

LENA

"STAY HERE, JAMIE," I directed before tapping on the door to Michael's hospital room.

"Come in," he croaked out, his voice weak and frail.

Wincing at the sound, I headed on in with a smile I wasn't feeling.

I didn't need a medical degree to know that Michael's cancer treatment wasn't working. I'd only been away two days to celebrate Declan's nuptials, but he looked to be even thinner than before.

As I plunked the carrier bag on the side of his bed and began pulling out some crossword books I'd bought him as well as some grapes, I chided, "You're looking like a hot mess this morning, Michael. Don't you shave for the ladies anymore?"

He sent me a sleepy smile as he reached for the remote on his bed to raise the backrest. As he did, the sleeve on his gown pulled taut around his arm, and when the loose fabric gathered high on his bony bicep, I saw the ink on the ball of his shoulder.

It was a testament to how thin he was that the fabric had shifted that much, but as I looked at the design, a design I'd seen practically every day during my childhood, for a second, I froze, unable to process that the past and the present were blurring in front of my eyes.

My father, his shirt off, suspenders hooked over his white undershirt as he ate dinner... Shoulders hunched because of how he ate, elbows on the table, one hand hovering over his plate as he scooped up food.

The flag that damnable phoenix was holding seeming to flicker like it was caught in the wind with the movements of his muscles.

Then my brothers had gotten one, and I'd been surrounded by phoenixes.

I thought I'd escaped them when I married Aidan, but the way Michael's hand snapped up to his sleeve and he tugged on it, I knew my eyes weren't deceiving me, and I knew they hadn't left me alone.

As I flashed him a look, he sighed and stopped fussing with his sleeve. Instead of trying to cover the ink, he raised it. Which was when I saw his pride.

God, they were always so prideful.

"How—" I broke off, tried again, "When?"

The time he'd have enlisted, seeing as he was a good fifteen years younger than me, Father would have been in the nursing home. My brothers were all dead, most of them in that bombing in London, and my connection to the ECD had been cut short.

By chance, I'd bumped into a *cheile* on the way out from visiting my father in the nursing home, and I'd learned the new leader was Eamonn Keegan. On a personal level, that was about all I'd heard of the group for over twenty-five years.

I guessed the when and the how didn't matter. He was a *cheile*. The web I'd felt certain I'd escaped years ago clung to me as tightly then as it did now.

My throat felt choked, but I managed to croak, "Does Aidan know?"

He nodded, and the sight had me staggering back, slumping into the chair beside his bed.

"It's been a long time since I've seen one of them," I whispered dumbly, staring at the phoenix that had haunted me for years, trying to reconcile that Aidan was aware of his real identity.

What did the ECD have on him?

That was what it boiled down to.

They had to have some leverage, otherwise he'd never have trusted Michael with me.

"Since your father?" Michael asked.

For a second, I didn't know what he was answering, then I realized it was about the ink and the last time I'd seen that godforsaken phoenix with the flag of a unified Ireland between its talons—a white shamrock on green.

I swallowed. "You knew Father?"

"Yes. Not well. I joined too early for that, but he's beloved. Your brothers too. Their memories live on through the *cheiles*." He tugged on his sleeve. "The phoenix doesn't mean much here."

"Wouldn't mean much to anyone," I countered, "unless they know what it signifies." Our gazes collided and I questioned gruffly, "How many ECD brothers are in the Five Points?"

His gaze shuttered. "Does it matter?"

"Is Fenris? Is he a *cheile*?"

"Whether he is or isn't, it doesn't matter," he said firmly, and his tone told me to drop it.

Michael had never spoken to me like this before; but then, if he were a *cheile*, everything we'd ever discussed, endured together, was a lie.

God, *everything*.

"It matters," I snarled, hands bunching into fists as I thought about how long and how deep this betrayal truly ran.

"Aidan Sr. is loyal to the cause," he grated out. "We're no harm among his ranks."

"You're a harm," I denied. "You *cheiles* always put the cause before anything else."

Why had Aidan placed him as my guard when that was nothing but the truth?

Michael's mouth tightened, confirming that we were on the same page—that he *would* put the ECD's goals before me.

They were all the same. Always sacrificing the people who mattered for a cause that would never come to pass.

"You lied to me. For years," I breathed. "Even though you know my roots." I wasn't a sympathizer, but I'd never go against the ECD.

Only a fool would do that.

He looked away. "I didn't lie."

"You lied," I reiterated. "If ever there was a time to come out with the truth, Michael Byrne, it's on your deathbed."

"I think you should go." He turned up the TV, and the news blared on before I could argue.

'Footage of a heated conversation between President Davidson and Irish Prime Minister Nathaniel O'Leary has leaked online.

'The recording appears to show both leaders standing in the Rose Garden, with the First Lady acting as a go-between for both men.

'A leak from within the White House said that the conversation was

tense, with Prime Minister O'Leary repeatedly raising his voice at the president.

'The video, since its posting, has had over two million views because of the unprecedented support the president has given to the concept of a unified Ireland—'

As I watched the footage, I lifted a hand to scratch at my neck, and from out of nowhere, a distant memory floated to the surface.

Elizabeth Davidson, our First Lady, taunting me outside Michelle Keegan's tearoom.

Michelle Keegan's death. By *my* hand.

Michael jumping into the car and yelling at me to drive away.

But what I knew now changed everything, didn't it?

It was all too much of a coincidence.

Aoife was Alan Davidson's daughter, not Aidan's.

Finn was Aidan's son.

Michelle Keegan had nothing to do with my husband. Nothing whatsoever.

Keegan.

Eamonn Keegan.

Aoife *Keegan*—her maiden name.

Why hadn't I made the link? Seen the connection?

Because I hadn't known Michael was a *cheile*, that was why. I'd had faith in a snake in the grass.

"You told me Michelle Keegan was Aidan's girlfriend."

I knew my words were barely audible over the TV, but I waited for an answer anyway.

Not that I got one.

I leaped up, snatched the remote from his hand, able to disarm him now he was so weak.

Switching off the unit and the news reporter's take on what a US president's backing of a unified Ireland represented, I snapped, "You told me Michelle Keegan was Aidan's girlfriend. Why did you do that?"

There were a hundred answers he could have given me. A hundred that would have appeased my confusion.

But he didn't give me one of those hundred.

He gave me, "I serve a cause greater than my own."

The news report whispered in my mind.

A US president's backing of a unified Ireland...

The ECD had gotten into the White House.

Oh, dear God.

I garbled, "You wanted Michelle dead, didn't you? Why?"

He didn't say a word.

It had to be because she'd given birth to Davidson's daughter. The ECD wanted him in office, and they always got what they wanted. Now, they had presidential support for their cause.

But...

"Her surname's Keegan. I know the ECD's leader is Eamonn Keegan. Are they related?"

Although, if they were, wouldn't he have protected her?

The second the thought crossed my mind, I almost laughed.

What was the blood between siblings if it came between the cause and a brother?

He stared at the wall, and I knew he wasn't going to say a damn thing. But still, I tried.

"If they're related, why wouldn't he protect her?"

He reached for some water.

"Why would you tell me she was Aidan's girlfriend?"

He hit the call button.

"Is Fenris one of you? Is Jamie?" I rasped, changing the subject, seeing if that would work.

He closed his eyes in dismissal. "I need to rest."

That could have been an affirmative, but I had no way of knowing.

I treated my guards like family. Everyone knew that.

Rogan's son was at St. Paul's Academy because of me—I was helping to pay Harry's tuition. When Fenris' daughter had gotten sick, I'd paid for Jenna's funeral.

Was I just a dupe to them?

Someone to con? To manipulate?

I thought about the young man outside.

Could Jamie be trusted?

Was he one of these cowards too?

Because that was all they were.

Men who claimed innocents were as guilty as politicians and treated them like collateral damage were cowards in my opinion, and the ECD was home to the worst of the worst.

Nothing mattered to them other than a unified Ireland. Nothing and no one.

My throat closed as I got to my feet. Knowing he wouldn't give me the answers I needed, I snatched up my purse and stormed over to the door.

I motioned to Jamie and strode down the hall toward the bathroom.

Brothers of the ECD were always marked. *Always.* And I needed to know. I *had* to know if Jamie was one of them.

Opening the door to the restroom, I held it wide and directed, "Go inside."

He frowned at me, but I was Lena O'Donnelly—Five Pointers obeyed me as if I were their queen—and for once, I wasn't afraid to act like it.

After he shuffled into the bathroom, I ordered, "Check there's no one in here."

Confusion in his eyes, he obeyed, opening the doors to the cubicles and peering inside. "It's clear."

"Take off your shirt," I further directed, holding my purse against my chest as if it were a comforter—how I wished it were.

At that moment, only Aidan's embrace would soothe the ache in my soul, but I couldn't tell him.

Not if he'd let a *cheile* guard me.

I couldn't trust him.

The only man who could give me comfort couldn't be trusted.

"Ma'am?" he queried warily, breaking into my terror.

"I'm not a desperate old woman who wants to see your body, Jamie," I snarled. "Take off your shirt. Now!"

At my order, he straightened, dragged off his coat, placed it on the vanity, then followed up with his suit jacket and shirt.

When he was bare from the waist up, I commanded, "Turn around."

The relief that filled me when I saw he only had ink that Aidan wouldn't approve of made me shaky.

Japanese tigers and koi fish were one thing, but there were no phoenixes or Irish phrases anywhere on his chest or back.

For all I knew, he might have one on his ass cheek, but I doubted it.

Tradition was tradition for a reason.

My da had that same damn phoenix on his upper arm, much as Michael had. And my elder brothers were the same, fools that they were.

High enough to be covered by a short-sleeved shirt, but easy enough to expose to prove to a fellow *cheile* they were of the brotherhood.

I pressed my back against the bathroom door as I ground out, "Get dressed."

"Yes, ma'am," he muttered and dressed at lightning speed.

Now I knew he wasn't ECD, I asked, "Do you know how to disconnect a PCA pump?"

"A what, ma'am?"

I took that as a no.

Sighing, I explained, "A patient-controlled-analgesia pump."

Jamie shook his head. "No, ma'am."

Damn.

Would Aidan Jr.?

Which of my boys would know how to do this? Would any of them?

The dread in my gut wouldn't abate.

The *Éire le chéile go deo* were bad news, and they'd targeted Aoife's mother. If the *cheiles* wanted Michelle dead, what was stopping them from wanting Aoife dead too?

If they'd gone for the lover, why not the love child?

I couldn't let that happen.

Aoife had been safe these last few years because she'd married Finn, but that was no guarantee, was it?

Aoife... I'd already caused that poor girl such devastation. The *cheiles* terrified me, and meddling was the last thing I wanted, but I had no choice.

I owed her; I owed Finn.

We needed answers.

I was under no illusion that my sons were cut from the same cloth as their father because I'd helped mold them into that. If I tossed Michael at them, then he'd be dead by the day's end. But dying for the cause was what the *cheiles* did.

Death was only a way to martyr them. They weren't afraid of it; they wouldn't be afraid of my children.

Well, that wasn't strictly true.

So I called the only man who'd be able to help me, the boy I'd let down, the son I'd failed. Whose soul, to my shame, Michael's death would rest on...

"Conor?" I whispered, wishing that I didn't need to do this, wishing there were another path I could take. "I need your help."

TWENTY-TWO

CONOR

MICHAEL RELEASED a moan that had me peering at him over my laptop.

Hatred filled me as he blinked at me, bleary-eyed from the drugs I'd dosed him with.

It wasn't often that I felt this level of hatred, but it wasn't often that my world was caving in around me.

Traitors—they were everywhere.

Every. Fucking. Where.

Callum O'Reilly had been my friend since I was a kid. He'd put up with my shit for as long as I'd put up with his. I was supposed to be his newborn's godfather, but he'd betrayed *us*.

More to the point, he'd betrayed *me*.

Rage spilled inside me like toxic sludge from an oil tanker into the ocean. It polluted everywhere it touched, turbocharging the hatred of moments before.

Ma had been betrayed too.

My whole family had.

I was so sick of this witch hunt, so sick of people who were supposed to have our goddamn backs taking pieces out of us like we were commodities.

"Where—" Michael broke into my thoughts as he panted a second, then slurred a word I didn't understand. "Where'mi?"

"Where are you? Just a warehouse."

An *anonymous* warehouse where no one would hear him scream.

"'Ow?'"

"I have contacts. It was a lot of fun hacking into your files, shuffling things around. Reminded me of the old days. The state believes you've been transferred to a hospice." I stared at him. "Welcome to your new ward."

His eyes flared wide before the lids drifted down as they darted around the space.

"See over there? That's your new roommate." The rat squeaked, and I murmured, "If you behave, you won't end up being eaten by him. If you don't, well, then your fate rests with him."

Michael moaned then jerked his hands and feet which had the cuffs around them rattling.

I ignored him and kicked up my legs so they were resting against the side of his 'mattress.'

"Ever heard of sirenomelia?" I asked as I scanned Aoife's medical records. Her doctor had received notification this morning, and I'd received them a minute later.

Michael rasped, "Lemme go."

"Why would I do that when it took me so much effort to get you here? If you don't know what sirenomelia is, then just say so."

"Need morphine."

"Well, let me just pop into something uncomfortable and become your nurse," I mocked. "Michael, what about this place is giving you the vibes that I give a fuck about how you feel?" I waved a hand around the room, further scoffing, "I mean, it's so hygienic, isn't it? What with the rats and the cobwebs?

"If you were someone I gave a fuck about, then this would be taped up better than an episode of Dexter, no contamination or germs allowed, but in your case, Mickey, you need to get friendly with germs."

"Why?" he wheezed.

"Because if you're lucky, they'll kill you faster than I do."

"You... don't—" He sucked in a pain-soaked breath. "Kill."

"What made you think that?"

"You're." He sucked in a breath, the sound raspy and Dalek-esque. "Soft."

"Remember that when you're screaming later." I stared at the test results on my screen. "I'd never heard of it before, sirenomelia, I mean.

"It's only when you realize how hard it is to get through pregnancy that you can appreciate life," I mused. "Quite ironic, of course, considering our current circumstances, but you matter to me about as much as that rat does, whereas my little niece or nephew..." My words waned before I ground out, "How can a kid's legs fuse together? It makes no sense."

"What." Inhalation. "You." Exhalation. "Talkin' about?"

"I'm talking about the miracle of life, Michael. A miracle that I intend to preserve."

There was nothing I could do for Aoife other than *this*.

Aoife was my sister.

Aela was my sister.

So were Inessa and Camille and Savannah.

I had five of them now.

I had five people who could create other people to watch over.

That was a lot of pressure, but it was worth it. More worthwhile than the other crap my father had me doing. I knew more than any doctor did now about pregnancy after a week's intense study.

It meant I was wired, but hey, wired and I went well together.

I was at my best when I felt like this.

And I could do nothing for the niece or nephew that was slowly dying in Aoife's womb, but I could protect the mother.

Aoife needed protecting.

She just didn't know it, but Michael knew. Michael knew more than he was willing to say.

"Feel those cuffs on your ankles and wrists? I adapted them. They've got a metallic plate running around them, and if I do this—" I fiddled with the program on my computer as I dropped my feet to the floor. "—it triggers a current." When he screamed, I tutted, "Oh, Michael, you disappoint me. That was only the first phase. Considering you're one of those *cheiles*, I thought you'd have more guts, but I see I was wrong."

"Bah-stard," he groaned.

I peered at the steam that wafted from his form and muttered, "Huh. More potent than anticipated. Interesting."

"Sick—" Inhalation. "O."

"Everyone thinks I'm so innocent. Don't you know it's the quiet ones you can't trust?" I rumbled. "Especially when it comes down to my sisters, Michael. My mother too. You fucked with the wrong family."

Lodestar: *Yo.*

The text bubble appeared on my computer, drawing my attention because Star had a habit of doing that.

There'd come a day when we would finally meet, and she'd suck out all the air from my lungs.

That didn't mean I was going to make it easy on her for being a pain. Our last conversation still stung.

I was *not* a weirdo for liking *Doctor Who*. And she was such a cheater when it came to *Call of Duty*.

aCooooig: *What?*

Lodestar: *You still sulking?*

aCooooig: *I don't sulk.*

Lodestar: *Seems to me like you do.*

aCooooig: *I don't sulk. I'm just busy.*

Lodestar: *Busy doing what? O.o*

aCooooig: *Testing a prototype.*

Lodestar: *For my Christmas gift?*

My lips twitched. So she hadn't forgotten.

aCooooig: *Not exactly.*

I deployed the program and ignored Michael when he screamed again.

Lodestar: *For what then?*

aCooooig: *Specialty cuffs.*

Lodestar: *You into bondage? Would never have pegged you as being into that.*

aCooooig: *Why?*

Lodestar: *I don't know. You don't give off sub or Dom vibes, I guess.*

I wasn't sure how I felt about that.

What was it with everyone thinking I was a pussy?

Lodestar: *Still, it's always the quiet ones.*

aCooooig: *You know, I just said that to someone.*

Lodestar: *Who?*

aCooooig: *You really want to know?*

Lodestar: *Sure. Wouldn't have asked otherwise.*

aCooooig: *Wanna go on cam?*

Lodestar: *Last time we went on cam, I got nothing but attitude from you.*

aCooooig: *You cheated.*

Lodestar: *I did not! I'm just better at shooting than you.*

aCooooig: *We need a rematch.*

My computer pinged as she started a video call.

"I started the vid solely so you could see me roll my eyes," she declared as she rolled her eyes.

I rolled them back.

Then, after flipping me the bird, she asked, "Where the hell are you?" She strained her neck as if that would give her a better view of the warehouse behind me.

"Somewhere secret." I tapped my nose. "Want to meet my current test subject?"

She squinted at me. "Why am I getting Norman Bates' vibes from you?"

I laughed. And it felt good. Nothing about this situation was nice, and the way I'd been feeling lately, after what had happened with Callum, laughter came as a relief.

It shouldn't have surprised me that she gave me that.

As I wondered if she knew the light she brought to my life, still chuckling, I told her, "I don't know. I don't think I have my mother's corpse in my apartment."

"Good to know."

Straightening up, I twisted the computer around so she could see what I was doing.

I'd hacked into her file at Langley, so I wasn't concerned about her reaction. She hadn't exactly bothered with The Hague Conventions on war crimes when she was an ex-CIA agent. And when I'd seen the reports on her when she was in captivity, the shit she'd done made this look like a day trip to the zoo.

Star sniffed. "There a reason for the *Dr. Death* setup?"

Impressed, I drawled, "You've been binging TV shows." TV shows that weren't even streaming yet.

"Maybe. You wouldn't talk to me! What the hell else was I supposed to do?"

Smiling, I told her, "It's been five days."

Five very busy days.

Getting this guy into the warehouse here was easier than arranging a wedding in Boston, but it had still taken some time to make it look seamless.

People would come calling if I didn't wrap this up nice and tight.

The ECD always collected their dead.

"Dude, don't 'it's been five days' me," she grouched.

"You can see why I've been busy now, right?"

It was a half-truth, but I knew she'd give me shit for being a wedding planner for my brother's nuptials.

"I do." She peered up at me. "What's he done?"

"You in a secure location?"

"Not really. Lily's kitchen. But everyone's out, including Tiffany's mom—old hag," she muttered under her breath.

"What about Katina?"

Kati was her foster daughter.

I wasn't sure how someone like Star got a foster daughter, but if I could redirect Michael into my very own private hospital, then I didn't think it would be too hard for a woman like Star to get herself a kid.

"She's at school."

I frowned. "What's going on with her bullies?

"I broke one of their arms."

Grinning, I told her, "I see being in a wheelchair for a while hasn't slowed you down any."

"Nope. God, it's good to be out of those casts." She stood up. "You've no idea how much of a luxury this is." She sat down. Then stood up again. Then walked over to the fridge and returned. "Heaven."

Her ass was definitely heaven.

"Dude, my eyes are up here."

Smirking, I told her, "You put it right in front of me."

"I expect an ass picture in return later on."

"You mean the ones from the satellite weren't good enough for you? I almost froze my balls off doing those snow angels for you."

"It was grainy—"

"*HELP!*"

I cast Michael a glance.

"Rude," Star grumbled.

"If you think that will help you," I told him grimly. "You're mistaken."

"*HELP!*"

"Can't you shut him up? That's why God made duct tape, Conor."

"I need him to talk or I'd tape his mouth. Want to see what my prototypes do?" I inquired.

"Sure," she said as Michael screamed again.

Turning the laptop around, I triggered the program, and as he yowled like a cat, Star laughed.

"That's awesome!"

The sounds of electricity whizzing along the airwaves sent shivers down my spine.

I loved electricity.

Without it, there were no computers.

No code.

Nothing to hack.

Life would be so boring without it, and there was nothing more fucking damaging than a live current.

When the program ran its short course, Michael started sobbing.

"He peed himself," Star pointed out.

"Yup. That's the second time he's done that now. How long does it take for ammonia to rot skin?"

She pursed her lips. "I'd say a day."

"That's something to look forward to." I plopped her on a makeshift table at the foot of the bed so she could get a better view of us both. "Star, meet Michael. Michael, meet Star."

"Pleasure to meet you, Michael," Star chirped.

"I don't think he's being rude," I murmured, "just trying to catch his breath."

"Why've you gussied him up? This isn't like you, Conor. Didn't think you were on the psycho end of the spectrum."

"I'm not a psycho."

I wasn't.

I was a fucking soldier in a war that people were waging against my family—the only people I gave a shit about.

"This setup gives me different vibes."

"He hurt my family."

"How?"

"You know what the ECD are?"

Star sniffed disdainfully. "Conor, what do you think?"

"I think you know what they are."

"Affirmative. He's with them?" She eyed Michael with more curiosity than before. "They're harder to crack than jihadists, did you know that?"

"I didn't. Had dealings with the ECD before?"

"A time or two. Like I said, hard nuts to crack."

"That's why I introduced him to my old friend electricity. Plus—" I held up a hand. "One second."

Getting to my feet, I rounded the bed where I had a couple of those humane rat traps waiting for me.

I picked one up then placed it on the bed.

"Rats?" Star shuddered. "I hate rats."

"They make good pets. I had one when I was a kid."

She arched a brow. "Did your mom know you had one?"

I grinned. "No."

"Typical boy. So gross. What are you going to do with them?"

"See how his head is secured?"

"Yep. Immobilized is the word you're looking for."

"I figure Michael won't like feeling his eyes being eaten by a hungry rat. Before that happens, I'm hoping he'll break. If not, he knows what's coming to him."

Michael started sobbing.

"That's it, Michael. Season Mr. Rat's dinner. I'm sure they'll appreciate the extra salt."

Star cackled. "You're crazy, Con."

I shot her a look. "I'm not crazy."

"You are. Totally. I love it." She rubbed her hands together. "If I didn't have shit to do here, I'd totally come for a visit."

Staring at her over the rat trap, I murmured, "I mean, you could visit anyway."

She shrugged, but a smile danced on her lips. "One day."

We shared a glance. Nodded.

"One day," I agreed, praying she wouldn't be someone else who let me down. Who betrayed me. Shoving those miserable thoughts aside, I placed the rat trap on the bed. "But I'm not crazy."

"Preaching to the choir."

I grumbled, "I'm not crazy. I just don't like it when my family is hurt."

"Who was hurt?"

"A lot of people," I said grimly. "Now, Michael, I'd like to know why the ECD needed Michelle Keegan to die." *And why they used my mother as the murder weapon.*

"Who's Michelle Keegan?" Star questioned. "Why do I know that surname?"

"You know Finn's wife?" I asked.

"Yep. I know of her."

"Her mom."

"Ah." Star's brow furrowed. "I see... this really is personal."

Did she sound disappointed?

If anyone was crazy here, it was her. Not me.

"Nothing more personal," I confirmed. "That's a problem for you, Michael. See, my father would just threaten to kill you, and you'd die, and that would be the end of that.

"You'd probably be feeling nice and smug that your death is going to have a purpose, so you're further encouraged to hold out.

"But I'm not my father. I'm not someone who delivers death lightly to people."

"No shit, Sherlock," Star muttered. "Death by rat? That's medieval-grade torture. I'd high five you if I were there."

"That's an ex-CIA agent giving me kudos, Michael. So I think we both know that this isn't going to be a pleasant death."

"Fuck—" An inhalation. "You." Exhalation.

I sighed and turned back to my computer. "There are five levels to this program. You've only experienced the first one."

I hit level two which had Michael's pain-filled shrieks morphing into an endless squeal.

"Wonder how long it will take for him to break?" Star queried.

Hearing a noisy crunching sound over the video, I turned and found that she had a bag of Flamin' Hot Cheetos on her lap.

"Settling in for the show?"

She nodded. "You'd better be entertaining."

I rolled my eyes. "This isn't Netflix, Star."

"Nope, it's even better."

TWENTY-THREE

AOIFE

A FEW DAYS LATER

"I'M AFRAID, Mrs. O'Grady, the pregnancy isn't viable."

I stared at my doctor, willing her to say this was a joke, but it wasn't.

I was already scheduled in for early screening because of the scars on my abdomen, but when the pain had returned during Aela and Declan's ceremony, I'd headed to the doctor's office the morning we returned from Boston, and they'd taken more tests.

Perhaps, in my heart of hearts, I'd known the truth, but I'd hoped I was wrong.

I stared down at my stomach where the bulge wasn't even that prominent yet, and I rasped, "You have to be wrong."

"I'm sorry but the tests confirm it. You know you're a high-risk candidate for pregnancy, Mrs. O'Grady." She shook her head. "To be frank, you're fortunate we caught this here and now.

"These kinds of birth defects tend to be caught at the twelve-week scan. We can terminate now to alleviate the undue stress on your body."

I jerked my head to the side. "I'm not going to do that."

The doctor frowned. "Aoife, the child won't survive past a few days without intensive, invasive surgeries that might not even work.

"Jake was a high-risk pregnancy, but he developed normally. This will be for nothing. You'll suffer for nothing. Miscarriage is likely. Why wouldn't you prefer to control when and how this happens?"

"I don't understand how this is possible. Why would the baby's legs fuse together?"

The doctor's expression turned sorrowful. "It's very uncommon, and the ultimate cause is unknown. What we *do* know is that babies born with sirenomelia have a host of other spinal and brain development issues." She sighed when she took in my expression. "You shouldn't be here alone, Aoife. Is your husband not attending with you today?"

Why did doctors always want to talk to the husband?

Mary Ellen, a friend of mine, had tried to get her tubes tied, but her prick of a doctor had made her get permission from her husband before he agreed to go ahead with the procedure.

Her husband.

Who should have had no say on her body and the right to do whatever she wanted with it.

Didn't matter that another child after the two sets of twins she'd already had might kill her. She still needed permission from her jackass husband who spent more time dipping his wick in other women than in her.

No, this was *my* decision. Not Finn's.

I needed to do some research. I needed to understand without this white noise whistling away in my ears, making it harder to understand what she was saying.

I got to my feet without replying to her and drifted out of the office as if I were in a daze.

She called out my name but I whispered, "I need to process this."

Needed to process the impossible.

But I'd seen for myself.

Where two small legs should have been, there was...

It was...

A tail.

Like a mermaid.

Two little bones fused together, wrecking my hopes for—

No.

There was always hope.

"Aoife, you need to consider discussing the option of Mr. O'Grady having a vasectomy—"

Deaf to her words, I made my way to the door. As it opened, my guard was standing there, and I almost sagged into him.

Like he knew I needed the support, John cupped my elbow, and I peered up at him while he frowned down at me.

"Is everything okay, Aoife?"

What did I say?

If Finn knew about this appointment, he'd want to know what was going on. If he knew, he'd make me—

I couldn't.

I just... I couldn't have an abortion.

Was that selfish or selfless? I had no idea, but the prospect of...

I blew out a breath.

"I just feel woozy. I think they took too much blood."

John frowned, but he nodded. "Damn doctors. You think they'd know when enough's enough."

"They should. You're right," I muttered, throwing my OBGYN under the bus because it saved face.

John guided me to the elevator, and I must have looked rough because he said, "Just wait here. I'll get the car."

Nodding, I leaned against the wall and waited for him. I placed a hand on my stomach then cringed when that pain hit me again.

It was such a weird feeling, and I'd gone through the gamut when I was carrying Jake. Abdominal scar tissue meant that pregnancy wasn't easy for me.

In all honesty, I'd imagined it would be just as hard as before, but this blindsided me.

The pregnancy isn't viable.

My child wasn't viable.

Was it wrong to take that as an insult?

My child was perfect.

Except... he or she wasn't. Because they'd live for a few hours if they survived long enough for me to give birth.

Pain slashed through me of a different nature this time. It had nothing to do with my womb, and everything to do with my heart.

Finn would make me terminate the pregnancy.

I knew he would.

The car pulled up and, still dazed, I drifted forward and didn't wait for John to open the door for me. Just clambered in with all the elegance of a giraffe eating grass and immediately hit the button for the privacy screen.

I stayed upright only for as long as it took for the screen to separate

John and me, then I slumped on the back seat, staring blindly at the ceiling, not even caring that I wasn't wearing a seatbelt.

The words 'not viable' rang around and around in my head until I thought they'd drive me crazy.

The twenty-minute car ride might have taken an hour or ten seconds for as much as I processed the journey.

The lunch I'd had with Jen could have taken place ten years ago and breakfast with my two favorite men might have been two weeks earlier.

Time was irrelevant.

Time was a void.

I managed to keep it together until I got into the elevator and made my way to the penthouse.

The second I did, I heard Jake's happy laugh and it triggered me. I had no idea why, but the relief that he was okay, that he *was* viable, hit me at the same time as the sorrow that I'd never hear *this* baby's joyous laughter, that I'd never hear him or her cry, that I'd never go through the myriad things a mother did in a day.

A single day.

I wouldn't have any of that if I had a termination.

I crumpled in on myself. Leaning back against the wall, I pressed into it, sliding down until I was sitting on the floor, my face buried in my hands.

That was where Lena found me.

She curved her arms around me, pulled me close, and hugged me.

I needed that.

I needed that so badly.

No judgment, no questions, just affection. Just care.

God, I missed my mom at that moment. Lena's arms were comforting, but nothing was like her hug.

She tried though. She rocked me like I was Jake's age, and I needed that too.

My tears were loaded with my pain, and the raw sounds that flooded the room sounded like an animal's. I didn't even know I was capable of making that noise.

I'd lost babies before, but this one... I'd been so cautious about not getting excited until the end of the first trimester.

Until things were supposed to be safer.

"Shhh, shhh, shhh," Lena soothed me, but I heard the tears in her voice.

She didn't know what was wrong with me, but maybe she didn't have to *know* to *know*.

"Not viable," I gasped out on a sob, turning my face into her throat and hugging her back.

"I'm sorry, Aoife. I'm so sorry."

And she was.

And she got it.

Like someone who'd gone through this too.

Maybe not the exact same specifics, but someone who'd been handed these shitty cards and had had to deal with them.

As sorry as I was for her, I felt like I was in a safe space with someone who understood.

With someone who'd been there, who had a uterus and had dealt with childbirth, and who didn't have a penis and who could make decisions about my body for me.

Right then, that mattered.

More than she could ever know.

TWENTY-FOUR

FINN

WHEN CONOR SENT me a video link, I knew my lies were coming to a head.

I was sitting at my desk when I received the email.

For a second, I ignored it because I received a thousand emails a day that needed my attention and I was in the middle of reading some R&D reports that were quite interesting, but Conor never emailed—he texted or called.

So when I saw his email address in my inbox, surprise and curiosity had me opening the link.

The second I saw where he was and what he was doing, I closed the site, ran the program on my computer that shredded anything that could be construed as evidence if the Feds ever decided to confiscate my hard drive, and as it ran, grabbed my phone and AirPods.

Tucking them in, I moved away from the windows and toward the corner of my office where there were no cameras.

My back to the wall so no one could peer over my shoulders, I tucked the earphones into my ears and opened the link on my phone.

Michael was on the table. Lena's favorite guard. I knew he was sick, but he clearly wasn't in any hospital I'd like to be treated in.

Grunge and grime laced every surface, and Michael was strapped down to the worst of it—a wooden board that had more stains on it than an artist's palette.

Conor didn't often get his hands wet, and we all knew why.

His creativity was beyond disturbing.

A buzz of electricity made the hairs at the back of my neck stand up.

Michael yelped then sobbed, "NO MORE! Please. No more."

"Then start talking. I don't have all day."

Michael's sobs turned into sniffles. "Michelle Keegan's death wasn't an accident."

Tension clutched at my spine.

"Ma told me that you were the one who informed her Michelle Keegan was my father's mistress. Is that right?"

He groaned in pain. "Y-Yes."

"Why? Why would you do that?" Conor huffed. "And don't tell me that bullshit about you cozying up to the Old Wives' Club. I spoke with them. Nobody had ever even heard a whisper of my father and Michelle Keegan together.

"You fed my mother that poison. *Why?*"

The buzz of electricity soared through the air. As Michael screamed, Conor's voice was indefatigable, untiring: "Why?"

"BECAUSE I NEEDED TO HAVE SOMETHING ON HER!" he screeched hoarsely.

"You wanted to blackmail her?"

"Y-Yes." He sobbed. "Let me die. Just let me die!"

"Why would I do that when you still have answers for me?"

"I don't, I don't!"

"Liar," Conor grated out. "Why did you want to blackmail my mother?"

"B-Because Eamonn had gone soft," he groaned. "We've been quiet, too quiet. With Britain leaving the EU, now's our chance to gain our freedom. I needed a way to tip the scales in our favor, and your father gave us that."

Senior had been a part of this?

"Eamonn? As in Eamonn Keegan? The leader of the ECD?"

As Michael nodded, my brow furrowed in consternation. *Keegan? As in Aoife's maiden name?*

"She was off her meds," he rasped. "A bullet just waiting to be aimed at someone. A ticking time bomb about to go off.

"I directed her at the target and just waited for it to happen." He started coughing, great hacking coughs that had him tensing against his restraints. "If she didn't do it, I was prepared to jump in," he croaked out, "but I was pretty sure she would. Your ma's violent. It doesn't come out often, but when it does, she's just as bad as any of us."

Hadn't I seen that with my own eyes?

Hadn't I seen her stamp her fucking heel into the Archbishop's eye before Christmas?

There was no denying Lena had it in her to do shit like that. No denying it whatsoever.

"Was Elizabeth Davidson involved?" Conor asked.

The First Lady?

"N-No, of course not. Why would you ask that?"

"Because Ma told me that was what tipped her over the edge." Conor stared into the camera, and it was like he was looking straight at me. "Elizabeth told Ma that Alan had investigated Da and had found out that Michelle was his mistress."

Totally confused, I watched as Michael shrieked when another surge of electricity flayed him alive.

"I think you're lying to me, Michael," Conor said grimly. "Is Elizabeth Davidson a part of the ECD?"

"NO!" Michael screamed. "I don't know anything about that—"

"I don't believe you. Especially not after today's news. The ECD wanted Michelle dead for a reason. Why?"

Today's news?

Oh, Christ. That bullshit from the White House about Davidson supporting a unified Ireland.

Fuck.

"There were reports of her and Alan Davidson cozying up to each other again."

My brows rose.

"Was Aoife a target too?"

Because she was Davidson's daughter.

"Y-Yes," Michael stammered.

"If she was a target, why didn't you take her out?"

"I couldn't get to her after Michelle was dead. She had guards on her."

Guards?

"Do you know who the guards were hired by?"

"No. But they kept a discreet distance—" He paused, and his tongue made a clicking noise before he pleaded, "Water. Please, Conor. I need water."

Kid grabbed a bottle and allowed a thin trickle of water to stream into Michael's mouth.

It took a while, and I watched on in horror but with a sense of relief too as it let my mind catch up.

Michelle had been targeted.

Aoife had also been in danger, and might still be despite what Davidson had told us.

I sank to the ground, the wall at my back, and I let my forearms hang over my raised knees so I could continue watching the video.

After a couple minutes, Michael gurgled, and Conor pulled back.

"Who were you working for?" Kid directed.

Michael sucked in a breath, and call me crazy, but I knew the next words to spill from his lips were going to be a lie. "I don't know. I just had a contact, and when I informed them of the guards' presence, he told me to pull back. To wait. But then Finn started seeing her, and they married, and that changed things."

"Is she still in danger?"

"Aidan brokered her safety into the deal."

"He's ECD, Finn," Conor called out. "Ma discovered that nasty truth the other day. It's taken me all this time to get him to talk."

ECD?

Those *cheile* fuckers who thought nothing of blowing up innocents in their fight for a unified Ireland?

How the hell had Aoife and her mom gotten onto their radar? Was it because of their links to Alan Davidson? Or the fact that Eamonn Keegan, with whom they shared a surname, was the leader of the group and he had enemies?

I needed answers so I phoned him.

"I'm busy, Finn."

"What the fuck is going on, Kid?"

"I don't know, brother, but something shady for sure. The ECD don't just target American citizens for no reason at all."

"Michelle wasn't a citizen. She was Irish."

Kid hummed. "She got her green card."

"She was still Irish."

Another scream sounded in the background.

"Can you stop that?" I muttered on a growl. "It's fucking distracting. Ask him. Ask him why they targeted Aoife."

"You heard him," he argued. "He just said he got his orders from someone up high."

"I don't believe him. I think he's lying about Elizabeth Davidson too."

Kid was silent a second. "I'll work on getting you answers."

"Thank you," I rasped, but I couldn't stop myself from inquiring, "Why has Lena gotten you involved in this, Kid?"

"Because she doesn't trust Da. Says he knew that Michael was ECD, but he never told her."

My eyes widened at that, but I persisted, "Why did she stick *you* on this? Why not Brennan? Aidan? Declan, or even me, for fuck's sake?"

Conor had a whacked up way of doing this because of his fascination with everything AC/DC—and we weren't just talking about the band here—but Lena didn't know that, did she?

"Because she knows I won't go to Da, and probably because Eoghan doesn't do close-up shit." He sniffed. "I might do his bidding, but it's on my terms. You're all up his ass."

I gritted my teeth. "You need to get us some answers, Kid."

"What do you think I'm trying to do? I ain't having a ball down here. You know how bad he stinks? He's lucky that I don't want him to drown or I'd just projectile vomit all over him."

Despite the severity of the situation, I rolled my eyes because I knew exactly how Michael would be smelling thanks to Cillian Donahue.

"What do we know about the ECD?"

"The leader, Eamonn, got served a sentence for thirty years back—"

"For that bombing in Canary Wharf in London, right? In 1992?"

"Yes."

"Think it's a coincidence that he and Aoife share a surname?"

"No. I know it's not. He's her uncle."

"I guess he's been in prison all her life. She never mentioned him to me." I sucked in a breath. "He's due out?"

"I checked. He's already out. Got released early."

Tension hit me. "Has he come to the US?"

"One of his known aliases that didn't get burned after the bombing flew into JFK just after New Year's."

That wasn't reassuring news.

"Aoife was born in ninety-two in the States. So Michelle couldn't have had anything to do with the Canary Wharf bombing." At least, that was unlikely to be the reason why she was targeted.

"Not the bombing there, but they've done other shit over the years. Saying that, the States wouldn't have granted her a green card if she had a record."

I rubbed my brow. "Don't kill Michael until we're sure we've got all the answers we need."

"It's not going to be easy to keep him alive," Conor grumbled. "His resources are depleted because of the cancer, never mind what I've put him through. If he lasts until tomorrow, then I'd be surprised."

"Christ. Give him an energy drink or something."

Conor snorted. "Since when was that an elixir?"

"It might help."

"I doubt it. But I'll stop zapping him. He's starting to rot."

I sucked in a breath at that imagery. "Just give me a couple hours."

"Okay."

Kid, never one to stand on ceremony, cut the call, and I used the number I'd memorized from Aoife's phone.

"Aoife?" her father greeted, his voice wary.

"Davidson, we need to talk."

"What do *you* want?"

His tone wasn't inviting, but it didn't need to be. We didn't have to like each other to have a mutual goal—protecting Aoife.

"Aoife—" The trouble was, where to start?

Had Aoife been targeted by the ECD because of her relationship to the current president?

"What about her?"

"I've just learned something about Michelle Keegan's death."

"Give me five minutes and I'll call you back."

He didn't wait for an affirmative response from me, just disconnected. I knew Davidson would phone. Though he'd tossed Aoife aside in a bid to hit the White House, the man had courted disaster by trying to have a relationship with her period.

He cared.

His care just wasn't enough, wasn't *worthy* of my wife.

A different number phoned me but it was exactly five minutes after Davidson had ended our last call.

"I can speak with more ease now," he said by way of a greeting. "What do you know about Ellie's death?"

My brows rose.

Ellie?

"The ECD targeted her. Aoife was also a target. But you knew that already, didn't you? You're the reason she had guards." I tossed that out like it was a lure, and he took the bait.

A hissed breath sounded down the line. "Are you in a private area?"

"Yes. No one can eavesdrop. Do you know why she was targeted?"

"I do."

The flat answer had me narrowing my eyes. "And you're not going to tell me?" When I received silence as a reply, I demanded, "Is the threat still active? Is it tied to the more recent threats to her safety?"

Davidson sighed. "It's complicated." I was about to call him out on his bullshit, but he said, "The ECD are a complex cell. When Ellie was killed, it triggered a power struggle. For a time, the leader lost power until he consolidated his position."

"What happened during the power struggle?"

"Someone decided to ensure that my rise to the top went unheeded."

"So it *was* because of her ties to you?"

"I loved Michelle, O'Grady. I'd have—" He fell quiet, then he repeated, "*I loved her.*"

I felt the truth in his words, but it didn't stop me from pointing out, "She died because of you."

"She did," he spat bitterly, "and that was the reason I left her in the first place, to keep her safe. I sacrificed a lifetime with her for nothing. She'd have died either way."

My brow furrowed. "Explain."

"I don't have to explain anything to you."

"You sure as hell do. I have to tell Aoife this. I have to share the truth with her. I'm not going to withhold this from her."

"What good will it do to tell her?" Davidson countered.

For four years, I'd lied to her about her mother's death.

I could feel the sword of Damocles hovering above my head with that one secret alone, never mind this.

For a second, I stared blankly ahead, and as I did, I was taken back in time.

Crouched on the floor like a rodent, shoulders hunched, fear of exposure making my stomach churn as I wondered where I'd spend the night, where I'd get my next meal—

It was then I knew I'd prefer to be back on the streets, to be without a home, to be without my family, rather than keep another lie from my wife.

She deserved so much fucking more from me than what I'd given her. I'd chosen family ties over her, a family that had taken me in when I was at my lowest, who'd given me a future—even if that was splattered with blood. They'd been my foundation, and that was why I'd sided with them. But Aoife was my heart. My soul—

"O'Grady?"

I heard the president barking in my ear, and it brought me back to the moment.

No longer was I sitting in a dirty alley that reeked of desperation, where the stench of trash was prevalent. I was in my office, the air redolent with some lavender and oat spray that Aoife insisted would make me calmer at work.

Blinking at the thought, I had to smile.

The only thing that would make me calmer at work was if they pumped Valium through the air conditioning.

But that was Aoife. Always thinking of me...and here I was, continually letting her down.

"Yeah?" I rasped when Davidson growled my name again.

"You don't have to tell her."

"I do."

I really did.

I had to tell her everything.

And rather than scaring the shit out of me, the notion came with relief. Like a bolder had been removed from between my shoulders. Like the truth was a key to a door that had been locked between Aoife and me for years.

"You don't. What good will it do, her knowing that her mother was killed for political gain?"

"Because she has a right to understand the puzzle pieces of her past that have brought her to this point." I sucked in a breath, letting the rightness in my words resonate.

I needed to go home.

Now.

I got to my feet and told him, "If you ever want a relationship with your daughter—"

His answer was immediate. "I do. I want nothing more."

"Nothing more? And you dumped her like she was nothing?"

A snarl sounded down the line, and I jolted in surprise because unless Davidson had a fucking lion in the Oval Office with him, he'd made that sound. "You think I wanted that? People in glass houses shouldn't throw stones."

"What the hell does that mean?"

"It means that you should look at your own people if you want to understand why I made the choices I did."

"The hell are you talking about?" I demanded, brow puckered with complete confusion.

"My family sold its soul to the O'Donnellys a long time ago, O'Grady. I got here with their help too. It was a bipartisan effort," he mocked. "The second she started associating with you was the second I had to back away because I couldn't raise attention to the ties between us.

"What the Five Points want, they fucking get. My family owed them a president, and they got one. Doesn't mean they have to like what I am."

"You're telling me the Five Points helped you get into office?" I rumbled.

"That's what I'm telling you." He let out a scornful laugh. "I'm not surprised Aidan Sr. doesn't boast about having a president in his pocket though. I'm not like my father. I'm not a puppet that'll dance to the Irish Mob's tune—"

A faint voice sounded in the background. "Sir? The meeting with the prime minister is about to start."

Davidson grunted under his breath. "I have to go. Just remember that everything comes at a cost. Even the truth."

When he cut the call, with those words echoing in my ears, my plans changed. I needed more answers before I returned home so I phoned Aidan Jr.

"You hear about Michael?" I asked by way of a greeting. "Or did Conor only send the livestream to me?"

"Michael? Ma's guard?"

That meant he was in the dark. I reached up and pinched the bridge of my nose. "Yeah."

"What's Kid done now?"

"What hasn't he done?" I snarked. "I told you to watch him."

"Watch him? Who the fuck can watch the watcher? It's as impossible as I said it would be."

"The second you told me about that amped up taser, I warned you this would happen."

Aidan huffed. "What in particular?"

"I'm sending you a link. That should explain everything."

"Want me to stay on the line?"

"Yeah." I sent him the link to the stream then listened as he sucked in a sharp breath.

"Jesus. Michael looks…"

"Like Chucky has been gnawing on him?"

"I was going to say like Freddy and Jason decided to team up."

"Exactly."

Neither of us were strangers to the darker aspects of the job; Kid wasn't either. I was averse to wetwork, Kid too, but that was because he just had a fucking way of doing shit that felt *wrong.*

I knew for a fact that neither of us had done anything like this for years. It was crazy to me that we'd both fallen off the wagon within a couple weeks of each other.

It was this fucking world we lived in.

Toxic. So fucking toxic.

"Why's he doing this to Michael? Conor doesn't do stuff for shits and giggles."

"Your ma asked him to."

"Ma? What the fuck? Why would she ask him to do this to her favorite guard?"

"Because he isn't her favorite guard anymore." I heaved a sigh. "Look, I have to tell you something but I need you not to ask questions, just answer mine. Okay?"

"No fair."

"Life ain't fair. This is urgent, Aidan. I need you to agree to answer my questions."

"I agree." He grunted. "Fucker."

"Aoife's Father… he's Alan Davidson. As in, POTUS." I let that sink in, and even though Aidan was Aidan and was used to dealing with the fallout from his father—i.e. drama worse than with the Cold War—I knew this wouldn't resonate quickly.

After a good couple minutes, where I felt the passage of each second like it was a year, Aidan grated out, "You're not joking, are you?"

"No."

"Okay. I have questions." He growled under his breath. "For later. Fucker."

"I'll answer them. Later." I rubbed my eyes. "Michael's ECD."

Aidan was silent a second. "You're really ramming these secrets home today, aren't you?"

"Sure am."

"You sure he's not one of those IRA assholes?"

"The ECD make the IRA look like teddy bears."

More silence as he processed a goddamn *cheile* had been guarding his mother for years.

"I'll kill him before the cancer does."

I got it. I totally fucking did.

Feeling ancient, I hunched my shoulders and muttered, "You don't need to worry about that. Conor's on the case, remember? The difficult part is keeping him alive.

"I can't believe I'm about to say this, but Aoife and her mother were targeted for their ties to Alan Davidson." I hesitated over the next part because I didn't have it in me to talk about Lena killing Michelle to anyone other than Aoife today, so I just said, "Michelle was killed for it."

"Jesus Christ, Finn, you know you sound like you're a conspiracy theorist, don't you?"

"Not my theory. Just what I've been told. Davidson confirmed it, Aidan. Look, that isn't what this is about." I sighed. "I just spoke with Davidson."

"Got him on speed dial, do you?"

"Would if speed dial still existed."

Aidan sniffed.

"He says his family owed the Five Points a president." Aidan's lack of response wasn't reassuring. "You know anything about it?"

Considering Senior had been grooming him for the throne, I was praying he knew something.

"No." I heard the sound of his fingers drumming. "You believe him?"

Jesus.

If Junior didn't know, then this was much worse than I could have anticipated.

"Why would he lie?" I rumbled.

"I don't know. You're right. It's not exactly something you lie about, is it? Not if you're a president." He hummed. "Why didn't you ask Da yourself? After Christmas, he'd probably be willing to answer."

"I didn't want to talk to him."

"Why not?"

I pursed my lips. "I just didn't want to deal with him today."

"Can't blame you. I *never* want to fucking deal with him," Aidan grumbled. "But he's the one who'll have answers. Not me."

"Hoped you'd know something I didn't."

"He treats us equally. You know that."

I did, actually.

Even before I'd known what I was to him, he'd always treated me like I was blood. It was what had made me believe him when he told me I was his son.

I didn't need a paternity test, just had to realize that for years, I'd been kidding myself. Aidan Sr. didn't have faith in me. He would never have trusted someone who wasn't in the family with the secrets I knew.

"You're his heir," I rasped, finding myself in the weird position of wanting to comfort Aidan.

"Doesn't matter."

"Doesn't it?" I rubbed the back of my neck.

"You having an existential crisis?"

"Maybe. I just... I'm sorry?"

"For what?"

Though I heard his confusion and knew it was genuine, I muttered, "For being born?"

Aidan snorted. "Get that shit out of your head. Thought we handled this at Christmas over the baptism by fire?"

My lips quirked as I thought about St. Patrick's Church going up in flames. "I'm walking proof, I guess," I mumbled, words waning.

"Proof that Da's no angel?" He scoffed. "Like I needed proof. Finn, you and me, we were blood before I knew about Da's wandering dick. I'd prefer for him to have cheated than for you not to exist at all and that's the truth.

"Anyway, Ma donked him over the head as punishment, and only God knows what else during their marriage... She'll have made him pay."

Payback.

I'd kept Lena's secret for years now, had protected her over Aoife, but I wasn't perfect—I'd resented her. I'd resented her for what she'd done and what I'd had to do to keep my family together.

I hadn't stopped loving her. Even though loyalty dictated I should. But our past made it impossible.

She'd taken me in when she didn't have to, when I was nothing more than her son's friend to her. Regardless, she'd brought me into the fold and had raised me like I was hers, never letting the difference between me and her kids shine through.

That wasn't gratitude talking either, but the truth.

Those first few months, she'd fed me twice as much as the others. Had made sure I wore clothes as good as the rest. She hadn't skimped or tried to make me feel like the poor relative...

How couldn't I love her for that?

Fuck, what a mess. Such a fucking mess.

"Finn? You there, bro?"

"Yeah. I'm here," I rumbled tiredly.

"Does it matter if the Five Points helped Davidson become president?"

"What if your da is ECD too?" There it was. The kicker.

"No fucking way," he disagreed. "Da can't take orders from the Internal fucking Revenue Services, never mind some fucker in jail in Ireland.

"He wants the motherland united and free from British tyranny but let's face it, he'll be donating to legitimate fronts so that'll be a nice tax break for him too. Bastard's never even been to Ireland. It's not that big of a cause to him."

I scrubbed a hand over my face, wishing I could trust that, but he didn't know about his ma's involvement in my mother-in-law's death. And none of us knew what the ECD's terms of blackmail were...

I didn't say a word, but Aidan steamrolled on, "I know my father, and you know what, Finn? You know your father too. Think about it. Having a president in his pocket—that's Da's idea of a wet dream.

"But answering to some zealous motherfuckers with less sense than a gnat and more memory than an elephant?" He sniffed. "I hate the asshole most days, but even I think that he's got more to him than that."

I didn't have the energy to argue, just told him, "Conor says the leader of the ECD ain't in jail anymore."

"Huh. Well, I don't see what that changes. He's been in jail for years, hasn't he? Anyway, you want to bring this up with Da?"

"I don't know." I couldn't trust him. Or could I?

"You know what's funny?"

"There's something funny about this shit show?" I sputtered in disbelief.

"Yeah. Remember last year when Da tried to get that law overturned about allotted airspace?"

My mind whirred. Manhattan airspace was as much of a premium as ground space. To build a skyscraper, you had to own the rights to not just the plot beneath a building, but above it too.

"Vaguely. We could only get the Danu building to sixty stories instead of the eighty Senior wanted because we couldn't buy rights from anyone on that street."

"Yeah. If Da does have the president in his fucking pocket, why didn't he win? Why's that law still active?"

"I don't know. Maybe Davidson couldn't do anything to change the law."

"It's fucking airspace. That's gotta be federal."

I blinked. "No, it's a zoning law. That comes under city ordinance. Either way, there'd be something he could help with, and Davidson didn't sound all that happy about his ties with the mob. Said he wasn't a puppet."

"That fits. Maybe he doesn't play ball like Da wants. It's not like Da wouldn't blow his own horn if he had a president in his pocket. I think Davidson doesn't do as he's told...

"Wonder what that's about and why Da lets him get away with it." He heaved a sigh. "Shit, now you've got me thinking all kinds of conspiracies."

"Me too," I said tiredly.

"Finn, what's going on with you? Aside from the crap you just told me, I mean. Where's your head at?"

"I gotta tell Aoife some bad shit, Aidan. Some real bad shit. I don't know if our marriage can survive it."

"Jesus, what the fuck have you done?"

I could have confessed to him. Could have shared the burden, split the load, but I didn't deserve that.

Sucking in a breath, I told him, "I can't tell you. Yet. She deserves to know first."

Aidan muttered, "Must be bad if you won't tell me."

"Yeah." I swallowed. "But I gotta share that shit about her mom being killed because of her dad as well..."

"I'll see you on the other side, *dearthái*. Later, I'll need answers, okay? You get away with this no asking questions bullshit now, but not tomorrow. Hear me?"

The words were simple, but they were genuine.

"Thanks, Aidan."

"No need to thank me. Tell me how it goes."

It wasn't a request.

"I will."

If I fucking survived it.

Every marriage had a defining moment. My father's and Lena's had been defined by the rolling pin incident. I just prayed that Aoife didn't have nefarious plans with a cookie cutter and my balls.

If she did, I'd take whatever she doled out though.

It was the least I deserved.

TWENTY-FIVE

WHEN THE ELEVATOR DOORS OPENED, the penthouse was silent so I heard the swoosh as if it were a clanging bell.

Lena had taken Jake on a visit to the zoo to give me some time to cry, but with every passing minute, I both missed him more and knew that it was nearer to Finn coming home.

Finn—the man I'd told my worst secrets to. The man I loved. The man I'd vowed to be with until death did us part.

Twice.

But who I couldn't share this truth with.

A truth that...

After researching sirenomelia, I knew what I was going to do, and I knew he wouldn't agree.

Over the hours of staring at nothing, of looking up at the ceiling and trying to think of a resolution, I knew what my next steps would be.

Knowing that the penthouse would have spat out a bubbling, gurgling toddler who'd be squealing happily if it were Jake and Lena returning from the zoo, I quickly shot up from the mattress and darted into the bathroom.

The second I saw my reflection, I winced because I looked like I'd been crying. That was the opposite of what I needed. I had to present a calm front, a *strong* and resolute front, so when I told Finn how it was going to go down, he'd listen and wouldn't take over.

Scrubbing my face with my cleanser, I wasn't surprised when there was a knock on the bathroom door.

"Aoife?"

My brow furrowed as I heard the note in his voice—sorrow? I knew my husband well. He was the king of the poker face, and that extended to most parts of his body.

Okay, not his dick. But everything else, he had complete control over.

If he sounded like that, it was because his guard was down, and that meant something had happened.

Something bad.

My own worries shoved aside, I dragged open the door, soap still on my face, and demanded, "Finn? What is it?"

His voice matched his expression which only augmented my worries.

Jesus, he looked like he'd aged a hundred years since this morning.

Finn was incapable of being unattractive, it was those O'Donnelly genes, but the way his shoulders were stooped and his expression—*his exhaustion reached out to me.*

Did he know?

That was all I could think.

Had the doctor called him? Had John, my guard, told him?

Finn looked like he was grieving.

He pressed a shoulder to the door and told me, "I need to speak with you, sweetheart."

"Isn't that what we're doing now?"

"No." Rubbing a hand over his face, he muttered, "I wish."

"What is it?"

He wafted a hand at me. "Wash your face first." Then, I watched the transformation happen—he went from being my husband to being the reason I'd love him until the day I died. He straightened up and questioned, "Do you need something to eat? How are you feeling?" He moved over to me and pressed his fingers to my stomach.

That hurt.

That hurt so bad.

I wanted to scream the truth at him. To tell him that I didn't want to eat again, that I felt like hell, but he wouldn't understand.

He couldn't understand.

He'd think that the baby in my belly didn't matter as much as Jake and him. He wasn't wrong, but I just... I just couldn't terminate the pregnancy. I couldn't. Not yet. There were all kinds of surgeries that gave me hope—

Biting my lip at the thought, I barely managed to stop myself from shoving his hand away and told him huskily, "I'll wash my face and be right out."

"You sure you don't want anything to eat?"

"No. I'm not hungry."

He nodded, stepped back and started tugging at the half-Windsor knot on his necktie. As he pulled it free, I watched him, watched as what should have been an easy motion took a good couple of seconds.

"Has someone died?" I blurted out before I finished washing up, my little face sponge still dripping suds and water onto the bathroom floor.

His head whipped to the side, and as our eyes caught and held, I knew someone *had* died.

Blinking, I took a step back, turned to the sink and quickly rinsed off my face. I saw him approach in the vanity mirror, but I didn't expect that the second I'd cleaned away the suds, he'd haul me into his arms.

He hugged me.

He hugged me so hard that it hurt.

But it hurt good.

God, I'd needed that earlier. I'd needed this hug when I got out of the doctor's office.

I sagged into him, barely managing to stop myself from breaking down and telling him the truth there and then, but Finn sagged into me too, and if I'd needed even more confirmation that everything was *wrong*, I had it now.

Sucking in a breath, I whispered against his shirt, "Finn? Talk to me, baby."

"I—" He tried again, "I—" He fell silent.

My hands tightened their clasp at the back of his jacket, and I pulled him even more into me, so much so that there was barely an inch separating us.

"I've been keeping secrets, Aoife."

Whatever I'd expected him to say, it wasn't that.

"What kind of secrets, sweetheart? To do with work?"

"I wish that were it. I wish that were all it was." He pressed his face into my hair then whispered, "I'm a fucking coward."

I tensed. "Why would you say that?"

"Because I wanted the best of both worlds, but lies... there shouldn't be lies between a wife and her husband."

When he started to pull back, I let him. Thoroughly confused by his statement, I tilted my head to look up at his tortured expression.

"What are you talking about, Finn?"

"For years," he rasped, "I've carried this burden, and I did so because I knew that there was nothing that could be done to bring justice to the people who deserved it.

"It's worn on me and worn on me, but that doesn't excuse what I did. That doesn't make it right or fair. I deserve that burden. I deserve worse. But don't think that I've felt like I've gotten away with—" His mouth quirked a second before he closed his eyes and shook his head. "—gotten away with murder," he finished.

"What are you talking about?" I demanded, folding my arms across my belly and hugging my elbows.

Of all the goddamn days for Finn to need to confess to whatever the hell it was that was going on, he had to pick this one?

I wasn't even sure if I had the mental capacity to deal with this, well, whatever *this* was, and truthfully, I knew I had to. Not because Finn clearly needed to get this off his chest, but because as much as that was true, he was struggling to do that.

Struggling to confess.

That really amped up my nerves.

"Will starting at the beginning help?"

"Where's the beginning?" he exclaimed, and then he stunned the hell out of me—he spun away from me and screamed, "WHERE'S THE MOTHERFUCKING BEGINNING?"

Brow puckered, I ground out, "Finn? What the hell?"

I almost moved closer to tug on his jacket, but he twisted back to look at me, and out of nowhere, there was a chasm between us.

It was wider than the Grand Canyon and just as impossible to cross.

At that moment, I felt more alone than I had in years.

After we met, I'd been lucky, I knew. I'd been swallowed up by his family. Absorbed into them. I wasn't used to feeling this way, and I didn't like it.

It happened in a glance.

Without a single word uttered.

That was when he started to break my heart.

"I don't know where to goddamn start, Aoife. I don't fucking know.

So many goddamn lies, so many secrets. It's starting to be like some kind of—" He dragged his hands through his hair. "I don't have all the answers. I just... what I'm about to tell you is literally all I know, you understand?"

Warily, I whispered, "Okay."

"Nothing's okay, Aoife." His jaw clenched. "When I'm done, when I've told you everything, I'll leave, and I won't come back—" Finn sucked in a breath, seeming to correct himself. "I won't come back *until* you let me in."

A gasp escaped me. "You're scaring me, Finn!"

Finn—leaving? Finn didn't do things like that!

"I deserve nothing less than for you to toss me out but, please, baby, please don't ask me for a divorce. I can't give you that. I can't. I'm incapable of—"

I rushed at him, and though he was taller than me, bigger and heavier as well, I surged onto tiptoe, grabbed his shoulders, and I shook him. It barely moved him, but I did it again.

"STOP IT," I snapped. "STOP IT. Tell me what the hell's going on."

"I know who killed your mother." His nostrils flared. "I've known for years."

For a second, I stared at him. Just stared.

Then I bit off, "Who?"

I'd break down later.

What was more grief on top of what I'd learned today?

My throat clutched so hard I wasn't sure if I wanted to cry or puke, but as I stared at him, waiting for him to answer, rage bubbled up out of nowhere.

"WHO?" I screamed at him when he remained silent. There was an apology in his eyes but that wasn't fucking enough, was it? "Who killed my mom?"

"It was..." He closed his eyes. "It's complicated. I knew what the ramifications would be. I've known since the beginning, but I swear to you now that if I'd known I could have gotten justice for her, I'd have fought for that, Aoife. I'd have fought for the truth to come out, but there was no chance of that."

"How do you know?" I ground out, well aware that I was in his face which was no easy feat seeing as he was so much taller than me.

"Because... it was Lena."

He said those fateful words on a sigh.

On a shaky breath.

On an exhalation so heartfelt that I knew it came from his soul.

Because that was goddamn confession for you, wasn't it?

Good for the fucking soul.

"Lena? Lena, the same..." I couldn't get my words together because as much as they'd liberated him, they'd imprisoned me.

I thought about my son who was currently with Lena, the woman who'd held me a few hours ago, the woman who'd become a surrogate mother to me—never replacing mine but helping me.

Guiding me.

When I'd had issues with breastfeeding, it was Lena I'd gone to—not Google.

When Jake wouldn't sleep, when I'd tried everything to make him settle for the night, Lena was who I'd asked for tips.

"You let me—" My throat choked. "You let our son—"

He stared down at the ground like he knew what I was about to say without me having to finish the sentence. "I did. I know." His shoulders slumped deeper, but even the sight of my husband like this, on the path to breaking, didn't stop the rage that surged to the surface once more when he rasped, "I'll go—"

"No. You fucking won't," I snarled, grabbing his arm. "What happened? Why—" I shook my head. There was no *why*. Unless... "Was Lena drunk? Is that why she drove off? Why wouldn't she just stop? If she'd have stopped—" I sucked in a breath as the world began spiraling out of control beneath my feet. "Maybe Mom would have survived!"

"I read the medical reports, Aoife," Finn murmured regretfully. "She hit her head on the way down. That injury was what led to her death."

"I'm the one who made the decision to turn off her life support, Finn. Don't talk to me about what happened." My mouth trembled as I stared at him, pleading with my eyes. "Make some sense out of this for me. Why didn't she go to the cops?"

"It's like something out of a damn spy movie, Aoife. I can't make sense out of the nonsensical."

He reached out, but before his hand could connect with my shoulder, I pulled back. I ignored his flinch, just hissed, "Explain, and stop talking cryptically."

"I'm going to tell you what I know," he rumbled. "That's all I can do."

It wasn't. There were so many things he could do, *could have done* over the years, but I didn't say that.

I needed answers.

I needed to understand.

"Hit me with it," I whispered.

"You have an uncle, sweetheart. On your mom's side."

My mouth gaped. "What? I don't! Mom was an only child!"

"She wasn't. I don't know what happened, but Conor looked into it. A man named Eamonn Keegan is your uncle."

"Eamonn Keegan?" I tried to rack my brain for a memory of that name, but I didn't remember Mom ever mentioning it. It rang a bell, just not because I'd heard her say it. "Why would she keep that a secret from me?"

"Because he's been in HMP Belmarsh all your life."

"HMP what?"

"It's a British prison." He slumped on the side of the bed. "He's... he ain't good people, Aoife. I can't blame her for wanting you to have nothing to do with him." He drew out his phone. "Recognize this man?"

My eyes widened. "That's the guy from *Verdi*! I thought he was just a barfly."

Finn pulled a face. "Me too. What did he say to you?"

"Nothing important. He called himself Dagda. Just..." My brow puckered. "I remember his voice sounded familiar. His accent was like..." The realization registered, making tears well in my eyes as a deep, painful longing for my mom hit me. "...like my mom's," I finally got out.

He tucked his phone away again. "I'm sorry, Aoife."

"Why was he in jail?" I whispered.

"Because he was a bomber." At my gasp, he kept his eyes on me. "With a faction called the *Éire le chéile go deo*. They're like the IRA, but worse."

Stunned, I staggered until my back hit the wall. Sliding down it, I stared at him as I whispered, "That's how I know his name. From the news."

He grimaced. "It made headlines around the world. One of the biggest terror attacks in the nineties."

"And my uncle was a part of it?"

"He was the ringleader, sweetheart."

"Jesus Christ." Horror hit me. "Was my mom involved with them?"

He hesitated. "We've no way of knowing."

"Is Eamonn why Lena killed her?"

He shook his head. "No. That was an accident, Aoife. It truly was. It doesn't take away from what happened, but Lena... You don't have to understand this, baby, but Lena's calmed down these past couple years because she's stuck to her meds.

"Before, she was a fucking lunatic some days." He swallowed. "I remember she had this habit of scratching at her neck. She'd do it until she bled, Aoife. What the Aryans put her through was fucking hell. I'm not excusing her. Don't you think that I am. But I'm saying she was sick and someone took advantage of her."

"How do you *make* someone commit a hit and run?" I demanded scornfully.

He rubbed his eyes. "Let me give you the truth in as much of a logical order as I can, yeah?" He sucked in a breath when I didn't reply then rattled off, "I spoke with your dad. Some of what I'm telling you coincides with what I just learned.

"Four years ago, your mother's death triggered a power struggle in the ECD. For all those years since his incarceration, Eamonn had remained the leader of the group even though he was in jail, but the year your mom died, something changed.

"Your father made it sound like the ECD wanted to ensure that there were no filthy little secrets that could ruin his journey to the Oval Office."

"Filthy little secret?" I breathed, watching him wince.

"I'm sorry, baby. But your existence is a secret worth killing for when you want a corrupt president in power and leveraged to the hilt."

I blinked at him, his words resonating, the heartache in his eyes, the grief and the pain and the apology, and that was when I knew the man I wanted to go to for comfort was also the man who was causing me this internal agony.

"My dad's..." Mouth working, I managed to get out, "My dad's enemies had Mom killed? Is that what you're trying to tell me? But Lena—"

"No, they were his friends," he corrected gently. "They almost got you too, sweetheart. He stopped them before... and then I met you, and you were safe."

My eyes widened. "Safe because the Irish Mob set their sights on me?"

"Who'd you prefer to be detained by? The Feds or Aidan Sr.?"

Shuddering, I rasped, "The Feds."

"Exactly."

Slowly, he got to his feet and walked over to me. I watched him. Watched that prowl of his that was capable of setting me alight when he was coming toward me with a different reason in mind, and I remained quiet as he seated himself by my side. I didn't say anything as he lifted his arm and curved it around my shoulders either.

Did it make me weak that I let him?

That I stayed there, huddled into his side, and took comfort from his supportive hold?

"Lena—" I whispered, needing him to carry on.

"Before your mom's death, Aidan had a health scare. It terrified him enough that he had to confess his sins to Lena."

"You?" I wheezed. "You're his sin?"

He nodded, but I saw pain shift into being in his eyes.

I hurt for him, then. I loved him enough that I felt his pain as if it were my own.

Who else knew what it felt like to be a filthy little secret?

Who else could understand other than me?

We were both bastards. Both born outside of someone's committed relationship.

I grabbed his hand, clasping it so hard that my fingers ached as I stared up at him, needing him to continue.

"Aidan told me this," he grated out, "and he said that she was off her meds and she was whacked up. Couldn't let it rest. He wouldn't tell her who it was he'd had the affair with or who the kid was because he didn't want to wreck the relationship I had with her." He clenched his teeth. "I'm so fucking sorry, baby."

My mouth trembled. "She thought Mom was his girlfriend? She thought *I* was his daughter?"

"Yeah."

"Why would she think that? What made her think we were his?"

"Michael, Lena's guard, he's with the ECD. We didn't know that until recently. He's the one who told her that your mom was Senior's girlfriend. He pointed Lena at her."

"Why? Why would he do that?"

He dragged out his phone again. "I got this on the way home. Conor sent it to me."

"What is it?" I rasped, squinting at the screen when I saw an article in a newspaper. There was a picture of a woman, half her face on display—

My brain screeched to a halt.

I recognized those laughing eyes, the smile that lit up a room.

Mom.

It was Mom.

I had photos of her all around the apartment, but this was different.

She was *lighter.*

Happier.

My throat tightened with tears as I stared at that smile—incandescent. She was capable of such joy, and I'd forgotten that.

For a second, my vision blurred as memories drowned me. Memories of what had felt like a simpler time but, in reality, hadn't been.

This intrigue had followed me since the day I'd been conceived.

This was a specter that was only just catching up to me.

Senator Alan Davidson spotted with mystery woman.

I managed to make out the article headline.

"This was printed a few weeks before your mom's death, sweetheart."

"They'd started seeing each other again?"

He nodded. "Seems like it. Rumors drifted in and out where he was concerned."

"He had a reputation? I never knew that."

But, hell, neither had I seen this headline, nor had I known that my mother was dating a presidential candidate.

Did I walk around with my head in the clouds?

Or was the flour causing problems with my eyes?

He shrugged. "You're not exactly into politics, and I get the feeling that shit was covered up."

"By whom?"

Finn hesitated. "I don't know for sure, but I think us."

"The Five Points?"

He nodded. "Senior never asked me to do anything like that, and I know Junior wasn't asked either—"

"Conor."

"Yeah, it could be him."

"Who was he with?"

"Did your mom date?"

"I-I guess. Toward the end not so much. We were busy with the tearoom but yeah, I guess... she dated more than I did."

"This is the only time I remember a picture coming out—what if they were seeing each other all along?"

"Why wouldn't she tell me they were together, though?" I whispered on a broken sob.

"I don't know, baby. I can't answer that."

He hugged me tighter to him and I let him. I let him because I needed him. It was shameful but I needed him so fucking badly.

"His wife was there the day your mom died, sweetheart. That can't be a coincidence, can it? And Conor told me that she's the one who confirmed Senior and your mom were together."

I reached up and rubbed at my temple. "Let me get this straight, you're trying to tell me two different sets of people wanted my mom dead, for two entirely different reasons?"

"It depends on whether Elizabeth Davidson is a part of the ECD."

"Is she?"

"I don't know. It would make a crazy kind of sense if she were, but Michael says she isn't."

Michael says she isn't.

I repeated the words in my head, then I looked at him, a plea in my eyes that I didn't know how to voice.

He pressed a kiss to my temple, and because I was so distracted, I allowed it. But Finn, of course, translated what the beseeching look I sent him meant and translated it perfectly. "Conor's dealing with him."

It took a second for his words to penetrate, but when they did, I was even more confused.

I reared back, spluttering, "Conor?"

"Trust me, sweetheart—"

"How the hell can I?" I snapped, and the words were like he'd tossed a live hand grenade at me. I leaped into action, shoving away from him as I launched myself onto my feet.

"You can trust me with this," he whispered, but I knew I'd hurt him, and all I could think was that I was glad I had.

I doubted it hurt as much as this ache in my chest. This gnawing, empty pain that could have been the start of heartburn or a heart attack for all I knew.

But as that ache took over, something filled it.

Something solid. Weighty. Heavy.

A need I'd never felt before, a need I didn't even know I had in me to feel.

"I want to see him."

He stared at me blankly. "What?"

"I want to see him."

My flat tone had him muttering, "You couldn't handle what—"

"I could." My words were grim. Loaded with resolve. "I want to ask him if Elizabeth was involved in this. I want details. I want to understand why my mom was murdered."

"He won't say anything new, sweetheart." He reached for my hand but I dragged it out of his hold. "What Conor does—"

"Conor's a fucking hacker, Finn. He's a *nerd*. What the hell can he do—"

"Let me speak, Aoife," he growled. "Conor's a nerd with a fascination for electricity. You don't see that side of him because it doesn't come out to party when he's with goddamn family eating roasted chicken as we bitch about the week we've had.

"If there's a brother who's like Aidan Sr., it's Conor. Where shit like this is concerned, where the family is *hurt*, where we're maligned and when he's interested enough to care, he's fucking wicked."

I tried to imagine Conor, the guy even his baby brother called 'Kid,' being *wicked*, but I couldn't see it.

"No," I denied. "Brennan's the fixer. Why isn't he handling this? He should be handling this. This is the worst kind of betrayal, dammit. I want Brennan to make him pay. To make him *hurt* like I'm hurting."

Finn got to his feet. "Listen to me, Aoife. There is no worse fate than Conor doling out his brand of justice."

I didn't believe him. *Couldn't.* It went against years of knowing his family. Of knowing who Conor was.

"I want to see for myself."

I *needed* to see that that fucker was paying. That he was suffering like I was suffering now.

Oh, God.

The pain expanded.

The grief was like a wave churning over me. Submerging me beneath it.

Grief didn't end. It didn't go away. It just became easier to manage. A person got better at swimming with the tide instead of letting it drown them.

But this, now, it was like I was back at the beginning.

I could see the tsunami heading my way and it was like I'd forgotten how to swim.

My mom... God, I missed her so badly.

"You can't," he denied me, and his words really pissed me off.

"You want to tell me that I can't do something? Finn, really?" I got in his face, hissing, "You lied to me. For years. You let me get close to Lena, you let Jake think of her as a fucking grandmother when you had to know that I'd never want her anywhere near him, you bastard."

I didn't see it happen.

I didn't even know I'd raised my hand.

Suddenly, I felt the sting in my palm and the ache in my bones as I slapped him.

I screamed, a long, loose warble of pain that wasn't eased as I carried on hitting him.

Loose hits, slaps, smacks, something I'd never have thought I was capable of, but I did it.

And he let me.

He let me hit him.

He let me slap him.

He let me smack him.

I screamed again, but this time, the torrent of grief poured from me in a bubble of tears.

"I hate you," I sobbed as my hands collided with his arms, with his chest. I knew I hurt myself more than him. "I love her—how could you do that to me? How could you let me love her when she killed my mom?"

After the day I'd had, this was more than I could handle. The starch in my bones disappeared, melting into dust as I sank to the ground, crying, shoulders rounded, hunched over as I grieved the loss of *two* mothers.

And when he huddled on the floor in front of me, I didn't shove him away as he tucked me into his embrace. As he hauled me into his arms and held me through the twister of grief that sucked me in with ragged claws and fangs as if Mom had died yesterday and not years ago.

TWENTY-SIX

FINN

LENA RETURNED at the worst possible moment.

Though Aoife was crying in my arms, I was still preternaturally aware of my surroundings, so when I heard the elevator doors rush open, I understood what it felt like to have one foot on either side of a fault line in the middle of an earthquake.

With each step that Lena took deeper into the apartment, the closer disaster came to striking and the more uncertain I grew as I tried to figure out how to fucking fix this.

Devastation imminent, I knew I had to appeal to Aoife's logic but there was no logic to be had in a situation like this. None whatsoever.

Praying that she'd let me fix this, I rasped against her hair, "Sweetheart, I need to go throw Lena out."

Aoife's gasping sobs stopped falling, and I felt her grow tense in my arms.

When she peered up at me, her face red raw from tears, I wasn't sure what her next move was going to be, but her question surprised me nonetheless.

"You'll kick her out?"

I blinked down at her. "Of course."

She licked her lips, and I watched the movement, half expecting her to start slapping me again.

Christ, I'd take every slap and every hit if it eased her pain, if it healed the gaping wound that I'd caused.

I *had* let her lean on Lena like she were a mother. I had allowed Jake to think of her as a grandmother.

Those were my worst sins.

As guilt threatened to choke me, I whispered, "You will always be my priority, Aoife. Always."

Teardrops quivered on her eyelashes as she stared up at me. "I'll deal with Lena."

Though I tensed, I nodded. "You do whatever you need to do, sweetheart."

She tipped up her chin. "Are you going to call Senior? Do some damage control?"

"No."

"Why not?"

"Because you're my priority. Not him. Not Lena."

I wanted to tell her that this particular situation was the only time I'd ever put them before her, but that was one time too fucking many anyway.

What kind of shit defense was that?

So I held my tongue.

I kept silent because words would only fuck things up even more.

"Help me up," she rasped, and I got to my feet and leaned down to support her as she stood on shaky legs.

I watched as, smoothing her palms over her cheeks, she said, "I don't want you to say a word to her."

"I won't."

"Not a single word, Finn," she warned. "I'm on my last nerve here. Do not push me."

I wasn't going to push her. Hell if I was. Like any man, I was capable of my dumb moments, but I wasn't that much of a fuckwit.

She hadn't thrown me out.

Yet.

I'd offered to go, but she hadn't accepted that offer.

Yet.

No way in fuck was I going to do anything that would have her shoving me out the door.

I let go of my hold on her waist and raised my hands in surrender. "I won't say or do anything that you don't want me to."

Her chin firmed before she nodded, and she twisted around and moved toward the hall door. As she dragged it open, I heard Lena say, "Look who's here, Jake? Mommy!"

Inside, I froze, but I pushed ahead as Aoife grated out, "Lena, I'd like you to leave my home."

I could almost imagine Lena's bewilderment, and I shook off that ridiculous need that had been inbuilt in me from adolescence.

We protected our women.

Always.

But in this instance, that was what I was doing. With the woman whom I'd chosen to make my own. Whom I'd always fucking choose.

"Aoife? What is it?"

Hearing my wife suck in a shaky breath, I stepped forward, unsure if she had the strength to go through with whatever she had in mind, and I placed myself at her back.

Lena looked at me in confusion, but I kept my glance straight ahead, pinned above her so that we couldn't make eye contact.

I was not and never would be her life raft in troubled waters again.

If only I'd made that decision years ago.

"I-I..." When I placed my hand on Aoife's waist, she sucked in a breath and intoned, "I know what you did. I know you killed my mom." Her head tipped up. "I want you to get the hell away from us." Her chin wobbled. "Now."

That was a lot calmer than I'd anticipated. I'd half imagined her throwing shit at Lena and chasing her out of the apartment.

Gently squeezing her waist, I backed her up silently as Lena whispered, "I'm so sorry, Aoife."

I didn't have to look at her expression to hear her devastation.

"Sorry isn't enough." She sucked in a breath, and then it came. She screamed loud enough for Jake to start wailing, "You killed my mom!"

Lena began backing away down the hall.

She'd been good lately, taking her meds, but I could sense that she was feeling hunted. Throw in her PTSD and this wasn't going to end well.

My gaze dropped and I watched her without making eye contact as she scrambled toward the elevator, her hand fumbling for the button.

"How could you keep that from me?" Aoife shrieked, the demand punctuated by the elevator doors whirring open. "Why would you befriend me?"

Only when Lena was standing inside it did she answer, and it was simple and not the right thing to say at all, "Because I had to atone."

With Jake wailing, I darted over to his side to pick him up.

Comforting him, I watched as Aoife grabbed an ornament from a console table and hurled it at the elevator.

But the doors were closing.

I caught Lena's eye, our gazes clashed and held for the first time, and I saw the muted apology in hers before she was cut off from me.

The vase exploded against the doors a fraction of a second later, and Aoife let out a wail as she hurried over to it and banged her fists against the wall.

"Atonement?" she screeched. "Atonement?"

"Sweetheart, stop it. Jake. The baby—"

That wasn't the right thing to say either.

I watched as she turned to the nearest console table, one that was loaded with photo frames, and swept her hands across it.

As the frames went flying and they crashed to the ground, I watched on, well aware that my borrowed time was ticking away.

I wasn't a man who watched on while his wife suffered.

But she had a right to grieve.

She had a right to express her anger.

She was also barefoot.

There was glass everywhere.

Every protective bone in my motherfucking body couldn't let this carry on.

I knew she'd escalate.

I'd been there myself.

She wanted the world to burn, and I had to help her control the inferno.

I placed Jake back in his stroller, strapping him in quickly, then I rushed over to her side and picked her up before she could throw the ornaments off another table.

I didn't know if her feet were bleeding from crunching on the glass, but I knew that was about two minutes away from happening.

As I picked her up, she screamed and her feet kicked out as she tried to free herself from my hold.

"Aoife," I ground into her ear. "You need to stop this."

"You bastard! I fucking hate you—"

The words sliced into me like she was armed with a knife.

I growled, "You can hate me all you want, but you will *not* harm yourself."

I backed away from the mess she'd made, and I strode us past a still sobbing Jake and into the living room.

The poor kid needed our attention but Aoife was kicking and screaming, trying to get out of my hold, and she needed all my focus.

She managed to clip my knee, and I almost went down, and that was when I lost my shit.

I didn't head for the sofa anymore, I went to the nearest wall. Twisting us around, I shoved her against it, pinning her in place as I snagged her hands, raised her arms, and pressed them to the wall.

Aoife bucked and battled but she was stuck between a rock and a hard place.

As she screamed and kicked, I let the battle rage on as I bit off, "You hate me, but I fucking love you. I love you more than anything. You're my wife, but you're my fucking life, Aoife. You mean every-thing to me. I will not let you hurt yourself. I will always protect you—"

"You're a LIAR!" she shrieked. "You protected *her*. You chose *her*."

She was right. To an extent. "I didn't," I snarled. "I didn't choose her—"

"You did. You fucking did. You let me love her—"

I had. There was no arguing with that. "I'm so goddamn sorry, sweetheart."

"Sorry isn't enough," she sobbed.

"It isn't, I know it, but I swear to you I didn't choose Lena."

"You're a liar!" she screamed again, the words armed with claws that made me bleed.

"I didn't!" I hissed. "I chose *me,* Aoife. I chose me."

I had no idea why but that stopped her shrieks, that stopped her from bucking against me.

Around us, the air seethed. As if our tempers made heat swell and bubble.

She grew still.

Hellishly still.

I tried not to savor these last moments of closeness, pretty damn sure this was it—the last time she'd let me hold her.

"Let me out," she breathed.

She sounded calmer. I was still unsure, however, if that was the worst thing to say or not. It appeared to have gotten through to her enough that it calmed her down.

"You won't keep doing shit that'll end up with you hurting yourself?"

"I won't," she bit off testily.

I moved a couple inches away so that she could turn around. I half expected her to try to knee me in the balls, but she didn't. She stared up at me with tear-drenched eyes that were red and weepy.

Unable to stop myself, I pressed into her, and I pushed my forehead against hers.

"I wanted my family, Aoife, and I didn't have faith. I-I didn't... I didn't choose her. I chose them. Why would you have wanted anything to do with them after this?" I shook my head. "I was selfish and so fucking wrong, and I'm so goddamn sorry. You're my life, Aoife, my life. My world—"

She was silent for so long that I felt sure I'd lost her anyway, then she rasped, "I want to see him."

I didn't expect her to say that, so it took me a second to reply, "I don't know if you could handle it, Aoife. We have to think of the baby—"

Her hands went to my shoulders, and she tried to shove me back and away. It didn't work, but she tried again anyway. In this, however, I would always be her safe haven in the storm.

She might not think she was safe with me, but she always would be.

"I can handle anything this fucking world throws at me, Finn. I'm still standing, aren't I? My husband betrayed me, the love of my life lied to me, and I haven't crumbled to dust, have I?

"I. Want. To. See. Him," she ended with a snarl. "You can help me or not but I swear, nothing will stop me from seeing him. Not you, not anyone."

This wasn't a hill I was willing to die on.

"I'll ask Aela to come babysit."

Whether Aoife would regret this later on was tomorrow's problem.

TWENTY-SEVEN

AOIFE

I SHRUGGED AWAY from Finn's grasp as he tried to clasp our hands together when we approached the warehouse two hours later.

It was dark out, cold too, but I didn't notice. He'd insisted I wear a coat, had insisted on gloves and a scarf for the baby.

The baby that probably wouldn't survive to term.

I complied because whatever he was, Finn was a good father.

I had to believe that, believe *in* that because otherwise I'd…

Well, I didn't know what.

I felt like I could keep on hitting him. Could keep on screaming at him. But all that would do is make me need to ice my knuckles again and my head was already pounding from all the crying.

The Five Points' business hadn't injured me since our wedding day when I'd gotten shot down in that drive-by shooting that had redefined New York's underworld, but this was proof that I was either naive or fucking stupid. I wasn't sure which yet.

What else was being kept from me?

What other secrets were whirring away behind the scenes that were reshaping my future and rewriting my past?

I peered around the grim set up, wondering how many steps it had taken me to get to this point. This moment…

A lifetime's, I guessed.

It was a standard warehouse, I recognized.

Grim and grody.

Old, and looking like it could fall down in a good gust of wind, but one of those buildings that somehow stood the test of time too.

It had streaks of red drifting down the façade from rust, and it needed a paint but, with a second glance, I saw that all the windows were new.

I also saw there were security cameras pointed right at us, shiny with their newness.

The façade within a façade—what the Five Points excelled at.

As the doors opened and I walked in, the first thing that hit me was a weird smell. Followed by a scream.

I jumped at the sound, jolting backward and straight into Finn who must have moved from my side to behind me to support me.

I hated that he'd been prepared for that.

I fucking hated it.

Because that was Finn.

Finn was a good husband.

The best.

He loved me. He showed me that every goddamn day. He praised me and celebrated my wins, he took time for me and Jake even though he was exhausted, and he showed up. Consistently.

I thought about the man I'd been raised believing was my father when really, he was just a stepfather, and I knew what a piece of shit dad looked like. A piece of shit husband too.

Finn was not that.

He wasn't.

And I believed him when he said he chose himself. Selfishness aside, I could deal with that better than I could him choosing Lena over me.

I froze in my tracks at the thought, and I twisted around and away from his support. I looked up at him and pressed a hand to his shoulder to maintain some distance.

Seeing the pain in his face at how I shoved space between us, I stayed strong as I demanded, "Are you lying to me about anything else?"

He straightened up. "I can't tell you shit about the Five Points, Aoife—"

"And I never asked you to. Why would I be interested in that? I'm talking about things that affect you, me, and Jake. Our personal lives."

"This was... I couldn't tell you." When I released a scoffing sound, his nostrils flared, but though I knew I'd aggravated him, his voice was calm as he said, "You might disagree but I knew Senior would never let her see a minute in jail, so I went along with it. I chose wrongly though. I knew that almost as soon as I headed down this path."

"Why didn't you tell me then?"

"Because the road to hell is paved with good intentions."

I stared at him. "How could you let me eat with them, break bread with them—"

"Because they're my family, Aoife." His words were wooden, cold. Like each one was chipped away from a block of ice. "Because they're the only family I've ever had, and because I didn't want to have to live without them.

"I know I was selfish. I know I was. But I... They took me in when I needed them most. Cutting myself out of their lives..." His throat worked and he straightened up taller and I heard his resolve as he ground out, "Whatever you need me to do, I'll do."

"You couldn't cut them out of your life before but you can now?"

I saw the pain in his eyes, and it made the open wound in my soul bleed.

"Every day I'm with you, I feel like there's more of a reason to live. A reason to wake up. It's to do with Jake, but without you, I'm a..." His jaw tensed. "I'm just putting one foot in front of the other.

"Asking me to live without you is like asking someone to live without the sun. I can't do it. Whatever you need me to do, I'll do because I need you more than sunlight, baby. I always will."

His words hit me like a slap in the face, but because I couldn't focus on this right now, because I couldn't waver in my resolve, I insisted, "Finn, tell me right now if you're keeping anything else from me."

He reached up and rubbed the back of his neck. "I mean, Christ, I don't think I am. Nothing like this, at any rate."

That probably wouldn't have reassured most women, but it did me.

Truth was, with as much as Finn had going on in a day, if he'd said that he was keeping nothing from me point blank, I wouldn't believe him. His lack of confidence seemed more earnest, and I needed that rather than bullshit assurances right now.

"Oh." He cursed under his breath. "Shit."

I scowled at him. "What is it?" *So much for reassurances.*

"I didn't know this until St. Stephen's Day," he admitted.

"What?"

"Callum O'Reilly was a Sparrow."

"Conor's friend?" I gasped. "He must be devastated."

"He is." His lips tightened. "Callum leaked the details of our wedding to the Sparrows, Aoife. It led to..."

"He's the reason..." My mouth gaped. "The drive-by?"

Pain darkening those cobalt blue eyes, Finn nodded. "Those fucking Sparrows."

Standing there, in the frigid cold, I went down the rabbit hole of everything I'd endured because of Callum O'Reilly...

Bitterness welled inside me, then another scream sounded from somewhere in the warehouse, and though I flinched again, it was out of genuine shock.

A guy was being tortured in here.

What did I expect? For him to be listening to that godawful *Baby Shark* piped on a loop for hours on end or for him to be made to pay physically?

I bit my lip at the thought, and like he knew I was wobbling, Finn rasped, "You don't have to do this."

"I do."

I surprised myself with how deeply the resolve in my voice was layered. There wasn't an ounce of give. As much as my body responded to the sounds, my mind was set on this path, and nothing was going to take me off it.

"Which way?"

"I'll guide you," he told me as his hand settled at the base of my spine, warning me, I guessed, that he was about to touch me.

A part of me wanted to slap that hand away, but when he steered me toward a section of the warehouse that was empty, I let him because we appeared to be walking into a blank canvas of space.

Frowning up at him, I saw that he cast me a look, but he remained silent, and suddenly, there was another scream. This time, I didn't flinch, and the source of the scream made me realize that the noise was coming from this area but there was nothing here.

Then a door opened, and the aperture was seamless. It blended in with the wall perfectly, I saw.

The second Conor clapped eyes on me, he demanded, "Aoife? Is everything okay?"

As he moved toward me, his concern genuine, he brought a smell with him that had my sensitive nose rebelling the second it collided with my olfactory senses.

"Jesus, Conor, what is that?" I shoved my hand against my nose to combat the stench.

"Did you know that pigs are a close genetic relative of humans?"

I blinked. "What does that have to do with how bad you stink?"

"Scorched flesh smells like bacon," Finn answered grimly.

My stomach twisted some, but I'd mastered butchery in culinary school. Sure, we'd chopped up pigs and sides of beef not humans...

"Why is he scorched?" I rasped.

"Because Kid likes electricity," was Finn's reminder, as I realized he'd said something like that before.

"What's not to like?" Conor replied with a frown. "Very effective at doling out pain without having to get your hands dirty. I need mine for typing. I tried dictating but it's not so easy with code. We adapt and evolve, don't we?"

"Sure, I guess." Uneasily, I looked up at Finn and saw he was shaking his head.

When he asked, "You sure you want to do this, Aoife?" it didn't come as a surprise.

Conor huffed. "The bastard helped kill her mother, Finn. Of course she wants to do this." He reached out and tugged on a strand of hair that hung loose from my ponytail. "All that red hair hides a fiery temper. This is the first time I've really seen it."

I didn't jerk away from his touch. Instead, I clasped his wrist with my fingers and asked, "Conor, why are you involved in this?"

Taking note that his pulse didn't jump, I watched his reaction as he answered, "Ma asked me to."

"Why?" I couldn't understand why Lena would get Conor involved. "Why would she drag you into this?"

"Oh, for many reasons."

"Can you tell me some of them?" I rasped, releasing my hold on his wrist as he gently dropped my hair. I huddled deeper into my coat as I stared at him. "I need to understand."

The problem was, I didn't want to offend him. Conor hadn't done anything wrong. It wasn't his fault this was happening. But he had a way about him that I knew, if I triggered it, he'd help me.

Conor's weakness was the underdog.

I'd seen that time and time again, especially in regard to Shay.

Finn said Brennan was teaching Shay self-defense because Conor had encouraged him to—before he'd stolen the trust funds of some of

Shay's bullies as punishment. If that didn't speak louder than words, I didn't know what did.

"The most pressing reason is she doesn't trust Da." He pursed his lips. "I also think she's scared he'll lose the plot."

"He lost that years ago," Finn grumbled.

Conor's smile turned darker. "Well, that's certainly true. But mostly it's because Finn and Aidan told them that I was raped as a child—"

Finn tensed. "Con—"

Conor's gaze never left mine. "Why the family insists on treating me as if I'm a kid I don't know. Da puts me in charge of monitoring everyone then doesn't seem to think I have the synaptic ability to put two and two together?"

Unable to hold back, I reached over and touched his chin.

Was he doing this because of Callum? Were the shadows in his eyes there because his friend had betrayed him?

Hurting for myself, hurting for him, I whispered, "They don't treat you like you're a child. They love you. They want to protect you."

"I don't need protecting." He tilted his face into my hand. "But thank you for saying that anyway. I understand that this can't be easy for you, Aoife. I'm so sorry." His gaze dropped to my stomach, and that was when I knew he knew.

Somehow, he knew that our baby wasn't... *right.*

My body turned to ice as I stared at him, stared into those beautiful eyes that could see the world for what it was, all while hiding the secrets of the universe.

"Thank you, Conor." As I drowned in his eyes, I found that was preferable to the waves of grief that kept hitting me like a sledgehammer to the heart. "If I wanted to torture your mom for actually killing mine, I guess you wouldn't help me then, though?"

He stared at me. "You have many reasons to hate her," he agreed.

"I do," I snapped.

With his spare hand, he booped my chin gently with a finger. "Do you blame the bullet or do you blame the gun or do you blame the man pulling the trigger?"

I swallowed. "Your mom's the bullet?"

"Yes." He cast a look at Finn. "Finn would probably like me to discourage you from coming in here, and maybe I should, but you have to know a few things before I let you see Michael."

I licked my lips. "What?"

"He has major burns. Some bones can be seen through the flesh. He stinks. He's pissed and crapped himself multiple times.

"The Geneva Convention doesn't exist within these walls, Aoife. There's no such thing as Amnesty International."

"You didn't beat him?" I asked gruffly.

"No. I don't work that way. That's for Brennan."

That was why I'd wanted him on the job.

For a second, my gaze darted to the open doorway where that stench emanated from. "What did you do to him?"

"I just made him talk. That's all."

"*Cheiles* don't just talk to anyone, Aoife. Don't underestimate what you're about to see," Finn warned.

"That man is the reason my mom is dead," I retorted.

"And you're of the world that believes prisons and the justice system are all it takes to make things right," my husband argued. "I'm from *this* world, but even I was shocked when I saw him."

"You've seen him?"

"I have."

I narrowed my eyes at him. "Is that something you're keeping from me?"

"No. You can see the livestream Conor sent. He probably has recordings of it." Finn shrugged. "But I have to tell you, sweetheart, that I've worked long and hard to keep you out of the business. With every step you take down this path, you're driving yourself deeper into a conspiracy charge."

Conor nodded, and his tone was easy as he reasoned, "He's right, Aoife. Conspiracy to commit murder comes with the same penalties as murder one."

A part of me wanted to scream at them, wanted to question if they thought I was dumb as shit if they didn't think I knew that already. But I saw that both of them were just trying to protect me.

That was what the O'Donnellys did, after all. They protected their women.

Just like they'd protected Lena.

But what about my mom?

My mom deserved protection too.

She deserved justice, dammit.

Jaw clenched, I shoved Conor aside, preferring to stop talking about this and to just get on with it. Only trouble was, my gag reflex began being triggered with every step I damn well took.

By the time I was at the foot of whatever torture device Conor had conjured up, my eyes watered with the need to puke.

Beholding the monstrosity of what was once a normal man who'd worn expensive suits like the rest of the Five Points, and who drove Lena around like she was Queen Bee, I wasn't going to lie—Finn was right.

I shouldn't be here.

Every instinct I possessed demanded I get the hell away from his hideous place, that I go and scrub off the atrocious scent that stained the air I breathed, that I erase every part of today and go down the selective amnesia route.

But I couldn't.

Because what I'd said earlier was right—this man was the reason my mother was dead. And I'd been next on his list of targets.

Only Finn shoving his way into my life had saved me. Only his extortion had spared me from the worst fate of all.

Though, as I looked at Michael, I had to reason that being mowed down wasn't so bad as this.

The man's blackened eyelids fluttered at the sound of our footsteps and the pain and despair hidden within those depths had my heart pounding double time.

A million questions surged into being, each one landing on my tongue before flittering away.

Eventually, I settled on: "Am I still in danger from your people?"

My voice sounded strange to my ears, but I knew I didn't sound that funny that he couldn't understand me. He turned his head to the side, and I knew he was ignoring me. Conor did too.

When I saw the flash of light snapping at his wrists and ankles, I almost heaved, especially as that scent hit me like a slap to the face.

Finn was there, holding me up, and it was so bad that I let him. His arms moved around my waist, and he propped me up, being my strength while I dealt with this horror show.

"YES!" Michael screamed before Conor stopped the electrical charge, allowing him to slur, "But only... if the... secret of who... your father really... is comes out."

He panted so hard it reminded me of an overheated dog locked in a car. I stared at him in horror, realizing that I'd never imagined this...

It needed to stop.

It had to stop.

"You look just like her." I jerked back in surprise as he smiled at me, a smile from his death mask. "At least you're not a slut like her."

"My mom wasn't a slut," I whispered shakily.

"She was. Even her own fucking brother thought so."

He sneered at me with so much hate from within that battered face of his that I knew his cruelty went bone deep.

I'd met him on dozens of occasions, but how he looked at me now was so different than those other times.

Was this the real him? With his mask gone and the act no more?

He jerked when Conor worked his horrors on him, and my brother-in-law snapped, "You don't speak unless it's to answer a question."

Finn moved into me, not touching but close enough that I felt his warmth. "Your mom was not a whore, sweetheart."

"She was a lying, filthy slag," Michael roared before Conor zapped him. "Betrayed... her... people," he stuttered on a scream.

Flinching at the sight, my mouth almost trembled before I firmed it. "Is Elizabeth Davidson a part of the ECD?"

He was quiet. Too quiet.

An electrical charge surged to life that made me feel like my hair was about to stand on end.

It went on for so long that I started to cry as his body twisted and morphed, bones and muscles straining.

Michael's scream pierced my ears and would, I knew, haunt my nightmares until the day I died.

"YES!" he screeched, a second before he fell silent.

I stared at his stillness with horror, wondering if he was dead, then Conor murmured, "That's the first time he's admitted that."

The First Lady was involved with a bunch of terrorists.

My life had turned into a Dean Koontz novel.

"He's not going to last long, Finn," Conor continued, "I know you wanted me to keep him alive, but—"

"Let him die." I pushed back against Finn's hold before I stared up at him and whispered, "Take me home."

And as we stepped outside of the house of horrors behind me, that was when I puked.

FINN

SHE DIDN'T ASK me to leave.

I considered that to be a good thing.

Instead, she stayed in the kitchen and she baked.

And she baked.

Then she baked some more.

But for all that her cookies and brownies usually had me sniffing around her, I stayed away. I hung out with Jake for the rest of that excruciating weekend, ignoring calls from both Conor and Junior. I didn't answer a single work email either.

The precariousness of my position wasn't something I was accustomed to.

I ruled over my world, dominating it in a way the homeless kid in me needed, but in this instance, Aoife held all the power.

As a result, I kept expecting to have the fight of my life, where I pulled out all the cards to convince her to let me stay, yet there wasn't one.

She stayed in her domain, I stayed in mine, and at night, we went to bed where things stayed the same—she remained on her side and I was on mine.

That Saturday night, when she came to bed, I was lying in the dark.

She shuffled around the room, making me realize that she thought I was sleeping, and I didn't do anything to make her believe otherwise.

I watched her as she undressed in the light from the bathroom. I watched as she scrubbed her face clean and applied some cream, and once the lights were gone, I watched the shadows as she headed over to the bed and climbed in at my side.

Marriage had changed me; I knew that. Throw happiness and love at someone who'd been perennially unhappy and unloved and it was like spreading horse manure in a garden—flowers were going to fucking grow.

I'd always felt unworthy of her, but these last few days, I had my confirmation. Trouble was, I was too selfish to leave her. To let her leave me.

Maybe that'd be the decent thing to do, but while I was willing to let sleeping dogs lie right now, I knew that I was too much of a scrapper to let her give up on what we had.

Registering that I was a piece of shit was the best way, I found, to spend every fucking Saturday night, so I just lay there, mind whirring while she settled down too.

Only, she didn't sleep. I felt her crying. Soft shivers, tiny gasps, each one was like a nail to my heart.

Regret and remorse consumed me, but I stared up at the ceiling as she cried herself to sleep.

Every second that passed as I just fucking lay there while her heart broke killed me. I'd gone through some shit in my life, but hearing her cry in secret twisted my insides, turned them ragged and raw.

I clenched my fists, wanting to grab a hold of her, wanting to hug her, but I knew it wouldn't be welcome—

The cries turned to sobs.

They'd escalated, not calmed down as she slept.

I couldn't stand it. I couldn't fucking bear hearing her like that, so I reached over, and while I prepared myself for her to hit out, I hauled her into me, trapping her hands against my chest as I hugged her and held her tight.

Her face burrowed against my throat, her tears wet my skin and the pillow beneath us, but as I held her, her sobbing eased some.

It might have been ten minutes or an hour, but we lay there, neither of us saying a word as her grief bubbled free.

"I shouldn't have hit you," she rasped out of nowhere.

I didn't tense up. "You needed a safe space to release your anger."

"That shouldn't have been on you," she denied, her voice nasal and raw from her tears. "I'm sorry I did that."

I wasn't.

"I deserved it."

"Violence is never the answer."

"I'm a Five Pointer, Aoife. Violence is always the answer."

"Not between us. You've never raised your hand to me in anger."

"There's a difference."

"Physically, yes. Symbolically, no." She tugged at my hold on her hands. "That's why you're holding them down, isn't it?"

Not wanting her to think I was tying her down, I released them. "I didn't want you to hurt yourself."

She fell silent at that, and when she didn't move away, I considered that to be a good sign.

"Why are you being so reasonable?"

I could have lied.

Maybe I even should have, but the truth was the only thing that belonged between us.

If I'd started our marriage that way, then we wouldn't be like this now.

This was on me.

It was all my fault.

"Because I'm fighting for my life."

"You're not dying," she ground out.

"I will without you and Jake."

The simplicity of my words had her whispering, "I'm not used to you being reasonable."

"Am I that much of a jackass?" I countered, brow furrowed.

I'd seen how Aidan Sr. was with Lena. I'd taken note of how my fucker of a stepfather had treated my mother, and I'd done my damnedest to make sure I never treated her like they did.

I worked too many hours, but I always made sure I had time for them, even if it meant giving up on sleep. I did my best, but I, more than anyone, knew that wasn't always enough.

"You're not a jackass, Finn. You're just... you're not..." She sucked in a breath. "When we met, what did you do?"

I winced. "Made you sign over the tearoom."

She scoffed. "Half the story."

"And had you come over here."

"It wasn't to play dress up, was it?"

My cheeks burned with heat. "I wanted you."

"I know."

"I always want you," I rasped, eyes burning as I stared up at the ceiling.

"I know. I don't think you ever understood what that did to me."

"What do you mean?"

"I knew what you were and who, Finn. I knew you could have any woman you wanted. But you chose me. I don't even know why I'm bringing this up."

"Because when I was all in, I was all in?"

Aoife hesitated. "Yes. I believed that."

Scowling, I asked the ceiling, "Past tense?"

"It was a lie, wasn't it?"

"No," I retorted. "How the hell was that a lie? Aoife, sweetheart, I made some shitty choices along the way, but you are the best fucking decision I ever goddamn made.

"You can doubt many things about me; you can doubt that I'm a good man, you can doubt that I deserve you, but you must never, ever doubt how much I love you."

My words were passionate, mostly because I meant them. Each and every one of them.

Loving her was the one honest and true thing I'd ever done with this fuckfest of a life of mine. That she could doubt it...

"Aoife?" I rasped.

She released a weary sigh and shuffled back to the other half of the bed.

"Go to sleep, Finn."

Curling onto her side, with the full expanse of the mattress between us, I stared at the chasm that separated us.

I was not a man who took things slow. I was a man who made things happen.

But here, now, I couldn't. She had every goddamn right to be angry with me, every goddamn right to be upset, but juggling the aftermath wasn't going to be easy.

That was why I got up and showered in the spare room when I heard her breathing change. As sleep overtook her, I headed out of the apartment to the garage and drove to my office building in my Porsche coupe.

A new status quo needed to be found, and me lounging around the place, waiting for her to explode, wasn't going to help matters.

The second I pulled out my desk chair from behind the desk, my cell phone rang.

Half expecting it to be Aoife, I sighed when I saw it was Kid.

"What?"

"Rude."

I narrowed my eyes at the black nothingness that was the Hudson this late at night. "I have shit to do."

"Don't we all," Conor sniped. "If anything, I have *more* shit than anyone else to do. Who's the one with their hands in all the Points' pies?"

"What do you want? A medal?"

"No. I just wanted to talk."

Without meaning to, I focused in on the background of the call. A part of me expected to hear Michael's screams even though Kid said the bastard had died late last night.

"What do you want to talk about?"

"Why you're going into the office on a Saturday night at eleven PM?"

Frowning, I glanced around the room. "Are you monitoring me?"

"Why does that come as a shock?"

"Swear to fuck you're worse than Big Brother."

Conor scoffed. "Little Brother is far more powerful."

"Only in this instance," I argued. "And I'll tell Aidan and Brennan you said that next time I talk with them both."

"Well, there's me shaking in my fucking Yeezys." Conor grunted, "You're my older brother too, Finn."

Tension crawled up the back of my spine and settled at the base of my neck—a headache was definitely brewing. "Heard about that, did you?"

"I hear all and I see all."

"You know how lonely that sounds?" I questioned, settling my ass at the edge of my desk and perching on it.

"You know how lonely that feels?"

I reached up and rubbed my chin. "You okay?"

"I'm not the one who needs to answer that."

"Look like a piece of shit, do I?" I flipped the room the bird and waggled my hand around to make sure he could see it in whichever camera he used to monitor me.

"You look rough," he agreed.

"Bad couple of days."

"Aoife tossed you out?"

"No. I get the feeling this is the calm before the storm."

"Think she's too scared to toss you out?"

My throat clutched at the thought. "She isn't scared of me."

"Isn't she?" I heard the shrug in Conor's voice. "She knows what happens in this world, doesn't she?"

"Meaning?"

"'Five Points until you die.'"

"She's different."

"Is she?"

"What's with all the fucking questions, Conor? Aoife ain't—" I massaged my temple where the headache was coming on thick and fast. "She..."

"She, what?"

I thought about what I'd told her—that I couldn't let her divorce me. That I wouldn't allow that to happen.

"I told her I'd leave."

Conor hummed. "Why didn't you? Or is this you leaving?"

"No. I've been hanging around, waiting for the other shoe to drop. It's not... It's not me, Conor."

"You asked her what she wants?"

"No. She doesn't want to talk." Unless it was to doubt that I fucking loved her.

Jesus, how could she think that?

Every fucking day, I made decisions *because of her*. Because of Jake. For them both. For our future.

I rubbed my temple some more.

"I'm no expert—"

"Yeah, I agree. You're no expert on marriage," I snapped.

"But women ain't like us, are they?" Conor chimed in, ignoring my snap of temper.

"Figured that out, did you? What gave it away?"

"No tits, pussy, or bubble butt," Conor grumbled. "But you know what I mean. Maybe she wants you to be there. Maybe distance is the last thing you need between you."

"Hanging around the apartment is like waiting for a bomb to go off."

"I bet," he consoled. "But maybe you sticking around is proof that you'll always stick around."

Staring down at my feet, I rumbled, "You think I should go back?"

"I do. Whatever work you got on your plate can be handled there, can't it?"

"Yeah. I need some files."

"Take them with you."

I scowled at my feet. "Am I really taking advice from my chronically single brother?"

Conor argued, "Single by choice."

"Aren't we all?"

"Nah. I was waiting on the one. I'm a man of discerning tastes."

Somehow hearing shit like that was perfectly acceptable from Kid. If Declan or Bren had said it, then I'd have ribbed them. But Kid said weirder shit over pancakes than most men did when they were pissed out of their skulls.

I scratched the stubble on my chin as I pondered his words, but the only thing I could think to say to any of that was, "I'd best get back home."

"Yeah, you'd best."

"Thanks, bro."

"I'm glad you're my blood, Finn. Always felt sure you were, but it's nice knowing it all the same."

"When did you find out?"

He hummed. "When you were seventeen. Same time as I found out O'Grady abused you."

My throat closed. "You knew before I did. About being Senior's son, I mean."

He didn't make it awkward. "Think about what you just said there, Finn, and wonder why you're surprised."

"You're such a fucking know-it-all," I groused, relieved that he was going to let it drop.

"Nah, I don't shove it in your face."

"That supposed to make it better?"

"Nope."

"Con?"

"Yeah?"

"That Lodestar woman. She's the one?"

"Yup."

"Does she know it?"

"Nah. Not yet. I'm gentling her."

My brows rose. "Gentling her? She ain't a horse."

"Never said she was," he countered. "She's been through a lot of shit, Finn."

"Haven't we all?"

"No. Worse than us."

"Both of us are child sexual abuse survivors, Conor," I pointed out, dragging it up when I hadn't meant to. "You're telling me what she went through is worse than that?"

"Da killed your rapist. My elder brothers killed mine. Our family came around us and showed us that we mattered enough to decimate those fuckers who dared hurt us."

"No one did that for her?"

"No. No one. She was on her own. But she ain't anymore."

"You... Do you..." For a second, my tongue wouldn't work, but of course, Kid helped me out.

"Do I forgive you for telling Da about Father McKenna?"

I could feel my goddamn Adam's apple bob. "Yeah."

"I dunno. I'm ambivalent about it. They were acting weird around Christmas, but they're getting a bit more normal. I don't want to talk about it with them, and I don't think they do either."

"Does that... do you wish they would? Isn't it like the elephant in the room?"

"No. Maybe I should want to, but I don't." He cleared his throat. "You think Aoife will come to Sunday dinner?"

"Doubt it. Why?"

"I don't want her to cut ties with us. I'll miss her."

An ache brewed in my chest. It had jack shit to do with a heart attack and everything to do with that fucking need I had, that we all had, to protect Conor. To shelter him.

"Maybe you should tell her that, Kid. Maybe that's what she needs to hear."

Conor just grunted.

"I wouldn't expect her tomorrow," I said cautiously.

Fuck, I didn't know when we'd be attending Sunday dinner as a family. I didn't even know if Senior would force us to attend.

As I wondered how that might turn out, if I was about to get kneecapped for refusing to force my wife to eat Lena's roast, Conor muttered, "Go home and be with your wife, bro."

"Yeah. Night, Kid."

"Night, Finn."

For a second, I stared down at my phone once he cut the call.

After a couple minutes, I stopped wondering if Kid could ever be happy with a woman who'd been through more shit than the pair of us combined, and I gathered the files together that I'd need.

In the morning, I'd have my assistant bring over anything I forgot, but I set myself up with enough work to get me through the night.

Loaded down with papers, I returned to my Porsche, headed home, and got myself situated in the office.

After I settled behind my desk, a half hour later, I heard Aoife stir in the bedroom.

I didn't lift my head to look at her when she hovered in the doorway, but I knew she was there, knew she watched me work for a couple minutes before she returned to our bedroom.

Proving, yet again, that Conor was right.

"Little shit," I hissed, hoping that one of his bugs picked up on *that*.

TWENTY-NINE

AOIFE

"WHERE'S FINN?"

I stopped whisking my brownie batter, the one that *We Cream For Ice Scream* was raving about and which had triggered a wave of interest in my bakery, and turned to Jen.

As I rubbed my side where that goddamn ache had started up again, I asked, "Why?"

"I want to talk to you about something. I don't need him listening in."

I blinked at her, feeling dazed. The day had been a long one. Deep inside, there was an ache that wouldn't go, and today, having received a voicemail from Lena telling me that I could send it to the cops like it was a confession, I'd heard the details of my mom's death.

On Lena's end, it was an accident.

I believed that.

But that didn't make the betrayal go away.

That didn't mean my family wasn't involved in a political conspiracy that was what nightmares were made of.

Woodenly, I told Jen, "Finn had to go out. No one else's here."

It was the first time he had since we'd gone to the warehouse together.

It was always interesting when he worked from home. I learned a lot of shit about the business that I really shouldn't have been listening in on.

Today's conversation with Aidan had been about ghost guns and the arrival of a shipment in the city. That was why he'd had to go out.

I didn't think Finn often got his hands dirty with stuff like this but Aidan had asked him to come with, and Finn had complied.

It had to be pretty important, though, if he'd left the apartment.

I got the feeling that he thought if he left, I'd get the locks changed and he wouldn't be able to get back in.

The thought had me blinking at Jen when I realized she was talking to me while I wasn't listening.

But three words resonated.

"You killed someone?" I gulped. "Jen, you killed someone?" She winced. And I didn't even care that I was repeating myself for the third time. "You killed someone?"

"Honey," she said carefully, "you're married to a Five Pointer. You're an Irish Mob wife. You're seriously giving me shade for killing that creep, Vlad?"

It wasn't like she was wrong. Especially not when I knew where Finn was spending his goddamn afternoon.

"Well, no, I'm not giving you shade, but..." I dropped the whisk which splattered onto the counter, making one hell of a mess, then staggered back to sit at the kitchen table.

The ache in my side morphed from a nagging, dull pain into a sharp one. Like something was clawing at me.

"Do you need some water?"

Her words broke into my thoughts. "No. I just—" My brow furrowed. "Why did you kill him?"

Jen had killed someone. Jen had actually killed someone.

I wasn't sure if that came as a shock or not.

The way she led her life meant that she put herself in a lot of danger. I guessed I'd known, at some point, that would lead to consequences.

It was why I tried to help her find a rich sugar daddy. If she found someone, then they'd protect her, keep her safe.

Still...

Her mother's boyfriend?

That blindsided me.

"Because he was attacking me." She rolled her eyes as she squatted down in front of me. "I didn't do it for fun."

I rubbed my temple as my mind warred with the knowledge that Jen had killed her mom's boyfriend, and it led to little spots dancing in front of my eyes. "Why were you even with him?"

"He came to my place. I didn't shut the damn door properly. It was my fault for being stupid, but he barged in, and then..." She reached up and fingered a tiny Band-Aid on her earlobe. "He dragged my earring off so he could pawn it."

"You're joking." But it wasn't a question. My gaze followed the passage of her fingers and I cringed, both with the idea of how much that would have hurt all while I felt the same kind of pain in my being.

"No. He groped me, started saying shit like he'd make more money if he whored me out instead of my mother. So... I stopped him."

"Why are you telling me this?" I choked, wondering if I looked like a pressure cooker that was on the brink of exploding.

God, after this weekend, this was just too fucking much.

She stared down at the floor, and I immediately felt guilty. Here she was, confessing this horrible thing to me and she probably wanted back up, and all I could think was that I wanted to huddle on the floor and cry.

God, that sounded so good.

The pain had abated this weekend, and it had made me forget about what the doctor had said. But there was no forgetting it when my body was giving me a reminder to end all reminders.

"I need your help with Conor."

Whatever I'd expected her to say, it wasn't that. "Conor?" I blurted out. "O'Donnelly? Conor O'Donnelly?"

"How many Conors do we know?"

I swallowed because she had a point, but I wasn't sure if I'd ever look at Conor in the same light again. "Why do you need help with him?"

"Maybe I don't. Maybe Finn will help." She sucked in a breath that she released on a whoosh, alongside: "But... I started dating someone."

Jesus. Would the hits never end?

I gaped at her. "You're dating someone?!"

"I'm sorry I didn't tell you. It was just a fling, until it wasn't. His name's Luciu Valentini. I think he's been arrested for Vlad's murder.

"I tried his place and the club he owns but... *nada.* I can't get any information. I need Conor, or Finn, to get me some."

My eyes felt blurry as I whispered, "Why? Can't you just ask this Luciu's family?"

"I need to know what's happening and his brother's a dick."

"I can't believe you didn't tell me you were dating someone."

"I didn't think it was serious."

"It's serious enough that you're here asking for a favor from the Irish Mob," I sniped before I reached up and rubbed my forehead again. "Why do I know that name?" It rang a bell, I just wasn't sure from where.

"He has ties to the mafia," she mumbled under her breath.

I clicked my fingers as I remembered overhearing Finn and Aidan talking about him during the holidays. "He's the Cheshire Cat smile guy."

"He only does one cheek," she defended.

Like that was a good thing?

"One's ample. Are you sure you're not happy he's been arrested? I mean, it's one way to get rid of him—"

"No! Aoife, I don't want him locked up for something he didn't do. I-I..." Jen heaved a sigh. "You won't believe me."

"Babe, I didn't think you could kill someone, but I believe that," I said carefully. "Trust me, I don't think there's much you could say that would surprise me."

"I love him."

She loved him.

I stared at her for a second, wondering if she'd started talking Urdu or something and I just hadn't realized it, but before I could even say a word, the dizziness and the spots dancing in front of my eyes turned into an all-out Irish jig.

There was no longer only one Jen looking up at me—there were five.

Suddenly, the muscles in my body that kept me seated upright seemed to turn to soup, and I felt myself falling forward just as that stabbing sensation in my belly morphed like the knife was being twisted and my insides were being attacked.

When the darkness came, and it brought with it some relief from the pain, I embraced it but it wasn't a total blackout.

I almost wished it were.

I still felt like my stomach was being torn apart but it was muted, like a shadow of the full sensation.

Jen caught me under my armpits. It hurt as she struggled to settle me on the ground. In the background, I could hear Jake sobbing, and I realized that was why the blackout wasn't total.

I could hear him.

He needed me.

As I tried to force myself to stir, to find out what the matter was, I heard Jen muttering something under her breath, and Jake stopped sobbing like his heart was breaking.

The waves of pitch black started coming in thick and fast as I smelled him—that sweet scent that was the baby cologne I sprayed him with and baby wipes—and I knew she'd brought him to me. Something that was confirmed as he started playing with my hair.

As he tugged on it hard enough to hurt, a moan escaped my lips.

Pain lashed at me with barbs that dug into my flesh and, eyelashes fluttering, I slurred, "Probably...call—Finn," and that was the last thing I remembered.

THIRTY

FINN

I'D DONE a lot of shit in my life.

A lot of shit that would undoubtedly see me spend an eternity in hell if hell even existed, but why was it my wife who paid for my sins?

As I sat outside the hospital room where she was being treated, Aidan's hand remained on my shoulder as more of a physical restraint than comfort as I kept trying and failing in not losing my shit.

Jake was asleep, thank Christ, resting in Jen's arms even though he didn't particularly want to be there. I kept jumping up whenever a doctor came barging into the waiting area, praying that the news was for me, so I figured he preferred sleeping on her rather than on me.

I knew what a wild animal felt like when it had been caged because within these halls, my wife was without protection.

She was being treated by doctors I didn't know, being aided by nurses my crew hadn't approved.

She was in danger in more ways than one and there was jackshit I could do to protect her.

The keys in my pocket jangled every time I tapped my heel against the floor, and my knuckles were aching from how hard I was gripping my hands, trying to stop myself from strangling the next fucking doctor who came in here without any news.

"Conor's on his way."

I blinked at Aidan's words, twisted to look at him and saw he was reading a message on his phone. "He's finished?"

"Scanning the hospital staff for any enemies?" Aidan's mouth firmed. "Yeah. He wouldn't be coming if there was a problem."

Well, that came as a fucking relief.

"He's certain?"

"It's Conor," Aidan groused. "When ain't he certain?"

Nodding, I muttered, "True."

Aidan squeezed my shoulder. "She'll come out all right, bro. You know she will."

I didn't know dick.

"Why is it that since we've been together, she's been hospitalized three times and I haven't even had to go to the doctor for chest pains?"

"Do you have chest pains?"

I scowled at him. "No. That's the point. I'm the one who lives the high-risk, high-stress life, and she's the one who bakes fucking brownies for a living and—" I released a breath as I reached up and rubbed my eyes.

I could feel Jen's glower, felt it like her eyeballs were goddamn lasers, but I couldn't look at her right now.

Couldn't look at the judgment and have confirmation that I'd failed my wife.

Again.

"The first time was... well, I mean, that wasn't like we asked for it."

No. It fucking wasn't.

Tension crept along the back of my neck and had me clenching my jaw as I thought about Callum motherfucking O'Reilly and how he'd set us up on my goddamn wedding day.

It was his fault she'd been hurt.

His fault.

I was glad the fucker was dead.

If I could get my hands around his throat here and now, I'd have strangled him again and again.

"Aoife's problems stem from those injuries, Aidan. Dipshit." Jen's voice was low enough that it wouldn't disturb Jake, but bitter enough that I felt each word like a poisoned lance to the gut.

"They do," I confirmed, rubbing my brow. "Goddamnit, when are we going to get any news?"

"There must have been complications from the miscarriage," Jen whispered, less sass in her tone now, more fear.

That I could fucking understand.

Christ, the guilt... I wanted to beat the shit out of Callum, but really, the person who deserved the beating was me.

I'd done this.

I'd put Aoife under so much strain that she'd lost our baby.

Bursting onto my feet, I started pacing, back and forth, and no one stopped me. I stayed pacing for another hour as my brothers and their wives drifted in, as Aidan Sr. and Lena did too.

She kept her eyes downcast but everyone was smart enough not to approach me.

As the waiting room filled up, I felt their presence though.

This was my family.

My fucking kin.

"When are we getting some goddamn news?" Senior grunted after another half-hour's silence from the staff.

I heard his question and felt his temper and was glad for it. So fucking glad.

That was on my behalf. On my wife's behalf.

My father cared.

Maybe it was a fucked-up kind of care, but I'd take it. Especially when he picked up his phone and started dialing.

"Calling the administrator isn't going to make them speed up, Da," Conor pointed out.

Senior glowered at Kid. "I just want them to realize that they're dealing with a VIP."

"If they didn't realize that already when we walked in, Da, they're fucking morons," Bren grumbled, his arm tightening around Camille's waist.

"Maybe they're fucking morons, then. They ain't given us jack shit for answers since we got here, and Junior said they didn't hear nothing for a good forty minutes before that."

"Calm down, Da," Eoghan intoned, but he jolted when, outside, a gurney squeaked its way down the hall. Inessa shot him a look and pressed a hand to his lap.

Eoghan's fingers tightened in hers as Senior spat, "We should have had her sent to one of our hospitals. At least there she'd have gotten the gold star treatment."

I winced at the idea of Aoife waking up in a goddamn warehouse like the one Declan had been treated in last year, surrounded by plastic sheeting in a makeshift ICU.

"James, good to talk to you," Senior boomed, loud enough to make even a deaf person flinch. "I wanted you to know that my daughter-in-law's being treated—" His eyes narrowed. "Yeah, Aoife O'Grady. No one could forget a name like that. Heard about her, have you?" There was a pause. "Then why the fuck haven't *we* heard anything for over an hour?

"I think you should remember who you fucking owe, James, and get your goddamn surgeons or doctors or whoever the fuck is treating my *daughter-in-law*, and you get them to tell us what's going on."

A second later, he cut the call, and I rasped, "Thank you."

Senior shook his head. "We all want answers, son."

Jaw clenching, I turned away and started to move over to the window in the waiting room, but Jake had stirred at Senior's call so I walked over to Jen and hauled him into my arms. He nestled against me, almost immediately falling back to sleep.

I clung to him as much as he clung to me, well aware that this might be the last fucking time Aoife let me anywhere near him.

Christ, we'd lost our baby because of the shit I'd put her through these past couple days... I had to... We needed to...

Fuck, I didn't know what to do.

I'd decided that I'd just carry on with life. Let her do her shit. I'd do mine. Eventually, she'd come around, right? She had to. But now, this was different.

We'd lost our child because of my bullshit.

I had to pay for that sin.

Squeezing Jake, I pressed my lips to his temple and breathed in his baby scent. It was a combo of baby shampoo and wipes and that sickly sweet softener that Aoife used for his clothes.

I wasn't sure how I'd cope not seeing him every day and every night, but if Aoife tossed my ass out...

With my back to the waiting room, I didn't see the doctor come in, but I heard footsteps.

Turning around to face him, I saw the combination of anger and fear in his expression—a sight I was accustomed to seeing when Senior waded into any given situation—and demanded, "How is she?"

When I stepped over to him, he backed down the hallway, and I moved with him, seeing that he wanted privacy.

"She's stable. It took some time because there were complications—"

"What kind of complications?" Lena asked, slipping beside me.

She had no right to be here, but when her hand found mine, nonetheless, I clung to her.

"More blood loss than anticipated in situations like these. With your wife's medical history, we were fortunate that we didn't have to give her an emergency hysterectomy.

"After speaking with her OBGYN, I understand that she advised this pregnancy be terminated, Mr. O'Grady." He cast a disparaging glance at me. "Everyone knows your family is Catholic, but when a doctor advises a termination, religion shouldn't be a part of the decision."

As I tried to process what he'd just told me, all I could think to say was, "The baby was..."

Lena squeezed my hand. "The pregnancy wasn't viable, Finn. Aoife found out that day you... she..." She sighed miserably. "You know, that day."

I tipped up my chin and untangled my fingers from hers.

Of course.

Of course, fate would be so fucking kind as to have my wife discover the truth about our baby on the day that I confessed all my sins.

I held it together for as long as the doctor explained how the next few hours were shaped, what would happen and when I'd be able to see her, and the second he left, I turned to Lena and demanded, "You knew?"

She shot me a commiserating glance. "I did."

Jaw clenched, I rasped, "Why didn't you tell me?"

"Because not only was it not for me to share, but I didn't have the opportunity to talk to you anyway."

She'd called several times since Aoife had thrown her out of our home, but I'd let the phone ring off on each occasion. I owed Aoife that and a hell of a lot more.

Even this, now, was a betrayal.

I rubbed a hand over my face. "What the fuck am I going to do, Lena?"

She hesitated a second, but then she rubbed my arm. "Miscarriages... men treat them like they don't matter, but you have to understand, son, that they do.

"To a woman, they do. We feel their loss and we grieve for them as if they were—" Her words waned. "Aidan might not be the best in certain situations, but he always got that. He felt the loss as much as I did."

"You miscarried?"

"Twice." She tipped up her chin. "Before and after Brennan. He and Conor were my rainbow babies."

"Rainbow babies?"

"They didn't have that name back then. We just had to grieve on our own and pretend we weren't grieving. Pretty much like we had postpartum depression, but it didn't have a name, and we had to get over it..." She cleared her throat. "You have to be there for her, Finn."

"Of course, I'll be there for her. Jesus, Lena. That wasn't even what I was asking. What if *she* doesn't want me to be there period? She could rest this at my door, and I'm not sure I'd blame her."

Her smile was sad. "The pregnancy wasn't viable, Finn. This could have happened at any moment. It isn't anyone's fault. It's just... It's just life."

"How the fuck am I supposed to make this better?"

"You can't. You just be there. And she will want you there. She loves you, Finn. You love her. These are the times that will bring you closer together or tear you apart." She reached up and cupped my chin. "I wish you hadn't gone through this already, but you have. You know what to do —just be yourself."

"It's different now." I gulped. "She knows everything."

"And she has every right to be mad and bitter about it," was her simple retort. Though the words *were* simple, her pain shadowed each one. "So let her. Let her get angry. Let her rage at you. Let her burn off her temper and her grief.

"But when she wants to cry, don't allow her to hide those tears." Her fingers traced underneath my eye where I could feel the slickness from my own. "Shed *these* with her, share them with her. Grieve together or you really will lose her.

"You have some dark days ahead of you, sweetheart. She... she hates me, rightfully so, and that will mean she won't want to visit on Sundays. Don't force her, okay?" She touched my arm. "I understand that she doesn't want to come and eat with us, and if your father doesn't, then I'll make sure he keeps out of it. Or try to. Just concentrate on getting things back on the right track."

"What if that's not possible?"

"Some people are just destined to be, Finn. You and Aoife are that." She reached up onto her tiptoes and pressed a kiss to my cheek. "You'll get through this, son. I know you will."

THIRTY-ONE

AOIFE

LIFE HAD a funny way of showing you your priorities.

When I woke up the first time, I wanted Finn. And Jen. But mostly Finn. I wanted him at my side. I wanted him there, bolstering me, having my back, and going through this with me.

We were a team, after all.

A team.

I figured that out fast when they tried to get him to leave the room, and the second he saw my tears, he growled, "I'm not going anywhere. I'll stand over there in the corner, but I'm not leaving her."

God, I needed to hear those words. I needed to hear them so badly.

His declaration made the tears dry up, and while the doctors were justifiably annoyed, it made it easier on me to have my eyes on him as they gave me a checkup.

It was insane but I missed Lena and my mom equally during those moments. I'd come to rely on Lena, but there was and always would be a gaping hole where she used to fit.

As for my mom, the grief doubled down, twisting me up inside until I sobbed myself to sleep.

Drifting in and out of consciousness, I was surprised when I woke up again and found Jake sleeping on Finn's chest. He looked uncomfortable as hell, and Finn didn't look that much better. His mouth was tight, his expression grim as he stared down at his feet.

The last few days had worn on him, but they had on me too.

My voice was croaky as I pleaded, "I need you to promise that you'll put me first, Finn. Before them."

His eyes were bleak as he stated, "You don't have to ask. I already promise you that."

The immediacy of his answer should have soothed me, but it didn't.

I knew what it must have felt like to be slashed with a double-edged sword because as freely as he gave that promise, there were repercussions that neither of us were ready to handle.

His family was no longer just *his*. They were mine too.

My life revolved around them.

Sundays were spent at the compound in upstate, the frequency in which I was meeting up with my sisters-in-law for afternoon tea had gone from once every couple of weeks to every Saturday now.

I talked about books with Inessa on the phone, and Aela was our go-to babysitter and my unofficial recipe sampler. I'd asked both Inessa and Camille for help with designing the nursery, for God's sake.

Cutting them out of my life wasn't going to happen.

But those women were tied to the men in Finn's.

And they were all tied to his parents.

I'd lived without mine for so long, and no one knew better than me how fragile life was. One second someone was there, the next they were gone.

Neither Lena nor Aidan were getting younger. How much longer would he have them around?

I hated him for giving me his family as much as, last week, I loved him for it.

"What are you thinking, Aoife?" he rumbled. "I don't like what I'm seeing in your eyes."

"What are you seeing?"

"Too much despair."

My bottom lip wobbled. "That's how I feel. The situation. Our baby—"

His hand snagged mine, and he entwined our fingers. "I wish things could be different."

"Me too." I gulped, and even though his family were a major problem, all I could think of was *her*. Because she'd have been a girl for sure. "I wanted to call her Imogen."

"So we will. Imogen O'Grady." His smile was tight. As tight as the times we'd named Gray and Lewis—the other babies we'd lost. "I bet she'd have had your red hair."

The pain in my chest stole my breath as I choked out, "Your blue eyes."

"Red hair and blue eyes?" He rubbed his chin with his free hand. "I'd have had to fight the boys off."

Wiping away my tears, I nodded. "All the boys."

"Especially if she had curves like yours."

"You're the only one who thought I was a bombshell." I sniffled.

"You were hiding out in a bakery, Aoife. I mean, I'm glad you were but you can't say I'm the only one who thought that when you were always working."

"I didn't hide out when I was in school," I argued.

"You were in a kitchen."

"So? There were men in class with me."

"They were idiots."

It seemed impossible that I could even contemplate smiling, but my lips twitched.

Here I was, looking and feeling like shit, but he was acting as if Marilyn Monroe were in the bed instead.

"Well, men *are* idiots."

He winced. "Yeah. I fell for that."

"Hook, line, and sinker."

"Anyway, what's with the past tense? You *are* my bombshell. No 'was' about it." Before I could argue, he gently stroked a hand down Jake's back. "She'd have asked for her ears pierced at seven."

"And I'd have told her she was too young a thousand times by eight." I swallowed down more tears, weaving the picture of the girl who'd never be in my mind.

God, I loved that he let me do this. Even if it hurt so badly it made each breath I took scorch my lungs with the agony of it.

He squeezed my hand like he knew what I was thinking. "She can live on through us, sweetheart."

"I'd prefer her to just live."

The breath that whistled through his teeth told me he agreed with me.

Watching him, I settled my head back against the pillows, and as I stared at his red eyes—proof he'd cried at some point—the way our son clung to his daddy, how Finn weathered the discomfort of the armchair to be with me, as well as how he'd fought to stay by my side, I knew what I had to do.

"Ask Lena if she'll look after Jake for a few days. I don't know how long I'll be in here, and he needs some good rest."

Finn's eyes widened. "Are you being serious?"

"Deadly."

I knew what she'd done, but Jake didn't. Jake just knew her as Grammy—the only grandmother he'd ever had.

"You don't have to do that," he denied immediately, tone fierce enough that it confirmed I was doing the right thing. "Aidan would look after him."

I had to snort. "Aidan and Savannah are the least parental people I know. He might be his godfather, but still."

"Aela could—"

Shaking my head, I told him, "He doesn't know her as well as he does Lena." She babysat, but most of that time was when he was asleep so it wasn't like he knew her better. "Lena is the sensible choice."

Sure, being sensible sucked for me, but acting as if Lena weren't there wasn't going to help matters.

She'd done what she'd done.

She'd burned a bridge between us that could never be fixed.

But that was on her. Not me. Not Finn. And certainly not Jake.

"I'm sorry," Finn whispered.

The broken words snagged my attention. I could have been sarcastic, asked him what he'd done this time, but I just didn't have the energy to resent him right now.

Not when seeing him sitting there, my hand in his, looking as broken as I felt, talking about the daughter we'd never see, reminded me of who he was. *What* he was.

Mine.

For better or worse.

In sickness and in health.

So, instead of being resentful and bitchy, I asked, "Why?"

"For Imogen. For Callum. For letting Jake think of Lena that way." He blew out a breath. "For letting him love her. For everything."

I got where he was coming from, but it made me feel ridiculously small.

My son was loved—was that such a crime?

Yet...

I stared down at my lap as a different kind of pain whispered through me.

Lena was the only grandmother he'd ever know *because* she had been the one who'd taken away Jake's other grandmother.

Finn tugged on my hand and broke my woozy attention span. "I love you, Aoife."

My mouth trembled as I pressed my other hand to my stomach. "Even though—" I couldn't finish the sentence.

"Forever," he grated out. "Nothing you could do would stop me from loving you, sweetheart. You're not the sinner in this marriage. I fucking am."

I wasn't a saint, but by comparison to him, I knew I was. But I didn't say that either.

It all seemed so fucking futile.

Hating him, resenting him, being bitter, none of it brought Imogen back, did it?

None of it brought back my baby.

My body was a maze of pain and discomfort, but that glaring emptiness where life had once blossomed was something I'd never forget.

I'd endured this several times now, several times we'd named our children who'd never see the light of day.

We'd talked about the things they'd never do and the amount of gray they should have added to our hair...

While this wasn't the first time, it still hurt as much as if it were.

I clung to his hand as I turned my face away from him. "Jake can stay with Lena and Aidan."

I didn't tell him he could leave though.

He couldn't.

I needed him.

And like always, when it mattered, he came through for me.

WHISTLER: *Got another target.*

Eagle Eyes: *Same.*

Dead To Me: *Against other sharpshooters?*

Whistler: *Yeah.*

Eagle Eyes: *Yup.*

Dead To Me: *Who the fuck is the target? I haven't heard any chatter.*

Whistler: *Me either.*

Eagle Eyes: *Same.*

Whistler: *But whoever it is, the ECD wants them dead.*

Eagle Eyes: *That's seven different sharpshooters all accounted for.*

Dead To Me: *At least we're making the world a safer place.*

Whistler: *Is that a joke?*

Dead To Me: *Apparently not.*

Whistler: *Zero chatter from your handler, Eagle Eyes?*

Eagle Eyes: *Zero. Business as usual.*

Whistler: *This is getting fucking weird.*

Eagle Eyes: *Same.*

Whistler: *I haven't been this busy since the war.*

Eagle Eyes: *Wish I could disagree but I can't.*

Whistler: *My PTSD is flaring.*

Dead To Me: *Same.*

Eagle Eyes: *Yeah.*

Whistler: *Maybe this will be over soon enough.*

Dead To Me: *In our line of work, it's never over.*

THIRTY-TWO

INESSA

"WHAT'S with the stick up your ass recently?"

Eoghan grunted. "Sassy."

Grinning, I slipped my arms around his waist and peered around his bicep to look at him in the mirror.

Okay, I did more than peer.

I pretty much drooled as I took in his naked top half, and when I messed with the waistband of his shorts, he scowled at me.

"You trying to give me a boner?"

"Don't have to try very hard, do I?" I retorted, watching the bulge in his pants grow with satisfaction.

"Shouldn't be so sexy."

"I didn't technically do anything."

"Apart from start playing with my shorts. That's the green light if ever there was one."

"I never said there was a stop light. Go and shower off the gunk and I'm all for you fucking me on the weight bench."

"The weight bench?" He arched a brow. "We haven't done that yet, have we?"

"Nope. Not since we broke the last one." I tugged on his waistband again. "Anyway, we can do that after."

"After, what? I shower?"

"Well, after your shower and after our conversation. Ya know, about why you're all grouchy.

"I'm not sure if a guy who gets laid as much as you should really be so grouchy. There needs to be a law against it or something."

He rolled his eyes. "I'm not grouchy."

"Sure you are." I tilted my head to the side. "Is it because I decided to go to college?"

"No," he scoffed. "If anything, I'm glad about that. You're too fucking smart to be drifting around these rooms like Bloody Mary just waiting to be invoked."

"Wow. That's really how you see me? An evil spirit just waiting to make people miserable?" I snorted. "Thanks, babe."

I reached down and grabbed his junk. He didn't flinch, and while I hadn't really tried to hurt him, the threat had been there, and I was reminded once again of what my husband had gone through over the years.

I was looking at G.I. Joe in the flesh. Except his hurts weren't sliced into plastic but flesh and bone, and his mind was... well, the nightmares had started up again.

Because he *didn't* flinch or chide me, just carried on with his bicep curls, I let go of him and frowned. "Eoghan, you're starting to worry me."

"Why?"

"Because you're being weird."

The joys of marriage had come as a surprise to both of us, I knew. Victoria moving in had definitely been a curveball, but she was out at school a lot, and she spent most of her time in her room anyway.

Thank God we were filthy rich because our bedroom was at the other end of the hall to hers, and because Eoghan's work was flexible, if he really wanted me to scream, we did that stuff through the day.

Adjustments were key.

We were going through that at the moment because of Finn and Aoife too.

Dealing with the aftermath of their loss was one thing, but Eoghan had been tense since we'd returned from Ireland.

"You've been acting strangely since we got home. What is it? What's wrong?"

Finally, he looked at me, and though his face was the same, his eyes were...

I blinked.

They weren't just cold.

They were *frigid*.

He never looked at me that way.

The instinctive response was to back off, but because this was Eoghan, and we'd already been forged in fire, if anything, I tightened my arms around him.

"You can tell me anything, babe. There's nothing you've done or could do that would make me turn my back on you."

His mouth twisted into a sneer. "That's only because you don't know the half of what I've done."

"I know you were a sniper for the Forces. I know you're The Whistler." His muscles bunched at that. Obstinately, I stared him down, just prepared for him to argue with me. "I know what you are, Eoghan, and I love you anyway.

"I'm from the same world as you." I placed my hand on his stomach, the flat of it settling against the divots of his abdomen. "I'm not afraid."

"Maybe you should be," he rumbled, his head angled down. "If I were you, I would be. I'm a fucking monster."

"Where's this coming from?" I whispered, not liking to hear him talk about himself that way.

My father was a monster.

Eoghan was *not*.

"It's coming from nowhere," he denied. "I need to shower. I got shit to do today."

"You have to do me," I pointed out, trying to tease him, but it didn't work.

He didn't laugh.

I let go of him, feeling the brush of that cold shoulder like it was a gust of wind from Siberia, and watched as he placed the dumbbells down on the bench.

He grabbed the disinfectant from the place where he kept it, and I watched him clean up everything we'd touched during our workout.

He was usually anal about being clean, but he left this stuff for the help.

Today, however, he didn't, and I'd know—I watched him wipe every piece of equipment we'd used.

Eoghan even cleaned the damn disinfectant after he was finished, then he left the gym and me behind.

Not once had he looked at me since I'd slipped my arms around his waist.

Not once.

And seeing as I was wearing a sports bra that shaped my tits and biker shorts that made my ass look *fine*, that was confirmation right there that something funky was going on with my husband.

Traipsing after him, even more perturbed than before, I headed into the bathroom and watched him wade under the rainfall showerhead.

"Eoghan, I want to know what's wrong."

Did he know the level of courage I needed to face him with this? After the shaving disaster that Cammie had helped me with, we'd grown closer, but it was still hard approaching him with these things.

He never disrespected me, always celebrated me, applauded my strengths and did his best to shore up my weaknesses, but he'd never been like this before.

Not since we were married at any rate.

Even that night when Aela had come into our lives, when she'd asked for help from the O'Donnellys in freeing a man who'd been kidnapped by the *Famiglia*, and when Declan had been injured in the fray, Eoghan had opened up to me.

I knew he'd done some bad things that night, knew he'd taken some lives, and he'd broken down, but I'd been his soft place to land. Why wasn't he letting that happen now?

Staring at him, I started to strip off and I wandered under the water too. I grabbed the shower pouf he never used, splatted some body wash on it and then started to take over for him.

He heaved a sigh, grating out, "Inessa, I don't have time for this."

"You make time," I insisted, staring up at him as I smoothed the sponge over his shoulders.

His mouth tightened, but he held his tongue as I washed him.

He was so tense it was a wonder he didn't cramp up, and the distance between us felt like an ocean, but with every moment that passed, I felt him come back to me.

Dropping to my knees, I moved the sponge over his legs, careful to clean him how I knew he cleaned himself—he was anal in the shower too—and when I looked up at him from my position, his dick was in the way, and his eyes were on me.

Then he stunned the hell out of me by intoning, "Run."

Pretty certain that I'd misunderstood him, that he was asking me to bend over so he could launch himself at me, I muttered, "What?"

"Run, Inessa. Run."

His nostrils flared when I didn't obey, and then he started to count, and I had no idea why, but his somber tone had me releasing a nervous chuckle.

I got to my feet, staring into those wildly frigid eyes of his, and that was when my heart started to beat faster.

"Eoghan?"

He pushed his forehead against mine, his breath brushing against my lips as the heat and the steam from the shower curled around us.

"Run."

From him?

Never.

He must have seen the answer on my lips because he rasped, "Please."

I could never be scared of this man. *My man.* But I could see that, for whatever reason, *he* was scared.

Of himself.

Around me.

There was a plea in his eyes as he begged me silently, and while I didn't understand, I did as he bade.

Darting out of the shower, being as careful as I could on the tiles, I took off. The only trouble was, I had no idea where I was running to.

Was this role play?

It wasn't the first time he'd chased me, but it was the first time he'd acted so weird beforehand.

Starting for the kitchen, I rushed inside only to hear the shower cut off. Ears pricked, I heard him leave the bathroom and then he whispered, "You can run but you can't hide from me, Inessa."

Instead of feeling sickened by his words—if that was his intent—my nipples tightened, and I felt the blood rushing in my veins as he approached the kitchen.

Lungs burning, my fight-or-flight instincts kicked in. He watched me as he moved around the island, but it was different than usual.

I felt... *hunted.*

I veered the other way, rushing off and through the door into the dining room.

His hand snapped at mine, and he almost caught me. I let out a shocked laugh as I sped up, rushing around the table.

As I made it to the doorway, my mind raced with the peculiarity of what was happening, and it keyed me further into the fact that my husband was *not* okay.

Hearing his heavy footsteps behind me, I rushed inside the living room. I made to run between the sofas, but he followed me, cornering me, until I was backed up against the window.

My heart was pounding like crazy from the run and the weird adrenaline rush this had triggered, and because windows and I were friends, I'd admit, my core started to ache.

Standing there, in my birthday suit, completely naked as I stared at my also naked husband, I had no idea what was happening when I found myself getting turned on, but Eoghan wasn't similarly afflicted—his cock wasn't even hard as he approached me.

This wasn't about sex.

So what the hell was it about?

I felt the glass against my spine, so cold against my heated flesh, and I slid to the side as he came nearer.

This was Eoghan.

He'd never hurt me.

Pissing me off was another matter entirely.

Whatever *this* was, it was about him.

Whatever it was that was keeping him up at night. That had him flinching at sounds and wearing sunglasses outside even though it was getting dark at six.

"Eoghan. What's going on?"

"Inessa," he crooned, like I was the wild beast here, not him.

Something flickered in his eyes, some warmth, like he was coming back to me. As if he'd been somewhere else.

I knew he had PTSD—whether he thought he did or not was another matter entirely—but this was the first time it had manifested like this.

It spoke of my confidence in him that I took a leap of faith.

Literally.

I hurled myself at him, and while he jerked in surprise at the move, he managed to steady himself but it was too late.

We fell backwards thanks to my tackling him like we were playing a goddamn game of football, with the only consolation being that there was a soft landing as we collided with the sofa.

Then, he was on top of me, looming over me, his face an inch away from mine.

Brennan had taught me enough self-defense moves that I could reverse this position if need be, but Eoghan whispered, "Imagine being at the end of my crosshairs. Imagine not knowing that your life was about to end. Imagine not knowing that I see every move you make.

"Instead of landing on a sofa, you get a bullet to the chest or worse, to the head." His mouth tightened as he pressed his forehead against mine. "Can you imagine that?"

So that was what this was about!

He was scared of losing me.

My husband was beyond intelligent, but where emotions were concerned, he was a Neanderthal.

Love filled me, concern and need warring with it as I tried to figure out how to help him.

How to reassure him about something that was entirely out of my hands.

That wasn't an impossible feat, was it?

I went limp under him then let my legs come up to cup his, lifting my arms to embrace him as I asked, "Why do you want me to imagine all those things?"

"Because I..." He sucked in a breath, and as I looked into those beautiful eyes that had graced me with so much affection over the length of our marriage, I saw the way his pupils were constricted.

They were so tiny, it was like he'd done drugs, but I knew my husband. As much as this situation was an anomaly, he didn't do drugs.

The physiological response was out of his control, and it made me think about all the other stuff he'd been doing recently.

He'd had bad headaches. Had complained about hearing weird noises when our apartment was so high up, the only thing you could hear outside were birds.

He never watched the TV above volume 10 because anything else was too loud so Victoria and I always needed subtitles to hear the damn shows.

He cleaned.

He worked out. A lot.

But worse than anything, his gun had moved from the nightstand drawer to under his pillow.

That was why I'd initiated the conversation between us.

"Because?" I prompted gently, wishing I could wrap him up in my love and fix whatever the wars and the military had done to him.

All the O'Donnelly sons were messed up because of their dad, but I knew Eoghan had it harder because of his time as a soldier.

As I rubbed my nose against his cheek, he whispered, "They always let you think that's the last time, but it never is."

I tried to figure out what he was talking about but the only thing that made sense was impossible.

Or was it?

"Have you done a job recently?" I asked, the words dripping slowly from my mouth as I registered how ridiculous the question was.

Then he shocked me.

A breath escaped him. "Yes."

"When? In New York? I haven't heard anything on the news..."

"It started in Ireland," he choked out.

"On our honeymoon?" I screeched.

"Where do you think I was when you were at that spa overnight?"

"I just thought you went to play golf, Eoghan. I didn't think you'd gone off to kill someone!" I yelped, annoyed beyond belief.

Of course, that annoyance was founded more in the fact that he'd ruined our honeymoon with work rather than the fact someone had died by his hand—yes, I knew I had skewed priorities, but I was a daughter of the Bratva.

Death and life were the only certainties, not death and taxes. And for me, it seemed predestined that I would always be a part of a murder investigation wherever I went in the world.

My honeymoon was now the makings of an episode of CSI.

Enraged and hurting, my hands went to his shoulders to shove him away, but if anything, he seemed to grow heavier.

"Let me up," I snapped.

"No," he argued. "You wanted to know what was going on with me, well, now you know."

I narrowed my eyes at him. "You didn't have to take that job."

"Didn't you hear me? They always say it's the last time, but it never is."

"What are you talking about? Who the fuck are 'they?'"

"I'm talking about—" He sighed. "Christ. What does it even fucking matter?"

That was when he flopped back on the sofa, letting me up, and of course, that was when I didn't want to get up.

With his admission, everything shifted.

I rocked forward, leaning over him as much as he'd done me. Studying the fatigue on his face, a fatigue that had grown worse since our return, I reached up and touched the lines of strain streaking across his forehead.

My anger burned off, the fanned flames dissipating when I caught sight of those pinpricks for pupils, and I muttered, "I'm sorry I freaked out."

I didn't think I owed him an apology, but I'd learned that 'sorry' got a woman farther than bitter words ever could. Unfair, but that was life.

"You don't have to be sorry," he said with a sigh, his chin tipping forward. As our gazes connected, he asked, "Where's your phone?"

"Huh?"

"Where's your phone?" he repeated.

"I left it in the gym. Why?"

"Never mind." Eoghan reached up and slipped a strand of hair behind my ear that had fallen forward and drifted above him. I almost flinched, but I managed to contain it. Just. He saw it, of course. He saw everything, and the regret in his eyes was apology enough. "Are you more pissed that I worked on our honeymoon or that I killed someone?"

My cheeks pinkened, but I admitted, "That you worked."

His top lip quirked slightly. "You look so innocent. You are so innocent. But the life tainted you before I could protect you from it."

"Is that a complaint?" My tone was wary.

"No," he denied. "I'm a lucky bastard."

"At least you know it," I said promptly and earned another twitch of his lips.

"I do. I didn't mean to frighten you."

"You did mean to," I countered. "You only didn't because I know you too well."

"I wanted you to understand," he rumbled huskily.

"How could I?"

His throat worked. "Every time you leave the house, I think about my enemies, and my family's enemies, potentially paying someone to do exactly what I do and for you to be at the end of the crosshairs. Do you know what that does to me?"

I frowned. "So this *is* to do with me going to college?"

"A little, but I'm not about to stop you from living." His nostrils flared. "There's no life to be had when you're trapped in a gilded cage."

"I have guards," I offered, well aware that if he were my father, gilded cage or not, I'd be locked up faster than I could say, 'No.'

"You do," he agreed.

"They don't protect me from snipers though, do they?" I whispered, our eyes still locked and loaded on each other.

"No." He breathed the word. "No, they don't."

"Am I at risk?"

"Not as far as I know, but you don't have to be for me to worry about you. Look at Christmas. What happened at the house. Look what happened with Savannah. There are no assurances."

My arms tightened around him. "You could be hurt too," I pointed out.

"I could," he agreed. "Look at Aoife. She didn't even have to leave her apartment to hurt. Life is pain."

His words made something inside me ache.

I cupped his chin and whispered, "That way of thinking is as much of a cage as this apartment could be for me."

For the first time, I felt a barrier between us, and I didn't want that so I knew I needed to prod.

Eoghan was the kind of man you could do that with. He wouldn't slap me if I asked the wrong question, he'd just tell me he couldn't answer.

He wasn't my father.

Cautiously, I questioned, "You said that they let you think it's the last time, but it never is. Who were you talking about? Who hired you?"

"They don't hire you; they recruit you," he corrected wearily.

Brow puckered, I questioned, "Who does?"

"Government agencies."

I processed that. "You work for, what? The CIA?"

"Something like that." He reached up and pressed a finger to my lips. "Best not to ask questions."

"Even though whatever they made you do hurt you?"

For a second, I wasn't sure if he was going to answer, then he said, "There are three people in this world who are as good a shot as me."

"Three?" More proof he wasn't my father. Papa was the best at everything. Always.

He nodded. "When I was in Ireland, I was sent to a small town, and after I set myself up, I realized I wasn't alone."

"You weren't alone," I repeated. "You mean, one of them was there as well?"

"I mean two of them were there, Inessa. Two. Do you know how fucking crazy that is? Three sharpshooters for one job?"

"Jeez. Who were the people you were targeting? Al Qaeda?"

"No. It doesn't matter."

"Doesn't it?" I argued.

"No, it doesn't. But I realized something."

"What?"

"I might never have come home to you."

I stilled. "They were targeting you?"

"They might have been, but they weren't. The people at the end of my scope were like me, snipers for hire... it could so easily have been me who was slotted to die that day." He leaned up slightly and pressed his mouth to mine. "I was embroiled in an international incident in the making, and as I dealt with the politics, all I wanted was to come home."

"To me," I whispered.

"Yes," he growled, the words torn from him.

I felt his love.

His fear for me.

His rage that I could be hurt.

His need to have me by his side.

His admission was so raw and real that it had me clambering over him as I straddled his hips.

Looming above him, my hair flying around us in a curtain, I whispered, "I always want you to come home to me."

"I may not be able to do that one day."

The pain in his eyes made tears burn in mine. "You need to make sure you do. You're not allowed to leave me, Eoghan."

"I can't control that, sweetheart. I lost that ability a long time ago when I was recruited."

I bit my lip. "I-I don't want you to go."

His hands slipped down to my hips. "I don't want to go either."

"Are we in danger now?"

"I wasn't in danger in the first place," he reasoned. "But I could have been. It never mattered before—"

A cry escaped me. "Of course it mattered! If you'd died, we'd never have had this! We'd never have been together. I'd never have known you and what it was to love you and be loved by you." I grabbed his shoulders. "And what would your mom and dad have done? They'd have lost it even more than they already have." I felt the tears pouring down my cheeks and knew they landed on his face, but they ran unchecked, and we both let them. "Eoghan, you might feel alone, and in those situations, you might be alone, but you're not. *You're not.* You never have been."

His mouth worked before he admitted, "How can we have a family, Inessa? I know you're not ready for one, and I'm not either, but in the future, how can we? I can't protect you from life and miscarriages and—"

This was about me.

Not him.

Not his own safety.

About mine.

This man, this control freak. My husband. The love of my life.

I pressed my mouth to his in a gentle kiss before I whispered, "You stand by my side, Eoghan. You do what Finn's doing. You be there. You show up. Nothing more, nothing less."

Before he could answer, I slipped my tongue along the curve of his lips, and as he parted them, I coaxed his into playing as I felt his cock stirring against me.

Whatever the hell this had started as, it had morphed as it always would, into him and me coming together, exposing our fears and baring our souls.

His hands rubbed the curve of my ass, his fingers pressing inward as they dipped between the cheeks, the tips slanted toward my labia.

As I rocked my hips, encouraging him to explore, I pulled back from our kiss and told him, "I want you by my side, Eoghan. Forever. Do you understand me?" I nipped his bottom lip to punctuate the point, and he growled beneath his breath. "I'm in love with you. I'll always be in love with you. You do what you have to do, what you're obliged to do, and I will never judge you for it. But you will come back to me. Always. Understand?"

His lips twitched into a smile that didn't reach his eyes. "Bossy."

I shrugged. "You knew that already."

His thumb stroked along the curve of my cheek. "You shouldn't trust me."

"You're the world's boogeyman, but not mine."

His nostrils flared as he leaned up to connect our mouths, and before I knew it, he was flipping us over so I was lying on my back on the sofa. It was like before, yet not. If anything, it was night and day.

When his hips slipped between my legs, I grasped a hold of him with my thighs, moaning when he bound us together, sliding into me with an ease that came as a shock.

I didn't think I should have been this wet, but hell, my body was as confused as my mind. Something that was compounded by his lack of movement as he stayed there, his cock burrowed away in my warmth as he hovered above me, his mouth brushing mine just, our noses kissing barely.

That seemed to go on for a lifetime. For hours and hours, months and years until I broke.

I caved in and whispered, "Eoghan?"

My hands moved over his head, nails scraping through his hair.

"Inessa?"

"Do you love me?"

"You know I do."

"That's all that matters." I tightened my thighs around him. "We're in this together."

"For better or worse?"

"Exactly."

"You're getting a raw deal."

"I don't think so. At least, I don't usually." My heels dug into his butt. "Baby, please," I panted. "Move."

He ignored me—of course, he did—and instead, he bridged our hands together and rested them over my head. "I have this core deep inside me, Inessa. It's ice cold. It never used to get warm until you. You're dangerous for me."

"You're dangerously in love with me," I countered as a wicked smile curved my lips.

"You should be going into PR, not interior design," he rumbled.

As I registered how surreal this conversation was, a conversation that seemed to be occurring despite the fact his cock was being soaked by my pussy, I rasped, "Maybe I'll do that after."

"Maybe you will," he agreed, confirming what I already knew—that he'd never hold me back—just as he urged our mouths into colliding.

His hips slowly started to rock, but each time, he barely moved inside me. I felt the vibration as I moaned into his mouth, which made him speed up.

Not much, not enough.

I groaned as he explored me, tasting me, savoring me, and I clenched his fingers hard to encourage him to quicken even more.

That was when he obeyed my silent demand.

From mega slow to super fast, I felt the change of pace like he'd taken me from zero to sixty in his Aston Martin.

He fucked me, all the while he stayed bound to me through our kiss and hands. The way my pelvis was arched, every thrust of his dick had him grinding into my mons, and I cried out when his fucking had me tearing my lips from his and screaming out my release just as he growled and poured his seed into me.

It was different than usual. Instead of feeling like I was soaring, it felt as if it tied me to him. As if he flew and I grounded him. But different wasn't bad. Different was just new.

I guessed that made sense.

Eoghan might be my hero, but every hero needed a heroine too, no?

Carefully, I nipped at his mouth, gently kissing him, sucking on his bottom lip as his hips twitched and his cock spasmed inside me while I breathed in Russian, "*Ty moyo schást'ye.*"

I half-expected him to ask me what that meant, but my husband was ever full of surprises as he pressed a kiss to my temple, and against my skin murmured, "You're my happiness too."

And as much as this morning had rattled me, that soothed the wounds he'd given me, eased the aches.

Just like I knew he always would.

FINN

"FINN?" I stared out of the window, looking at nothing as Eoghan mumbled in my ear, "For fuck's sake, are you listening?"

"I'm listening."

"You really sound like it. Jesus."

"What are you whining about now?"

"Ma asked me to ask you when I should pick up Jake. Why she couldn't just call you herself, I don't fucking know."

I rubbed my eyes, feeling even more exhausted than before. The last few days hadn't been easy, but now Aoife was back home, things felt both settled and chaotic.

The apartment was too quiet without Jake, but he was so rambunctious and Aoife was so fragile... I didn't even dare hug her. I just held her hand when she let me, feeling like a complete and utter failure as I wished I could do something to make this better, wished like fuck I could take away her pain, all while knowing I couldn't do dick.

"Aoife and Lena have had a falling out," I rasped eventually, staring into the sky where a cluster of birds were flying in a 'V' formation.

"They have? Since when?" Eoghan queried, his surprise clear. "I didn't think Aoife had spoken to anyone."

The family gossip mill was churning along as per fucking usual, it seemed.

Only three days had passed since Aoife had come home from the hospital, but it felt like an eternity had drifted by us too.

"Does it matter?" I heaved a sigh. "What a goddamn week, Eoghan."

"I'm—"

"Don't say you're sorry."

"Why not? I am."

"So am I. I'm overdosing on that word. Sorry won't bring Imogen back."

"Aoife named her?"

"*We* named her," I growled.

"Does that help?"

"Doesn't fucking help me, but it does Aoife. That's all that matters."

If anything, thinking of her, when Imogen would never exist anywhere other than in our imaginations, hurt as badly as what had happened to me as a kid.

Never in my wildest dreams would I have thought that was possible, but it was.

Rubbing the back of my neck, I muttered, "You don't need to hear any of this shit. I'd appreciate it if you could bring Jake home. Lena will have a car seat."

"If I can help, I will. You know that. I was only bitching because Ma was being cagey. I got your back, Finn."

"I know you do. Same goes."

"What time should I come around?"

"Whenever's easiest for you." I placed my hand against the glass and leaned into the window. "You don't realize how quiet a place is until they're not hanging around. I swear, Eoghan, kids... they'll break your fucking heart."

"They're terrifying."

I knew what he meant. "They are," I agreed. "They're so goddamn breakable. It's a wonder we even make it to adulthood."

"Inessa and I will head upstate within the hour, okay? He'll be home before dark."

"Don't mean to cramp your style, but you can't take the Aston Martin."

He snorted. "I'm not that dumb."

My lips curved of their own volition. "I needed to hear something funny today."

"Fuck you." He grunted. "Sorry. Shouldn't have said that."

"Why not? We never stand on goddamn ceremony, do we?" The soft tapping of footsteps came to my attention, and I turned away from the window and stormed over to the hall. "Eoghan, I gotta go. See you later."

"Yeah. See you later."

Dumping my cellphone on the table, I headed out into the hall and saw Aoife slinking into the kitchen. I managed to snag her hand and tug her to a halt.

Since she'd miscarried, neither of us had mentioned the weekend before when shit had hit the fan, but we weren't talking as much as we should.

I didn't know if that was because of the secrets I'd kept or if it was a genuine silence that came from grief.

"You shouldn't be up," I chided. "You need to be back in bed."

Dressed in one of the nightgowns she only wore out of bed, or when she was sick, she looked so washed out with the white cotton against her pale skin.

Her auburn hair was a stark contrast to the white, and I saw just how much weight she'd lost, how gaunt her cheeks were, the shadows beneath her eyes.

"I need to do something."

"What do you need to do?" I countered.

"Work."

I narrowed my gaze upon her. "Work? What kind of work?"

"My work." Her frown turned stubborn. "Louise is coming over. Would you mind going downstairs and grabbing the receipts she's brought with her?"

"Are you joking?"

"Do I look like I'm busting a gut over here?"

My mouth tightened, and for a second, we waged a silent war. Her daring me to say anything, *anything* at all. Me trying to keep my fucking mouth shut.

I felt my blood pressure creep up as we stared at each other, me longing to say the words—*I'll spank your ass if you don't get back into bed.* But I was here on borrowed mercy.

I knew that.

She fucking knew that.

We both goddamn knew that.

I stared her down far longer than she stared me down, her gaze drifting away to the counter as she slithered off to the refrigerator and began pulling out butter and eggs then headed to the pantry for flour and sugar.

Hovering there, watching her, I knew I was standing on a tightrope.

A man like me was not built for a tightrope.

One false move and I'd fall.

But I was destined to fall anyway.

The buzzer saved me.

I was on the brink of striding over there and hauling her over my goddamn shoulder and getting her back into bed but she muttered, "That'll be Louise."

"Why the fuck are you doing the accounts, anyway?" I snapped. "Hire an accountant."

She snarled, "Because it's my business, and I like doing it. It's relaxing."

"You'll be missing out on a shit ton of tax breaks. I set you up with Jenkins, didn't I?"

"I chose not to use him."

Jenkins, the guy I'd used for a long time for my own personal accounts, would be hearing from me about that.

"Why would you choose not to use him?"

"Because I wanted to know that I'd done this on my own, so I get Jen to do most of the filing and sort out the rest." Her chin tipped up. "She supervises things, don't worry. This way, though, I know that the bakery is where it is because of me."

"It would have been that anyway. The place is nothing without your recipes." I narrowed my eyes at her, well aware that she didn't go in as often as she used to because of... well, being pregnant. "You'd better not even think about going into the bakery until the doctor says you're ready."

She sniffed. "Why do you think Louise is here? I'm not an idiot, Finn. I know not to push until I'm ready, but that doesn't mean I can laze about in bed all day and night. I'll go crazy.

"When are you going to get Jake anyway? I miss him."

"Eoghan's bringing him tonight."

"Eoghan?"

"I'm not leaving you." I pursed my lips before I growled, "Good thing seeing as I'd come back and you'd probably have headed into the bakery for the first shift."

She slammed the flour jar on the counter. "I lost Imogen, Finn, not my brain."

"You're grieving."

"So? Aren't you?"

"Yeah, another reason why I'm not hard at work in my office, dammit. You think I can focus—" My voice cracked at that, and she stopped slamming more shit on the counters to turn and face me.

Aoife and Jake and our family were the only source of normalcy in my life. When there was chaos here, it triggered a butterfly effect.

Naturally, her grief was more detrimental than mine, and she was the one who needed looking after, but she wasn't alone in her suffering.

Her lips quivered as she looked at me, seeming to see that she wasn't the only one drowning, and she whispered, "Oh, Finn—"

I swallowed down her pity and stepped back and away, not able to deal with what was happening right now. I heard her call out my name, but I ignored her and headed to the elevator when it buzzed again like the annoyance it was.

If she were anyone else, if it were Billy, for example, I'd have let Louise come up to the penthouse. I didn't like her though. Aoife trusted her, but that didn't mean I had to.

Pressing my back to the wall, I stared at my reflection as I descended to the lobby.

"When did you start looking so fucking old?" I rasped under my breath.

"Do you want a statistical analysis on that?"

"What the fuck?" I growled, peering up at the elevator ceiling as I straightened. "Conor? Is that you?"

"Yup, it's me. I can run your pictures through a program and give you a time lapse if you want."

"A time lapse of what?" I snapped.

"We can pinpoint when you started to look ancient."

"Beating the shit out of you would be one way to ease my goddamn mood, Kid. Watch yourself. What the hell are you even doing?"

Warily, I eyed the console where the speaker was then looked up at the magic eye in the ceiling.

He sniffed. "I was doing routine updates."

"Nothing's routine about you."

"That didn't sound like a compliment, Finn."

"That's because it wasn't." As the elevator approached the lobby, I growled under my breath with impatience as, barely thirty seconds later, the doors opened.

I saw her immediately, and everything about her put me on edge. I wasn't sure how Aoife didn't see it, but I sure as fuck did.

The first time I'd had the misfortune of meeting her, she'd had blonde hair.

Now, she was auburn, and she wore green goddamn contacts too. She'd started wearing her hair in a similar style as Aoife, and the clothes weren't exact replicas because my wife's wardrobe was expensive, but Louise did what she could within her budget.

The second she saw me, she smiled and strolled over to me.

"What's Aoife doing in the lobby?"

Conor's voice was softer now, as sotto voce as he got, and that he'd mistaken her for Aoife pissed me off even more.

"Louise," I greeted curtly.

"Finn." Her smile dampened down as she gave me an apologetic look. "I was so sorry to hear about Aoife and the baby." She reached out and pressed her hand to my arm. "If there's *anything* I can do, just let me know."

In the background, I heard a gagging sound.

How I managed not to smile, I'd never know.

Louise jerked in surprise. "What was that?"

I shrugged, but primarily, it was to get rid of her hand on my arm which was clinging on like she'd stuck it there with Gorilla glue. "What was what?"

Her brow furrowed, but she pinpointed me with her attention. "How are you doing, Finn?"

"My wife just lost our child, Louise. How do you think I'm doing?" Though she flinched, I ignored it and demanded, "Aoife said you had some accounts for her?"

"Yeah. Here they are."

As she handed me a box, she gave me a limpid smile that I also ignored as I asked, "Why couldn't you email these over?" I opened the lid and peered inside. "It's just a bunch of receipts."

"The system isn't online."

I nodded my understanding and retreated into the elevator. As I did, she joined me. Her audacity had me snarling, "Did I invite you in here?"

"Well, no, but I wanted to visit Aoife..." Her voice waned.

"Not today," I dismissed. "Maybe some other time."

"Oh, but I'd really like to catch up with her."

"She's not feeling up to it." Whether Aoife would agree with me or not was another matter entirely. Regardless, *I* wasn't damn well capable of dealing with her cooing and simpering over a coffee. I dismissed her by saying, "I'll pass on your well-wishes to her."

She shot me a disappointed look. "Oh, okay, then."

As she stepped back and out into the lobby, I didn't even have to tap the button for the doors to close.

"Thank you, Kid," I told Conor the second we were ascending.

"My pleasure. Want me to arrange for their system to go online?"

"Please."

"I tried to do it a few years back, but Aoife wouldn't let me."

"Yeah, well, I'm not asking her, and neither are you."

"Good, good. I'll be discreet."

I snorted. "Yeah, I just saw you being discreet. What was that gagging about?"

"Am I the only one getting *Single White Female* vibes here?"

If I wasn't pissed, I'd have laughed. "You're not."

"She wants to fuck you."

"I know," was my grim reply.

"Aoife doesn't see that?"

"No."

"She looks like Aoife."

"Yeah, a watered-down version."

Like the diet version of anything when full fat always tasted and looked that much better.

"What's that about?"

"God knows, but Aoife doesn't see it, and I'm not about to cause a problem for her that isn't necessary. I see the freak a couple of times a year, and Aoife says she's good at her job."

We could agree to disagree with that one.

Conor hummed under his breath. "It's weird."

"You think I don't know that?"

"Well, I'm just making sure you do."

I grunted as the penthouse floor approached. "Ever fucking helpful."

"Here if you need me, Finn."

His words had me tensing up. No apologies or commiserations from Conor. Not because he wasn't polite but because he had his own way of working.

"I know, Kid. I know." I reached up and rubbed my forehead, wondering why he was the easiest to talk to when he was the craziest. "My whole fucking world feels like it's collapsing under my feet."

"It is. For the moment. You'll find solid ground soon. You and Aoife are too strong to let this tear you apart."

My throat was too tight to reply, so I just nodded. But as the doors opened, I finally managed to grate out, "I hope you're right."

THIRTY-FOUR

AOIFE

THE SECOND I heard Senior's voice, I cringed. Deep inside.

It was stupid.

Ridiculous.

But I was just waiting to hear Lena. And the reason it was ridiculous was because they were talking business, and just as always, business wasn't discussed around the womenfolk so it wasn't like I'd hear her voice anyway.

But the dread was there.

Dread I disliked feeling.

My phone pinged with a text from Jen, but though I recognized the ringtone, I didn't look at the screen. My focus was too intent on the call, on listening to who was speaking rather than the content of the conversation.

When Finn eventually put the phone down, I realized that I'd been listening to that damn phone call for forty-five minutes.

"Mommy's getting obsessed," I told Jake who clambered into my arms when I swooped down to pick him up.

He garbled away at me, totally uninterested in what I was doing, and I hugged him to me, enjoying the feel of him in my arms, the weight of him.

He was so solid.

So strong.

So healthy and alive.

My throat closed as I pressed a kiss to his forehead.

The second I did, he started scrambling to get down, and it was as crazy as me listening to a damn phone call, waiting to see if my husband was lying about cutting ties with the woman who'd raised him better than his own mother had, but my eyes pricked with tears.

I could feel them welling on the lash line, ready to spill over.

Pushing my back against the wall, I let myself droop, let it take my weight as I slid to the ground.

I slipped my arms around my knees and hugged myself while Jake carried on playing at my side, proving that he didn't want to be far away from me, just didn't want to be hugged for the millionth time today.

Staring at him, watching him, so goddamn grateful for him, I sucked in a sharp breath after a good ten minutes of doing nothing other than that and reached for my cell phone.

Jen had called and texted me so many times over the past week, but I'd been a shitty friend and had let it go to voicemail and had often ignored her messages.

When Finn's phone rang again, I knew I'd go insane if I kept on listening to him, so I found Jen's number and called her.

Her voice was frantic as she hissed, "Where the hell have you been?"

I closed my eyes. "Sleeping mostly."

"I tried to visit but the doorman said you weren't in," she complained.

I bit my lip, well aware that Finn had likely vetoed any visits from friends or family. I couldn't be angry, though. I just couldn't be. I didn't want to see anyone, didn't even want to talk to anyone.

Not even Finn or Jake.

I wanted to watch them.

Know they were safe. Sound. But I didn't want to talk.

Words got me nowhere.

Feelings got me nowhere.

Because she'd bitch if she knew Finn was behind it, I lied, "Finn told me."

"Five times this week, Aoife," she grumbled. "I know you're sad, sweetheart, but that's what I'm for. I cheer you up. It's like my job."

I chuckled, but the sound was watery. "Better than Prozac, that's you."

God, if only that were true.

"Damn straight," she joked before her tone softened and she asked, "How are you feeling?"

"Been better, been worse."

There, that didn't sound too pathetic, did it?

Didn't broadcast that I was going insane over the secrets my husband had kept, didn't reveal shit I couldn't talk about even with her.

"Only natural," she said softly before a knock sounded at her door and she called out, "One second!"

I shouldn't have felt relieved, but I did. "You're busy," I told her. "I should go."

"No, it's okay—"

"I'll speak with you later. I just wanted you to know I was fine."

God could strike me down for that lie and I wouldn't have blamed him.

"Take care, darling," she whispered, but I didn't have the words to reply so I cut the line.

Blowing out a breath, I pressed my face to my knees and tilted my head to the side so I could do what I really wanted to do—watch my son be healthy, happy, and safe.

And if I cried, he didn't know. He was none the wiser. He was just pleased that he had all my attention and that he was at the epicenter of my love.

My cell buzzed, and disinterestedly, I turned my head to look at the screen.

Alan: *I'm so sorry, Aoife. I just heard the news.*

Nausea swirled inside me, and the urge to hurl my phone across the room hit me hard. My nails dug into my thighs as I fought the urge, but then I heard footsteps in the hall.

Distracted, I didn't have it in me to get up, to put on a façade, I just stayed where I was, slumped with my back to the wall, but Finn surprised me by joining me.

I didn't know if it was because of Lena or if it was because we'd lost Imogen, but he kept on shocking me by doing things I didn't expect of him.

He was being infinitely patient, which definitely wasn't in his nature, and it was beginning to freak me out.

When Finn didn't say a word after a couple minutes, I asked, "What did Senior want?"

"You could hear?"

I hummed.

"He was talking about business. He asked about you," he said after a moment's hesitation.

"Of course he did. I'm the useless broodmare who can't carry a grandchild to term without—"

"Don't you dare say that again. Not within hearing distance of me," he snarled, startling Jake and making him burst into tears.

"You frightened him," I told him coldly.

When I held out my arms, Jake, wailing all the while, hurled himself at me, and I took full advantage of hugging him like I wanted to.

"You needed to hear that. I wanted Imogen, Aoife. I wanted her with every bone in my body, but you—" He shook his head. "I know you put yourself at risk. I know you should have had a termination."

I tensed up. "I don't want to talk about it."

"No? Tough shit. We need to talk about it. We need to talk about the fact that you put yourself in danger when Jake and I can't fucking function without you."

I could feel the tears lodge themselves in my throat like I'd swallowed an orange whole. "Don't be ridiculous."

"Ridiculous? Look at him, Aoife. He's a baby. What would he do without you? If you think having children is the only reason I married you, you're wrong. I married you, Aoife. *You*. Not your goddamn womb."

"Why don't I think Senior agrees?" I retorted, even though his words were a punch to the gut.

I knew he meant them. I knew that. So why did I feel like such a failure?

"He didn't say anything about that. He wanted to know if we were coming on Sunday. If you were ready for that or not. I told him you're not."

"Maybe I want to go."

"What?" he drawled. "You want to go and eat dinner with the woman who—"

"The woman who murdered my mother?" I queried as sweet as saccharine, watching his eyes narrow upon me.

It wasn't the first time I'd invoked his anger, but I knew I was testing his temper. Testing *him*.

His fury poured out of him in great waves, and the heat of it warmed the parts of me that felt frozen solid.

My husband was one of the most controlled men I'd ever known, but around me, I knew I could shatter that control.

I wanted that.

I wanted him to be as shattered as I was, and I didn't care if that made me a bitch or not.

"We're not going on Sunday."

His flat tone got my back up.

The last thing I wanted was to break bread with fucking Lena, but that he was telling me I couldn't go made me determined *to* go.

"We are. Jake misses her."

His nostrils flared. "We'll talk about this later when you're in a better mood."

"This is about as 'better' as I get," I retorted, kissing Jake's head when he finally stopped crying and began to suck on his thumb. "You should know that by now."

Finn sucked in a breath, and just when I expected to be hissed at again, he rumbled, "I don't know what the hell you're doing, sweetheart, fucking with my temper, trying to addle my self-control, but it won't stop me from looking out for you.

"If you haven't realized yet, you're the priority here."

I didn't look at him. "If I'm the priority, then we should do what I want."

"You don't want to go to the compound."

"Maybe I do."

He squinted at me, and I could feel his brain ticking away as he tried to figure out what I was thinking. If I didn't feel so messed up, I'd have laughed.

If I needed proof that men were from fucking Mars and women were from Venus, I had it.

"Do you want to start a fight? Is that it?" he asked, the words coming out slowly as if he were still trying to reason it out.

"Daddy's so smart when he wants to be, Jake, isn't he?" I crooned, my gaze on Finn now.

"Fine," was his gruff reply as he started to get to his feet. "If that's the way you want it, we'll go on Sunday.

"If you want to set the dinner table on fire, throw her roasted chicken into the trash, and grab the TV off the wall, we'll go." His arms flailed up into the air in a move I was starting to see more and more often, as if he were washing his hands of trying to understand me. "If that'll make you feel better, we'll even drive over her fucking flowerbeds—"

"That sounds like a trip."

"A trip to the ER," he ground out, shaking his head. "I'll tell Senior to expect us." He stormed off, but I heard him mutter, "And to expect fucking fireworks too."

Though Jake jolted when he slammed the door, my lips curved. "We're gonna have a blast on Sunday, aren't we, baby? Daddy's got the best ideas."

Just thinking of our Range Rover sliding into her beloved flowerbeds was enough to ease my mood.

I didn't see why Lena shouldn't suffer some of my misery too.

PART 4

THIRTY-FIVE

PAST

AIDAN SR.

AS I FINALLY SETTLED LENA INTO bed, I held her tight to me as she sobbed against my chest.

It had been a long fucking day, and I knew it would be a long fucking night.

It was right what they said—there was no rest for the wicked.

I hadn't earned my rest, and in seeking atonement, I'd caused my wife, the love of my life, to commit the worst sin of all, earning damnation for us both if I couldn't get her to church for confession.

Pressing my lips to her forehead, I rocked her against me.

I'd doped her up with a couple Valium, and she was drowsing against me, however I was in no rush. Michael was downstairs, but he could wait until the heavens and the earth started burning for all I cared.

When her silent sobs ceased and she rested, I closed my eyes. "You'll be safe, my darling. You'll be safe. I'll make sure of it."

Guilt lashed at me like a whip, and as I let go of her and rolled off the bed, I felt every single one of my years as I straightened.

Peering down at her, seeing that she was resting, I heaved a sigh and headed out of the room.

The ECD and I had a fragile understanding.

I stayed out of their business, they stayed out of mine, and together, we worked toward a unified Ireland.

So far, I'd only been in their debt to a certain extent. There were

Five Pointers who were *cheiles*, and one of them guarded my wife. That was about as much as I owed.

But the scales had just tipped out of my favor.

As I trudged downstairs, I headed into the living room where Michael was sitting. He had his feet up against the coffee table and, beside his shiny leather Oxfords, there was a bottle of my finest whiskey.

That immediately set the tone.

I didn't like it, but I didn't have a choice.

He smiled at me, a smile that set my teeth on edge and had my top lip snarling up with distaste.

"Spit it out," I snapped. "What do you want?"

"That's a loaded question if ever there was one," Michael drawled as he dragged out a pack of cigarettes from his pocket. "I mean, what do I want? I suppose it all depends on what you're willing to do to make sure I keep Lena's secret."

I narrowed my eyes upon him. "She'll never see the inside of a jail cell. No matter what you fucking do or say."

He shrugged. "I like Lena. I've always liked her. She's good people."

She was. That was the kicker. She'd been good people when I dragged her into this marriage. She'd been good people when she whacked me on the head with a rolling pin. That had only changed when the Aryans had gotten to her. And whose goddamn fault was that?

Mine.

Mine for giving a boy a man's job.

Grinding my teeth, I snagged the bottle beside his feet and pressed it to my lips.

Swallowing a big gulp down, I let the fire consume me. "What do you want, Michael?"

"Eamonn's getting soft," he murmured into his glass, referencing the leader of the ECD.

I actually liked Eamonn. He had reasons for being the way he was, reasons that were beyond honorable, and his loyalty went soul deep.

This fucker? Not so much.

I watched as Michael swirled the amber liquid around the crystal tumbler. "We should be taking advantage of what's to come, planning accordingly, but he's more interested in seeing how the politicians will fuck things up."

"And you're not interested in letting the lawmen pave the future for the country?" I guessed.

He sneered at me. "Are you? With O'Leary in power?"

I wanted a unified Ireland as much as the next man, but I wasn't as zealous as these ECD bastards.

I'd never regret making Lena my own, but I sure as fuck wished her father hadn't been the leader of these nutcases.

Wifing her had drawn me into this mess, and betraying her had only deepened it. Maybe that was exactly what I deserved.

No sin should go unpunished.

"Brexit's going to stir the Troubles to life again," he predicted, his mouth forming a sneer. "Hard borders, soft borders, whatever the fuck it is—it's our land and the British want to control if we can access the North.

"Do I want to wait on the politicians? No. I don't. But with the right people in power in the US, maybe they can help steer those assholes into siding with us."

Though I knew what he was talking about, I shook my head. "Davidson's the only future president in our pocket, and it's not likely he'll fall on his sword for this cause."

"Leave that to me."

I narrowed my eyes at him. "What do you want from me?"

"It's time for someone else to take charge of the *Éire le chéile go deo.* Someone working on the ground. Someone who's been a second-in-command for too fucking long."

I wanted to sneer at him, but I couldn't.

My hands were goddamn tied.

"Mutiny'll get you killed if you fail," I informed him as I took a deep sip of whiskey.

"I won't fail."

"Eamonn's kept the *cheiles* together since the late eighties when Cormac lost it, Michael. If you think you'll get them on your side without a struggle, you're stupid."

"That's where you come in. Not only are you going to back me up, not only are you going to help me, but if you're right and I can't turn them, you're going to make sure that Eamonn doesn't kill me."

"That's a lot of requests from a man skating on thin ice."

Michael smirked at me. "The only person skating on thin ice, Aidan, is Lena."

THIRTY-SIX

BRENNAN

PRESENT

"DO you think Aoife and Finn will come today?"

I stared at Camille in bewilderment. "It's Sunday dinner."

She arched a brow. "So? She wasn't here last week."

"She was in the hospital. That's different. This is tradition we're talking about."

"She just had a miscarriage, Brennan."

"It's Sunday dinner," I repeated. "You don't miss Sunday dinner."

"You don't understand women," she groused.

"I understand you."

"Barely."

My lips curved. "You didn't say that last night."

She grumbled something in Russian under her breath then asked, "Why do you even call it Sunday dinner when it's two PM?"

"I don't know." I shrugged. "We've just always called it that. She'll be here," I predicted.

"She's grieving. She's bound to be in pain."

"Roasted chicken, gravy, and potatoes fix all wounds."

"You're being obtuse on purpose," she complained.

Laughing, I hauled her against me, letting her feel my boner as I grabbed her ass. "I do most things with a purpose."

Waspishly, she informed me, "I will have sex with you in most places, Brennan, but not in your mother's living room."

"Do I look as if I have a death wish?"

She squinted at me. "What does that look like? The same as constipation?"

"Funny, very funny," I teased, smirking at her and giving her ass a final tap before I positioned her under my arm. "Why do you like this room so much?" I asked after a second.

To me, this was the same as having a bunch of mugshots on the walls.

Ma had hundreds upon goddamn hundreds of photos here, so many that you couldn't see if it was wallpaper or paint beneath the frames.

We were all there in various stages of childhood and adulthood, sometimes cleaned up, sometimes looking like we'd been dragged through a dirt pile in the backyard.

Finn's cold stare peered back at me from beneath the brim of a graduation cap as he held up his diploma, looking about as cheerful as the sun during a blizzard.

Conor's cocky smirk beamed at me too, but he held about a million diplomas in his hands.

Around them, there were also shots of my uncles and my grandparents on both sides.

"This is your family," Camille explained.

"I know it is," I retorted.

"Well, I like seeing them. They're my family too."

"Poor you," I joked even as I squeezed her. "They're pains in the ass, but they'll kill for you so that's better than that piece of shit father of yours, I guess."

She tilted into me so she could rest her hand on my stomach. "They are my pains in the ass too."

"They are." I bopped the tip of her nose with a kiss. "You ready to eat?"

"Ten thousand different vegetables and potatoes four ways?" she mocked. "Sure."

Grinning, I started to make my way out of the room, and it was quite by chance that I saw it.

Hovering in front of one of the picture frames, this one in a spotty black and white, I squinted as I took in my grandfather on Ma's side.

"What is it? He's your grandfather, right?"

Humming under my breath in confirmation, I pointed at his arm. "You see that?"

"It's a tattoo."

"It is."

"Wasn't Lena's grandfather a wealthy man?"

I peered down at her. "How do you know that?"

She sniffed. "I was Russian Bratva—"

"Past tense is right, baby," I slotted in with a growl.

"—they do their homework on the enemy. I know plenty of things about our family that I learned before they were mine," she tacked on dryly.

I grunted, "Nice save."

"Yeah, I'm pleased with it too." She squinted at the picture. "Wealthy men didn't have tattoos back then, did they?"

I moved us closer, trying to make out what was happening in the picture, saying, "I guess they could do whatever they wanted."

Grandfather had his shirt off and was wearing a wifebeater beneath it. He was laughing as he ducked his face into a barrel of apples as he bobbed for them.

All around him, there were boys—Ma came from a bigger family than ours—and they were laughing too. Some had wet hair that had nothing to do with Brylcreem and everything to do with a turn in the barrel.

"They have tattoos as well," Camille pointed out.

She wasn't wrong.

Brow furrowed as I tried to make out what the tattoo said, I heard laughter coming from the hall before Conor hurried in.

"You have to see this," he boomed as he ran over to the window.

Not wasting a second, we joined him. I was well aware that one of the last times we'd been huddled around a fucking window in this house, we'd been waiting for a goddamn battalion of Sparrows trying to smoke us out.

On this occasion, however, there was no truck full of soldiers.

There was Finn's Range Rover.

I didn't even have it in me to be smug over the fact that I was right about Sunday dinner being sacred in this house, not when said Range Rover was making donuts in the front yard.

"What the fuck is he doing?"

Conor hooted. "I don't give a shit. Oh, my God! I'm jealous as hell. Why didn't he let me jump in the back?"

Camille's unease was clear. "Are they stoned?"

"Not with Jake in the car," I disregarded immediately.

Conor pointed out, "Maybe he's not with them."

"Who else would they leave him with? Aela's in the kitchen with Ma," I argued.

"True," he muttered before he started cackling when the Range Rover surged forward, mowing through Ma's prized flowerbeds.

"What the actual fuck?" I rasped, watching as Finn pulled a J-turn and rammed into what, in the spring, would house Ma's favorite daffodils.

Dirt kicked up everywhere, spraying into the tracks the heavy vehicle had left behind.

Because it was Finn, and everyone knew that silver Range Rover was his, guards had run out to watch the show, but no one was laughing—everyone was just gaping.

Including the folks who'd finally figured out that something was happening, and who, without me even knowing it, had rushed outside onto the front driveway. Ma included.

A few minutes later, another couple of flowerbeds destroyed, the car pulled up outside the house, but Finn didn't jump out of the driver's side.

Aoife did.

Even more goddamn bewildered, I blinked at the sight of the carnage before us, a sight that had only just been rectified when Da had brought in a bunch of landscape gardeners to fix the mess from the holidays, and turned to study Ma.

"She's going to shit a brick."

"Nah," Conor denied, folding his arms against his chest as he too watched our mother.

The second Ma's eyes crashed into Aoife's, I saw the change in her.

Her shoulders hunched, and instead of hurling curses at her, instead of getting in her face like our mouthy mother was more than capable of doing, she twisted on her heel and retreated into the house.

I blinked again.

Then I shoved Conor's arm. "What the fuck is going on, Kid?"

He smirked. "Sucks not to be in the loop, doesn't it?"

"When are you *not* in the loop? You're always in the goddamn loop. Declan and I are the ones who are cut out of shit when you, Aidan, and Finn get together in your fucking fancy-assed high-rise offices. We're the brawn in the goddamn docks and the Hole, and you're the brains—"

"Not my story to tell." Sniffing, Conor brushed off his sleeve. "You should have told me about Callum sooner," he sniped.

"I'm not getting into this with you now," I growled.

"Your dad looks like he's going to have a stroke," Camille interrupted uneasily.

Distracted, I shot Da a look and saw she wasn't half wrong. But Aoife, showing more guts than any of Aidan O'Donnelly Sr.'s kids combined, strode past the man whom most of New York was terrified of, who had a face redder than a beet, with Jake now in her arms—his smiling face telling me he'd enjoyed the ride in the Range Rover—and moved into the house.

"I'll find out what's going on," Camille assured me, darting onto tiptoe to press a kiss to my cheek before she scampered away, on the hunt for information.

As Conor made to follow her, I grabbed his arm and demanded, "What was that about?"

"Ma had it coming."

"What the fuck?" I shook my head just in case I'd gotten a shit ton of water in my ears during my shower earlier. I'd been between Camille's thighs for some of that, so it'd explain a lot.

"You heard me. I know you're a momma's boy, Bren, but she ain't perfect."

"Never said she was."

If anything, I knew more than anyone else that she wasn't. He was right that we were close, but I'd seen how she'd let us down over and over again, but that was what parents did.

They fucked up.

They made mistakes.

But Ma had always bounced back. Like a fucking boomerang, you couldn't get rid of her.

Same thing with Da.

"What did she do?" I demanded.

"Finn's story to tell, not mine."

Before I could clip him around the ear, I saw the glint of a vehicle in the distance. That wasn't extraordinary, but on a Sunday, with all the family here now, it was unusual.

"We expecting guests?"

Conor peered out of the window and muttered, "Huh. No. I don't think so."

Both of us watched as the guards scrambled to get back to their stations to deal with the guest, but a few minutes later, the gates opened and Da, who was hurling curses at Finn like a hungover witch the day after Halloween, paused to pick up his phone.

When his beet-colored face blanched, and he staggered back, leaning on Finn who darted forward to support him, Conor and I shared a look before we ran outside.

We weren't the only ones who'd seen the show. Declan was on his way, and Aidan, thanks to his knee, was hobbling outside too.

"What's going on, Senior?" Finn ground out, shaking his arm as if that would give us answers.

"I-It can't be," Da rattled off, but his gaze was pinned to the car that was driving nearer.

"Who is it, Da?" Aidan demanded.

He licked his lips. "Jackie says..." He paused. Broke off. Tried again. "Jackie says it's your uncle Padraig."

Conor snorted. "He's dead."

"Well, it ain't a fucking hearse that's driving toward us," Declan groused. "How can Uncle Paddy still be alive, Da? Jackie must be wrong."

A wall of O'Donnellys turned to face the chaos that was about to blast our way. Because the guards wouldn't have let just anyone inside the gates, and definitely not Jackie who'd been with Da since the beginning.

Whatever was going on here, however, we were all in the goddamn dark but we were united together.

No matter what.

That was how the O'Donnellys fought their battles.

THIRTY-SEVEN

FINN

THE SECOND he got out of the car, I knew it was him.

Uncle Paddy.

The guy who'd been like a second father to me, and to Junior too. Who'd been our confessor, our confidante, and the guy who'd helped bury the bodies we'd left behind because we were too young to deal with corpses and crime scenes ourselves.

I knew why Aidan Sr. looked like he was about to pass out, because I fucking felt it too.

I'd gone to his funeral. I'd stood by his grave...

Casting Junior a glance, my eyes widened in surprise when I recognized that he didn't look shocked. His interest was clearly piqued, but he wasn't stunned.

Not like me.

I felt like I was seeing a ghost and finding a long-lost message in a fucking bottle.

"This has to be some kind of joke," Senior rasped.

"It's him," I countered at the exact same time as Conor muttered, "It's definitely Uncle Paddy."

"I don't remember what he looks like," Declan said.

"Me neither," Eoghan agreed.

Paddy, for all that he was a walking corpse, looked pretty good. Unlike Senior who ran on the lean side, he had round cheeks and a big gut that squeezed over a pair of pants which definitely weren't tailored. His suit was clean, and the jacket was nicely pressed, but it wasn't the suit of a wealthy man.

Now I knew what I was looking at, *whom* I was looking at, I studied his car—a mid 2010s Chevy.

I nearly got whiplash when I saw it had Canadian plates.

"Paddy's been living in Canada," I mumbled under my breath.

"Canada?" Senior choked out.

"Look at his plates," I explained.

Senior didn't say anything for a second, but then, as Paddy approached, he whispered, "You can't be Padraig. I buried you. I fucking mourned you. I destroyed half the goddamn city for you." His head whipped from side to side. "This is a nightmare—"

"It's me, Aidan," Paddy denied, his voice husky. "It's me, *deartháir*."

Hearing the nickname we all used between us, that we'd picked up on because Aidan Sr. was as tight with his brothers as his sons were, I knew it shook the lot of us. At the same time, no one had a clue what to do.

Gone were the recriminations about a hundred grand's worth of landscape gardening that had just been wasted on Aoife's joyride through Lena's pride and joy, gone was even the memory of it—it might as well not have happened.

Instead, we stood there like a bunch of marionette dolls waiting on someone to pick up the strings.

"I-I..." Senior stammered. "I need a drink."

"You're not the only one." I grunted.

Senior backed away without another glance, leaving us all behind, and whether Paddy was shocked or not at his greeting, he didn't betray much with his expression.

As Eoghan, Declan, and Brennan followed Da, Aidan, Conor, and I just hovered there, staring at him.

The betrayal was real. Not just for us, but the ones who'd left without a word of greeting.

"You pretended to be dead?" Conor asked flatly, then his jaw clenched. I turned to look at him, took in the fact he looked like he hadn't slept in two weeks before he spat, "What kind of fucking godfather pretends to be fucking dead when his fucking godsons fucking need him?"

Paddy flinched. "I was a dead man walking, Conor. It was either make it look like I'd died or get my skull caved in for real." He reached up and rubbed the back of his neck. "I know I've got some explaining to do, boys, but—"

"You can tell Da at the same time as you tell us," Aidan remarked, "but I want you to answer one question, Paddy, before I let you go through that door."

"What is it?" he asked uneasily.

"Why the hell are you back?"

Paddy's Adam's apple bobbed. "I need money."

Conor shook his head. "Of course you do."

Without another word, he trudged off after the others, and staring at him, I felt much the same desire.

I'd grieved for this fucker, had felt his loss as if it were another parent I'd buried, but he was back now.

For money.

I gritted my teeth at the sight of him, but Aidan was calm and cool still as he questioned, "Did the Sparrows get to you?"

Shooting him a look, I demanded, "Did you know he was alive?"

"I found out a few years back, when Da sent me after Savannah who'd gone hunting for some of our family secrets." His mouth tightened. "Figured out that when Da killed Jurkavic—"

"Rammed him in the gut with a sword, didn't he?" I queried, frowning as I tried to remember which of the many murders my biological father had committed we were talking about.

"That's the one," Aidan said with a nod. "He was drugged. The Albanians sold him out.

"Savannah uncovered evidence that proved the bastard on the autopsy table, who Jurkavic supposedly killed, was a couple inches too short to be dear Uncle Paddy." He narrowed his eyes at his godfather. "Did you run because of the Sparrows?"

Padraig slammed his hands into his pockets. "Birds?"

"No, not fucking birds," I snapped. "You must have heard about them on the goddamn news."

His eyes widened. "You think I got something to do with those fucking pigs?" He pshawed. "I wish my life had been that simple. Once you mess with the ECD, boys, that's it, you're screwed."

"The ECD?" I rumbled, trying not to show that his revelation staggered me.

Why did this feel like it was coming full circle?

"Yeah. Those goddamn *cheiles* ruined my life. You think I'd have left everything behind if I had a choice?"

"I don't know anymore," Aidan retorted, "I just know that you're back and it ain't for a good reason."

"My boy's been taken, Aidan."

"You got kids?" I spluttered.

"A son." His chin jerked up. "He's a hockey player. Done real well for himself in the NHL." He gulped. "Name's Liam Donnghal, you might have heard of him."

"Jesus. He's the hockey player who got fucking kidnapped, ain't he?" Aidan commented, for the first time looking surprised.

Paddy's expression crumpled, and it messed with my head.

Unlike this generation, Frank, Aidan, and Padraig had all looked eerily similar. Like they were triplets, just with an age gap. So, seeing Paddy like that reminded me far too much of Senior over the holidays.

I knew what it looked like when a father felt as if the world were crumbling beneath his feet, not just because I'd experienced it myself, but because I'd seen it with my own eyes.

Two men I'd goddamn loved, who'd felt it too.

"He is," Paddy whispered. "I need your da's help, boys."

Aidan shuffled on his feet, pain creasing his expression. "I think, first things first, you gotta make him believe you ain't dead."

Though he grimaced, Paddy nodded. "I get that. It was a shitty fucking thing to do, but I didn't have a choice."

"We always have a choice."

"Not when you fuck with the ECD's plans, Aidan," Paddy discounted.

His words had someone walking over my grave. The hairs at my nape stood to attention like good soldiers, and a shudder worked its way down my spine, because I knew he wasn't bullshitting.

Better than Aidan, at any rate.

"Liam Donnghal—" I paused, corrected, "Liam, he's been gone a few weeks, hasn't he?"

"I couldn't get the money together. They sent me his fucking ear." Tears welled in his eyes, great big drops that poured over his cheeks. One thing could be said about the old generations—they weren't afraid to show their emotions. "That's why I came here. I knew Acuig was doing well, and I knew Aidan would help if it was for family."

I stepped back and away from him, Junior did too, pretty much at the same time.

Warily, though, I said, "You should come inside."

"Da's private office is on the compound, but I haven't heard the golf carts so he must still be in the house," Aidan reasoned, prompting me to nod my head in agreement.

Heading inside first, I looked around, half expecting to find an audience, but the foyer was eerily quiet.

In fact, I couldn't hear voices from any part of the house, not even the kitchen where the women tended to congregate.

Either Lena had disappeared and gone to her room or Aoife was hiding out somewhere else.

Concerned, I turned to Aidan and I muttered, "I'll be five minutes."

"Where are you going?"

"I need to find Aoife."

"Why?" he argued.

"I just do."

I didn't wait for a discussion or his goddamn approval because I needed neither. I headed to the kitchen, only to find that my assumption was right—Aoife wasn't in there. No one was aside from Lena who was cooking on her own.

She must have heard my shoes against the tiles because she looked up and shot me a sad smile. "It's okay, son."

Her words had my jaw clenching. "Nothing is fucking okay, Lena." I wanted to hurl at her that I wasn't her son, but that was my anger talking. For all intents and purposes, I goddamn was. Emotions battling inside me, I rasped, "Where's Aoife?"

"They're all in the conservatory." She pressed her hand to her throat. "I didn't expect you to come today."

"Neither did I. I won't apologize for the flowerbeds."

"After what I did, I deserve worse. I'll…" Lena swallowed. "I don't know what to do, Finn."

"You think I do? She made me promise not to put the family before her again. I intend to stick to that promise, Lena, but this is her family too now. How the hell—" I shook my head. "How am I supposed to make this right?"

She stared down at the potatoes in her hands. "If I had the answers, I'd give them to you."

Mouth tight, I stepped back.

I wished it were different.

I wished she hadn't done what she'd done and that things could revert to how they'd been, but... "I choose her, Lena. I'll always choose her."

This was her punishment.

The only punishment she'd ever get, and she should have endured it sooner.

It was on my shoulders that she hadn't.

"As you should," she whispered, her gaze darting to mine. "Go on with you now, son. Be the husband she needs and the man she loves. She deserves to have both."

Agitated by her understanding, and needing to see with my own eyes that my woman was okay, I slinked away and headed over to the conservatory to check on her.

Lena's grief hit me hard, and as guilty as I felt, it was nothing to the abyss growing larger inside me. Something that made whatever Lena was feeling seem inconsequential.

Out of nowhere, I felt the ticking of a clock start to rumble in the back of my mind.

It had been fainter before, but now, it was like tinnitus.

The countdown to when Aoife left me.

It was, I knew, only a matter of time.

Striding down the hall, trying to tune out that goddamn noise, along the way, I saw Victoria and Shay hanging out in the family room, watching an MCU movie.

The volume was so loud that they might not have even heard the racket going on outside.

As I heard their laughter, I found myself jealous—had my life ever been that simple? I didn't think so. But I prayed theirs stayed like that.

Wasn't that what I was striving for?

An easier path for the next generation—not just my own kids, but my brothers' too?

When I made it to the greenhouse, I found Aoife surrounded by her sisters-in-law.

Inessa cooed over Jake, all while they drank coffee and kept their heads together, a motley crew of women who were clearly discussing what had just gone down in the yard.

Aoife sat there, straight-backed, her face tense, but her eyes clear.

She didn't see me because I retreated once I saw she was safe, once I realized she wasn't upset or crying.

Destroying the flowerbeds had clearly brightened her mood, but that was only a temporary fix.

Destructive behavior only derailed and grew more erratic.

That was what scared me the most.

Preferring to deal with Paddy's bullshit, I escaped to the office but found there was more of that eerie fucking silence.

When I headed inside, Senior was turned away from the room, his gaze on the wrecked yard as he drank from a tumbler that was sloshing around the brim with whiskey.

The rest of my brothers were dotted around the office-cum-library, each of them nursing a whiskey of their own, all while staring at Paddy who was the only man standing.

I headed in, poured myself a good measure of whiskey, did the same for Paddy, and as I passed it to him, I leaned on the edge of Senior's desk.

After I took a sip, I drawled, "You should start at the beginning, Paddy. Maybe that'll help us make sense of it."

THIRTY-EIGHT

FINN

THE SILENCE CHANGED at my words. Went from tense stillness into buzzing curiosity.

I much preferred that.

Paddy cleared his throat after he shot me a grateful look then rattled off, "After all these years, Finn, I still don't know if I can make sense of it, but things are plenty clearer now. Remember that year when Alan Davidson came to us, Aidan?"

My ears pricked up at that. "Alan Davidson? The president?"

Padraig corrected, "His father. Alan Sr."

"What is it with the fucking fathers in New York?" Conor muttered. "Junior, Senior... there are millions of other names out there."

"He's got a point," Junior agreed, his lips twitching as he sank back into the chair, one hand curved around a tumbler, the other absentmindedly rubbing his fucked-up knee.

Conor smirked. "You know when you're called Junior... your mom has probably moaned your name during sex."

Eoghan groaned. "Jesus, you filthy feck—"

"Takes one to know one," Conor interrupted, snickering all the while.

"Think I give a shit about first names?" Senior snapped, twisting around to glower at his brother. "You're dead. So why are you standing here, gracing my office, and drinking my whiskey?"

"Because I need your help, Aidan."

Senior's nostrils flared, but he cut through the BS like usual. "You need cash." It *wasn't* a question.

"Not because I'm broke."

"Then why?" His nostrils flared and that was the only clue we got about the imminent explosion. "*WHY?*" he roared, hurling the crystal glass against the wall.

As it shattered into a million shards, whiskey spraying everywhere in a graceful arc, I figured it was a testament to how accustomed we were to his volatility that not a single one of us flinched—not in surprise at his scream nor at the smash of the glass colliding with the brick wall.

Padraig didn't either, but his pinched features blanched even more. "Because my boy's been kidnapped, Aidan."

I wasn't sure whether that was the right thing to say or the wrong because Senior rasped, "I've got a nephew? My sons have a fucking cousin and I didn't know about it."

His head rocked back and forth, leaving me wondering if this past Christmas, on top of everything else, was more than my old man could stand.

He already subsisted on the verge of insanity. I felt certain he was shuffling nearer and nearer to the edge until he was dangling above it by his fingertips.

"Da," Junior rumbled. "Padraig had a reason for what he's done. You don't listen to him, you'll regret it for the rest of your life."

"Praise Jesus I won't be living that much fucking longer if this is how life is going to be—"

At his complaint, Eoghan snarled, "Shut up, Da. You'll die an old decrepit bastard because only the good die young."

Senior narrowed his eyes upon his youngest, proving yet again that only Eoghan and Conor could talk to him that way because he merely huffed. With Dec, Brennan, Aidan, and me, he'd have clipped us around the ear.

"Speak, Paddy. Let us know why you betrayed your family, why you lied to us for decades, why you broke your mother's heart—"

Paddy choked, "I didn't want to have to do it, Aidan. I didn't have a goddamn choice."

"Neither did Ma when her heart stopped beating because both her youngest had died." Senior tipped his chin up. "You're the one who has to live with that knowledge, not me."

Like a lightning bolt meeting a lightning rod, their tempers arced between us until Paddy blurted out, "I saw Elizabeth Ó Cléirigh fucking Michael Byrne in her wedding dress."

Senior stilled at that, his mean gaze narrowing with all the precision of a laser on his younger brother.

He wasn't the only one.

Michael goddamn Byrne. *Again.*

Conor and I shared a charged look as Senior repeated, "You saw Elizabeth Ó Cléirigh and Michael Byrne together on her wedding day?"

"Yes," he admitted.

"And you didn't think to tell me that?" he asked quietly. Too quietly. So quietly that it was fucking dangerous. "When you've known for as long as I have that those *cheile* fuckers have had me by the balls for decades?"

Well, that was goddamn news to me.

Conor and I shared a look before I inserted, "What hold do they have on you?"

"The *cheiles?*" Brennan queried. "Those Irish independence zealots?"

"They're the ones we break bread with on a daily basis." Senior bared his throat and sliced a finger across it. "Got me up to here with their bullshit."

"What? Why?" Declan demanded, sitting up, his interest clear. "Why do the Five Points support the *cheiles?*"

Senior's mouth tightened. "Because your grandfather, on your mother's side, was the leader at one point. Only reason he gave her to me was that I agreed to help the cause."

Junior quoted, "'He gave her to you?'"

"Second I set my eyes on her I wanted her," Senior concurred. "Knew she was mine."

"If you wanted her so fucking badly, why did you cheat on her?" Brennan spat.

Padraig flinched at the question, and Senior's expression darkened, but before anyone could say a word, I reasoned, "Seeing as I'm living proof that you couldn't keep your dick in your pants, Aidan, I think that merits an answer."

"You're Aidan's boy?" Padraig blurted out, his eyes rounding, his shock clear.

"I am." I rubbed my chin, well aware that no one in the room other than Paddy was surprised by that news.

It was the worst kept secret in our family, and in a group of people who were currently being deepthroated by the truth, that was saying something.

"Who's your ma?" he demanded.

"Fiona Davenport."

"The girl you had married off to that O'Grady fucker?" Padraig's eyes widened, but I saw a sliver of *something* make an appearance in his gaze. "You lying bastard. All that time you were grumbling at me for not getting married and for sleeping around and you were cheating on Magdalena? After all the shit we got into so you could have her—"

"Shut the fuck up," Senior snapped.

"What shit?" Conor chimed in, his curiosity pricked.

"Your grandfather was a head case. Never mind your uncles on her side. You were fucking lucky that most of them got their asses exploded before you were born or got shoved in jail while you were kiddies. Otherwise, you'd have to deal with them.

"You think your father's got a problem up there—" He tapped his temple. "—consider yourself blessed you didn't meet them. I didn't have that luxury. Neither did Frank.

"Aidan only went and started a war with those nutcases because he snatched her from her debutante ball."

Junior's mouth gaped. "Ma had a debutante ball? Like a socialite?"

Senior sniffed. "Your ma was well-connected."

His shoulders hunched when Padraig hissed under his breath. "Well connected?" he scoffed. "With the worst people, meaning that everyday folk were too fucking terrified to deny Cormac O'Shea's daughter an entry into society.

"How the hell did you keep that from me?" He smacked his forehead. "I should have known. I always thought you looked the spitting image of Frank, Finn."

"I thought you and Ma had an arranged marriage," Conor demanded.

"More like an *arrangement*," Padraig muttered.

"Look, this isn't about me," Aidan retorted. "I screwed up, I know I did, and I've repented and Lena probably added to my brain damage but I didn't pretend to be fucking dead. I didn't—" He shook his head. "You mean to tell me that the Albanians were in on it? They had to be for me to butcher Jurkavic the way I did."

"They had a problem and so did I."

"They bribed you?" Aidan guessed, tone flat.

"Needed the money to set up elsewhere, *dearthár*."

"Don't give me that '*dearthár*' bullshit when you've pretended to be dead for almost three decades!

"Not when you could have just told me what was happening, and I'd have slapped Byrne upside the head. If you fucking knew the shit you'd have spared me if you'd have come to me—" He slammed his hand against the table. "You used that as a reason to get out. You never did have the stomach for our work."

Paddy snapped, "I had your back from the first day I was thrown into the Points. Don't you dare—"

"Is it really a bad thing not to have the stomach for murdering and killing and torturing?" Eoghan questioned before he sank down some whiskey. "I don't think that's the worst crime, Da."

"He was supposed to reign by my side, goddammit," Senior snarled, and I wasn't surprised when his fist went flying and it collided with the mirror behind his desk. Fist bleeding, knuckles bloodied, that didn't even stop him as he hissed, "Leave us, sons—"

"I don't think that's wise," Junior rasped.

"You'll kill each other," I agreed.

"It's okay, boys. Leave us be. If he wants to beat on me, then he can. I don't give a fuck. I just need to get Liam home." His eyes collided with Junior then Conor, and whatever they saw within his gaze had them getting to their feet.

"Come on," Junior urged.

Conor started for the door. "Let's leave them to it."

Shaking my head, I followed them, as did Declan, Brennan, and Eoghan. As we left the room, leaving the brothers to duke it out, Brennan grumbled, "Well, that was informative."

"Wonder why there aren't any pictures of Ma at a debutante ball?" Conor mused.

"Probably because Senior stole her before they could photograph her," I muttered.

"He's your da too," Conor pointed out. "You can call him that."

My brow furrowed. "I can't."

"Why not?"

He was the one who asked, but I knew I was at the center of their attention.

Uncomfortable, I retorted, "Because he's been Senior a lot longer than he's been my father."

"He's always treated you like family," Declan pointed out softly. "Hell, most of the time, he was nicer to you than he ever was to me."

Though I cringed, I couldn't deny that was the truth. "You always did get the short end of the stick."

"The short, pointy end," Declan groused.

"No arguing with that," Brennan agreed with a sigh.

"Anyway, we have a problem."

Aidan turned to Declan just as the sound of something crashing came from Senior's office. "More of a problem than that?"

Another crash echoed down the hall. It warred with The Clash's 'Should I Stay or Should I Go,' from the soundtrack of the movie Victoria and Shay were watching.

"Think that was the Chippendale?" Brennan asked wistfully. "I wanted that cabinet when the fucker finally died. It'd look perfect in my office."

"Yeah, more of a problem than that," Declan said with a grimace.

Aidan hobbled away from the office door and limped into the nearest den. As he slumped on one of the chairs, he muttered, "Come on, then. Hit me with it."

I was the last to head into the room, and as I did, I saw Aidan sitting in Senior's armchair.

The move was probably accidental because it was the closest to the door, and I could see that his knee was paining him, but it seemed more like fate.

We congregated around him, each of us taking our place close to his seat all while our father lost his shit in the other room.

It felt... *right.*

Like stepping away from the past and walking into the future.

I shook off the thought as Declan mumbled, "I didn't mention anything because I didn't want anyone to know, even went as far as to hire private guards for the event, but Aela was recently invited to the White House."

Arching a brow at that, I asked, "Why?"

Brennan sat up. "Your wife, a woman known to associate with a mobster, was invited to the White House?"

"Well, it wasn't official until we got married, was it?" Declan retorted. "But I wouldn't be surprised if that whole administration was as crooked as Da."

"What makes you say that?" I asked, even though I knew truer words had never left his lips.

"Aela was commissioned by the First Lady to make the Davidson official china set." He crossed his feet at the ankle as he told us, "I feel like a real dumbass for not registering it sooner, but she wants the words *Éire le chéile go deo* inscribed into the dishes."

For a second, none of us said anything, then as I processed that we no longer needed Michael's word for it, Brennan growled, "You mean to tell me that the First Lady is a fucking *cheile*?"

THIRTY-NINE

AOIFE

"SHE DID *WHAT?*"

I grimaced at Aela's screech, but I had to admit, how my sisters-in-law gathered around me made me feel better.

A hell of a lot better.

I'd been isolated since the miscarriage, with most of that being self-imposed.

I hadn't meant to put up barriers between my family and friends and myself, but right now, everything was much too much, and I needed to shut down. Go into turtle mode to lick my wounds.

But seeing Inessa's round eyes, Camille's furrowed brow, Savannah's clenched jaw, and the way Aela was practically vibrating, hands fisted at her sides as she loomed over me in the large conservatory, I felt embraced by their horror. Warmed by their outrage.

I mattered to them.

I knew that, but seeing was believing.

"She killed my mom," I repeated after a couple seconds of basking in their care.

"This is fucking nuts," Aela hissed, dropping to the seat next to me then quickly leaping up again. "Why isn't she in jail—?" She snapped, "Goddamn Senior. You shouldn't be here, Aoife. Why are you here? You're not going to eat at the same table—"

"Finn told Aidan I wasn't coming, and I wanted to spite him," I admitted sheepishly.

"He can't have known," Inessa whispered, her pallor pinched.

"He did." I stared down at Jake's hands as he tugged on her bright blonde hair.

"He's lucky you didn't kill him."

Savannah was new to this little circle, but her cool words drew my attention.

I wasn't sure if she meant it. Wasn't sure if she was joking. But she sipped on what appeared to be a mimosa, one arm slung along the back of the sofa like she was ready to be photographed for a magazine.

Picture perfect.

How I wished that I were like that.

We'd had a couple fallings out because of Jen, our mutual best friend, and how Savannah had treated her, but her words made me realize that she was on my side too.

"It's the men who kill. Not us," Camille rasped. "That's not our job."

"Our job?" Aela mocked. "What's she supposed to do when the guy with that job is the one who needs killing?"

Her staunch defense soothed me, but it made me feel bad for admitting, "I love him."

Inessa's soft eyes landed on mine. "Oh, Aoife."

"Doesn't mean you have to forgive him," Aela grumbled, but my admission seemed to take the wind from her sails.

She sat down heavily, her arm rubbing up against mine in comfort, not happenstance.

"I don't," was my prompt reply. "I really don't, but I don't want to kill him. I don't—" I sighed. "I thought we were solid."

"You are," Camille whispered.

"How can we be when he's kept this from me?" I cried. "When he let me love Lena? I know you're not a fan of her, Aela, but Inessa gets it, don't you?"

Untangling a lock of hair from Jake's clasp, Inessa flinched but confirmed nonetheless, "She's good to us."

Aela scowled. "Your definition of good is different than mine."

"No, it isn't. You just haven't been around her long enough to see. Plus, you're—" I winced.

"Rebellious? Opinionated?" Aela threw in, but she was smirking as she did so.

"Yes." I blew out a breath. "I feel like Mom died yesterday. I feel this hate inside me for who took her from me like it's still a raw wound. But Lena did that, and I love her.

"Jake's teething, and she gave me a rusk recipe that I can't find. I want to ask her for it but I can't.

"Jake wants to go to her, because she's his grammy, and I don't want her anywhere around him." I covered my face with my hands. "I want to cry all the time, and I want Finn to comfort me, but then I remember what he kept from me. So I argue. And he's being so patient. So, so... *reasonable.*"

"Being reasonable isn't necessarily a bad thing," Savannah said carefully.

"My husband isn't reasonable. He's fair, but..." I shook my head. "It's difficult to explain."

Camille reached forward and snagged my hand in hers. "Try, Aoife, it might make you feel better."

I stared into her kind eyes and clung to her fingers. I didn't know her as well as her sister, but I was grateful for her presence in my life.

All of these women had been a part of my world for such a short space of time, but we'd endured so much together.

We were O'Donnellys.

Through and through.

"I keep pushing his buttons," I whispered. "I say things I know will piss him off. I—"

"You want a reaction out of him," Savannah inserted softly.

"Yes." I clung to her words as much as I clung to Camille's hand. "I want a reaction from him. I just don't know what kind of reaction I want."

"Do you want to break up with him?" Inessa questioned. "Is that it? You want him to throw in the towel?"

The pain her words stirred in me was akin to the raw agony I felt over losing my mom.

"No," I ground out on an agonized breath. "He can't leave me. He's not allowed to do that."

Camille's voice was gentle. "She didn't ask that, Aoife. She asked if *you* want to break up with *him?*"

My head whipped from side to side. "No."

"If you wanna stay with the jackass," Aela mumbled, "then you just have to ride this out. Men do stupid shit all the time. Granted, nothing on this level. This is a grade A fuck up, but if you keep pushing him, you'll get that reaction you want out of him."

Her words were a warning, and I knew she was right.

I plucked at my bottom lip, muttering, "He'd never leave me. He'd never let me go."

Aela shrugged. "Then is it worth pushing for a reaction you won't be able to control?"

Savannah took a deep sip of her mimosa. "How did it feel to drive over her flowerbeds?"

I stared at her. "Satisfying."

For a second, I thought about Finn's other suggestions, but I knew I couldn't go through with them. A part of me wanted to set fire to the dinner table, after I'd thrown all her food onto the floor, but it was wiser to leave.

To head back home.

Home.

I rubbed my temple as I wondered exactly where home was.

That place where Finn had told me something that was proof he'd been lying to me for years?

Where I'd lost my baby on the kitchen floor?

The desire to go to him, *my real home*, hit me, but I didn't have anything to say. Didn't want to be held by him. Didn't even want to look at him.

"I think I'm going mad," I rasped.

"If you were, I don't think any of us could blame you," Savannah murmured.

Aela slipped her arm around my shoulders, and I tried not to cringe when I felt her baby bump rub up against me. "We got you, babe."

"Do you want to come and stay with us?" Inessa offered.

I shot her a shaky smile. "Thank you, Nessa, but no."

A chasm had made an appearance between Finn and me. Like a crack in the earth's crust after a quake, I could feel it spreading. Staying with Nessa would only exacerbate that.

If I wanted my marriage to work, then I couldn't run away. But how did I cope with what I was feeling? How did I purge myself of the poison that was killing us both?

I cleared my throat at the thought then, needing to change the subject, asked Savannah, "When's your next article coming out?"

"Have you been talking to Jen?"

I blinked. "What?"

"Never mind."

"I meant the Sparrows—"

"Don't talk to me about the fucking Sparrows," Aela spat. "I finally decided to get a workshop, and because of those bastards, Declan wants to choose it for me. He showed me this poky little place in the East Village. The man's got no idea."

Inessa snorted. "He's protecting you. Not just from the Sparrows."

Chills whispered down my spine. "Speaking of the Sparrows... You guys remember Callum O'Reilly?"

"That dude who's gone missing? With the bitch for a wife?" Aela clicked her fingers. "Priestley? Thinks she's God's gift to womankind when she's probably the reason he ran off?"

I had to smile at her description, but it died as I rasped, "Finn told me he was a Sparrow."

"What?" Aela boomed.

Ears aching with her outburst, I muttered, "Calm down, Aela."

"Your blood pressure," Camille tutted.

"He's a fucking Sparrow?!"

"Yes." I swallowed. "Finn said that he's the reason..." I couldn't get my words out. "He told the Sparrows about our wedding. He's why the drive-by shooting happened."

None of the women had been there, but they shuffled nearer to me, as if that would take away my pain.

"Those scars are why you—"

"Can't carry a baby to full term?" I answered Inessa. "That's right."

"I am so sorry," Aela whispered, rubbing her hand absentmindedly down her belly as if she were comforting both the baby and herself.

The sight had me jerking to my feet. She hadn't meant to upset me, but it was too much. Much too much.

"I-I need to go." They all jolted in surprise as I grabbed Jake from Nessa's arms. He screeched in outrage as I reached for my purse, muttering, "I'll text you later."

A hand snagged mine before I was clear of the seating area, stopping me from surging forward and leaving.

"Jen's our common ground, Aoife, but our men are the best of friends too. I'd like it if we..." For the first time, Savannah didn't look her regular composed self. "I'm here if you need me," she ended eventually.

Swallowing, I nodded then hurried away.

I had no idea where Finn was, and I didn't care either. I heard furniture clattering at one side of the house, and though it made me jump, I was glad everyone's attention was elsewhere.

When I was outside, I saw John standing by the garage, huddled in a coat as he smoked and checked his cellphone.

"I need to go back to the city, John," I called out the second I registered the glint of the glowing tip of his cig.

He saw me, and his eyes widened. "Where's your coat?"

I started shivering, just as Jake did.

God, I'd left all our stuff inside!

What the hell was I doing?

Maybe I really was losing my damn mind.

John darted into action, though, and he dragged open the door to the Range Rover, demanding, "Get inside, Aoife. You'll drop from exposure in a minute."

When I leaped into the back and settled Jake in his car seat, I wasn't too dumbfounded to realize that he'd shot off a couple of text messages in that time.

How did I know?

Finn appeared at the doorway, and he stood there, watching me watch him as John, permission granted, climbed behind the wheel and drove us home.

With each yard that separated us, I felt the agonizing pain as if our arms were tied together and they were being pulled from the sockets as the distance grew.

But away from him, away from that house, I took the first deep breath since I'd jumped behind the wheel earlier and had destroyed something Lena loved and held dear.

As I leaned back, I processed the conversation I'd just had with my sisters-in-law, and while they'd all said something that had made sense, it was Aela's words that resonated the most with me.

Is it worth pushing for a reaction you won't be able to control?

FORTY

AIDAN JR

"WHAT'S GOING ON WITH THEM?" Brennan rasped as Finn jumped out of his chair and took off after his cell buzzed and he read the message.

"I don't know," I answered.

I knew it wasn't a medical emergency because he'd have shouted an explanation, but Eoghan got to his feet and headed toward the same doorway Finn had used to leave the room.

I monitored my youngest brother's movements, saw him drift over to the windows behind me after a couple seconds, and I let him be my eyes and ears until he finally said, "Aoife left without him."

My brow puckered. "She just took off?"

"She did," Eoghan confirmed before he demanded, "Kid? What do you know?"

"Why would Conor know?"

I didn't mean to sound peeved, but Finn was my best fucking friend. If anyone should know what was going on with him, it was *me*.

"Keep your panties on," Eoghan sniped. "Boy Wonder over there has all our phones bugged."

"That's creepy as fuck," Brennan growled.

Declan snapped, "Since when?"

"Christmas." Conor frowned, rubbing his eyes tiredly. "I'm not listening in because I get a sick kick out of it. I was *told* to do it, and like a good fucking soldier, I *obeyed*."

Studying him, wondering when the last time he'd slept was, I retorted, "You can't possibly be listening in on all our conversations."

"I have a program that scans for keywords."

"That doesn't sound like it could go wrong at all," Brennan mocked.

Yawning, Conor flipped him the bird but agreed, "I have a system. It's working so far."

"Because of the Sparrows?" I questioned. "He thinks we can't be trusted?"

"More that the people around us can't."

"His daughters-in-law?" Brennan demanded.

I ignored that to ask, "How did you know about this, Eoghan?"

"I did a sweep of my rooms. Found a bug, then, when I realized the only person who'd come by to visit was Conor—"

"Conor came to visit?" I asked suspiciously.

"Hey! It's not that fucking weird," Kid grumbled.

Ignoring him, Eoghan retorted, "Exactly. It was weird. Anyway, his visit prompted me to look deeper, and I found spyware on my phone."

"And you didn't think to tell us?" I retorted, incensed.

"No, I didn't," Eoghan groused. "What use would there be in you knowing? Conor keeps getting hacked. He had to up his game at some point. I just thought it was him trying to recover lost ground."

"I take offense at that."

"So you should. Slow poke." Eoghan's mouth quirked up at the corner. "Plus, I thought it'd be funny, you guys finding out on your own, but, apparently, I'm the only one who does security checks like that."

Brennan grunted. "I'll start scanning my place every week."

"Same," Dec concurred with a glower.

"I don't always use bugs." Kid's sniff was disparaging, as was the eye roll he aimed at no one in particular.

"No, you use spyware too," I drawled.

"Is that a threat?" Brennan rumbled, his eyes narrowing on Kid.

Deciding to save Conor's neck from being broken by Brennan, I asked, "He's trying to weed out more Sparrows, Kid?"

"It's why I agreed to do it." Conor shrugged. "But who knows why Da does what he does?"

I heard footsteps down the hall and watched Finn, pale and tense, head back in.

"Everything okay, brother?" I asked him quietly.

"Nothing's fucking okay," he snapped, and he stunned me by raising his hands to his head and gripping his hair in his fists. The room throbbed with his wrath before he snarled, "No more secrets. No more. I can't deal with any fucking more."

Conor leaped to his feet, and just when Finn looked like he was going to let loose and punch the wall, Kid grabbed his shoulders and rasped, "Finn, I'll explain. Just leave it to me, okay?" He shook him when he didn't answer. "We'll get those out in the open."

As he shoved his forehead up against Finn's, I knew I wasn't the only one watching on, wondering what the fuck was happening.

Finn was supposed to tell me what had gone down with Aoife, but shit had gotten in the way and I'd forgotten. Was this what that was about? Or was Aoife's miscarriage the problem?

Ashamed of myself for forgetting, my hands tightened around the armrests of the chair I liked to think of as Da's throne, and I ordered, "Conor, what are you going to explain?"

Finn muttered something under his breath, but then slowly pulled back.

Conor's hand tightened around his shoulder. "Aoife's mom died in a hit and run."

I cast Finn a confused look. "This isn't news to any of us."

"Ma was the one driving the car that knocked her over."

Eoghan spat, "What?"

"No fucking way," Brennan griped.

"You can't be serious," Declan hissed.

"It's true," Finn mumbled. "I found out at the same time as I learned Senior was my father."

"Ma just knocked some lady over and Da covered it up?" Declan hesitantly guessed. "That's why this is news to all of us?"

Conor's grip tightened on Finn's shoulder. "It took some time to unravel shit," Kid started, "but basically—"

"Basically, Aidan told Lena that he'd had an affair and he had a kid," Finn ground out. "Because he didn't want to fuck up our relationship, he never told her who his girlfriend was or who his kid was."

"Genius move, Da," I grated out under my breath.

"Jesus Christ, that'd have driven her mad," Brennan bit off.

"It did," Conor said. "According to Da, she was off her meds too."

"Until this week, I just thought it was... I guess a tragic accident," Finn confessed.

"You've known for four years?" Declan asked slowly, measuringly.

Finn rubbed his forehead. "Yeah. I really am that much of a dumb fuck."

Brennan grunted. "Kept it from her for all this time?"

"I did. Senior assured me that nothing I did would make shit better. Lena was never going to jail, he'd see to that, and it was either—" He sucked in a breath. "It was either lose my whole fucking family or keep this shit a secret."

Brennan frowned. "What changed?"

"Ma went to visit Michael in the hospital and learned that he's a *cheile*," Conor explained grimly. "She saw his ink, that damn phoenix. Then she realized that he was the one who'd told her Aoife's mom was Da's girlfriend and knew that had to be for a reason seeing as Aoife's mom was a goddamn stranger to the family.

"He was the one who told her that he got the info from the Old Wives' Club so she believed him. But learning he was a *cheile* made her question everything."

Finn's gaze shuttered as Brennan demanded, "Where the fuck's Michael? Why didn't you bring me in on this?"

"I dealt with it," Conor retorted.

"It being Michael? Or the situation?" Declan asked carefully.

"Both."

Having seen how he'd handled it, it wasn't like I could argue.

"Why wasn't I involved?" Brennan snapped.

"Because Ma thought you'd get Da in on this, and..." Conor seemed to brace himself. "She doesn't trust him."

If anything could have silenced the others, it was that.

Until Brennan grumbled, "About time she fucking learned that lesson."

Rubbing my chin, because I didn't disagree, I muttered, "Then, we have the issue that Aoife is President Davidson's daughter."

Declan and Brennan's eyes widened, but it was Declan who sniped, "That can't be a coincidence."

"Nothing is a fucking coincidence," Finn retorted. "And we learned that Aoife's got this secret uncle, Eamonn—"

"Who's the leader of the ECD," Conor finished.

Eoghan twisted to face Finn at that, then he demanded, "Eamonn Keegan is Aoife's uncle?"

Conor nodded. "He's been in jail since the nineties—"

"I know, Conor," Eoghan grated out. "I know more about the fucking *cheiles* than you do."

"Yeah? Like what?" I inquired, curiosity stirred.

My baby bro rarely brought up the war or his time in the military, but when he did, it was always like fucking story time for adults.

Eoghan pulled a face but said, "He served in the British Army during the Troubles in Northern Ireland.

"They say his skills are one of the reasons the Falklands War only lasted two weeks. He got deployed in Belfast then went AWOL. He got arrested, escaped, resurfaced again as the leader of the *cheiles,* then the soldiers hauled him in one last time, and the rest is history. He goes by the alias Dagda."

"He approached Aoife in a bar just after New Year's," Finn murmured. "I wonder why he introduced himself to her as that and not his real name?"

"Anonymity? Maybe he didn't know that his sister had never mentioned him?" I turned to him. "If he instigated a meet, she's clearly a priority of his."

Finn nodded grimly. "She needs a battalion of fucking guards on her."

"Why is he one of the reasons the Falklands War went on for two weeks?" Brennan asked.

"Didn't even fucking know there *was* a Falklands War," Declan groused under his breath.

Conor snickered. "If it isn't art history, you're not interested."

Eoghan ignored Kid. "Because he was one of the best goddamn sharpshooters in the British Army. They say that he lost his edge when the British arrested him. But I don't know if that's fact or rumor."

"Why?" I asked.

"Ever heard of the Five Techniques?" Eoghan's tone was grim.

I winced. "Torture methods, aren't they?"

"They are. Illegal torture methods that were supposed to be decommissioned a long time ago. Long before Keegan was ever captured." His mouth firmed. "They said he got some kind of brain damage after soldiers banged his head against a wall during interrogation.

"That little stay with the Brits is why the ECD went from being pains in the asses to terrorists."

"You know a lot about this shit," Brennan rumbled.

"I know a lot of shit about a lot of shit," Eoghan rasped. "And let's bring it down to the bare bones. Aoife is both the daughter of the man who leads the free world and the niece of the man who's terrorized the free world for over twenty years. Am I getting that right?"

Finn's jaw clenched as he nodded, but it was Kid who said, "Funny how she's the gentlest of all the women, ain't it?"

Funny?

More like fucking hilarious.

"I don't get it," Brennan groused. "If the ECD are led by Eamonn Keegan, then why the fuck would Michael be working to kill Eamonn's sister?"

"Michael wanted leverage over Da," Conor inserted. "Michelle's death triggered a power struggle in the ECD. I'm guessing from what Da said in there that he helped make that happen."

"Eamonn's out of jail now," Brennan said. "Right, Kid?"

"He is."

"Then why's Michael still alive?"

I nodded. "That's a good fucking point, Brennan."

"Well, he's dead now," Conor mumbled.

"Not by Eamonn's hand." Brennan frowned. "Aoife really does need extra guards, Finn. Who the hell knows what a whacked up mother-fucker like that's got planned now that he's out."

"Why would he want to hurt Aoife? She hasn't done anything," Conor argued.

"He might want to take her from Finn," Brennan reasoned. "We need to make sure that doesn't happen."

"Does Ma need extra guards?"

"No one outside of this house knows what Lena did," Finn told Declan.

"You don't know if that's true," Brennan denied. "Michael could have told anyone."

"Or no one," I said softly, mind whirring as I processed all this information.

"Michael said he involved Ma in this because he wanted something over Da," Conor murmured. "Probably wanted his support when he pulled that coup. There's a reason he's still alive, so I have to figure that reason is Da."

"Maybe he's the one who needs the extra guards, then." Brennan grimaced.

"If he's the reason the power struggle happened, then he sure as fuck does." Finn ran a hand through his hair.

"So, let me get this straight," I stated. "We have a president with a love child who happens to be our sister-in-law.

"His First Lady is in bed with a bunch of terrorists. Or *was* at some point. And seeing as Davidson's backing a unified Ireland, I think she's the one who encouraged *that*.

"Finally, we have a newly released ex-con who may or may not be looking to get his revenge after what happened to his sister... am I missing anything?"

FORTY-ONE

FINN

"NO, you're not missing anything, but I think we need to get some shit out into the open."

Junior arched a brow at me. "More shit?"

"There's *always* shit," Conor declared. "If we get everything out in the open, then we'll be here all day."

"Ain't that the truth," Declan said on a huff.

Staring at Junior, I ground out, "There'll come a day when you're in charge, Aidan, and this is it. It's us. We're the council."

"That's gloomy." Brennan frowned. "Da ain't in his grave, yet."

"No, but he would have been if I hadn't dragged him from the cathedral when he and your ma tried to burn themselves to death." I shot him a pointed look when his mouth gaped. "See? This is the kind of stuff we need to be transparent about."

"Ma tried to kill herself?"

I wasn't surprised that Brennan focused on that. He had a better relationship with Lena than the others, but that was forged on guilt. Guilt he only had on his shoulders because his father had given a man's job to a teenager.

Declan, on the other hand, demanded, "Da was behind the arson attack on the cathedral? Do you know how many pieces of art were lost in that fire?"

Eoghan murmured, "And the Archbishop? Da killed him?"

"Ma tried to kill herself," Junior rasped, staring down at his shoes. "Da killed the Archbishop, but the Valentini Don kidnapped him for us—"

Brennan snapped, "When were you thinking of telling us all this?"

He shrugged. "When it was important."

"Jesus Christ," Brennan hissed.

"Your folks both set fire to the cathedral," I tacked on calmly.

"But why?" Eoghan muttered. "What the hell made them do that?"

Before I could answer, Conor stated, "I think it's my secret to tell."

"What secret?" Eoghan inquired.

"A couple months before Paddy disappeared—" Disapproval laced Kid's tone at his uncle's behavior. "—a priest groomed me."

Tension had Brennan's shoulders stiffening. "Groomed you?" he repeated, his words like ice.

By contrast to the threat of danger in Bren's voice, Conor sounded conversational as he explained, "Yes. He raped me multiple times over a period of about six weeks."

I closed my eyes at that news. After *that* day, we'd never spoken about it. What we'd seen, what we'd done, I knew it fucked us all up.

Aidan had gotten real angry, so much so that his da had whupped him to 'beat the devil out of him.' Unsurprisingly, that didn't help with his anger issues. Conor had turned to his computers. I'd just tried to ride through it by studying as much as I could, knowing that one day, I'd be able to leave wetwork behind.

"Conor, fuck, you—" Declan rambled, sitting forward like he wanted to *do* something but couldn't.

"Who was the fucking piece of shit bastard son of a bitch?" Brennan growled, jerking to his feet to loom over the lot of us.

"Give me his name," Eoghan whispered. "I'll kill him. No one has to know."

Conor smiled, but it was a weird one. Neither edgy nor gleeful, mostly... entertained? Satisfied? "It's okay. He's already dead."

"He is?" Brennan started pacing. "He better have suffered."

I cleared my throat. "Aidan made sure of that."

Their heads whipped around to glance between Aidan and me.

"You knew?" Declan barked. "And didn't say anything?"

"You and your fucking secrets. You're always keeping things from us," Brennan spat.

"And that's why we need to do this," I said as calmly as I could.

"Haven't you noticed? Your parents aren't doing well, and what's going to happen now... it could be the nail in their coffin.

"Aoife came today out of spite. She wanted to hurt Lena by hurting something she loved. But why the fuck would she come next week? Or the week after?

"You think I'm going to make her come eat chicken and potatoes when I'm clinging onto my marriage—" I scrubbed a hand over my face. "Senior won't like it, but he ain't got a choice. I'm protecting my woman, and I'm taking her out of a toxic environment—"

"You don't have to explain," Brennan said. "It makes sense."

"Total sense," Declan agreed.

"Of course it does," Junior concurred.

Eoghan gave me a nod, but actions always did mean more to him than words.

"After our last call," Conor admitted, "I was surprised when you came today."

"So, you don't know *everything*," Brennan mocked.

I held up a hand. "Don't start arguing. We've all got a lot of ground to cover."

Clearing his throat, Conor continued, "He's right. While I was being raped, Aidan and Finn entered the church, grabbed McKenna—"

"That fucking pedo? Jesus, I remember him! I knew he was a piece of shit—" Brennan snarled while Conor ignored him, saying:

"—and Aidan clubbed him to death. We called Paddy in, and he got rid of the body."

Junior rubbed his chin. "I've known Paddy wasn't dead for five years."

Declan's mouth gaped. "You gotta be shitting me?"

"Savannah discovered the truth."

"Five years ago?" Eoghan asked. "You've known her that long?"

"Yeah. It's complicated. Ain't seen her for most of that time."

Conor hummed. "Wondered why there were guards allocated to my building that weren't on me."

Aidan rolled his eyes but murmured, "Da threatened to kill her. She was digging into sensitive family secrets, and he didn't like that."

"That's how you met?" Declan questioned.

"Yeah. She worked out that Paddy wasn't the person on the slab in the morgue."

"Why didn't you tell anyone?" Brennan grouched.

"Thought it must have been to do with the Sparrows." He shrugged uneasily. "Instead, it's to do with some other fanatical fuckers. Jesus Christ, what screwed up legacy am I going to inherit?"

Declan muttered, "You remember that war with the Haitians?"

"How could we forget? That was fucking brutal."

He wriggled his shoulders. "I might have started that."

"What?!"

Junior whistled. "You might have had a point here, Finn."

"Apparently." I stared at Declan. "Finish your story."

He rubbed his eyes. "My crew, back when I was a teenager, we started pulling heists on pawn shops. Without Da's approval.

"One day, there's an argument over who's getting the bigger cut, guns go off, and half the crew's dead.

"Not gonna lie, brothers, Cillian Donahue and I were shit scared. We were the only ones left, and we knew we'd have to explain what went down... so we blamed the Haitians."

"Fucking hell," Junior drawled. "You changed the face of the city with that stunt."

He cleared his throat. "Did more than that. Cillian, that rat bastard, blackmailed me over that shit for years. Got me tied to that cunt of a sister.

"I hated Deirdre with every bone in my body. Aela was my side piece at the time when she should always have been my woman. Worst day of my life was when I had her tagged as mine like she was fucking property because I had to have a ring on that bitch's finger and not hers."

Junior's mouth gaped. "You hated Deirdre?"

"I did." He pulled a face. "Made her pay in the end though. Her death wasn't as... well, I might have been able to stop it from going down that way."

"Fuck."

"About sums it up," Declan agreed. "Then, of course, there's the fact that I'm pretty fucking sure Shay's grandparents were killed by the IRA—"

I straightened up. "What?"

"Yeah. Shay told me this story about him being shoved in a closet by his grandma and then hearing an argument and shots fired. I think that's it for my secrets." He looked sheepish. "Anyone else got something to share?"

Brennan blew out a breath. "'Round about the time you were pulling heists on pawn shops, Dec, I was fucking Mariska Vasov."

My eyes rounded. "The Pakhan's wife?"

"Your wife's mother?" Declan spluttered. "That's fucking sick, man."

"Fuck off. It was a long time ago. Anyway, Camille came to me." He grimaced. "You might as well know... she's the one who offed Vasov." His tone turned proud. "Hit him over the head with a glass paperweight. Maxim Lyanov helped clean shit up." He scratched his chin. "He wants Victoria for his bride, but I promised Camille that if she doesn't want him, she doesn't have to have him for a husband."

Junior blinked at him. "You gotta be shitting me."

"I wish I were, brother." He wriggled his shoulders. "But I'm not."

"You guys know Jen, right?" I tossed in.

"Aoife's best friend? She came for Christmas? The one who kept trying to bang you, Aidan?"

Junior snorted at Brennan. "That one. She's related to us."

"How?" Declan spluttered.

"One of Paddy's progeny," Conor intoned grimly.

"How the fuck did you know—" I shook my head. "Those goddamn bugs are going to be the fucking death of me."

He just smiled. "I think that's most of the secrets for now. Unless... Eoghan, you feeling up to sharing with the class?" It was more of a command than a request.

I glanced at Eoghan who murmured, "I'm MI6."

Conor smirked. "My brother's James Bond."

Though most of the brothers' mouths gaped more than Ghostface's, Declan was the one who rasped, "Wait a fuckin' minute. They're English! We're goddamn Irish!"

My lips twitched.

I'd never looked at it that way until now.

FORTY-TWO

SAVANNAH

AS A JOURNALIST, I'd always known this family was fascinating.

But being a part of it was a thousand times better.

That made me sound like such a bitch, especially in the face of what Aoife was going through, but I was utterly absorbed in the entire process.

"We should boycott the family dinners," Aela was saying, blood-thirsty as ever as she started storming in front of the seating area where we were gathered together in the conservatory.

"What use will that do?" Inessa replied.

"As a stance so Aoife knows we have her back."

Inessa frowned. "Aoife knows that already. We can't just..."

"What? What can't we do?" Aela snapped.

Camille's voice was calm as she said, "Aela, one, losing your temper won't be good for the baby. Two, we come from a different culture than yours."

"You from Mars?"

My lips twisted as I took a deeper sip of my drink.

"No," Inessa countered. "We come from a world where we always look after family."

Camille shifted on her seat, her discomfort clear. "Or we try to."

"Lena's a snake," Aela pointed out.

"She's still Shay's grandmother. Jake's grandmother," Inessa said, but her voice was miserable.

This news was going to tear the O'Donnellys apart.

I could feel it.

Sadness hit me.

Making me feel as miserable as Inessa clearly was.

Change always sucked, but this was a devastating blow.

I thought about Aidan, about how he had a weird relationship with his parents. He didn't like them, didn't respect them all that much, but he came here every week. He listened to his da. He obeyed...

It was very 1950s.

From the outside looking in, they had an unusual dynamic. I wasn't sure how this would pan out, and the side of me that was his fiancée pitied the people around me.

It was *not* going to be an easy year.

"She *is* still their grandmother," Eoghan agreed, stepping into the conservatory and drawing our attention his way.

Behind him, Brennan, Declan, and Aidan were talking among themselves as they approached us.

Aidan was a little slower thanks to his limp, but when he saw I was watching him, dear God, it was like he shoved a vibrator between my thighs and turned it on max.

Everything about him got to me.

Everything.

I crossed my legs to reduce the ache, watching that serious look on his face morph into a smug smile.

Anyone else, I'd want to slap them.

With Aidan, I'd happily drop to my knees and suck his cock.

It was bizarre, but that wasn't a complaint.

The men all moved over to their women, sitting beside them on the massive sofa.

Aela didn't let Declan tug her down though, she sniped, "I don't care if she's their grandmother. What she did was fucked up."

"Agreed," Eoghan said easily. "But we're not a regular family."

She scowled. "Regular? There's regular and there's the fact your mom killed Aoife's."

"I'm aware of what happened."

Aela growled under her breath, and Declan stated, "You don't have to come as often."

"We don't?" she asked warily.

He shook his head. "You don't."

I was surprised by the concession, doubly surprised he hadn't told her to calm down like men always did. But while it soothed Aela's temper, she sagged and shuffled over to the seat, cuddling into Declan in the most tender move I'd seen her make.

They were an odd couple.

They bickered a lot in front of the family. I got the feeling Declan liked that though. She wasn't afraid to stand up to him.

"You could stop coming too," Aela said in a small voice.

"Finn knows we have his back, and we support Aoife wholeheartedly," Aidan commented, "but it's different for us."

I turned to shoot him a surprised glance. He grabbed my hand, squeezed it, and while I was still the noob here, and I was well aware that I had no rights to wade into the fray, I knew I had to change the subject onto one that was less incendiary.

Inessa looked like she was about to cry, which was an interesting response. Lena wasn't *her* mom, but she was clearly distressed.

Torn, I guessed was the right way to describe it.

Camille was much the same. Both of them had huddled in to their other halves the second they'd approached.

"Did Finn leave with Aoife?" I asked, deciding to shift gears.

Aidan shot me a grateful glance. "He just left. Conor did as well."

"I heard fighting earlier."

Eoghan snorted. "Fighting? Not likely."

"Who was it? None of you look bruised."

"Didn't you see the man who came by to visit?" Declan inquired gruffly, pressing a kiss to Aela's temple.

"No. We came in here to start a council of war," I said, to which Aidan laughed, but it wasn't mocking.

"After you guys became the UN, our uncle stopped by."

"Uncle?" Camille questioned, tipping her head to look up at Brennan. "I thought they were dead?"

"They were... Paddy faked his death."

"What?!" Aela straightened up. "Padraig faked his death?!"

"Yeah," Declan said on a sigh, tugging her back down against him. "Da didn't take it well."

"I can imagine," I drawled, shooting Aidan a glance. This wasn't a secret to us. We'd known for years, after all. "So your da and Padraig were fighting?"

"Think it was more a case of throwing furniture at him," Aidan said.

"Makes sense from all the crashing sounds," I replied. "You looked like you'd been brooding when you came in. What's going on?"

He pulled a face. "We had a hard talk."

"What about?"

"Secrets, and the shit we've been keeping from each other." Brennan shrugged. "Think it's time we came clean with you ladies about some of that."

"What like?" Inessa asked, her curiosity pricked enough that she didn't look so torn.

Declan grimaced and pressed a kiss to Aela's temple. "Shay told me about your grandparents, and about how he saw them being killed. I've believed for a while that they were killed by the IRA."

"You don't know that for sure," Aela muttered, but her cheeks had turned pale. "It was just a robbery—"

"In County Louth?" Declan scoffed. "This isn't the Bronx we're talking about, babe. Armed residential robberies aren't exactly common over there unless they're tied to the IRA."

Eoghan turned to look at her. "Your grandparents were in County Louth?"

"Yes. That's where our family is from."

He pursed his lips.

"What?" Declan demanded.

"Arrest warrants were out for a couple of ECD sharpshooters who took out an old couple in County Louth. Could be a coincidence."

"ECD?" Aela questioned.

Declan sighed. "You know that phrase the First Lady wanted tied into the glassware you're making for her?"

"Yeah. What about it?"

"It's a tagline for an extremist faction of the IRA. The ECD."

Aela looked like she'd been slapped in the face with a fish. "Is this a joke?"

"No. I wish it were, sweetheart."

"That means the First Lady has ties to them," I said slowly, every journalistic bone in my body tingling with that news.

Aidan tugged on my fingers. "We need this to be kept under wraps for the moment, Savannah."

While I pouted with disappointed, Aela whispered, "That cunt."

Declan agreed darkly, "That's one way of phrasing it."

She leaped up and started striding back and forth again. "She kills my grandparents and wants me to make some fucking glasses for her?"

"Well, she didn't pull the trigger," Eoghan pointed out.

"She was one of those fuckers." Aela paused. Then wagged her finger at Declan. "Don't you think this means the hunt for an atelier is called off. You're not about to keep me barefoot and pregnant and tied to the goddamn stove."

Declan sniffed. "Never thought that."

"Bullshit. I know you, Declan O'Donnelly."

His sheepish smirk told me that he *had* been hopeful about the barefoot and pregnant stuff.

"You guys remember Jen? Aoife's friend?" Eoghan tossed into the mix, clearly wanting to change the subject when Aela and Declan started eye-fucking each other over the coffee table. "She came for Christmas?"

He got some nods, but it was Brennan, who was toying with the hand Camille had laid on his lap, who said, "She's Padraig's daughter."

Inessa gaped at him. "Jen's an O'Donnelly?"

"Apparently," he muttered.

Camille frowned. "You didn't know?"

"Not until recently," Aidan confirmed, and I was grateful he didn't drop me in it.

I was trying to make a good impression on my sisters-in-law and going around admitting that I'd stolen DNA wasn't going to win me any awards.

Aoife already bore a grudge about that, and while I was trying to get friendly with her, it hadn't been easy.

Today was the first day she hadn't looked at me with disdain.

"Then there's the fact that Finn's not just our friend, he's our brother," Aidan murmured.

Aela grunted. "Is that all?"

Camille blinked. "I thought everyone knew that now?"

Inessa snickered. "I knew it the first time I came for Sunday dinner."

My lips curved when I saw Aidan's consternation. "You're surrounded by very smart women, boys," I declared, taking a final sip of my mimosa. "You need to get better at keeping secrets if you're going to try to pull the wool over our eyes."

Declan chuckled, Brennan grinned, and Eoghan, dear Lord, his lips actually twitched.

Surprised and delighted by the response, when I usually garnered nothing more than a grunt over potatoes, I preened when Aidan, clearly amused, tucked me into his side.

"They're starting to like you," he whispered in my ear.

Which, naturally, made me squirm.

Some mobsters liked me.

That made the inner thirteen-year-old in me squeal with glee.

FORTY-THREE

FINN

MY WEEKEND HAD ENDED after my brothers and I hashed out a conspiracy theory worthy of a novel and had confessed to enough sins that we were never entering the kingdom of heaven.

The following week started with Baggy, Tink, and Forrest—Brennan's crew—reenacting *Rambo* as they were given the coordinates to the location where Liam Donnghal was being held captive.

After a brief tussle with the bastards holding our cousin hostage, with Eoghan's skills reportedly keeping the Five Pointers in one piece, Liam had been freed.

I didn't get involved with that side of shit, but I'd heard the details, and that was more than enough for me.

Knowing he'd been locked up with some poor Triad kid made me glad that the Points and the Triads had worked together to kill every kidnapper on the compound.

While I was relieved for Padraig's sake that his son was safe and sound—aside from a partially missing ear and psychological trauma that would haunt him for the rest of his life, small fry in the grand scheme of things—I had my own problems to deal with so I stayed out of the loop.

And if that sounded selfish, then I was fucking selfish.

Aoife was my priority right now, and she wasn't making it fucking easy on me.

I'd told her about Aidan and Padraig, had even shared the news about Liam being a long-lost cousin who'd been kidnapped, and while she'd listened, she hadn't really conversed with me about the fuckfest that belonged on a daytime talk show.

I didn't know if her silence was telling me she wanted nothing to do with the O'Donnellys, or if she was just too grief-stricken to process more family drama.

Either way, stuck between a rock and a hard place—yet again—I'd shared what I could in the interest of being transparent, but it wasn't getting me anywhere.

Case in point now.

"Aoife?"

She didn't look up from the bowl of frosting that she was lacing with lemon juice.

"Sweetheart," I said with a sigh. "You need to eat."

"I can eat when Paddy gets here."

Her flat words had me frowning at her because she hadn't eaten at breakfast, nor had she eaten much last night at dinner.

My curvy wife was starting to look emaciated, and while I was all for her doing whatever the hell she wanted to her body, this wasn't her choice.

This wasn't her dieting to fit into a bridesmaid's dress for Savannah's wedding whenever the bride decided the wedding would be.

This was her starving herself because she had no appetite.

What scared me the most was that the loss of appetite wasn't just for food but for life as well.

Strolling over to her, I watched as tension struck her, straightening her spine and stiffening her shoulders.

The physical rejection was something I deserved, but that didn't make it hurt any less.

Even knowing I was skating on thin ice with her, it didn't stop me from continuing to walk over to her, moving behind and resting my hands on either side of the counter to lock her in.

"Finn, leave it," she intoned grimly, her hand whisking the thin, syrupy goop in the dish.

It smelled of spring, fresh and citrusy, but my appetite had died with Imogen.

That was the bitch of it.

I understood *why* she wasn't eating, but I still did it.

"You need to eat," I rasped, ignoring her warning.

"I'm eating enough."

"To get by?" I scoffed. "You're getting thinner by the day."

"Thought you'd like that," she snapped.

She couldn't see my scowl, but that didn't make it any less ferocious. "When have I ever done anything but celebrate your curves?"

Her gulp was audible. "Just leave it."

A plea.

She was itching for a fight.

I got that too.

Closing my eyes, I longed to press my head to her shoulder, to hug her, wrap my arms around her waist and hold her, but that wasn't in the cards yet. I didn't think she'd want that from me right now.

My impatient nature warred with knowing that I was doing the correct thing by taking this slowly.

With a care I wasn't known for, I murmured, "You're starting to look gaunt. It's winter, sweetheart. If your defenses are down, you'll get sick."

"Finn, I'm a grown woman. I can take care of myself—"

"You proved differently when you didn't immediately book an appointment for a termination, Aoife, so excuse me if I feel like I have to check in with you."

The words were a gauntlet I tossed down, but my tone was calm.

A shocked gasp escaped her as she whirled around to glare at me. "You did not just say that." Her hands went to my chest, and she shoved me away, but I didn't budge.

"I did," I continued in that calm tone. "Do you know the doctor who treated you blamed *me* and my Catholic family for you not going through with the abortion?" Her cheeks turned pale, stark white like she'd accidentally faceplanted in the powdered sugar. "I read the files, did some research. What the fuck were you thinking, Aoife? Imogen wouldn't have survived more than a couple of days—"

"There was surgery she could have had."

"Invasive surgery that would likely have killed her!"

"There might have been a chance of her surviving," she yelled shrilly.

I could feel my anger starting to grow as I saw how righteous she was. "You'd have put yourself through a high-risk pregnancy, would have risked *yourself* to have a baby that would have died within hours—"

"You don't know that," she rasped.

"I do know that. I read the statistics. I looked into this. The second your doctors accused me of putting *my* religion before my wife's health and welfare, you bet your ass I looked into it. I just didn't say anything because of—"

"Your withholding of the fact that you knew who murdered my mom," she interrupted with a sneer. "And *you* were the one who made me promise to always put our children first."

"Not above your health!" My mouth tightened, but I ignored her interruption and continued, "Jesus, Aoife, wasn't that obvious? You need to slow down. You're obsessed with baking—"

Her hands went to my chest, and this time, when she shoved me away, I rocked back on my heels. "Is our son clean? Fed? Happy?"

"This isn't about Jake."

"Answer the question," she snarled.

"He is."

"Is the kitchen tidy at the end of the day?"

I narrowed my eyes on her. "Yes."

"Then what I do or do not do with myself is none of your business."

"You *are* my business, Aoife," I rumbled huskily, staring down into those eyes that used to look at me like I set the stars in the fucking night sky and now looked at me as if I were a stranger. "That you could put yourself at risk when Jake and I can't function without you—"

"I did what I thought was right."

And that was what terrified me.

How could she think that path was the right one?

Mouth tight, I informed her, "I'm getting a vasectomy this week."

Her eyes flared wide. "You wouldn't do that. Jake's not supposed to be an only child!"

"No, baby, this proves that he *is*. I'm not putting you through this again. Even if the pregnancy was viable, I'm not watching you suffer for nine more goddamn months.

"Watching you sitting with your back on the floor and your legs against the wall to keep our kid inside you... I won't let you go through that again. Jake is our blessing. We need to accept that and move on."

"If you have a vasectomy, Finn, I *will* file for a divorce."

I'd set the gauntlet down.

She'd just picked it back up and she'd slapped me in the fucking face with it.

For a second, her words throbbed throughout the room, and as I stared down at her, seeing the tears in her eyes, but the otherwise frigid expression on her face, the gaunt cheeks, the shadows beneath her lashes, how her lips were colorless, how her shirt hung loose on her, I took note of it all and I weighed my words.

I would never let her divorce me.

Ever.

I'd get it tied up in court so fucking fast she'd be stuck with my married name until Jake was eighteen, and by then, I'd have wormed myself into her good graces once again.

There was no way that this was the end of our journey.

There was no way that this was where we threw in the towel.

That didn't make it any easier to say, "To protect *you*, there's nothing I won't do, Aoife. You want a divorce so badly, then I'll get you a good attorney.

"Instead of threatening me with something neither of us want, maybe you should realize what you're asking for—"

Before I could finish, her hand snapped out, and with the stark white fading beneath the bright spots of cherry on her cheeks, I knew she'd been about to slap me.

Not allowing her to let her outrage wither away at her control, I caught her wrist.

"I took that from you before, Aoife. I deserved it. I do *not* deserve it now. You will not lay another hand on me in anger, just as I would never dream of treating you in that way."

She dragged her hand out of mine and held it to her chest as if it were red hot.

Guilt flickered in her eyes, and she whispered, "I'm sorry, I didn't mean..."

"You *did* mean to," I said coldly, watching the heat of her shame burn color into her cheeks. "And you know why? Because giving up on *us* is enough to make you violent. Just like it is with me. You think I'm not furious that you'd threaten me with a divorce? You'd be wrong.

"You do not get to give up on us," I bit off, "and you do not get to use our family planning as an excuse to break us apart when having another child could *kill* you."

Hope stirred in my chest when she didn't interrupt me.

Praying that she realized I was right, I made to continue, but I heard the buzz from the elevator, and it stopped me in my tracks.

It was too early for Paddy, and the doorman had a list of faces who were permitted to enter.

Still, concerned, I backed away from her, watching her nurse her hand like it was a foreign entity, before I turned toward the door then strode down the hall.

My brows rose when I saw Jen, Aoife's best friend, standing in the elevator.

While she *was* on the list, it was still unexpected to see her, especially this Jen.

She was... *happy?*

"Jen?"

She frowned at me. "Yeah? I'm Jen. Is it that long since you've seen me that you don't remember what I look like?"

"No."

"Then?" she asked grouchily when I carried on looking at her. "What's the problem?"

Jen had that pouty look of constant dissatisfaction about her. She was a bitch, but Aoife loved her, so did Jake, and truth be told, she was good fun when she let her hair down.

But that was why I was staring.

The pouty look of constant dissatisfaction was no more.

"There's no problem," I countered gruffly. "You just look... happy."

"Did I look constipated before or something?"

"Maybe. You just look different."

"Is that Jen?" Aoife called out before she stepped into the hall.

Twisting back to look at her, I saw she studiously ignored me as she moved toward Jen.

It seemed her friend picked up on the atmosphere because Jen hovered there awkwardly before she blurted, "You freezing me out, Eef, is a low blow."

Aoife stilled then whispered, "I was just going through some stuff."

I almost snorted at *that* understatement.

"Yeah, well, you don't cut out your BFF, bitch."

My temper flared. "Watch it, Jen." I growled the warning.

"It's okay, Finn. She's right." Aoife's chin tipped up. "I've been ignoring everyone."

"I'm not 'everyone.'"

"Agreed. Do you want some cake? I made some for a guest who's coming over this afternoon."

"Oh, shit. That's who the doorman thought was coming over, right? I figured he wouldn't let me up—"

"I didn't put a block on you coming up, Jen—"

She wasn't to know that I had.

"—jeez, I just didn't feel like talking." Her smile was wan. "I still don't feel like it, but I have to get on with life, right?"

Where the hell she got that idea from, I had no idea.

In no way, shape, or form was I encouraging her to 'get on with life.' Not when getting out of bed in the morning was hard as fuck for me, and I hadn't gone through the physical torment that she had.

I frowned. "No. You take it as slow as you want."

I just wanted her to fucking eat and get some sleep.

"Flopping around the apartment crying isn't getting me anywhere." She wafted a hand at Jen, answering me while somehow acting as if I weren't there. "Come on, let's eat. Padraig is coming to see Jake and Finn."

"That's not true. I'm sure he wants to get to know you too," I argued, but again, she ignored me, retreating to the kitchen as Jen followed her.

With my concerned gaze clinging to my wife, I hovered outside the kitchen, wanting to give them privacy but needing to monitor the situation.

I watched Jen plunk the gift bags I finally noticed she was carrying onto the counter, then she took me by surprise because Jen wasn't exactly affectionate, and she moved over to Aoife. She gave her a hug from behind, and when Aoife stiffened, I had to admit that relief washed through me.

She was pulling away from everyone, not just me.

Then, I realized what a jackass that made me for being relieved. Throwing away the negative shit, I wished to hell that she'd spin around and take comfort in her friend.

I even said The Lord's Prayer, but no dice.

She didn't hug her back, not even when Jen groused, "I missed you."

"Missed you too, Jen," Aoife whispered.

"Then why cut me out?"

"Because I-I don't know... I just wanted to be alone."

Another understatement.

"You're not made to be alone," Jen reasoned. "I'd have come and hung out. You didn't have to isolate yourself."

"I did. I wasn't fit for company. I was crying all the time, either that or sleeping. I just..." She blew out a breath. "It was difficult. I was really happy, and then, I just wasn't."

"I'm so sorry, Eef. I shouldn't have sprung my news on you. I just, well, I tell you everything."

What news?

My brow furrowed as Aoife muttered, "It wasn't your fault."

"No?" Jen whispered.

"No." She patted her hand. "The OBGYN said it was high-risk. She even said..." Her gulp was audible. "She told me that I should terminate the pregnancy."

That was the first time she'd said that aloud without coercion.

I closed my eyes as her admission had a cocktail of emotions roaring through me.

Anger. Concern. Fear.

A potent combination that put my back up.

"Finn never said—"

"He didn't know. I went without him to that appointment." She bit her lip before she conceded, "I knew something wasn't right before they even did the exams."

"Oh, my God, Eef."

"I knew what he'd say. I didn't want to hear it. I knew what you'd say too," she muttered mulishly. "I didn't want to hear that either."

"Were you in danger?"

When she didn't answer, I couldn't stop myself from growling, "Yeah. She was. If she hadn't miscarried, and if the baby had gone to term, it could have killed her."

That she'd shut both of us out just pissed me off all the more.

"Our baby wasn't an 'it,' Finn," Aoife snapped, twisting to face me, her hands balled at her sides.

"I could really do with some cake."

Jen's feeble words fell to the wayside as I snarled, "What the fuck would Jake and I have done without you, Aoife? How the fuck would we have—" My voice broke off when that goddamn arrogant righteousness seemed to filter the air around her.

She breathed it in.

Sucked it down, not realizing it was toxic.

Poison.

Her gaze was loaded with a hatred I'd earned, but not with this.

I wanted to protect her.

I loved her so fucking much, and she was talking about throwing her life aside as if Imogen meant more than her. As if all our *deceased* babies meant more than her health.

I wanted Imogen. I wished to fuck she were still going to grace us in August, but that wasn't to goddamn be. And I definitely didn't want to have my daughter if it cost me my wife.

If that made me evil, then I'd take the title, and I'd own it.

Nothing and no one was worth sacrificing Aoife for.

But I knew she didn't see it my way. I knew we were on two different sides, and I couldn't stop myself from flopping my hands up into the air, letting them fall, then turning away and walking out of the kitchen.

I felt like a flotation device that had been pricked with an ice pick as I headed down to my study.

But as I looked around the workspace that I'd turned into a semi-permanent office and not just somewhere to finish off a couple pieces of work over the weekend, I didn't feel at home here either.

With Aoife and me at war, nothing felt right.

Nothing.

I didn't have much time to dwell on it before the elevator pinged again.

Checking my Patek Phillipe, I noted the time, registered that it would be Padraig, and I headed over to the drink tray on my desk, poured myself two fingers of whiskey, and downed it.

The burn resuscitated a few of the more frozen parts in my soul, and I headed out to greet my uncle with it warming me up from the inside out.

Conor and Aidan, his godsons, hadn't welcomed him with open arms, but I knew he'd visited Brennan and Eoghan this week.

I thought that was in thanks for their help in getting Liam back, something that the new Italian Don had facilitated by sending us the coordinates to the site where our cousin was being held hostage. But either way, he'd visited with them, and now it was my turn.

When I saw him, I had to admit, the changes in his appearance were difficult to process. The last time I'd seen him before Sunday, he'd been a grown man and I'd been a teenager.

I'd looked up to him. I'd respected him. He'd been larger than life and a welcome tonic to the craziness of Aidan Sr.

Now, he looked washed out.

A sepia version of the man I'd known and loved.

"Paddy," I greeted, heading down to shake his hand.

Everything else might have changed, but his grip was the same. A handshake was a handshake with him and not an act of war like it was with Senior.

After, we stood there awkwardly until Jen laughed, and it stirred me into action.

As I shuffled him down the hall toward my office, he asked, "Who's laughing?"

I could have told him who Jen was to him right then and there, but I didn't have the energy. That explosion in the kitchen had taken everything out of me. I just wanted to get into bed and sleep for a goddamn decade.

"A friend of Aoife. Aoife's my wife."

"I remember."

Nodding, I chivvied him down the hall, keeping it low because it was Jake's nap time.

Only when the door was closed behind us did I drawl, "Never thought I'd see a day where a ghost would be in my office."

"You've come up in the world," was all he said, his gaze circling the space as he shook his head. "You all have. Penthouses, the lot of you." His smile was sheepish. "And I thought we were flush with cash when I left."

"Times change." I arched a brow at him. "Need a drink?"

"Thought you'd never ask," he said dryly, heading over to the sofa in front of my desk and taking a seat.

Aware he was looking around the shelves that lined the room, each loaded with books that he had no way of knowing were first editions and taking note of the artwork on the walls that cost a cool couple million, I poured him a drink, myself another, then moved over to the sofas.

Passing him the tumbler, I took a seat then sipped deeply from the glass.

With his eyes back on me once he'd done the same, he asked, "Brennan said the family's made it because of you and Conor. That true?"

I shrugged. "I'm good with figures."

He scoffed. "Good with figures? There's being able to do trigonometry, Finn, and then there's creating a billion-dollar industry."

"Surprised you know what trigonometry is," I mocked.

The O'Donnellys didn't exactly applaud educational endeavors.

"Had to help Liam out with school. Amazing what you learn as they grow up."

Tipping my chin up in understanding, I explained, "You'd already set the groundwork. You, Frank, and Aidan had a great portfolio of properties thanks to your da, and I couldn't have done this without that."

Pride had his shoulders straightening. "Really?"

I nodded. "Really. Conor's good with figures, so he helped me earn more profits—"

"By cutting the IRS out of the loop?" Paddy queried, a gleam in his eyes.

I smiled over the rim of the glass. "Maybe." I tilted my head to the side, took in the shitty suit and the collar on his shirt that had been laundered several dozen times. "Liam's gone back home? That's what Aidan told me."

He pulled a face. "It's the middle of the NHL season. He didn't want to miss any more games.

"Didn't he need a break?"

"I think that was the last thing he needed. My son's very determined."

"I wonder where he gets that from."

Paddy snorted. "Yeah. I wonder."

Curious, I asked, "You don't speak much, do you?"

He leaped to his feet and blustered, "What makes you say that?"

That he bristled merely confirmed my suspicion.

"He's a rich NHL star. Your suit saw better days ten years ago, Paddy."

"You think I'd take money from him?"

"I think a good son with a father he respected would figure out a way to maneuver around any pricked egos."

His nostrils flared and his jaw clenched, and for the second time that day, I prepared to be struck down, only he settled back against the sofa and muttered, "You always been this perceptive and I just didn't notice it?"

"Few people notice it," I mocked. "Until it's too late."

Paddy tapped his nose. "That's smart, Finn. Real smart."

Hitching a shoulder, I asked, "What went wrong?"

"His manager turned him against me."

"And you were the completely innocent party?" I mocked.

He grunted. "No. I said shit I shouldn't have."

"About what?"

"His ma. She was a stripper."

"You stuck around for math classes," I pointed out. "So you weren't totally deadbeat."

"It's complicated." He heaved a sigh, but he didn't argue with my description of him as a father. "Liam's made a lot of bad decisions lately—"

"That why you had to pull a Lazarus and resurrect Padraig O'Donnelly?"

His mouth turned down at the corners. "He lost a couple million to some shady investors in Quebec."

"Give the names to Conor. He'll get the money back," I said softly.

"Conor don't want nothin' to do with me. I get it. I did a shitty thing."

There was no self-pity in the words, and that was probably what made me say, "Conor's been betrayed recently. We all have—"

"I didn't—"

I held up a hand to stall him. "Wasn't talking about you. Yours is the least problematic of a bad bunch. You know Mark O'Reilly?"

He sniffed. "That dipshit Aidan thought was a best friend?"

Amused, I said, "Well, he's still a dipshit. Callum was on Con's crew. They were best friends, but we found out recently his son was a Sparrow."

"Jesus!"

"Exactly. You notice Junior hobbles around?"

"Yeah, what's with that?"

"He got gunned down on my wedding day, alongside Aoife. But Callum is the reason that drive-by happened."

Paddy sank back into the sofa then, with a statement worthy of an award for understatement of the decade, muttered, *"Tabarnak.* The Sparrows have really messed with the Points, haven't they?"

"The fuck is *tabarnak?"* I asked.

His cheeks turned ruddy. "Means 'fuck' in *Québecois.* Picked up the language over the years."

Though I arched a brow at that, I merely said, "The Sparrows really have messed with us. And then there's this shit with the ECD."

"Never liked dealing with them. Getting into bed with the IRA's one thing, but those fucking nutcases?" He scoffed. "But Aidan just had to have Lena. He's such a goddamn hypocrite."

"You only just figured that out?"

His smile was wry. "No. Spent a lot of time pining for home, Finn. Not going to lie, some days, I thought it would have been better if I'd let the ECD take me down. Then Liam happened and shit suddenly made sense. Until it didn't no more."

"It's never too late," I said softly, feeling the words impart some of their wisdom onto me.

He was silent a second, then he murmured, "You're right."

"This is proof of that, in fact."

Nodding, he said, "I'll be returning to Quebec soon. I'll try to straighten things out with him."

"See Conor, Paddy," I insisted. "He'll help get Liam's money back."

He winced. "I'll think about it."

I scratched my chin. "How are you for cash?"

His gaze darted around the office, but he surprised me by saying, "I don't need charity. Only when my boy's life is at stake."

I respected that. "You got any savings I can invest?"

"You'd do that for me?"

"Don't see why not. It's what I do, after all," I commented.

"I'd appreciate that, Finn. Don't have much."

"Not for long."

His lips quirked up. "Would be nice not to worry about paying rent."

With a nod, I told him, "Consider it a done deal. Would you like to meet Jake?"

His smile was earnest and genuine. Some of that came from his relief at my offer, but I also knew it was from the joy he found in reconnecting with his family. "I'd love to."

And because I believed that, it was with pleasure that, twenty minutes later, I introduced Jacob Padraig O'Grady to his namesake.

FORTY-FOUR

AOIFE

PADRAIG, oddly enough, was nothing like his elder brother.

He was cheerful, kind, watchful, and, most importantly, *sane*.

As I fed him and Finn, while picking at my own dinner, I watched them interact, and even though I felt raw after our earlier argument, I liked listening to their stories.

"Remember that time when Senior got Aidan that hooker?" Paddy queried with a laugh, shooting me an apologetic look.

"I know what a hooker is," I said dryly.

"I remember," Finn mused, his lips forming a smile that didn't hit his eyes. Like the memory was there, it was funny, but it was in shadow. "He got a crush on her real bad, didn't he?"

Paddy cackled. "Your da found out he wanted to marry her—"

"No way," Finn countered, laughter finally bubbling from him. "How old was he?"

"Thirteen."

Jesus.

Thirteen? Senior had set Junior up with a hooker at *thirteen*?

Well, *that* took my mind off the fact that I'd almost hit Finn again.

Not for long, though.

The shame I felt soured the roasted chicken I'd cooked for today's meal, and it made me quiet.

Finn had done many, many wrong things, had made some of the shittiest decisions, but he'd never physically hurt me.

He'd been right to restrain me.

Right to tell me that he wouldn't let me do that again.

I couldn't believe I had, to be honest.

Yet, when he talked about Imogen, when he tossed his opinions down, when he declared he was going to take away our chances of having another child, I wanted to shake him because that felt like the only way he'd listen to me.

That he'd hear me.

Paddy stayed for around four hours. I was polite and spoke when he asked me something, but when we finished dessert, I retreated to the kitchen until he left.

When the elevator descended, taking him with it, I half expected Finn to return to the kitchen to hash things out again.

It was only when he didn't that my heart sank.

I felt like a candle flame with a wet wick. It kept fizzing in and out, the flame dying before it surged back to life.

Finn did that to me.

He made me feel alive when I was sure parts of me were dead.

And that triggered more guilt.

He'd hidden the truth from me. He'd stopped my mother's murderer from finding justice.

How could I still feel so reliant on him?

My mom would hate it, might even hate me for being weak... but maybe I was.

Maybe that was a character flaw of mine.

Maybe the reason Finn and I worked so well together was because I let him take charge.

"Maybe you're just fucking weak," I muttered to myself as I baked.

When Finn left me to it and went to bed without saying goodnight, I baked some more.

And I carried on through the night until the following dawn. I barely ate, and I didn't drink all that much. I stopped to put Jake to bed twice, to nurse him and change his diaper when he woke up, but then I went right back to it.

At five AM, I messaged Billy, my runner, to come to the apartment to pick up all the things I'd developed.

Most of them were new products, things I was trying out. My life was a mess, but the only thing that made sense were my recipes.

I had more stacks of Tupperware than a Tupperware party by the time the elevator buzzed. Heading into the hall as the doors opened, I frowned when I saw Billy wasn't alone.

"Louise? What are you doing here?"

She shot me one of those pitying smiles that made me want to curl up into a ball and die.

In my kitchen, no one pitied me.

Outside was another matter entirely.

"When he told me what he was picking up, I said that he'd probably need help. So, here I am."

Nodding in understanding, I jolted in surprise when I heard the heavy padding of feet behind me.

It wasn't like I didn't know it was Finn, but Louise's eyes lit up like a stoplight and that had me narrowing mine as I turned around and saw him in a pair of gray sweatpants, striding forward, his destination? Me.

He approached with a frown, demanding, "What the hell's going on?"

I might have been upset with my husband, but every instinct I possessed wanted to rage at the way Louise was eying him up like he was one of my brownies. I could feel my claws extending with the desire to swipe them at her. That was when I knew I was losing it.

Louise had been a trusted member of staff for years.

And as big of a jackass as Finn was, I knew he'd never cheat on me.

Still, I cast him a look, curious if he reacted to Louise's evident attraction to him, but unsurprisingly, his focus was all on me.

"Aoife?" he bit off angrily.

I pursed my lips. "They're here to collect the prototypes I've been making."

"Prototypes?" he repeated.

"While interest in the bakery is at a peak, it's a good time to gauge response to new recipe ideas," I said quietly, stepping away from him and heading for the kitchen.

As I did, I noticed the gun he had tucked into the back of his sweatpants and had to shake my head.

I was well aware that he didn't realize I'd noticed, but I had extra guards despite the fact we were so high up even the birds felt nauseated when they looked down.

With extra security in the lobby and all the alarms we had now, I had no idea who he thought would get to me.

Even if it stirred something in me that he was so protective, I shoved it away as Billy was saying, "Holy crap, Aoife! Do you think we should hold off on producing our regular menu to work through this stock?"

I shot him a look, well aware that Louise was out in the hall with Finn still.

Ears pricked to see if I could hear their conversation, I murmured, "Do the minimal of all our base products, but I'm hoping there'll be a clear winner by which of these run out of stock first."

"You sure that's wise?" Finn asked, moving into the kitchen, his lips firmed with his displeasure. At, I assumed, the fact I hadn't gone to bed yet.

"Why not? I'd like to know what customers want. Most of the influx are new so they're not used to the staple items anyway, and then the old clients can buy their favorites."

He considered that before he nodded. "You're right."

"Funny, isn't it?" I rasped. "Me, knowing my own business."

Finn conceded that with a grimace. "Sorry."

Mutinously, I raised my chin even as I started unfolding the packing crates so Billy could stack the Tupperware in them. We had these crates for this explicit purpose.

While my set up wasn't industrial in size, it was in layout. I had a double oven as well, commercial grade, and it was surprising how much I could output in a short space of time.

"How are the new guys working out?" I asked Billy. Louise said they were slackers, but I liked to get Billy's take on things too because she was more front of house and he worked in the bakery itself.

"They're great. One of them made some homemade puff pastry the other day. It was delicious."

Before I could answer, Louise wandered in a second later, and annoyed, I asked, "Where've you been?"

"I had to use the bathroom," she said with surprise.

I frowned but shook it off as being irrational, and in silence, we packed up the boxes and the crates.

Finn wouldn't let me carry anything, so he and Billy took everything to the elevator.

"Thanks for coming, Billy," I told him once we were finished. "Are you going to be able to manage getting all this into the truck?" We had one for deliveries.

"Yeah, sure. It'll only take a few minutes. We're parked right outside."

Finn muttered disgruntledly, "Let me grab my coat and I'll help."

Louise grabbed his arm and said, "That's so kind of you, Finn."

"We can manage," Billy countered, shooting her a frown.

"You know I hurt my wrist yesterday," Louise complained.

"Did you file a claim for it?" I questioned, my voice sharp.

"It wasn't at work," Louise said, hesitating long enough that I knew she was lying and that she hadn't filed it.

Gritting my teeth, I watched as Finn retreated to the closet beside the door. He shrugged into a hoody, then an outer coat, and shoved some sneakers onto his feet.

When Louise looked up at him like he was Chris Hemsworth, settling into the elevator at his side, too close for my liking, I pursed my lips and watched as the doors closed, leaving me behind.

I stood there for a couple minutes, trying to understand my agitation, but it warred with the memories of sweeping up the glass and the porcelain from the vases and the photo frames I'd thrown at Lena.

Cringing, I retreated to my safe place, the kitchen, but as I did, I found myself looking at the part of the floor where I'd collapsed.

I'd never asked who cleared it up, but I knew there'd been blood. Jen had told me that earlier.

Why did this place feel haunted?

This was my home.

My haven.

So why didn't it feel like that anymore?

Tired, I trudged over to the counters and cleared away the mess I'd made. It didn't take me long to load the dishwasher and clean up, just enough for Finn to come back.

"Jesus Christ, it's cold out there," he grumbled as he stripped off, loud enough for me to hear over the dishwasher.

Stepping into the hall, I greeted, "Louise was a bit much, wasn't she?"

I almost winced at how bitchy that was, but Finn popped his head around the closet door. "You're talking to me?"

I huffed. "Apparently."

His brow furrowed as he closed the door behind him, stepping over to me as deliciously bare as he'd been earlier.

Which reminded me.

"Why are you armed?"

"I always am."

"In bed?" I scoffed. "Who do you think can get to me here?"

"There are several active threats we're dealing with right now," he rasped. "But the gun has nothing to do with it."

Wiping my hands on a dishcloth, I asked, "Why then?"

"Because I'm on edge. Because my woman is in danger. Because I want to kill anyone for even thinking about hurting her. Because I love you and need to make sure you're safe."

I tipped my chin up. "Okay."

"Okay?" He frowned his confusion. "Really?"

Thinking about Louise, I said, "Yes. Okay."

His consternation was clear, but he surprised me by asking, "Earlier, Jen said she shouldn't have dropped her news on you... what news?"

I pursed my lips. "She's dating. She told me she loved him."

His brows rose, and he said, "Knew there was something different about her."

"What?"

"She was happy."

Now that he mentioned it, he was right. She had looked... *content.*

"Louise is always like that."

It took a second to figure out what he was talking about. When it registered, I sputtered, "What?"

He shrugged. "You never noticed before?"

"No, of course not," I sniped. I thought back to the last time I'd seen her with Finn, but it had to be last summer. "You're not together that much, so I don't think I'd have noticed."

"No. I make sure of it."

His wry remark put me on edge. "Does she make inappropriate comments?"

Finn scoffed, "Aoife, I handle it. Don't worry. You need her for the bakery. I get it."

When he started to walk away, shocked, I almost watched him go, then I called out, "That means she does make inappropriate comments!"

You need her for the bakery. I get it.

What was that supposed to mean?

He looked at me over his shoulder. "You have nothing to be jealous about."

"I'm not jealous," I disregarded.

"Well, then? What's the problem?" he retorted, no longer looking back at me, just heading to bed.

Uneasily, I watched him go.

My husband was a beautiful man. I knew women looked at him. I knew they wanted him, but I wasn't jealous because he never gave me reason to be.

He hadn't done a damn thing to encourage Louise; if anything, his scowl should have had her running for the hills. But the idea that she'd been drooling over him for a while was creepy. At least, it sure as hell creeped me out.

Turning off the lights, I dashed down the hall too. When I found him getting into bed, I demanded, "What inappropriate things has she said?"

"Aoife, I'm a grown man. I can handle this."

His tired tone just pissed me off even more. "Finn, answer the damn question."

His stare turned bewildered. "I'll answer yours if you answer mine."

"Fine," I snapped, folding my arms across my chest.

"Did you notice that she's made herself look like you?"

"What?"

"She was blonde before, now she's a redhead. She wears green contacts—"

"Lots of people wear colored contacts and have dyed their hair."

He studied me a second then shook his head. "I asked, you answered. Your turn."

"Is she coming onto you?"

"What do you think when she looks at me like she's a starving dachshund and I'm a steak? And no, I'm not interested." He punched the pillow a couple times before he rammed it beneath his head and turned away from me. "The day I met you was the day I stopped seeing other women."

Another man might mean that in the figurative sense. That he didn't date anymore.

Not Finn.

He was being literal.

He didn't see other women because I was all he saw.

The simplicity of his statement packed more of a punch than Hiroshima. It had me closing my eyes a second as I hovered there, torn between anger and concern and a desperate need to go to him. To feel his arms close around me.

When the tears came, I didn't know. But I stood there, bawling my eyes out for no particular reason aside from the other million reasons I had to weep.

It took him less than thirty seconds to register what was happening, and once he did, he was out of the bed and storming toward me.

When he dipped down and grabbed a hold of me, I let him. I climbed him like a tree, legs around his hips, arms around his shoulders, and I burrowed my face in his throat.

The second his arms were around me, it was like coming home.

The agitation I felt when he'd left the apartment disappeared, and as he clambered into bed—a move that was made awkward when I wouldn't let go of him—he shifted us around so that he was sitting up with his back to the pillows so I could keep burrowing into him.

I had no idea how long I sobbed for. It might have been a few minutes or an hour, but the scent of him, combined with the cold touch of his body from having left the apartment, the strength of his arms around me, it soothed something in me. Something that would always respond to him.

He didn't say a word.

Not to calm me down, not to annoy me, not to make me laugh.

He was just there.

Like I knew, no matter what, he always would be.

My nails dug into his shoulders, but he didn't complain, and rawly, I whispered, "I'll never divorce you."

"I know you won't."

He pressed a kiss to my temple then carefully lowered us both deeper into bed. I had to shuffle around a bit, but he didn't make me get off him.

If anything, he grabbed the covers, tucked them around us, encouraging me to stay exactly where I was.

"How do you know that?" I breathed, my face still pressing into his throat where I could feel the slightest trace of his pulse against my forehead.

"Because you and me, we're it for each other, Aoife. You could leave me, but it would be a half-life you'd be resigning us both to." He squeezed me. "I fucked up. I admit it. It was a horrific thing I did, and I will spend the rest of my life making up for it. Even then, it might never be enough, but I am yours. You are mine."

I thought about the tattoo on my arm, and I whispered, "The air I breathe—"

"—belongs to you."

With a shuddery sigh, I nuzzled his throat again, then I closed my eyes.

FORTY-FIVE

FINN

WE SPENT the night like that.

Her covering me, me holding her.

I woke up about an hour or two after dawn and just savored the closeness because her threats of divorce might have been hurled at me in a tantrum, but a threat was a threat.

I'd never let her go, but that didn't mean she had to love me, and her love was...

Jesus Christ.

Once upon a time, I'd thought love was a weakness. When Aoife came along, I figured it was a strength.

Now, I was reminded that my earlier belief was fucking right.

No one had the power to decimate me like she did.

Aidan Sr. could nail me to a goddamn cross, and he could slice me up like I was deli meat, and it wouldn't be as excruciating as this agony inside me.

So I held her for as long as she'd let me. I was her calm as the wild winds of her grief overtook her, and only when she mumbled in her sleep and slipped off me, falling flat on her back in her flour-dusted tee and sweatpants, did I get up.

Knowing she was exhausted, and that she needed to rest, I showered in the guest bathroom, got changed, then I started to get Jake ready too.

But after I changed his diaper, I was surprised to realize he wanted to sleep.

Yesterday had taken a lot out of him, I knew. Meeting with Paddy, and then staying up late, I'd intended on taking him with me, but seeing that he wanted more sleep, I decided to leave him.

I needed to head to the office to access some private files the Points had gathered on Hanover Corp., files that couldn't be computerized.

The last thing I wanted was to leave, but I didn't have much of a choice. We stored that shit on paper, not computer.

While we'd sent a contract over and they were due to sign it, I got the feeling they were going to dick us around, and I liked to have my leverage firmly in place before I negotiated.

So with my family still resting, I left my apartment with the baby monitor in my hand and went to the floor below where my crew had a place of their own. My guys had fewer tasks than my brothers', and they acted as guards and drivers for my family.

As the elevator doors opened, Braden got to his feet, dropping a breakfast burrito on the table in front of him. "Everything okay, boss?"

I nodded. "I need to head out."

"Okay. Want me to go up?"

A part of me did, but another part knew that they'd disturb Aoife, and I wanted her to rest for as long as Jake would let her sleep.

"Here," I told him, giving him the monitor. "Listen for Jake. Go on up if he stirs."

Braden shot me a wary look. "You want me to babysit?"

I rolled my eyes. "You have three kids of your own."

"Yeah, and Nevaeh looks after them!"

"You got three kids and you don't know how to take care of them?" Ollie muttered, stepping out of the kitchen too. In his hands, he was holding a BLT. "That ain't something to be proud of, dumbass." To me, he said, "I'll handle Jake, boss."

"Appreciate that. I won't be long. Just keep an eye out."

"Will do. Want Sam to drive you?"

"No."

They nodded, and I retreated to the elevator then pushed the button for the garage.

Moving over to my Range Rover, I climbed in, and I set the radio to blasting. The beat seemed to rage in time to my anger and fears, so I felt calmer when I approached the main headquarters of Acuig.

With one of my PAs notified of my arrival, Ethan was there waiting for me as I climbed into the elevator.

As he passed me some coffee like this was a regular day at work when it wasn't, I murmured, "I won't be here for long."

Of course, the coffee must have been some kind of fucking test because I ended up spending the next eight hours locked in discussions over some changes to the contract that Hanover Corp. sent over at nine AM.

Their actions proved that hostile takeovers were the best way to make corporate moves because when you did shit diplomatically, they thought you were a punk-ass bitch and could make demands that were beyond their worth.

Angered by the wasted morning, I was on the brink of storming off when Ethan popped his head around the corner and said, "There's someone called Louise waiting down at reception for you, Finn."

I glowered at him. "Who?"

"Louise? She says she works with Aoife?"

Louise?

"Send her away," I dismissed.

"You don't want to see her?"

"I sure as hell don't."

He hesitated. "She says she has something for you."

A bunny she could boil later?

I grunted, "Tell her to leave it at the front desk."

Seemingly aware that I was on the brink of getting him to send security, Ethan said, "She won't. Says the receipts are important and she wants to show you that someone is stealing from Aoife."

Achilles' heel well and truly tested, I snapped, "Send her up."

I had no way of knowing if this was a ploy or not, but if it was, I didn't give a damn that the bakery had nothing to do with me—I was firing her.

Ten minutes later, I finished sending an email to one of our attorneys when a knock sounded at the door.

Ethan waited a second before he popped in. "She's here, Finn."

"Send her in."

"Want some coffee?"

"No," I sniped. And encourage the bitch into thinking she was welcome here?

"Oh, but, Finn, it's so cold out. I'd love some," Louise chimed in from behind Ethan.

He flicked a glance at me but I shook my head. Ethan backed off, letting Louise stride inside.

She wore the same outfit as earlier this morning: skintight jeans with a tee tucked into them. A thick cable-knit cardigan swung around her hips, and she had a winter coat over the top. With calf-length boots, gloves, and a hat, she was dressed for winter.

Not for seduction.

Praying this wasn't a ploy and genuine for the sake of my patience, I beckoned her forward and remarked, "Ethan says you have proof someone's stealing from Aoife?"

She shot me a wary smile. "I didn't want to disturb her with this."

"You were right to come to me first," I told her coldly as she approached the desk.

From her bag, she pulled out a folder, and instead of handing it over to me, she rounded the desk and moved closer.

"You're fine where you are," I groused, incensed when she ignored me and shuffled even nearer to my side.

"I need to show you where there are clear signs of theft," she argued with a somber smile that I didn't trust.

Jaw clenched, I snatched the folder away from her and drew out the receipts. I saw she'd circled some totaled amounts in red pen, and that she'd scribbled a name at the top: *Billy*.

It was difficult to discern what was going on with the figures, mostly because products were itemized under a single number, and without knowing what each digit represented, I didn't know what was allegedly being stolen.

Determined to hurry Conor along with his computerization of Aoife's sales, I questioned the one thing I could make sense of, "You think Billy's stealing from Aoife?"

"Every second time he rings up a purchase, he isn't including some items that he gives to the client."

"You've seen him charge the client and serve them more than they'd ordered?"

"Yes." Louise patted my hand. "Was I right to bring this to you?"

I stared at the receipts then shuffled them together and began tucking them away in one of the sleeves she'd used to keep a day's worth of tickets separate from another day.

Beneath that was a printout of unsold items at closing and the day's takings.

Finding myself impressed by Aoife's turnover, I inquired, "What's he giving away?"

"The cake pops. They're a dollar a piece. But in the quantities he's doing this, it's costing Aoife thirty bucks a day."

A vague memory of Aoife discussing cake pops over dinner drifted to the surface. I was pretty sure she'd been talking about them as potential loss leaders.

Staring up at her, I asked, "Why do you think he's stealing?"

She frowned at me. "Because he is."

"Cake pops are a dollar a piece, but if I remember rightly, Aoife said to give them to customers. To their kids.

"Billy isn't charging them because Aoife told him he didn't have to." Her mouth gaped as she tried to argue with me, but I merely held up a hand to stall her. "I'll go through these and will determine if you're lying or if Billy is stealing, but to be frank, I have more faith in him than I do in you."

"That's not fair! I work hard for Aoife—"

"Yes, you do, so why are you here trying to cause her extra stress with a bullshit lie about theft?" As I stared up at her, with her diet version of Aoife's hair and the green contacts that couldn't match my woman's beautiful eyes, I spat, "You saw her this morning. Do you think she looked like she was ready to be dealing with this kind of crap?"

"That's why I brought it to you!"

"Even though I have nothing to do with the company?" I shook my head. "This was just to have some ridiculous excuse to see me, wasn't it?"

"I think you're full of yourself. If I can't report this to Aoife, then who can I report it to other than you?" she argued, trying to grab the folder from my hands.

I snatched it back. "No, you're the one who's full of yourself. If you could leap into Aoife's skin, you still wouldn't *be* her, Louise." I held the folder away from her. "This is my wife's property. I'll go through it to determine there is no theft occurring on the premises, and you can bet I'll go through it with a fine-tooth comb."

Her brow puckered. "Why are you being so mean to me? I was only trying to help."

"You were trying to throw a colleague under the bus so you'd have a reason to come see me." I thought about this morning when she'd tried to kiss my cheek in thanks for helping and had 'accidentally' brushed my mouth and bit off, "Even if you didn't, this is a case of Peter and the wolf."

I was ninety-nine percent certain she was spouting bullshit, but that didn't mean I wouldn't do due diligence.

"I didn't want to disturb Aoife," she whined.

"Well, you didn't. You disturbed me." My mouth tightened. "I think it's time for you to leave."

Her hand came to my shoulder. "Finn, I didn't mean to anger you."

"No? You did." I pushed her arm away then jerked in surprise when she grabbed my face and dove onto me.

I shoved her away before she could kiss me, but she sobbed, "Let me make things better for you, Finn."

Pushing my feet back had my desk chair rolling away as I snarled, "What the fuck do you think you're doing?"

But she was as demented as she was stupid.

She tried to plant another kiss on my mouth with lips that were like suckers, but I shoved her away again. That was when she let loose a sob, and eyes wild like the bunny boiler she was, Louise darted out of the office fast enough for me to hear Ethan's chair scraping back as he ran over to the door to peer inside.

"Is everything okay, Finn?"

Jaw clenched, I shook my head as I reached for my phone. As weird as that had been, as *ridiculous*, there was no way this would end well if I didn't inform Aoife before that psycho had the chance to.

"She left at the right moment. Jim Hanover's here."

"He's in the building?" I ground out in shock.

Ethan nodded. "He wants to see you."

The last thing I wanted was to see him. Beat his ass for wasting my fucking time? Damn straight.

"Tell him I'll be with him in five minutes," I snapped as I called Aoife and waited for it to connect.

"Finn?" she asked.

"I need to speak with you about Louise. I don't have much time, though. I have a meeting."

Confusion laced her tone as she queried, "Louise? You saw her again? Are you at the bakery?"

"No. She came to my office, Aoife. She tried to kiss me. Tried to spout some crap about Billy stealing from you by giving away cake pops.

"Anyway, I don't doubt that she'll call you and try to tell you all kinds of lies, but I wanted to let you know what happened from my side first."

I heard her breathing, but she didn't reply as I made my way out of the office and headed for the conference room.

Her silence felt damning.

"Aoife? You have to know I'm not interested in any woman but you. I thought we cleared this up earlier this morning," I grated the words out, pissed beyond belief that she might think I'd cheated on her. Maybe it made me more snappy than I'd have liked, but I spat, "I'll speak with you tonight. I'll be home late."

Infuriated, I headed into the impromptu meeting with Hanover.

If he thought I was going to be his whipping boy, he could fuck off. Today was not the day to want to fleece me out of a couple million more just because he felt like it.

FORTY-SIX

AOIFE

I STARED at the loaves of bread in front of me.

Golden brown, pillowy. The tops so beautifully curved that they were like cartoon drawings.

They were my olive branch.

Finn loved my bread.

I didn't make it for him so much anymore, but I knew he'd see them and would know what I was thinking.

This was not forgiveness.

This was not me forgetting what had happened.

This was me saying that I wanted to take a step forward. That I wanted his hand in mine as I did so.

Forgiveness would take time, and letting my resentment die would as well, but I didn't want to do any of this without him. Didn't want to wake up tomorrow without him in my bed like I'd done this morning. Didn't want to go to sleep without him at my side.

And that was what divorce would mean.

An empty bed.

One set of silverware at the table for dinner.

One plate in the dishwasher.

No hand to hold as I watched TV.

And it wasn't just that I'd be alone. It was that the other set of silverware, that the hand I should be holding, belonged to Finn.

My Finn.

Finn and Aoife, that was us.

We were a team.

We were a team.

I twisted away from the counter, leaving the loaves to their pristine perfection. But as I did, I stared at the space where I'd collapsed.

Where my blood had pooled.

I could remember Jake twining my hair with Jen's as she sobbed and tried to help me.

I could remember the pain of my baby dying.

And even more recently, I felt the anger and the hate that had seen me raise a hand to my husband. Again.

Needing to escape, I stepped out into the hall, but as I walked away from those memories, I dove deep into some new ones.

Sobbing on the floor as Lena comforted me, the news my baby was malformed a lead weight in my heart.

Watching Lena scurry away at my request that she leave my home, her telling me our friendship was atonement before I hurled a vase at her.

I stepped into the living room where, years before, I'd seen Aidan Sr. torturing one of his business associates—that had happened the very first day I'd met Finn.

Veering into my bedroom triggered memories of the tears I'd shed when I'd researched the surgeries it would take for a baby with sirenomelia to survive.

It wasn't the first time I'd cried in that bed, either.

I'd suffered three miscarriages now, and all of them had happened within these walls, under this roof.

Then there was my recovery from the drive-by shooting on our wedding day... something that had only happened because the Points had been infiltrated by the Sparrows. Where this apartment had been invaded, where my safety had been compromised. *Yet again.*

Changing the decor hadn't changed what I'd endured here.

The pain of the past, the memories, choked me.

But as much as they did, it was nothing to Finn's revelations.

His secrets had sunk into the walls themselves, lining each inch with words that would never be erased.

There was regret built into the foundations of the building. Lies. Resentment.

And I knew I didn't want to be here anymore.

Simple.

"I can't be here anymore."

I said the words aloud, but it was only then that I realized how out of control my breathing was.

When Finn had called, I knew my heart had started racing, but it was only now that I felt like I was running even though I was standing still.

My ears raced with the sound of my pulse, and my skin felt clammy.

I staggered over to the bed, widened my thighs, and plopped my head between them.

It took a hellishly long time for my heart to calm down, for my lungs to stop burning.

I felt sick, but for all that I was shaken, resolve filled me, and it gave me the strength I needed to stand up. To take a deep breath and to exhale, and to do it again.

Slowly.

To calm myself down.

Gradually.

After five minutes of self-soothing, I knew what I had to do.

Grabbing my phone, I tucked it into my purse before I headed into Jake's room. He'd been napping off and on all day, and I watched him squeeze his toes with his hands so I knew he was awake.

There was joy in this room, but it wasn't enough to make me want to stay here.

I picked him up and got him ready to head out, and as I did, Louise rang me.

Finn's call was the final straw for this apartment.

I believed him.

I was well aware that he wasn't interested in Louise.

I'd seen the way she looked at him, and I knew how he looked at me.

But it was me reaching the end of my rope.

Me needing to be somewhere else.

Me needing to be somewhere different.

Somewhere fresh. Clean. Untarnished.

As I dressed my son, I hit connect and I prepared myself for whatever she was about to say.

"A-Aoife," Louise sobbed. "F-Finn just tried to assault me."

I narrowed my eyes at the wet wipes, but I stayed silent.

"Aoife?" she shrieked. "Can you hear me?"

"What do you want me to do about it, Louise? If he assaulted you, then you should go to the cops."

A shocked breath sounded down the line. "What?!"

"If he assaulted you, then you should go to the cops."

"I-I don't understand," she whispered.

"What's not to understand? You need to report him if he hurt you."

"But you—"

"No buts," I said calmly when I was the opposite of calm. "However, if you're lying, and I know you are, then I wouldn't go to the police. They don't appreciate having their time wasted."

"How could you say that, Aoife? Why would I lie?"

"To save face? To make sure that I didn't fire you even though you came onto my husband? I can think of several more reasons but I'm pretty sure you'll sue for wrongful termination whatever I say.

"But I'll tell you this, Louise, you have two choices. You either go to the cops and report the assault or you're fired."

"You can't do that!" she snarled.

"I think you'll find I can. There are several occasions where you've underperformed recently, and I'm well within my rights to fire you for them."

"What like?"

"Failing to file a claim for an injury is a health code violation, and it could cause trouble with OSHA," I said flatly.

"I can't believe you're doing this!"

"No? You must really think I'm a fool then." I pursed my lips. "Of course, just show me that you filed a report with the cops and you're more than welcome at the bakery in the morning."

She cut the call.

I leaned over to press a kiss to Jake's belly and said, "Let's see what that snake does, baby, hmm?"

He chatted away at me, totally unaware of what had just gone down, totally unaffected because I'd kept my voice pleasant and calm at all times.

I had faith in my husband when it came to other women.

I trusted him in this when my self-esteem, before him, had always been shitty.

That trust and faith had to get us through the next weeks and months ahead.

He'd made a mistake. He'd protected the wrong people. But I knew he'd never do that again.

But I needed a fresh start.

We needed a fresh start.

So with Jake clean and ready to leave, I put him on the floor so he could shuffle around as I stocked my diaper bag up for a day.

With that packed, I reached for my phone, and I reserved a hotel room for us before I picked Jake up again. That done, I walked into the hall with him, where I called downstairs through the intercom.

"John?"

It took a second for someone to answer. "It's Braden, Aoife."

"Oh. I need to go out. I have a spa appointment," I lied, knowing full well they'd never let me out of the apartment if they suspected my intentions. And the second they did, they'd call Finn, and he'd make me stay here.

He wouldn't understand what I was doing.

So I had to show him.

"Sure. I'll get John to head downstairs and warm up the car."

"Thank you. You can ride with us. You don't have to pretend to be in another car."

He was silent a second. "Okay. Thank you."

I cut the line, then I waited for Braden to come up to tell me I could descend to the garage.

As I stared around the space, I told Jake and I meant it, "I hope I never see this place again."

FORTY-SEVEN

FINN

I GOT the message about Aoife leaving the apartment the second it happened.

My meeting with Hanover could only be described as frosty by that point, but it turned glacial after that.

While Braden assured me Aoife was visiting a spa, that it was at the Victoria Hotel, and because I knew my wife, I was well aware she'd used that as a reason to leave the apartment.

To leave me.

With Arctic winds blowing in the conference room, Hanover's bluster faded as the temperatures continued plummeting, and he finally signed the contract we'd agreed upon four days ago before he'd sent in the amended one.

Once that was dealt with, I told Ethan, "Hold all my calls. Deal with my emails. I'll contact you when I'm back in the office."

He didn't have a chance to answer me as I stormed out. My temper filled the elevator, my hurt throbbed beneath the surface, but as I looked at my reflection in the mirrors, it wasn't a defeated man who stared back at me.

I wasn't about to lose Aoife.

Not without a war.

Straightening up, I headed for my car, and as I jumped in, the music from this morning blared on. It eased me, much as it had done earlier as I raced through the traffic to make it home.

Maybe it was ridiculous of me to need to check things out, to have my suspicions confirmed before I got myself suited and booted for battle, but when I got there, I didn't expect to see drawers that were full of clothes. Jake's closet was still loaded with his things too.

My cell rang, but I ignored it as I saw, in the kitchen, there was freshly baked bread.

The loaves mesmerized me.

What they represented held me in a thrall.

When I realized that the phone call could have been Braden or one of Aoife's guards, I blindly hit the missed call and blinked when Aidan Jr.'s voice sounded down the line. "Conor says Hanover signed the contract? Well done, Finn!"

She'd baked me bread.

That was all I could think about.

Did that mean she was coming home? Or had she finished baking them before I'd called? Had I misunderstood what was happening here?

"Finn? You there?"

"I'm here," I choked out.

"Are you okay?"

"Aoife—"

Aoife, what?

"I don't know…"

"You don't know where she is? How she's feeling?" Aidan prompted after more silence, "Is she sick?"

"I don't know where she is precisely," I said carefully.

"What? Don't your guards know?"

"She's in a hotel—"

Though he couldn't see it, I shook my head at myself. I was talking nonsensically, but that *bread*.

It floored me.

It was a token of peace because Aoife knew I adored her bread.

But why had she gone to the Victoria?

Maybe it really was to go to the spa and I was just being paranoid.

"Finn? You there? She's in a hotel? Which hotel? Don't you know? Did I hear you right?"

"I'm here, but I have to go, Aidan."

"You sound weird, brother."

I felt weird.

"I can get my crew onto finding her," he was saying, making me realize I had to speak out before I had the Five Points roaming the city for a lost wife who wasn't lost.

"No. It's all right. I-I need to go, Aidan."

"I'm here if you need me, Finn."

His words settled in my chest. "I know you are."

"Always."

"I know. And it works both ways."

I cut the call because I needed to text Braden.

Except I saw that he'd already messaged while I was on the phone.

Braden: *Finn, we have a problem.*

Me: *What is it?*

Braden: *I swear, we all thought she was going to the spa, Finn.*

I goddamn knew it.

So what the fuck was the bread about?

Me: *She checked in?*

Braden: *She did.*

Me: *Wait for me in the reception with the key. I'm coming over now.*

I returned to my car empty-handed and drove like a crazy person toward the Victoria. It was only around the block from my office building, and the traffic hadn't abated since leaving earlier.

When I made it to the hotel, I paid for valet parking, and as I headed into the reception, I found Braden waiting on me.

"Sorry about this, boss," he muttered, shuffling from one foot to the other.

That he called me 'boss' told me he knew he'd fucked up by letting Aoife check into a goddamn hotel under the guise of going for a 'spa day.'

"Which suite is she in?"

"The penthouse suite."

"Did she tell you not to let me in?"

He shook his head. "No. She even gave us a key. John, Ollie, and Sam are all in there. No argument or fuss."

My eyes narrowed as I held out my hand. "Key card?"

Braden passed it to me and, ignoring the grandeur of the hotel that had seen dignitaries and royalty staying under its roof, I retreated to the elevator alone and hit the button for the penthouse.

I wasn't sure what I expected when I got there.

Angry words? Recriminations? Tears?

I didn't get that.

Unlocking the door, I found a pleasantly appointed suite. A little traditional for my tastes, very ornate and with a lot of antiques, but I saw there was a pen for Jake to sit in, and he was watching my crew playing cards over by the dinner table.

When he saw me, he called out, "Dada," and I dipped my chin at my men as I moved over to him and picked him up.

At his squawk, I heard footsteps, and I twisted around to find Aoife watching me from a kitchen I knew would have her approval.

"Leave us," I intoned, my gaze on hers even as I spoke to my men.

Chairs scraped, booted feet trod on the Persian rugs, and a door closed, shutting us in together.

I tipped my chin up. "I won't let you leave me."

"I won't let you leave me either," was her flat response.

Surprised, I bit off, "What?" I squeezed Jake when he jolted at my tone, and hugging him, I asked quietly, "What the fuck is going on, Aoife? You have to know I didn't touch her."

"Having a miscarriage didn't make me dumb," Aoife retorted, folding her arms across her chest. "If there's one thing I can trust, it's that you think I'm some kind of Marilyn Monroe reincarnate." Though I frowned at that, she narrowed her eyes. "I've never worried about you cheating."

"I've never given you cause to worry," I said stiffly.

"No," she agreed.

"Then what's this about?"

"My New Year's resolution."

"It's March."

She shrugged. "Better late than never. I didn't want to stay in the penthouse tonight."

"You couldn't have just said that?" I growled.

"You told me yourself you'd see me tonight, and I knew the guards would keep you in the loop about my location—"

"You moved out of our apartment!" I snapped. "And you didn't tell me dick."

"I moved to a hotel around the block from your office, Finn," she retorted. "You can walk to work in less than five minutes. If you think this was me leaving you, then why would I have moved so goddamn close to where you spend most of your days?"

Logically, I knew she was right. I'd gotten into my car and two minutes later, I could climb out of it again in Acuig's parking garage. But this wasn't about logic, was it?

"You should have talked to me."

"I couldn't talk. I was having a panic attack. But I knew I had to get out of there."

Hurt flickered inside me, as well as concern. "Are you okay now?"

I started to step closer to her, my hand outstretched, but I hovered in place, uncertain of my welcome.

Her gaze drifted to my hand. "Don't I look okay?" was all she said.

I took her in, saw her cheeks were bright pink, and she...

Surprise welled inside me.

She wasn't covered in flour. Her color wasn't phenomenal, but her pallor was better. She didn't wear that harried frown I was growing used to seeing, and it was an odd thing to notice, but I swore she stood taller.

"You left our home," I repeated.

"I did. That place is..." She straightened her shoulders. "I don't want to live there anymore."

"What?" I barked, groaning under my breath when Jake started sniffling.

"I don't want *any of us* to live there anymore," she clarified, and while her words made my heart stop racing, I still had to pick apart what was happening here.

"You want me to move out?"

"No, Finn. Have you got selective hearing or something? I'm not leaving you. We're not splitting up—"

"But you... I... we..." My mouth firmed as relief hit me harder than Brennan's fist in a fight. I stared at her, so fucking thankful and relieved and agitated all at the same time, but I had to get this out, had to remind her of a truth that wasn't going anywhere. "I arranged for a vasectomy."

Hurt brought shadows in her eyes. "I understand."

"Do you?" I demanded. "Do you understand that I can't live without you?"

She shuffled forward and surprised me by sliding her hand around my waist and pressing her face to my other shoulder. I hugged her back, tucking her tighter into me, holding my world in my arms.

"I understand," she breathed, but I heard her sadness.

"All the money in the world won't fix this," I whispered against her hair, rubbing my chin over the crown of her head. "I wish it would. I'd throw millions at it if I could give you what you wanted."

"I know you would," she whispered.

"We could—" I almost bit back the words, until I continued, "We can adopt, Aoife. I can throw money at that so our ties to the Five Points fade away. I can get you the family you want that way. But I can't risk you, baby. I can't knowingly endanger you. Please, don't ask me to do that again."

She squeezed me. "I won't. And I'll think about it. Finn?"

Sagging with relief that she accepted what I was going to do without argument, I leaned against her as I asked, "Yeah?"

"I need to never step foot in that apartment again."

Carefully pulling apart that sentence, I queried, "You know the penthouse's done nothing to you, don't you?"

"Yes. I'm not crazy. But I don't want to be there anymore."

"I understand. I'll set a realtor on it, and we'll find something different."

"You don't mind?"

Did I?

"I don't care where I live so long as you're there," I rasped, knowing I was speaking the whole truth and nothing but the truth. "Where do you want to live? Westchester? Somewhere like that?"

"No. Not in the suburbs. Your commute would be too long. Somewhere in this neighborhood. So you're close by."

I pressed a kiss to her forehead. "I can work from home."

"There'll be some days where you can't. Like today." She huddled into me. "I-I need things to change, Finn."

"Like what?" I asked quietly. "I already promised no more secrets."

"Do you know what I was thinking about when I had that panic attack?"

"What, baby?"

"That the walls were closing in. Over eight thousand square feet of space, Finn, and the walls were closing in." She shook her head. "I'd pushed you away and you left me in bed, left the apartment... I thought about you not being there every morning. About waking up alone and eating alone and raising Jake alone, and it made my panic attack worse.

"I don't forgive you," she said, blunt enough to make me wince. "I might never forgive you, but I don't want to be without you, and that's something to work toward. But I need compromises. The way things were... I don't want that anymore."

Her words resonated more than she could know. "What *do* you want, sweetheart?"

"No more fifteen-hour days. No more getting in when Jake's asleep. No more working yourself so hard that you'll break."

"You know why I'm doing that."

"I do, and I agree to a point, but I don't want—" She pulled back, and though I held her firmer against me, not wanting her to drift away, she didn't. She just stared into my eyes as she whispered, "My mom had no idea that that day would be her last. She left me in the tearoom thinking she'd see me later that evening. And as devastated as I am, I know that we did so much together over the years, that we made the time we had count.

"Jake won't have that with you if you keep on working so many hours. It's different now. He won't remember these times, but as he gets older, he will. He won't know you. You'll become a stranger to him.

"I understand that you want him to have choices down the line, and I'm all for you striving to achieve that, but Acuig doesn't stop running when you start working eight-hour days.

"Hire more people. Get your brothers in on it. Declan's lost in the docks. He could work for Acuig easily, and be so much happier too. Brennan's wasted just being your father's fixer. What else could he be doing for Acuig? He and Camille will want kids soon. He won't want his kids doing what he's had to do. Aidan's the same.

"Senior might be a problem, but he won't be around forever, Finn. Aidan will have to handle the fact that none of his brothers really want to be in the mob, and when he becomes a father, that will resonate more than ever too."

Staring into her eyes, seeing her resolve and her fear that I'd reject what she was saying, I bowed my head and ran my nose along her temple. "When did my wife get to be so wise?" I questioned.

Her hands tugged at my jacket. "When she grew up and realized her husband wasn't a white knight, but that didn't mean he couldn't still be her hero anyway."

I sucked in a breath at her words and whispered, "I never tried to be your white knight."

"You became that, but you're not perfect, and I shouldn't have put you on a pedestal. Things will change between us, Finn. I can't stop that from happening."

"I know," I agreed sadly. "I'm sorry I broke that, baby."

"Maybe it needed to be broken. Mom's death, how she died, there was no closure for me. I think, for the longest time, that I've been nursing that open wound.

"Now, it can start to heal. I know who did it, I know why, and I know that I can't have justice." She tipped her chin up. "Lena sent me a voicemail. It's her confession. I could take it into a precinct tomorrow, but I know you're right. No matter what happens, she'll never see the inside of a jail cell." She swallowed. "I don't know how..." Her mouth worked. "I need you to understand that I might not be able to go to Sunday dinner for a while."

"I don't expect you to," was my immediate retort. "Baby, I didn't expect that of you last week."

"I was being spiteful."

"You're allowed to be. You're allowed to be mad at me. You're allowed to grieve, and you're allowed to hurt. You're allowed to shout at me and to sob when I'm there so I can hold you. All of those things you're allowed to do, sweetheart. You're just not allowed to leave me."

Our gazes collided, and softly, gently, I lowered my head and pressed a kiss to her mouth.

It was a simple promise.

A silent vow.

"I choose you, Aoife. Always you."

When tears appeared and began to trickle down her cheeks, I pressed my lips to those trails and kissed each one.

"I choose you, Finn," she choked out. "Always you."

But she didn't have to make that vow.

I wasn't the one who'd been betrayed.

"I'll spend the rest of my life working toward your forgiveness, Aoife."

A shaky sigh escaped her as she shook her head. "A fresh start, Finn. That's what we both need."

"Is moving apartments enough?"

She appeared to consider that but admitted after a couple seconds, "I love my sisters-in-law; I even love my brothers-in-law. I don't want to be away from them. I don't want Jake to be away from them either."

"Maybe it's time we started our own traditions?"

An interested gleam appeared in her eyes. "What do you mean?"

"How about a Saturday night dinner?"

"So they can still go to their parents' but we won't lose touch?"

I nodded. "What do you think?"

Hope appeared to unfurl inside her, tipping the corners of her lips into a beautiful smile. "I like the sound of that."

PART 5
EPILOGUES

FORTY-EIGHT

FINN

"CON? LET ME UP."

A yawn sounded on the intercom. "It's four."

"Yes. I know."

"Four, Finn. You know I don't get up until six."

I shot Padraig a look and watched him squint at his watch. "I know you don't, but this is different. And it's four in the afternoon, Con, not pre-dawn. Let me up."

He yawned but I heard the buzz as the elevator drifted down to greet us in the lobby of his building.

When the doors opened, Padraig and I clambered in, and he remarked in confusion, "It's late."

"Not for Conor. Anyway, this is the only way I'd get you up there. He'll be too tired to check the video feed."

"It's a lot more high tech than it was when I was younger," Paddy admitted uneasily.

"Yeah, you hung around in the back of restaurants—"

"Huh, do I look like a fucking Italian? They did that shit. We went to bars, Finn. *Bars.*"

My lips twitched at his sudden descent into full on New Yorker. "You can take the man out of Hell's Kitchen, but—"

"Yeah, yeah. Can't take Hell's Kitchen outta the man." He hunched his shoulders in his coat. "You know him well, don't you?"

"Con?" I frowned. "Of course."

"It's good to see. Frank, Aidan, and I, we were tight, but I can tell you and your brothers are closer."

I pondered that a second and mused, "I think in your position, I'd have no fear about going to Junior."

He grimaced. "Times were different back then. Had shit with the Haitians and the Aryans going down. This was before the wars, but shit was rough. The eighties were harder going. Lots of territory disputes. Your da made Stalin look friendly where his paranoia was concerned."

"That sounds about right," I said gruffly.

"Wish I'd been as tight with him as you guys are. Makes my soul pleased, ya know? Looking at the lot of yous, I know somehow, those fucked up folks of yours managed to make some decent sons."

My brows lifted at that character assassination. "You sound... critical."

"I am. Wasn't at the time. But with distance and the passage of years, and then the fact I got Liam now, I saw what he did and realized it was fucked up." He reached up and scratched his chin. "Our da was of the same school as yours. 'Spare the rod and spoil the child.'"

"You weren't like that with Liam?"

"Nah. I had two choices. Knew I could be like Aidan or I could be like *me*."

"And you decided to be like you?"

"I did, but I still fucked it up anyway." He heaved a sigh. "I fuck up a lot of shit. That's another reason why I didn't tell Aidan. There's only so much shit you can dig your way out of."

The doors opened to an empty hall. With his words drifting around my head, I beckoned him out and hollered, "The fuck are you, Kid?"

"In the kitchen," he hollered back.

Aware that Paddy followed me, I headed to the kitchen and found Kid with a mixing bowl full of cereal.

Peering into it as I approached, I asked, "Honeycomb?"

"You're not having any."

I scowled. "Why the fuck not?"

"You brought him." He sniffed at Paddy. "What do *you* want?"

"Could you sound anymore petulant, Kid?"

"Yeah, I could if I tried." He pointed his spoon at Paddy. "You knew I depended on you. You left me anyway."

Paddy's nostrils flared and his shoulders hunched again, his ears pretty much diving under the upturned collar on his coat.

Watching him turn into a tortoise, I asked, "What did you depend on him for?"

"Everything Da never gave me." Con shoved a heap of cereal into his mouth.

"Which was? You were his fucking favorite," I pointed out, bewildered.

"Con and I used to talk, didn't we?" Paddy rasped.

"We did. About everything and anything. You were the only one who got me, Paddy. But you left me." Con's brow furrowed. "How could you do that?"

"Your da wasn't wrong, Conor. I was never any good at the Firm. I fucked up all the time, and that was the final straw. When my life was on the line, I guess I took my chance."

"And left me behind." Kid's voice wasn't plaintive, just matter of fact. He squinted at him, malice in his eyes, as he declared, "You're a piece of shit godfather and an even worse dad."

"Fucking hell, Con, that's hard," I bit off, shooting our uncle a glance.

Though Paddy had blanched, Conor merely said, "You can say that knowing he left Jen behind?"

I hissed.

Fuck.

I'd forgotten about Jen and her ties to us.

She was an O'Donnelly.

"What a clusterfuck," I muttered. "Did you know you had a daughter?"

Paddy frowned. "Shut up. I don't have a girl. I got Liam. He look like a girl to you?" He straightened up. "I know I'm a piece of shit godfather, Con, but there's still time to make it right, ain't there?"

"Why? What do you want?" he sniped.

"Finn said you'd help Liam with some funds of his that were stolen, but that's for him. Not me. I won't see a dime." He raised his hands. "I missed you, little fecker. So many times I wanted to pick up the phone and call you, but I—"

"Didn't. You know I can keep a secret," Conor ground out. "You know I fucking can. Why would you keep that from me?"

"Because of all the shit that went with it! I knew what would happen. You'd want to come live with me—"

My brows rose at that. "What?"

Paddy sighed. "Con always wanted to come and stay with me."

"Because you got me," Con said, his tone pained. "You accepted me."

"I don't get it. Senior accepted you."

"Da thinks I'm a fucking machine. He treats me like I'm an iPhone," was Conor's bitter response. "Need to bug an office? Send Con in. Need a program that'll protect the family homes? Doesn't matter that I fucking hate coding security programs, nope, Conor'll do it.

"Want to record every single soldier in our Firm? Con will trawl through the millions of recorded minutes." Then, pointedly, he snarked, "Want to get money out of someone's account because they stole it from you? Con will get it back."

I blinked. "Shit."

"You think I want any of that?" Kid rasped. "I'm his fucking monkey, Finn. He makes me dance."

Shoving a hand through my hair, I stepped back and plunked my ass on a stool. "I just thought you liked doing that shit."

"I got used to it. I didn't have much choice." He grunted. "It's okay. I accepted that's my lot, and I'm fucking good at it. I never thought about complaining either because what was the use?" He jabbed his spoon in our uncle's direction. "But he's the reminder I didn't need."

"Doesn't mean you shouldn't have a relationship with Paddy. This is a second chance for both of you."

"I'd like that," Paddy said. "I missed you, Con."

He tipped his chin up. "What about Jen?"

"Who the fuck is Jen?"

Conor narrowed his eyes. "Your daughter."

"I ain't got no daughter," Paddy sniped.

"You do," I said softly. "It's been confirmed several times."

"Who the fuck is this Jen?" His bewilderment was genuine—I'd tortured enough men to know the difference between candor and bullshit.

"Jennifer MacNeill. Her mom's name is Diana." Conor bit off, "Don't make out like you don't know her. You put her up in one of the buildings over on 35th."

"Diana MacNeill?" His face scrunched up in confusion, but slowly, it cleared. "She had a kid?"

"Yeah, she did. And she wasn't raised right, neither." Con slurped up some milk from his bowl. "That's on you."

"I didn't know she had a kid," Paddy whispered, staggering over to join me at the kitchen counter. "I got a daughter?"

"You do," I confirmed, shooting him a look, curious as to what he'd feel about this.

His eyes rounded. "I got a little girl?"

"Yes," Conor snapped. "Which part aren't you understanding?"

I glared at Kid. "Leave him be, Con. I think he's glad."

Paddy's mouth worked. "Does she know I'm her dad?"

Scrubbing my hand over my hair, I admitted, "She does. You know when you came to my place?"

"Yeah."

"Jen was the friend with Aoife in the kitchen."

He cringed. "She knew I was there?"

"Yeah. Aoife would have told her."

"She didn't want to meet me," he said mournfully. It wasn't a question.

Conor, eating his cereal with more aggression than was warranted, watched Paddy with eagle eyes, scanning him for truths and lies.

I figured that our uncle had shocked him. His response was unexpected.

Conor, for whatever reason, liked the unexpected.

And maybe it was wishful thinking, but that gave me hope for them.

It really did.

SAVANNAH: *Holy shit, you should have seen the Aidans today.*

Aoife: *Why? What happened?*

Savannah: *Look at you low key trying to bullshit the bullshitter. You and I both know it's the first Sunday you haven't come to eat at the compound since Paddy pulled a Lazarus.*

Aoife: *I'm not in the mood for this, Savannah.*

Savannah: *You don't have to be. I'm telling the story. You just have to read. And trust me when I tell you it was beyond sexy.*

Aoife: *Sexy?*

Savannah: *Yeah. My man butted heads with Aidan O'Donnelly Sr.*

Savannah: *I thought I was going to come.*

Aoife: *LMAO.*

Aoife: *Well, I can tell you now... I didn't expect this convo.*

Savannah: *I'm not sure what Finn said to Senior when he told him you guys weren't coming to eat with them anymore, but it riled him up something fierce.*

Savannah: *Aidan was all, 'Finn's a grown man. If he doesn't want to eat dinner with us, then he doesn't have to.' And trust me, this is the PG version.*

Aoife: *Can't imagine that went down well.*

Savannah: *No. Like a lead balloon. God, my man's hot.*

Aoife: *You really get off on this mobster stuff?*

Savannah: *Oh, yeah. It's better than porn to me.*

Aoife: *Well, that's TMI.*

Savannah: *You're friends with Jen. Don't lie to me about TMI. She's the queen of it.*

Savannah: *Whether you like it or not, and are pissed at me or not about betraying Jen, we're gonna be in each other's lives, Aoife. I'd prefer to be friends, wouldn't you? And friends share things.*

Aoife: *True.*

Savannah: *You're a woman of few words.*

Aoife: *You're a woman of many.*

Savannah: *Ha. That's not a lie.*

Aoife: *So? What happened?*

Savannah: *Aidan went to battle and won the war. It was sad actually. I thought Senior was going to cry.*

Aoife: *Cry?*

Savannah: *Lena ran from the table when they finished arguing,* *and Senior just stood there, looking at her like she was running away from him.*

Savannah: *Anyway, just wanted to let you know that there was an argument and Aidan Jr. won it.*

Aoife: *I knew there'd be arguments. It's weird. I don't really want to cause shit between the family.*

Savannah: *You're kinder than me. Lol. If Lena had killed my mom, I'd be poisoning those brownies of yours and giving her a fancy gift basket.*

Aoife: *You're going to make a fine mob wife, Savannah.*

Savannah: *This I know.*

Aoife: *Is Aidan aware of what he's in for?*

Savannah: *Half of it. The rest will come with time.*

Savannah: *Won't that be a hoot?*

Aoife: *ROFL.*

Savannah: *Anyway, the fun didn't stop there. After we ate, this guy came storming in. Mark O'Reilly? Started yelling at Senior. Demanding to know where his son was and why Aidan wasn't helping out more. It was better than a TV show.*

Aoife: *Sounds like you had a ball.*

Savannah: *Yeah. I know I'm sick. But I own it, right?*

Aoife: *You do.*

Savannah: *Guessing that's the Mark O'Reilly who's the father of Callum? The one who betrayed you?*

Aoife: *Yes. What happened?*

Savannah: *Don't know. They went into Senior's office. I tried to suck the info out of Aidan, but no dice.*

Aoife: *LOL.*

Aoife: *Thanks for telling me, Savannah.*

Savannah: *Savvie. We're friends now. We'll be sisters at some point too.*

Aoife: *I know Aidan would have told Finn, but Finn's being quiet about Lena and Senior.*

Savannah: *He'd be an idiot to bring them up. Finn knows he's a lucky bastard that you're not asking for a divorce, so he isn't going to test the waters.*

Aoife: *I don't want him to keep things away from me like that though.*

Savannah: *Can't have it both ways, Aoife. I mean, it's not really a secret. I guess that's what your concern is, right?*

Aoife: *Yeah.*

Savannah: *Don't think of it as if it is one. Think of it as Five Points' business. They're not family anymore, after all. Not to you. So they're business.*

Aoife: *You're right.*

Savannah: *I often am.*

Aoife: *Thanks, Savvie. That makes sense.*

Savannah: *My pleasure.*

FORTY-NINE

AIDAN JR

TWO WEEKS LATER

WITH MY HANDS behind my head and flat out on the bed, I watched Savannah undress.

"Should I be jealous?"

She turned her head to look at me and, serious as a funeral, told me, "Yes. Always."

My lips quirked up at the edges. "You don't even know what I should be jealous about."

"My pussy's prime real estate."

Laughing, I leaned up on my elbows and demanded, "What's my dick?"

"The only buyer it'll accept."

Her eyes twinkled so I knew she was kidding, but I whistled under my breath as she stripped out of her bra, opening the front clasp and letting the cups drift to the sides.

We were in her apartment, the one below Conor's penthouse, because she'd decided to go all maidenly on me.

"When are you moving into my place?" I ground out as she stripped off her panties and then crawled onto the bed.

When she straddled me, my gaze drifted to her core, and I immediately reached for her, only for Savvie to grab my hands then pin them over my head.

Because I wasn't a fool, I didn't complain. Not when that put her tits in my line of sight.

"When you marry me."

I narrowed my eyes at her. "You're the one who wants to wait."

"No. I said I wanted to marry before Jen does."

Fucking Jen.

My fellow godparent, cousin, and the bane of my goddamn existence.

"That wasn't what you said before," I argued.

"No, well, things changed when she got with Luc."

Jen's ability to piss me off was second only to my da, but I had to admit, her friendship with Savannah had led to a nice alliance with the Italians.

Luciu Valentini was a man I'd prefer to have in my corner than against me.

Rocking my head forward to motorboat her tits, she laughed and squirmed against me which had my dick reacting to the softness of her pussy.

As she rocked against it, moaning now in response, I murmured, "We'll get married tomorrow."

"I don't want a shitty wedding."

"Then what the fuck do you want?"

Her smile hit me right in the chest. "You. Every filthy hot inch of you."

"You're difficult. You know that, don't you?" I complained, even as I maneuvered upright so I could snag her mouth in a kiss that told her how much I liked what she had to say.

When she groaned, I pulled back with a smirk then tugged on her bottom lip, dragging it away from her teeth.

"Jerk," she grumbled a second later when I released her.

"Always. But, by your own admission, your jerk."

She huffed. "What are you jealous about anyway?"

"You wore garters for the news program."

Her eye roll was so exaggerated that it must have given her eye cramps.

"The day is coming," I warned, "when I'm going to have to put you over my knee whenever you roll your eyes at me."

"Is that supposed to be a threat?" Savvie flounced her hair, tossing it aside, but I saw how her cheeks lit up with heat.

"It's a warning," I countered. "Now, who did you wear the garters for?"

"You." She tutted. "You're the one who canceled lunch."

I hissed, "Shit." I *had* canceled. "Fuck."

I only knew about the garters because I'd happened to see them in the bag she had for dry cleaning.

"You snooze you lose," she taunted, rocking her hips along my dick in a way that spread her slickness over us both.

"I fucking lost today." My scowl was ferocious, and I knew it pleased her because that smug smile was delicious. "How did it go?"

"The report? Quite well." Her smile broadened. "I enjoyed manipulating the city. It was fun."

I snorted. "I don't know why you had to."

Her article about Eva Martinez had gone live a few weeks back, but the TV news shows had yet to stop inviting her on air.

The rogue ex-cop who'd been accused of everything from genocide to granny-butchering had become Savannah's current pet cause, and the networks were loving the uptick in their audience.

Savvie was becoming quite the celebrity. In her own right, too. Not because of her famous father.

Naturally, she hadn't keyed me into *why* she was defending the cop because I, and everyone else in the underworld, knew that Eva was guilty as fuck.

"Someone asked me to write the article as a favor."

Narrowing my eyes at her, I demanded, "Jen?"

"You like to think the worst of her, don't you?"

"That means it *was* her." I saw the truth in her eyes. She could convince the city that the sky was green, but her lies meant shit to me. I knew the stench of her particular brand of bullshit. When she lied, she held people's gaze too long. "What did she want? Why did she want Eva Martinez to look innocent?"

"She wanted nothing." She arched her back which did interesting things with her pussy and my dick.

Further proof that something was going on that she was trying to hide.

The distraction didn't work.

"Did Valentini ask you to do this?"

"No." Her quick frown told me the truth—*that wasn't a lie.*

"Did Jen ask you on his behalf?"

Her eyes caught mine. Held. "No." Untruth. "Can we drop this?"

What purpose did it serve for the new head of the Italians to try to prove the innocence of a dirty cop?

Curiouser and curiouser.

Staring up at her, I rumbled, "You owe me your loyalty above anyone else."

She shuddered, but it wasn't in fear. "Oh, fuck, you sounded all mobster just then."

I almost rolled my eyes because Savvie had a thing for mobsters. I even felt the difference when that slick, pretty cunt of hers grew even wetter.

"You should be scared," I ground off, but who the fuck was I kidding? Those four words were to get her hotter.

She gulped. "Oh." A hiss escaped her as she wriggled around, managing to get the tip of my dick to rub against her clit.

This was her idea of dirty talk.

"One day, when you're my fucking queen, Savvie, you know what you'll have to do, don't you?"

Her pupils were like pinpricks. "What?"

"You're gonna have to pay your king his dues."

A low groan escaped her. "Every morning and every night," she promised breathily, and she let go of one of my hands and slipped it between us.

When the tip of my cock felt the pressure of her tight slit, I gritted my teeth as she groaned, slowly taking every inch I had to give.

When her hand returned to mine, we bridged our fingers as she began riding me.

"How you gonna do that, little one?"

She licked her lips. "I'll suck you off. Make sure I send you out into the world nice and relaxed."

I grinned. "Savvie, that mouth of yours ain't relaxing. Just makes me want inside this pretty pussy."

"O-Okay—" Mewling, she pressed her forehead to mine. "We're going to have to get you a throne."

"You're not supposed to make me laugh when we're fucking."

"I'll fuck you on it," she argued. "Every king needs a throne."

Biting back another grin, I told her, "You ready to be my queen, little one?"

"You know it." She whimpered when I arched my hips up.

"Then why are you holding out on me?" I caught her lips with mine. "Set the date."

"Give me a time and a place, and I'll be there."

The words set fire to something inside me.

They gave me hope.

They made me *happy*.

As I smiled up at her, I rasped, "I want a spring wedding. You in a sleeveless white dress, the sun shining behind you. Our families relaxed and happy, none of this stress and tension with what's going on..."

She blinked, sighed. "I want that too."

"You know how this works, little one. Whatever you want, you get. You just have to tell me."

"I want to be your wife," she whispered.

"And I want to be your husband."

I tightened my fingers around hers, and with my good leg, leveraged up so that I could take us back to where we'd been before I derailed shit.

My woman's pussy was the only paradise a sinner like me would ever experience, and luckily for me, I intended to savor it for the next fifty years.

AIDAN: *I finally pinned her down.*

Finn: *Who?*

Aidan: *Savannah. She's a sly witch, I swear.*

Finn: *Lol. You know that's your future bride you're talking about, don't you?*

Aidan: *Oh, yeah. I'm not complaining about her being a sly witch. It's one of her better qualities.*

Finn: *Then... what?*

Aidan: *She agreed to get married at the end of May.*

Finn: *You're going to wait that long?*

Aidan: *I like the idea of a spring wedding.*

Finn: *You? Not her?*

Aidan: *Yeah, yeah. Give me shit about that.*

Finn: *I will. At a later date. Thank you for the ammunition.*

Aidan: *Welcome.*

Finn: *Why spring? Summer's nicer.*

Aidan: *You want more ammunition, huh?*

Finn: *Why not? You're among family.*

Aidan: *Remember I bought my estate from that old woman?*

Finn: *I remember.*

Aidan: *She planted a massive garden in the back.*

Finn: *So?*

Aidan: *In the spring, there are a bunch of peonies.*

Finn: *That you know this is disturbing. Where's my brother and what did you do to him?*

Aidan: *Fuck off.*

Finn: *I will not. You texted me first.*

Aidan: *I was dumb to do that.*

Finn: *You were.*

Aidan: *Anyway. Peonies are Savvie's favorite flower.*

Finn: *This is cute, Aidan.*

Aidan: *Cute?!*

Finn: *Yeah. We're talking like teenage girls ABOUT WEDDINGS! Jesus Christ. Give me mob talk, please.*

Aidan: *Fuck off.*

Finn: *I will. If it'll stop this conversation in its tracks.*

Aidan: *You know you're going to be my best man, don't you?*

Finn: *Aidan, I'd love to, but I can't.*

Aidan: *Why the fuck not?*

Finn: *Because getting Aoife there when Lena and Senior are too... it's going to be impossible if I'm standing at the altar with you.*

Aidan: *Fuck.*

Finn: *I'm sorry, bro.*

Aidan: *Christ, I hate this.*

Finn: *Me too.*

Aidan: *It is what it is, I guess.*

Finn: *Yeah.*

Aidan: *You can be my honorary best man?*

Finn: *I'd love that. Ask Brennan, Aidan. And don't tell him you asked me first.*

Aidan: *Why?*

Finn: *Because he's going to be your second-in-command, and he already feels excluded.*

Aidan: *Stop being wise.*

Finn: *Lol, that's what you need me for. I'm your right-hand man, aren't I?*

Aidan: *True.*

Finn: *I'll help arrange your bachelor party, though.*

Aidan: *No Reno.*

Finn: *Haha, just wait.*

JEN: *That bitch!*

    Aoife: *What?! Who?*

    Jen: *Savannah. Can you believe it? She's getting married before me.*

    Aoife: *Lol. Is that all?*

    Jen: *IS THAT ALL? She did it on purpose.*

    Aoife: *Yes, Jen. I'm sure your best friend decided to get married first just to spite you.*

    Aoife: *I swear you've turned more melodramatic since you got pregnant.*

    Jen: *Charming!*

    Aoife: *What conspiracy have you cooked up?*

    Jen: *I bet she wants me to be her bridesmaid. She'll pick one of those skank sisters of hers as maid of honor.*

    Aoife: *So?*

    Jen: *So?! I should be her MATRON of honor. But she's getting married first.*

    Aoife: *Take that up with the bride, lol.*

    Jen: *Like you'll escape that fate. She'll ask you to be a part of the bridal party too.*

    Aoife: *I asked her not to.*

    Jen: *She won't listen.*

    Aoife: *She will. Finn talked with Aidan about it.*

    Jen: *Do you think Jerkface Junior will listen to Luc?*

    Aoife: *I doubt it. Lol.*

    Jen: *Damn. Fucking Irish. Always sticking together.*

    Aoife: *Like you can argue with that! You're Irish too!*

    Jen: *Pfft.*

    Jen: *By the way, you're not getting out of it with me. I hope you know that.*

    Aoife: *I know, lol.*

    Jen: *Matron of honor. That's on you where I'm concerned.*

    Aoife: *Well, I won't mind then.*

    Jen: *You'd better not. I'll get Luc to make sure that cunt isn't invited. I never did like Lena.*

    Aoife: *Thanks, babe. <3*

    Jen: *I'm still mad that it took you so long to tell me what she did.*

    Aoife: *I'm sorry for turning into a turtle.*

    Jen: *Gah, just remember I'm always there for you next time, yeah?*

Aoife: *I won't forget. :* Anyway, I don't want to cause any problems between the Irish and the Italians.*

Jen: *Like Luc would allow that.*

Aoife: *He isn't God, Jen.*

Jen: *He is in bed.*

Aoife: **snorts**

FIFTY

FINN

THE KNOCK at the door had me grimacing because I could hear it in my skull.

"Aoife?" I called out.

No answer.

Damn, did that mean I had to open the door myself?

I was pretty sure I'd prefer to climb Everest stark naked than do that.

Huffing, I flopped onto my back and stared up at the ceiling. Seeing the ornate mural above me, I groaned, remembering where I was.

"Aoife loves it here," I muttered to myself. "Aoife loves it here."

If I said it enough, I'd stop whining like a little bitch about this hotel room.

Everywhere I turned, there were ornate vases and lamps and things that were destined to cost me a fortune when I tipped them over.

Grunting when the knock came again, I flopped onto my knees as I tumbled off the sofa.

"Aoife?"

When there was no answer, my hungover brain finally remembered that she was in LA with Savannah, Jen, Aela, Inessa, Camille, and Jake for Savannah's bachelorette party.

That was why I felt like shit.

While the women were in LA, we'd gone to goddamn Reno.

Brennan and I had organized Junior's bachelor party. If he felt as shit as I did, then I knew he'd be thankful the wedding was in a month's time and not tomorrow.

"Reno, never, ever, ever again," I mumbled under my breath as the knock sounded at the door.

More insistently this time.

Instead of 'tap tap,' it was like an oversized hummingbird was pounding it.

"I don't want the place cleaned!" I called out.

"Finn! It's Priestley!"

Priestley?

Who the fuck was Priestley?

It took me far too long to figure out who it was, then I heard the gusty sob of a baby.

Fuck.

Callum O'Reilly's bride.

Rubbing a hand over my head, I stomped over to the door and pulled it open. "Priestley," I greeted gruffly.

She looked like hell.

I hadn't seen her since her wedding day, granted, and brides were supposed to look their best then, but she was about forty pounds lighter, and seeing as the kid was only young—

I squinted at the bundle in her arms. "He's small, ain't he?"

"Niall was premature," she rasped, and her eyes were huge in her face. "The stress... Callum..."

As I stared at her, pity filled me. Her husband had nearly killed my wife, but she was innocent in all this.

Niall too.

I shoved the door back and said, "Come in."

She peered around the entrance then whispered, "I-I just needed... I just needed to talk. I don't need to come in."

"Yeah, you do. You look like you're going to drop." I beckoned her forward. "Sit down before you fall down, Priestley."

Niall cried harder and, grimacing, I murmured, "Is he okay?"

"He's hungry," she whispered forlornly.

"Don't you want to feed him?"

She pressed a hand to her forehead and started weeping.

Right there in the doorway.

I shepherded her forward, hustling her toward the sofa and carefully taking Niall because she looked like she was about to drop him.

That she didn't notice I picked him up told me a lot about her state of mind. In a similar situation, Aoife would have battled me for Jake.

"Do you have a bottle?" I asked grimly. "I'm an expert at feeding babies now."

She sniffled and reached into the soft diaper bag she'd brought with her. When she shoved the bottle at me, I took it then slumped down in the armchair beside the sofa.

Niall's face made a prune look smooth, but I smiled down at him, laughing when his big blue eyes peered up at me in shock.

"I know, little man, I stink."

Of stuff he shouldn't really be smelling: cigars, whiskey, beer, vodka, tequila. My clothes were probably flammable now.

"You're good with kids," Priestley commented, wiping her hand over her cheeks as she looked at me.

"Had plenty of practice," I replied as I started feeding Niall. "What's going on, Priestley? Why are you here?"

"C-Conor won't see me."

"You visited him?"

She nodded. "I did. Well, I tried to. I wanted... Callum wanted him to be Niall's godfather, but... he wouldn't let me up."

"How do you know he was in?"

An exasperated growl escaped her. "Why will no one answer me? Why will no one help? Why is everyone stonewalling me? Callum worked for Conor. He worked for one of the O'Donnellys.

"When a man goes missing, there's an investigation. When someone from an O'Donnelly's crew goes missing, the entire city is overhauled!

"Knowing Callum and Conor were tight was one of the only things that used to help me sleep at night. There was security there. But Conor isn't doing anything to find him. What kind of friend is he?

"Callum's father is friends with Aidan Sr. himself as well! But I haven't heard a word from Callum in months!" She leaped to her feet and snatched Niall from my arms. "He has a son. A wife. *A family.* Why aren't you telling me where he is? You have to know!"

I stared up at her and rasped, "You should be talking to Mark about this. I'm sure he's been running his own investigation into—"

"Without authority from Aidan Sr., you know any attempt to find him is stonewalled." She gulped and started rocking Niall when he began crying. "I want answers, Finn. It's driving me crazy, thinking of him out there—" Her mouth quivered. "If he's even alive."

Somberly, I studied her, wishing for a fucking vat of whiskey to make this easier. This had nothing to do with hair of the dog, either.

"What do you want me to say, Priestley?"

She let out a sob. "I just want to know where he is."

"I don't know where he is," I told her, and it wasn't a lie.

Her gaze latched onto mine, as if she recognized I was taking her seriously. She staggered toward the sofa and sat down heavily.

"Why isn't anyone looking for him?"

I tilted my head to the side. "Why do you think, Priestley?"

"I don't know!" she shrieked.

Tension hit me when Niall started crying.

"Calm down!" I barked. "You're scaring him."

"Tell me! Finn, God, I have to know. I've tried the others, but they don't..." Her grip on Niall turned fierce. Enough for me to wince. "They don't have kids yet, Finn. They don't know what it is to be a father."

"Declan does."

She sniffed. "Not really. He's barely been a father for five minutes. You, *you* know what it is to raise a son. You know what it would mean to miss out on your baby's early years. Declan doesn't have that experience, but you know what my man will never get back."

I scowled at her. "Declan missed out on those early years—"

"Finn! You're not listening to me. Please, *please*, I'm begging you. Tell me something. *Anything*. I'm going out of my mind here."

Her words hit me in the heart, an organ that was quickly becoming a liability, but what could I say?

A woman in her position could easily turn nasty, and if she went to the cops, her son would be an orphan before he was a year old. Aidan Sr. would see to that.

Scratching my stubbled chin, I rasped, "Some truths are too hard to handle, Priestley."

"W-What are you saying?"

"You said it yourself. He was in Conor's crew."

Her mouth trembled. "Was?"

I didn't comment. "Why do you think we'd forget a man like that?"

She stared at me for so long, and so silently, that I wasn't sure if she'd ever let the dots connect. Then, Priestley whispered, "No."

I arched a brow.

"No, I won't believe it."

"That's down to you."

"He isn't a Sparrow!"

I rubbed a hand over my face. "You sure about that?"

"He's my husband. Of course I know," she spat.

"And yet, I know Callum was the reason my wife lost three babies, has to take daily antibiotics, and spent our honeymoon in a hospital ward."

Her eyes rounded, and in a hurry, she gathered all her things together, rasping, "I won't believe it."

"And like I said before, that's down to you."

But she didn't hear my words. She scrambled out of the room, slamming the door behind her.

Once she left, I sighed, clambered to my feet and made it to my bed. That was when I let the hangover pull me under.

Priestley was tomorrow's problem.

FINN: *We may have a situation.*

Brennan: *I have a hangover. That's my only situation right now.*

Finn: *Me too. I drank more than Conor weighs.*

Brennan: *Lol. Think you'd be dead if you had.*

Brennan: *Okay, what's the problem?*

Finn: *Priestley came around this morning.*

Brennan: *Callum O'Reilly's Priestley?*

Finn: *Yeah. Did you know she had her kid prematurely?*

Brennan: *I didn't.*

Brennan: *Stress?*

Finn: *Yeah.*

Brennan: *What did she want?*

Finn: *Guess.*

Brennan: *Smart ass. What did you tell her?*

Finn: *That he was a Sparrow.*

Brennan: *Fuck. How did that go down?*

Finn: *Not well.*

Brennan: *I can imagine. Think she'll be a problem?*

Finn: *Refer to the start of this conversation.*

Brennan: *Wow, someone's in a mood.*

Finn: *Bet your fucking ass I am. That wasn't my idea of fun.*

Brennan: *No, I'll bet. Think she's a threat?*

Finn: *Perhaps. How's she coping financially?*

Brennan: *There's no difference. I've made sure that she gets Callum's take.*

Finn: *From the state of her, you wouldn't know.*

Brennan: *Want me to monitor her?*

Finn: *Think it's for the best.*

Brennan: *Understood.*

FIFTY-ONE

"MARK O'REILLY CAME to see me again," Da rumbled as he took a deep sip of whiskey.

Conor tensed up. "What did he want?"

"Wanted to know if I thought Callum was a Sparrow."

"What did you say?" I asked.

"I said that I hadn't sanctioned his death. But if a Five Pointer had decided to take out a Sparrow, then they'd done us a service."

He sank back the last finger of whiskey then poured himself another. It sloshed over the sides, pooling on the desk.

"Think you need to slow down, Da," Declan said cautiously, frowning at the sight of the mess he'd made.

"I know my limits," Da snarled.

"I don't think you do," I retorted, backing Dec up.

I narrowed my eyes on him, well aware that his volatile nature had been off the charts for the past six months.

Whatever sanity he had left was starting to fade away like the gray in his hair. White was slowly winning that particular war, and the batshit in Aidan Sr. was becoming more and more prevalent with every passing day.

"Calm down, Da," Junior sniped. "What did Mark say to that?"

"What could he say if his son was one of those bastards?" His hand clenched around the tumbler before he raised his other hand to cup it too. The move caught my eye as he demanded, "How's Finn?"

Declan's voice was free of inflection as he said, "He's fine."

"I can't believe Aoife pussywhipped him into breaking our family apart."

My brow furrowed but it was Junior who bit off, "Finn ain't a pussy, Da. Ma killed his mother-in-law. You think Aoife finding that out wasn't going to change things? Did you expect her to come around for Sunday dinner and make no mention of that?"

"How the hell did she find out, that's what I want to know." He glowered down at his tumbler and rasped, "I miss him. Your ma misses him. I even miss Aoife even though she broke everything up."

Uncomfortably, I shifted in my seat. I didn't say anything because I understood. Our lives had changed, and not necessarily for the better.

I backed Aoife one-hundred percent and totally understood why she refused to come here and why Finn had put a blockade between her and the folks. That didn't mean it didn't hurt or that there weren't Aoife, Finn, and Jake-shaped holes around the dinner table.

Our new tradition of Saturday night was one thing, but it didn't make up for Sundays.

"You talk with Finn," Junior retorted.

"About business. He doesn't want to talk about anything else. I'm his fucking da," he snapped. "How could he do this to us?"

"I think you need to stop drinking," I told him, watching liquor slosh around the rim of his glass.

"I need for my boys to stop telling me what to do." He dropped the glass against the table and turned to face the yard.

At first, I thought he was doing as we suggested, holding off on the whiskey, but I watched him clutch at his wrist and rub it as if it were hurting him.

When he fell silent, we looked among each other, and Eoghan was the first to speak out, "No one else going to talk about the elephant in the room?"

"Which one?" Junior mocked.

"The one shaped like a phoenix. The Sparrows aren't our only concern anymore. If you think the ECD have gone away—"

"Leave things alone, Eoghan," Da sniped.

"They're dangerous."

"You think I don't know that? Been managing those assholes all my life. Just let it be."

"Isn't that a song?"

I snickered at Conor. "That's 'Let It Be.'"

"That's right. John Lennon."

As he hummed the melody, Eoghan scratched his jaw, but I could tell he was mad at the conversation derailing even if he was going to let the topic drop. "Are you doing anything special for Orthodox Easter?"

I shrugged. "I don't know. Camille didn't mention anything. Has Inessa talked about it?"

"Orthodox Easter," Da griped, his dismissal and disapproval clear.

"You married us into the Russians, Da," Eoghan stated calmly. "That comes with consequences. What do you want them to do? Wear green for the rest of their lives?"

Da's shoulders hunched, slurring, "Green would suit them."

Was he drunk already?

"So does red," I said softly, earning myself a glare. "Are you feeling okay, Da?"

He sniffed. "I'm fine."

"Ma told me you fell down the stairs last week," Conor remarked, his focus on his phone.

"She's exaggerating."

"If you say so," was Conor's retort, but it was clear that he didn't believe Da.

I couldn't say that I blamed him.

Something was definitely going on with him, but what were we supposed to do? Torture the answers out of him?

The phone on the desk rang, and Da straightened up, slurring, "That'll be your ma."

"You drunk?" Junior demanded. "How many have you had this morning?"

"I'm fine."

"You don't look fine," Declan agreed, but he shuffled over to him and helped him straighten up. "Come on, you old bastard. Let's sober you up with some of Ma's roasted chicken."

As they hobbled out of the room, Junior turned to me and demanded, "You need to talk with Ma. Get her to make him see a doctor."

"He'll do what he wants to do. Ma can't make him do jack," I argued.

He glowered at me. "Just fucking do it, Bren."

"Yes, boss," I muttered under my breath.

How much fucking longer until I could get my ass out of here?

As Junior followed Da and Declan, Conor murmured, "Don't worry too much, Eoghan. I've got things under control."

Eoghan frowned. "The ECD? There's no controlling them."

He wiggled his head. "Might have tipped off ICE that there was an illegal alien living in a certain hotel in Manhattan."

"Keegan's out of the country?" I questioned, sitting up.

"He is for the moment. I don't think it will keep him out, but it buys us some time."

"Or pisses him off even more. Look, the ECD hired several sharp-shooters to kill a high-profile target. That target has yet to be killed. I'd have heard.

"Don't think they've gone for good, because they haven't. They might have gone underground for the moment but that just means they're planning something."

"Fucking know-it-all, James Bond."

Eoghan grunted then flipped me the bird. "Da's wrong. You don't manage the ECD."

"Not saying you do," Conor denied. "I'm saying that you put road-blocks in their way."

"That won't work forever."

Frowning, I asked, "Eoghan, what aren't you telling us?"

"I'm telling you what I know. The ECD were shopping around for a sniper for a high-profile target. There have been no assassinations so far." He got to his feet. "This is a waiting game."

"Isn't life a waiting game?" Conor asked, his tone almost wistful.

I squinted at them both then shook my head. "It's too early and I'm too hungry for conversations like this. Let's get some food."

The sooner we ate, the sooner I could get the fuck home, and my new pool table had just arrived.

I had plans for it. Very specific, very detailed plans.

FIFTY-TWO

CAMILLE

A SHARP CRY escaped me as Brennan ran his knife along the outer length of my thigh.

The fabric of my skirt parted like butter, and I moaned as I felt the tip whisper over my skin, close enough to leave a mark but I knew he wouldn't.

Brennan bit.

He sucked.

He didn't cut me.

My back arched against the blue baize of the new pool table, and I moaned again when he hooked one of my heels in the bottom right pocket and the other in the bottom left.

Legs spread, the now useless skirt flopped between my thighs until he lifted the flap and shoved it against my stomach, revealing lacy cream panties that had him groaning.

My eyes stayed on his face, remained on the rigidity of his features that showed a tension which had been present since we'd stepped foot on his parents' compound.

Something had happened, though.

Something specific.

Something he didn't want to tell me about. And whatever it was, it made his expression stern and his gaze somber.

A soft sigh escaped him, however, when he saw my panties, and I hissed when he pressed the flat of the blade in his hand against the gusset.

I felt that chill along my core and whimpered in response to that, and his rumbled, "So fucking wet for me, Camille."

"Always wet for you," I rasped, needing him to know that, hoping that it would give him some comfort.

He always comforted me. Always.

It hurt that he wasn't letting me do and be the same source of harmony for him.

It was why I was here.

The pool table back at the Satan's Sinners' compound had been a place where clubwhores were often fucked. I'd seen women slipping pool balls into their asses, had seen hardcore sex take place on a surface that was anything but hygienic.

For no other man would I put myself in this position.

Not when the memories of my time with the Sinners were real and raw.

But he needed this. And this was something I could give him.

Reaching out, he snagged a finger beneath the crotch of my panties and pulled it away from my sex. A quick flick of his wrist and the blade tore through the expensive silk, and from the waist down, my clothes were left in shreds.

"I was hoping you'd be wearing a garter belt," he said as he rubbed the knife's handle against my clit.

The faint friction had my eyes flaring wide as he touched my most tender part with a deadly weapon.

I felt his volatility at that moment, and my mind began to war.

Life made me hesitate, doubt what was happening here. Experience told me he'd never hurt me, told me to trust him.

"You ran through my stockings," I told him, voice breathy with a combination of nerves and need.

"I ran through them?"

I eyed his knife. "I need to buy some more," I croaked when the butt moved down and slipped inside me.

He hummed in response, then stunned the hell out of me by shifting his hand away and flinging the knife across the room.

With a thud, and a weird vibration, I knew it had connected with the wall, and I tipped my head back to see where it had landed—the dartboard.

"Bull's eye," I whispered.

Another hum.

His fingers slipped over my legs, and he dragged me down the table, making me feel the strain of the stretch in my inner thighs.

His digits rubbed the taut muscles and I moaned, butt rocking as he touched a place I really didn't need touching, focusing his caresses there instead of where I wanted.

My glance locked on him, I remained silent, sensing that he was testing me, and I was rewarded when he slipped his thumb to my gate and pressed inward, hooking up and back against the front wall of my pussy.

"Camille?" he crooned.

"Y-Yes?"

"Do you know who you are to me?"

Maybe he'd struck me dumb because my only answer was to croak, "Your wife?"

Brennan shook his head. "You're more than that. Wives can be ignored. They're chattel. Bargaining chips. Empty wombs that are to be filled." He moved his thumb from side to side, rubbing confused tissues that didn't understand if this was him teasing my G-spot or stretching the quivering flesh. "You're not an empty womb. You're not chattel. You're not a bargaining chip."

I licked my lips. "I am all those things, just not to you."

"And who else matters?"

He was right.

I smiled. "No one else matters."

His head rocked forward, and finally, his gaze moved from my pussy to meet with my own. He said nothing, just held my stare as he dipped down and pressed his mouth to my clit.

Immediately, he sucked hard against the nub, and I groaned as he kept me captive. Not just with his touch, but with his stare.

His tongue flexed and teased the sensitive bead of flesh, and the straining muscles of my inner thighs somehow turbocharged what I experienced, making the sensations hit more ferociously than normal.

When his hand pressed against my stomach, I gasped, back arching of its own accord as I reared up. Yet not once did our eyes break the connection that bound us together.

I dug my heels into the pockets, uncaring that they tangled with the netting, and I rocked my hips so I could grind into his face. His expression morphed at that, turning from moody and pensive to lit with a fire I expected from him.

It was then I realized he'd been holding back.

He smashed his mouth into my cunt, not even an eighth of an inch parting us as he gorged on my flesh like he wanted to swallow me whole.

I screamed.

No one would hear.

I let go.

No one cared if I wasn't the perfect Bratva princess here.

My head wanted to flop back on my neck, but I didn't let it, just kept my gaze trained on his, knowing that the way he looked at me as if I were his universe, his reason for getting up in the morning, triggered sensations even more powerful than what he was achieving with his tongue and teeth and lips.

His thumb retreated, replaced with three fingers that he scissored inside me. A groan rumbled from my lips as a fourth made an appearance, and all the while, he sucked.

He licked.

He flicked.

Those fingers spread wider and wider until I screamed again as his knuckles pushed up against my slit. At that, my head fell back some, but I remained locked with him as he carefully started to thrust into me, back and forth, stretching and teasing and torturing my hungry flesh.

I had no idea why I came when his knuckles pressed into my pussy, no idea why that massive hand flexing into a fist had me releasing a guttural groan so deep it seemed to find its source in my soul.

My fingers snapped out, and they sought his ears. I'd never done this before but I guided him, shoving my pussy against his face, fucking him back as he sent his fist into me, taunting me with tiny movements that made me think he was going to open up his hand, but I knew I wasn't ready for that. So did he.

This wasn't the first time he'd pushed my limits, and I knew I was in for a lifetime of that because Brennan's brand of filthy sex was all I wanted.

All I needed.

The pleasure was wicked. Deep and dark and bewitching. It felt better than *good*, but it didn't stir a high in me. Didn't make me feel like I was flying. If anything, it made me think I was drowning.

It was a dull throb that seemed to spread into my bones, that sank into my blood, poisoning every vein and artery it came into contact with.

I didn't whine with pleasure, I groaned with the sheer agony of it.

It hurt.

It hurt so good.

When he didn't stop sucking on my clit, just continued making those teasing stretches with his fist, I slurred, "Your cock. Need—"

His tongue flickered against my clit one final time.

He sucked it hard *one final time.*

Then he pressed a kiss to it *one final time* as he straightened up.

Mouth and chin and jaw drenched with my juices, I slung my arms around his neck as I hauled him into me. I wiggled so my butt wasn't flat to the pool table, uncaring that my inner thighs screamed with the position, and I glued our mouths together in a kiss that tasted of me.

When he started to retract his fist, I whimpered and moaned, writhed and wriggled against him, understanding how a fish felt when it was hooked on a line.

The panic inside me was strong, enough to make my heart pound as I felt sure his hand would be stuck inside me or something—

An internal pop.

Logically, I knew that didn't happen, but I felt it anyway when his fist pulled back and the relief inside me had me sagging into him as he thrust his tongue against mine, taking over the kiss.

I felt the gush of liquids release onto the pool table, but though I knew it would stain, he didn't seem to care. If anything, I felt his slippery fingers pull away and heard the noise of his zipper parting.

Pushing my forehead against his, I broke our kiss and stared down at his hand, wanting to watch as his slick fingers grabbed a hold of his dick. He jacked off for me, using my wetness as a lubricant.

The sight had my empty pussy clutching down against nothing, and I reached between us, slipping my hand around his balls, holding them firm in my grasp.

With his breath brushing my lips and mine his, I whispered, "A husband is a burden. An albatross around a woman's neck. Something to endure." I pushed my forehead against his. "You're a storm to weather, my darling, but you're no burden, you're not something to endure— you're someone to love."

My words weren't poetic. They were drawn from my soul when I was hungry for his dick, but his nostrils flared in response, and the way he tore at my mouth was clue enough that I'd pleased him.

That my words had pleased him.

As he feasted on me, his dick found its way home, and as he slipped inside, his hands shifted.

He drew one heel out of the pocket, then when the other got stuck, he didn't relinquish his hold on me, just shuffled me down the table, one hand holding my leg high against his waist, while the other was stuck in the netting.

I'd have laughed at any other moment, but nothing about this was a laughing matter.

Whatever had my husband all riled up, I was soothing. I was born for this, I knew. Born to ease the path of a man who fixed everyone else's problems but rarely focused on his own.

As his hips pumped into me, his dick dragging over tissues he'd stirred to life with his mouth and hand, I fell over the edge so quickly it was practically shameful.

Only, nothing about what we did together, about what we had together, could ever be deemed shameful.

I knew that now.

As I screamed through my orgasm, I felt him pump his cum inside me. Felt the snarl as it rumbled past his lips, heard the groan that was from the soul, sensed the rage and the need battering him as he exploded into me, letting me absorb this, allowing me to ease his strain.

I clung to him, weathering the storm much as I'd told him I would, and moaned through my release as he held me just as tightly.

Together, we melted into one another, a puddle of extinguished need and want that was just waiting for another match to set us alight.

It took us ages to come back down, to hold each other upright.

Beneath me, the blue baize was itchy against my arms, and the flat surface that had zero give to it, along with the way my leg was starting to ache, should have had me fidgeting, but I didn't want to move. He didn't either. He stayed where he was, slumped against me, letting me run my fingers through his hair.

I thought he only came back to reality because his phone started ringing, and I wished I could spare him that, but I couldn't.

I didn't grumble because I knew what he was, *who* he was. A man like him didn't get vacation times, and federal holidays were *not* a part of his life, so an unofficial holiday like Orthodox Easter Sunday meant very little in the grand scheme of things.

He straightened up, but surprisingly, he didn't reach for his cell immediately. His hand smoothed over my calf, and he freed my heel from the net with a patience that always came as a surprise.

As volatile as he was, Brennan was infinitely patient with me. That was why I refused to panic when he did something that confused me.

He'd hurt himself before he hurt me.

I knew that like I knew he loved me.

Love for him made me sit up so I could cup his cheeks and hold him closer for a kiss that had him sighing into me.

"Answer your phone," I told him softly when I pulled back, smiling when I saw his eyes were closed. He huffed at my smile as they opened but did as I said—answered his cell.

"Inessa?" He blinked a couple times. "What's wrong? Is everything okay with Eoghan?"

My legs clamped together as concern hit me while I waited for Brennan to tell me what was going on.

The next second, however, his shoulders relaxed. "We'll be over shortly."

"What is it?" I demanded.

"Victoria made *Kulich*. Apparently, I'm supposed to know what that means."

Though he butchered the pronunciation, my brow furrowed. "Victoria cooked?"

"She cooked. They invited us over." He joked, "Apparently, it's a feast for both her sisters. And a chance for Irish heathens to know what Russian food tastes like."

"I didn't even know she *could* cook," I said dryly. "Inessa and I sure as hell can't."

Brennan snorted. "Don't I know it. Although those burgers you made last week weren't bad."

I shoved him but muttered, "I wonder why she cooked?"

"Maybe because this is her first Easter without that poisonous prick of a father?"

Humming, I murmured, "Maybe."

I'd prefer that to some surprise news that she was five months pregnant or something.

Cooking might mean nothing to Brennan, but to us? That was a red flag. That was 'I need to fix this and food is the way to anyone's soul' kind of logic.

"Hey, chill. We'll go and eat and you can spend some time with your sisters without worrying about my da breathing down your necks if you speak Russian. I'll hang out with my baby bro and watch sports." He shrugged. "Sounds like a night."

His words had me relaxing. Not because they were soothing, but because Bren had just done what he always did—he fixed.

So whatever shit Victoria had gotten herself into?

Bren would fix that too. I just had to have faith, and with every passing day, he kept on proving that, kept on proving himself to me.

I knew he always would.

FIFTY-THREE

VICTORIA

I GIGGLED when Shay's head appeared through the crack in the door, his face smushed as he whispered, "All clear?"

Nodding, I made grabby hands with the food and raised a finger to my lips to keep him quiet.

Not that it worked.

"You're lucky Mom let me out," Shay complained.

"Quieter," I hissed. "Anyway, I'll make it up to you."

"I didn't think this was how you wanted to hang out."

Grinning, I shoved his shoulder. "You mean you don't like being my glorified errand boy? If you're going to become president, then you should get used to it."

His brow furrowed as he dumped a lot of bags onto the counter in front of me. "The president doesn't go and pick up takeout that you fake-cooked to serve to your fam."

"Nope, he's the whipping boy of the Senate and the Congress." I sniffed. "You need to watch *The West Wing*. You'll see what I'm talking about then. We all have a boss. Even you if you become the first filthy—"

"The president doesn't have a boss," he interrupted. "He's the most important man in the world."

"You keep on believing that if it makes you feel better," I drawled, amused when he rolled his eyes at me. "How much do I owe you?"

He waved a hand. "It's okay."

I scoffed. "Shay, there's over five hundred dollars' worth of food here."

"You can owe me one."

"Accruing favors already?" I mocked.

"Yeah, you can pay me back with some political machinations when you're thirty."

"Thirty and married with squalling babies?" I retorted. "Not sure I'll be in a position of power then."

Shay stilled. "You can be so much more than that, Victoria."

"Mama said there was no greater job than being a mother."

He shrugged. "I'm sure she's right, but it's not a job, is it?" Before I could slap him, he murmured, "I mean, Mom can switch her phone onto 'Do Not Disturb' when she doesn't want to talk to her agent. But she'd never do that just in case something happened to me.

"Being a mom is worse than a job. It never ends."

"You'd know," I said stiffly, not trying to be bitchy, but my mom had died when I was young. Too young to even remember her that well.

Awkwardly, he patted my shoulder. "Sorry, Vicky. I didn't mean to—"

I raised a hand. "It's okay, Shay."

"It isn't. I shouldn't have..." He sighed. "Foot in mouth disease."

"Is that why the boys in your class keep trying to beat you up?"

"'Try' is the right word since I broke Jessop's hand."

"You sure it's that and not the fact you held their trust funds hostage for a little while?"

A smile lit up his eyes. "That was all Uncle Conor."

I smiled back at him, amused by how amused *he* was at his uncle's antics. For a kid who wanted to be president, he didn't mind using lawless tactics for his own gain...

Not that that was too unusual in politics.

Still, the O'Donnellys were like no family I'd ever met before. I didn't mean that in a bad way, either. It was a good way, a very good one.

A sound outside the kitchen drew my attention. I heard Inessa's moan and groused, "Those two never stop, I swear."

"They're still newlyweds."

"Hardly," I pshawed, but I didn't miss the puppy eyes he shot at the door. He had a crush on Inessa, and he wasn't good at hiding it.

Eoghan might seem placid in most things, but I'd heard him arguing with someone called Driftwood on the phone a few times—I'd almost peed my pants. He was *not* a man whom you messed with.

And crushing on his wife was exactly that. Shay needed to get over his crush. Yesterday.

"I'd better go. If I missed anything, tough. I'm not going back to that deli. The butcher looked like he wanted to cut off my hand and sell that."

"Would you say that if he wasn't Russian?" I sniffed.

"It had nothing to do with his being Russian," Shay grumbled, "and everything to do with how he kept twirling that frickin' cleaver of his." He backed away to the door that led to the maintenance elevator and waved at me as he said, "Let me know if you sucker them or not."

Smirking, I told him, "Game on."

He stuck out his tongue as the door closed behind him, and I took advantage of the fact that Eoghan and Inessa were making out to carefully empty the carrier bags and to lay all the items on the counter.

If I served it right, they'd never be able to tell that the items were store bought and not homemade. It didn't matter if I lost, except Shay and I had a bet running—if I won, then he'd teach me how to kiss. And if he won, I had to teach him Russian.

I emptied the containers, carefully unwrapped the festive treats that I'd been raised eating, and tried not to think about the fact that Papa wasn't with us this year.

He hadn't been the best of fathers, but he was all I had. Now, I was an orphan, but it hurt that I was safer than I'd been with him alive.

The thought had me biting my lip as pain stung me, and I focused on making everything appear as if I'd been the one cooking it, disposing of the containers in the trash shoot outside so I wouldn't get caught.

Forty minutes later, I heard the sounds of voices and knew Camille and Brennan had arrived.

Unlike Inessa who wasn't particularly nosy, Camille was curious and asked a lot of questions because she felt bad about leaving us.

I didn't hold it against her like Inessa did, and I was grateful for her interest. Grateful for her, period.

The door opened, and while I saw her, knew it *was* her, for a second, I didn't see the Camille of today.

I saw her from before.

It hit me out of nowhere.

The flashback—blood on her mouth.

Hatred in her eyes.

My sister was my hero, and she didn't even know it.

I hated that this kept happening, but I tried to shove it away to deal with later. She didn't deserve for me to act weird around her because I kept thinking back to that day when we'd been kidnapped. Held hostage in a room—

No.

Stop thinking about that, Victoria!

Blinking a couple of times in an attempt to shift the memory of watching her bite off the penis of the old man who'd wanted me to be his bride, I rasped, "*Zhelayu tebe schastlivoy Paskhi.*" Wishing you a happy Easter.

She tipped her head to the side. "*Schastlivoy Paskhi,* Victoria. Is everything okay?"

I nodded then cast my hands out wide. "A festive feast to remind us of home. Of the good days at home," I corrected.

Her smile grew as she took in the dishes, and it hit her eyes as they glanced over the Olivier salad, deviled eggs, *Kulich, Pashka,* and the *peljmeni.*

"You made all this?"

"I started before we left for upstate New York. The cookies aren't as good as they were," I lied.

"I didn't know you could cook."

"Lots of things you don't know about me," I pointed out, not to hurt, just to deflect, but I regretted it when she winced. Quickly, I tacked on, "You might hate it. I might be a terrible cook."

"It looks beautiful." She stepped over to me and said, "I'll help you take things into the dining room."

"*Tak.*"

When she approached, however, I slipped my arms around her and hugged her quickly. She smelled like soap, as if she'd just showered, and she was wearing different clothes to the ones I'd seen her in back at the compound.

"My pleasure, baby sister," she breathed, kissing my temple as she pulled back.

"Camille?" At her nod, I mumbled, "Eoghan and Inessa are going on another honeymoon soon."

"*Another* honeymoon?"

"Yeah. Inessa said he owed her another one." I shrugged. "I have a feeling she'll go on a yearly honeymoon."

Her lips twitched at first, but her shoulders stiffened some. "And you don't want to stay with Brennan and me again?"

I shook my head. "I wanted to ask if I could?"

Her smile was so bright it nearly blinded me. "Of course! You don't have to ask! You're always welcome." She squeezed me. "I'm looking forward to it. I had a ball last time."

"Me too."

It wasn't a lie.

This had nothing to do with the bet between Shay and I about who could pull off the greater con on our families.

The past six months had been tough, but that I got to spend more time with my sisters was a blessing I'd never expected.

Everything was changing, and it would continue to do so. Shay acted like I had a choice about what would happen when I was thirty, but girls like me didn't have choices.

Our destinies were written in the stars long before we were pushed out into this world.

Camille had spared me one particular fate, but that didn't mean she or Inessa could keep on saving me.

Exactly like them, I'd be expected to marry as soon as I hit eighteen.

I just had to pray I was as in love with my husband as they were, and wasn't as unfortunate as my darling mama...

FIFTY-FOUR

AOIFE

IT WAS a beautiful day when I climbed out of the Porsche and peered over my sunglasses at the façade of Aidan's estate.

"Looks like it's been hit with a flower bomb," Finn murmured from behind the wheel.

I smiled.

He wasn't wrong.

"Savvie likes peonies."

"Trust me," he said, "I know. Aidan told me."

"You guys talk about flowers?" I laughed. "So, it's not all about tax evasion and hostile takeovers?"

His mouth cocked up in a smirk. "It's eighty percent that. Three percent flowers. Seventeen percent shit that would turn your hair curly." He slipped his glasses down his nose. "Oh, wait, it's already curly."

I'd embraced the curl today, thinking, 'fuck it.' It was a late spring wedding, why couldn't I go boho chic when I wasn't a part of the bridal party?

And no, that wasn't a complaint.

His eyes clashed with mine and...

Damn.

Double damn.

A shiver rushed down my spine.

It was the first time in months that I'd felt that way.

I looked at him and saw a beautiful man. Much like I made a pan of brownies and knew they were delicious but didn't eat the whole tray.

I'd been... I didn't want to say dead inside because that was extreme. But how he looked at me had my mouth working as the lightning bolt that had always existed between us surged to life once more.

He felt the zap of it too.

His head reared back, his mouth firmed, and a look that was pure predator overtook him. Everything in me responded to that. Flickered to life because of that glance.

I sucked in a breath.

"Aoife?" he rasped, his voice sending more shivers down my spine.

"Finn, I—"

"Aoife!" Jen screeched from the doorway, making me jump.

I twisted around before I could finish my sentence and found my friend waddling over to me because of the toe separators she wore to keep her nails dry.

My brow furrowed at the sight. "I thought you went for a pedicure yesterday."

"I did. I chipped a nail." Jen shuddered. "I had to do them."

Behind me, I heard Finn mutter to Jake, "Cockblocked, buddy. But never get between a woman and her friends. That's advice that'll take you through life."

Lips twitching, I asked, "Why did you have to do them?"

"Because Savvie got a team of estheticians in who are all guys."

"So?"

She shrugged, but a kitten-like smile curled her lips. "Luc doesn't like other guys touching me."

I rolled my eyes. "Jesus, Jen."

Her smile morphed into a grin. "I love it." She raised her hands together, clasping them in front of her chest in true Disney princess fashion. "I don't want him to ever change."

"Just wait until you're married, then you'll hit him over the head with a frying pan," Finn drawled unsympathetically as he rounded the car with Jake struggling for freedom in his arms.

"When have I hit you with a frying pan?" I countered, but even as I asked the words, ice overtook me.

I'd hit him.

Guilt made the ice shatter inside me, leaving shards behind until he moved beside me and snagged my hand.

Squeezing it, he retorted, "I've never told you not to get your nails or makeup done by a guy."

That hand squeeze was him giving me forgiveness.

But it was easier said than done.

I was still ashamed that I'd hit him. Violence might be the answer in his world, but it wasn't in mine. Even if our borders did rub up against each other.

"This is true," was all I said.

"I like my man to be all in my face." Jen boasted, "It's the Sicilian in him."

Finn snorted. "Yeah, you keep telling yourself that. I'm plenty in Aoife's face, but there's a time and a place."

Sensing a brewing argument, I decided to butt in, "Why did you waddle out here?"

"Because Savvie's being bridezilla and I need moral support."

My lips twitched and I leaned up on tiptoe to give Finn a kiss. "I'll act as referee."

When my hands moved toward Jake, he shook his head. "We'll go and have some men's talk."

I grinned. "Good thinking."

"Come on, Aoife!" Jen had already started toward the door, and as I joined, he snagged my hand and pulled me against his side.

"Hey." His timber was low enough to make my pussy clench.

"Hey," I breathed.

His fingers let go of mine with another squeeze, and he reached up and tugged on a curl before he trailed a finger along my neck. "You feeling okay?"

Well, that *really* made my pussy clench.

I swallowed. "Yeah."

That finger trailed to my pulse, and as he felt it speeding away, he smiled. "Did I tell you you look beautiful?"

"You did," I whispered, watching his gaze drop to my outfit.

It was only a silk chiffon maxi dress, but I knew I looked good.

Sweeping sleeves that floated thanks to the chiffon, with a deep V that showed off my breasts, while it hugged my waist and hips before swirling down to the floor. It was a bright blue and was patterned with thousands of beads shaped into flowers.

I felt pretty, but when he looked at me like that, I felt *hot*.

"Did I tell you that you look handsome?" I tacked on, taking him in in his casual suit and patting his lapels so I had the excuse to touch him.

He wore a navy one for once, no pinstripe, a white shirt that was open at the collar, and tan loafers. On his wrists, he wore the anniversary cufflinks I'd bought him last year.

Yum.

"You did." He smiled as his finger continued tormenting me. "Later?"

The question made my heart stutter, and nerves hit me. Which was ridiculous. But the nerves were soon drowned out when his finger drifted between the deep V of my neckline.

It was an innocent caress, but so filthy.

Heart skipping another beat, I nodded and sighed when he pressed a kiss to my lips.

Just a simple one.

Then, he shifted when Jake started struggling to get down, and in my ear, whispered, "Today might be hard, sweetheart, but I'm here. Always. Okay?"

Nodding again, I whispered, "I know you are."

And that was the truth.

I did.

He ran his nose along my temple, and though it shot shivers of sensation through me, I whispered, "Thank you for being patient with me."

Tension hit him, and he pulled back, shaking his head. "I wasn't being patient, sweetheart. I was grieving too."

My mouth rounded at that, the simple honest statement.

"You didn't want—"

"I always want you," he said simply. "But I know I'm lucky to have you by my side. That you climb into bed with me. That you want me at all in your life.

"That's been enough for me, and it would have been enough." His gaze tangled with mine. "I saw that you wanted me back in the car though."

"I always want you," I said, using his words. "I've just been..." I tried to explain, and when I heard Jen squawk my name again, it forced me to speak when I might have stayed silent. "I felt like I was in hibernation."

"I felt that way too." He kissed my forehead. "But it's sunny today, isn't it?"

"It is," I confirmed. Jen's subsequent shriek had me grunting under my breath, and this time, I was the one who growled, "Later."

He smiled, and I hurried away after I kissed a squirming Jake then snarled at Jen the second I was in the entryway, "You totally cock-blocked me!"

She was standing at the top of the stairs, glowering down at me, but her mouth rounded in surprise at my snarl. "I did?"

I huffed as I rushed up the stairs. "Yes. You did."

"But I thought you and Finn weren't doing the nasty."

"Well, we sure as hell weren't doing it in the driveway," I grumbled, "but, you know how it is."

"In the air love is," she intoned as if she were Yoda.

I snorted.

"You look gorgeous, babe," Jen complimented. "No wonder he wants on top of you."

My nose crinkled. "Charming."

She grinned. "You totally wanted to bang him. Now that I think about it, you were definitely eye-fucking him." She made a moue with her mouth. "Do you want to go back and find him? I'll look after the monster if you want to go and get it on somewhere."

My eyes widened in horror. "With his family and Savvie's and everyone here?"

"Girl, trust me, you need to try it before you judge."

"I couldn't."

"Finn's vanilla, huh?" Jen queried sympathetically.

I thought about one of the last times we'd had sex before the miscarriage. When he'd fucked me on the baby grand piano...

Squirming for real now, I rasped, "No, but he wouldn't like it if anyone heard me come."

"Luc's like that too," she said breezily. "But he's started shoving his tie in my mouth to stem the sound."

Jen had never believed in TMI, but she was getting worse because her and Savvie egged each other on.

With an eye roll, I demanded, "Why's Savvie gone bridezilla?"

She shot me a look. "I'm asking you to come up because I know Lena's gone downstairs, okay?"

Jen knew about Lena. She'd heard the confession that Lena had sent me, and was pissed at me for not taking it to the cops.

Inside, tension crawled through me like I always knew it would at the mention of her name, but I merely nodded. "I understand."

"Well, she's bitching about how deep the neckline is on Savvie's dress, and well, the fact it's black." Jen grinned. "It's an awesome dress, just a little non-traditional. Anyway, Savvie isn't used to being told what to do."

My lips twitched. "That's total BS."

"Being told what to do by Aidan is one thing," she said wryly. "Orgasms make everything worth it."

"You and Luc should come to ours on Saturday. You'd see how he's got her panting after him."

"I already see that whenever we're together," she grumbled. "The only bright spark is that Junior looks like he's got a dildo up his ass whenever she snarks him. I can't make out if he's pussywhipped or if she's cockwhipped."

"Like you're not the same," I chided. Her smile was coy, and before she could take me back into the land of smut, I murmured, "Did Lena make Savvie cry?"

"No. She made her get mad. It took three hours to get her hair into a certain style and she ruined it when she dragged off her dress and told Lena that she wouldn't get married at all if she wouldn't leave her and her dress alone."

My mouth rounded. "She threatened to call off the wedding?"

"Yep," Jen said cheerfully. "Anyway, Lena toddled off like the she-bitch she is, and now we've got a hairstylist crying because 'the hair is ruined.'"

"He phrased it that way?"

"He's one of those guys, you know? Super melodramatic."

"You'd know, Ms. Melodrama," I teased.

She laughed. "See? If I think he's bad then he is."

Finally making it to the end of the landing where Savvie was getting ready, I tugged on Jen's hand. "You ready to see Paddy?"

He was standing up at the ceremony for Aidan. I felt bad because Finn should have been there, but he wasn't going to be a groomsman so that he could stay with me.

"Nope," she muttered. "I'll be opposite Brennan though, and Savvie made sure Paddy was at the bottom so I don't have to look at him."

"Finn says he didn't know you existed."

She shrugged, tossing her hair over her shoulder in a move that was pure sass. "I don't care."

I grabbed her hand. "I'd do anything to have a relationship with my parents, Jen. I know how it ended with your mom... maybe you could have something decent with your dad."

Her mom had tried to use Jen to pay off her debts. Thank God Luc had smelled a rat and had been there to protect her.

She bit her lip. "Don't fuss, Eef."

"I'm not. I'm just saying it how it is."

"I miss Ellie too, you know?"

Tears made it harder to choke out, "I miss her every day. It was an ache before, you know? Like, it had faded some.

"I could think about her without wanting to bawl, but it's dragged it back to the surface so it's fresh." I sucked in a sharp, pained breath. "It hurts," I said simply.

"Oh, sweetheart, I know," she whispered, tugging me into her arms for a hug. "I'll talk to him today, okay?"

I muttered in her ear, "More than a 'hello, sperm donor?'"

"You drive a hard bargain," she complained.

"You could ask how Liam is. Maybe talk about how often he's going to be visiting New York now he's back in the fold," I prompted. "If you want, I could invite him around for Saturday night dinner and you and Luc could come then. But you know you're always welcome."

She squeezed me. "Thank you, sweetheart. You're the best, do you know that?" Jen pulled back and cupped my cheek. "I learned something today."

"You did?"

She nodded. "I impart this knowledge to make up for the fact I cock-blocked you."

I groaned. "Jen, I'm trying to be serious."

Clucking her tongue, she said, "Do this."

She crossed the thumb of her left hand across her palm, then tightened her fingers over it. With her other hand, she pressed the tip of her pointer finger to her chin, before she opened up her clenched palm and pinched the soft meat between thumb and pointer finger with the same digits on her other hand.

"What on earth? Is that some kind of secret handshake?"

"Do it," she ordered.

I huffed, did as she said, then demanded, "What now?"

She smirked. "Now you can choke on Finn's dick tonight without gagging."

Cackling at me as she raced into Savvie's room, I shook my head and experimentally pressed my finger to the back of my throat.

Holy shit.

It worked.

ALAN: *Just wanted to check in. Make sure you were okay.*

Aoife: *I'm fine. Everything's fine.*

Alan: *If you need me, I'm here.*

Aoife: *Are you sure about that?*

Alan: *Yes.*

Aoife: *What's changed?*

Alan: *Life's too short.*

Aoife: *Has something happened?*

Alan: *Something's always happening.*

Aoife: *Maybe I could call you? Sometime this week?*

Alan: *I'd love that. You're sure?*

Aoife: *Yes. Today's a good day.*

Alan: *I'm glad it is, but why in particular?*

Aoife: *My friend is getting married.*

Alan: *Oh! Well, have fun.*

Aoife: *I will. I told my friend that she should give her dad a second chance. It's funny that you messaged me today.*

Alan: *You're always on my mind, Aoife. I have many regrets.*

Aoife: *Maybe we can talk about them? I'd love to know more about you and Mom.*

Alan: *I'd love to share our stories. It wasn't*

Aoife: *It wasn't what?*

Alan: *Sorry, got distracted. We were in love, Aoife. So, you tell me when and I'll make sure I have time for us to talk.*

Aoife: *I will.*

Aoife: *xo*

FIFTY-FIVE

FINN

STROLLING INTO THE YARD, I cast a quick glance around and found where Aidan Sr. and Lena were sitting.

I was going to ignore them, but Jake shrieked, "Grammy!"

"Little traitor," I muttered under my breath, but seeing I had their attention, I walked over there.

Lena, who'd been sitting with Senior's arm over her shoulder, sat up with a happy cry, her arms outstretched. I plunked Jake on her lap and shot them both a look.

Senior looked sick. Conor told me he was drinking too much, and I could see it for myself. He was starting to look that odd yellow color—jaundice. Thin and weedy too.

Lena wasn't doing much better. Though her neck wasn't scratched red, so she wasn't doing too badly and was clearly taking her meds.

I tried not to feel guilty, but it was their actions that'd brought us to this tipping point, not mine.

It had been two months since we'd gone to the compound for dinner. Two months since our lives had changed. Two months of silence from the ECD, the Sparrows too.

I was under no illusion that we were in the eye of the hurricane right now.

I wasn't looking forward to coming out of it.

"You okay with watching him?"

Lena cooed, "Of course," as she bounced Jake on her knee "You go and enjoy being with your brothers."

The words had me swallowing, and I tipped my head at Aidan.

As I walked away, I heard her say, "Leave the boy be."

She never pressured me, whereas Aidan glowered at me as if his displeasure would be enough to make me toe the line.

A part of me wondered if she'd ever told him about going to Conor to handle Michael... and another part questioned if marriages were always so rife with secrets or if that was just how mob life worked.

I didn't want that for Aoife and me.

I wanted open honesty between us; that was why I'd told her when I'd gotten my vasectomy. That was why I was being candid with her about my grief.

Maybe it was harder being transparent, but it was worth it when she looked at me the way she had in the car.

As I moved away from the arbor that was entwined with the goddamn peonies Aidan had driven me crazy over for the past six weeks, I heard Victoria's softly lilting voice say, "Shay, are you reneging on our deal?"

I arched a brow at that then heard Shay mutter, "No. I don't renege. I'm an O'Donnelly."

She sniffed. "Then teach me how to kiss!"

My shoulders straightened in surprise.

"You lost our bet," she argued. "I played it better."

"You didn't. I was unlucky. Mom's nesting or she wouldn't have noticed."

"Or maybe you're just a crappy actor. You need to improve on that if you're going to be president."

My lips twitched at her sass.

To be honest, I hadn't heard more than a couple dozen words out of Victoria and thought she was a shrinking violet. I was pleased to know that I was wrong.

Shay huffed. "I actually vomited."

"She didn't think you had food poisoning though, did she? And still made you go and sit that exam, no? That means you lost and I won. Pay up."

Shay had pretended to have food poisoning to get out of an exam and Aela had caught him in the lie?

"Teenagers," I muttered under my breath, relieved I didn't have to deal with that for another eleven years.

Deciding to leave them to it, I headed onto the decking at the back of the house and found Padraig having a smoke.

"Finn," he greeted, beaming at me as he went in for a hug.

I smiled at him and said, "Good to see you, Paddy." I meant it. He was free from the BS guilt and anger that filled me whenever I saw or dealt with Lena and Senior. "Nice flight?"

He whistled. "You shitting me? Didn't realize Junior was gonna send me first-class tickets. I had a ball."

"You'll get used to it." I laughed when he shook his head.

"Nah. Things have been tough, Finn. Been in some rough places. But being back with the fam, it's good, you know?"

"Why don't you move back to New York? You miss it, and we can find you someplace to live. Hell, you could even stay in my penthouse. No one else is living there."

He gaped at me. "Me?"

"Yeah. You."

"You want me, by myself, to live in that massive penthouse of yours?"

"Well, it's empty because my realtor says it's ten million over market price. You might as well use it."

His mouth rounded at the 'ten million,' then his shoulders hunched. It was his massive tell. He did it in life and in poker. "I don't know, Finn. It might not be safe."

"You weren't an enemy of Eamonn Keegan," I pointed out. "Just Michael Byrne. He's not a problem anymore, is he?"

Paddy pulled on his collar. "No. Conor told me about that."

I shot him a look. "How's he doing? I still can't believe you used to be his confessional."

"Well, I ain't exactly a priest, Finn," he said with a chortle. "But Con and I..." He twined his middle and pointer fingers together. "...like that. I always wished Liam and—" He sighed. "Some shit isn't meant to be."

I clapped him on the back. "I know Con's glad to have you here."

"Wish Jen were," he said mournfully.

"You keep calling her?"

"Yeah. This is the first time I'm seeing her. I'm nervous *en tabarnak*." He raised his hand, and I saw the wobble, but it was the shift into

Québecois that rammed his anxiety home. "Look at me. Shaking like a virgin on her wedding day."

My lips quirked. "Not this wedding."

Paddy snorted. "Nah, Junior's not the sort. Locked her in nice and tight. Some women you've got to do that with before they fly off. You seen him in a temper?" He whistled. "That kind of fire needs a woman like Savannah. She'll be a good match for him. Won't let him get away with shit."

"I agree. I didn't push Aoife, but I kind of told her some stuff about you. Tried to get her to ease the path."

"You did that for me?" he asked rawly.

"Sure. I can see you want to know her. Jen's difficult though," I warned. "She's not an easy person to get to know."

I watched him preen. "She's an O'Donnelly, Finn. She was born difficult. Your grandma used to say all O'Donnellys are born breech."

My lips curved. "I can believe it. Did Conor help you get shit sorted with Liam's finances?"

"He did. Got it all back. Liam actually thanked me. Thought there was a great big hole about to open up beneath my feet. He should be here, but it's the playoffs."

"I get it. I bet a couple grand on him, so he'd better win."

Beaming from ear to ear, he tugged on his tie. "Thanks to you as well, son. Appreciate the help with my finances. Feels good to be in a new suit that I bought."

"My pleasure." I clapped him on the back. "Okay, I'm going to go check on the groom."

"He's nervous she ain't gonna show up."

"Why?"

"Some hairstylist ran wailing out of the mansion or something after Lena waded into the fray. Savvie called him and said if he didn't get his ma off her back there wouldn't be a wedding." He wafted a hand. "You know, the usual shit."

I chuckled. "Yeah, usual around here." Before I left, I told him, "Think about it, Paddy. New York's home, and Jen's here..."

"Liam's in Quebec though." He looked torn. "I will think about it, Finn. Don't mistake me for being ungrateful."

I shrugged and squeezed his shoulder in a farewell, wondering if Conor was likely to get Liam transferred to NYC whether he wanted to move or not...

Aidan was sinking back a shot of whiskey when I found him; Brennan and Declan were as well. Conor was seated at the piano in the room and was playing—

I rolled my eyes. "Ozzy Osbourne shouldn't be played on the piano, Kid."

He paused to flip me the bird then continued playing.

"Heard it's chaos here today," I said to the room.

"Savannah's gone ape shit," Declan agreed.

"Can't say that I blame her. Ma never did know when to butt out," Eoghan said as he wandered into the room, handing me a bottle of beer.

With a nod of thanks, I took a sip as he sank down on the sofa while we watched Aidan limp from one side of the room to the other.

"She's not going to cancel," I told him. "She spent too long getting this place how she wants it."

"Aidan, want me to go and deal with Ma?" Brennan asked, getting to his feet and fastening his topcoat.

He'd been taking his role of best man deadly serious. That was the only reason I didn't tell them that Lena had Jake to distract her now.

"If Savvie doesn't calm the fuck down, then yeah, please." He scrubbed a hand over his hair. "I'll fucking kill Ma if she wrecks this for me. Best thing that ever fucking happens to me and she decides to get in my bride's face because the dress has a deep V and it's the wrong color."

"I won't let her, bro," Brennan soothed, grabbing Aidan's shoulder and squeezing it.

"I think you should tell us your speech, Bren," Conor mused. "Let's make sure there aren't too many curse words in it."

He squinted at Kid. "You looking to pick a fight?"

The smile dancing on his younger brother's lips confirmed Con was up to something.

It was like being around a communist dictator—Orwell was probably doing the fucking tango in his grave.

Aidan shot Brennan an alarmed look. "What the fuck does it say? Don't embarrass me in front of my in-laws, Bren. Jesus. They're already marrying into the mob and that meeting with Da didn't exactly go down well—"

Bren's ears turned pink. "Look, it's okay."

"Nah, you're blushing," Declan mocked. "That means we need to hear it to make sure you don't embarrass yourself."

Brennan sent him a look that promised retribution.

Declan hid his grin in the beer bottle in his hands.

"You gotta be fucking kidding me. You want me to—"

"Yes," we all declared at once.

His nostrils flared. "I'll get you fucking back for this, Con," he warned, dipping his hand into his pocket and dragging out a piece of paper.

Clearing his throat, he announced:

"I never thought I'd see the day where I stood up as best man at my oldest brother's wedding. I was pretty certain he'd ask our brother Finn to do it, and to be frank, being here, giving this toast, is the proudest day of my life.

"Standing up here for him, after all he's been through, with a woman who's his choice and his equal, I couldn't be more pleased for him.

"In the grand scheme of things, I'm the spare heir, but I've always looked up to Junior. He's got something about him that compels people to listen. I don't share that talent. In fact, I'm probably boring you. But with these weak words, it's important I convey to you that my brother is a better man for having Savannah in his life.

"I recently got married myself, and while I was happy single, it wasn't until I met my Camille that I realized what it is to actually have a wife. To have a partner. To have someone who'll stand by your side no matter what. I have that now, and I'm happy that Aidan's found that too.

"My brother's soldiered through so much to make it here, gone through more than you know to stand at the altar, to walk his bride back down the aisle. There were times when I wasn't sure if he'd make it, if his demons would cling too hard and we'd lose him forever, but I should have realized... he was waiting.

"I recently found out that he's known Savannah for five years, and even though he wouldn't say it himself, that's why he never let go.

"So, this speech isn't my send off to Aidan, but my thank you to Savvie. Thank you for coming into our world, for becoming a part of our family, but more than anything, thank you for being the reason my brother's still standing and fighting today.

"Let me propose a toast to the bride and groom."

As he finished speaking, he clearly expected for us to joke around and to have shit hurled at him, but there was silence.

Aidan and I shared a glance, and I watched him dip his chin in thanks.

Thanks for letting Brennan be his best man, a role that was clearly an honor for him.

"Brilliant speech, Bren," Dec muttered into his beer. "Better than the shitshow Conor gave me."

Conor grunted. "I planned your fucking wedding. I didn't have time for fancy speeches—"

Sensing a brewing argument, I was glad when a knock sounded at the door.

As I yelled, "Come in," I saw Aidan and Brennan clap each other on the back and smiled to myself.

"Hey, I'm looking for the kitchen?"

Aidan tossed a look at the door, dipped his chin, then waved a hand at the coffee table. "Come in, Camden. You want a drink? Some snacks? Con brought the entire fucking pantry in here when Savvie threatened to cancel the wedding."

When Conor shot Camden a look, Ozzy Osbourne morphed into Noxxious—his favorite band, and who Camden and Savannah's father played for.

Unlike Savannah who'd gone into the entertainment industry as a journalist, Camden was a rockstar too.

"I wouldn't worry about her canceling," Camden told him. "Savvie's a bitch but she got the tantrum out of her system."

Aidan's shoulders wriggled. "You don't want to hear this, Camden, but I'll spank her ass until it's red then I'll fireman's lift her down the fucking aisle if need be."

Camden mused, "She probably needs a good spanking. She always was more vinegar than honey."

"Well, this conversation got weird fast."

I smiled at Declan's grumble.

When the door popped open, and I saw Aoife's face drift into view, I wandered over there, trying to keep it low key and probably failing. Camden had broken some of the tension and they were all shooting the shit as I left, so no one noticed my departure.

"Sweetheart?"

She peered into the room. "Jake?"

"With Grammy."

Distaste flickered in her gaze, but she nodded her understanding.

Jake loved Lena.

There was no fighting that, and because my wife was a goddamn angel, she didn't try.

Every other Wednesday, Lena came into the city and I took Jake back to the penthouse so they could spend some time together.

Was it awkward? Yeah.

Was it all my fault? Yeah.

"My dad messaged me."

Studying her expression, I asked, "Is everything okay?"

"I want to start talking to him again."

Cupping her cheek, I nodded. "I think that's for the best."

"You do?" She bit her lip. "I thought you'd fight me on this."

"I might have before... There's more to what went down with him and your mom than you know."

"I told him as much and he agreed." Her chin jerked up. "I don't need your permission."

"I know you don't," I said calmly, watching as she relaxed some at my statement. Frowning, I asked again, "You okay, baby?"

She swallowed, stared up at me, then, without answering, grabbed my hand.

"Where are we going?" I rumbled when she dragged me down a hallway that I knew led to a suite of rooms.

She raised her chin. "I want to try something."

Blinking, I shrugged. "Fine."

When she shoved open a door and strolled into it, I closed it behind me then jerked in surprise as she flung herself at me.

Aoife usually let me instigate things, but that she came to me here, now, fuck, it made my dick ache.

Her mouth tore at mine, teeth and tongue fighting fire with fire as she dominated the kiss. Her hands went to my belt and her fingers found my cock.

I was crazy hard already, not just after months of abstinence but because this was her, coming onto me after the crap we'd been through.

Her fingers grabbed a firm hold of my cock, and I groaned as she jacked me off. Her lips pulled away from mine and she pressed heated kisses against my chin and down to my throat.

When she bit me there, I jerked in surprise because that was *my* signature move, not hers, and then she rasped, "You're mine, Finn. You're mine."

"I know I am, babe. I know I am."

Her grunt had me lifting my hands to cup her head, to hold her in place as I devoured her mouth, thrusting my tongue against hers this time, feeding her passion, stoking the flames.

Dropping one hand to her hips, I started to drag up her maxi skirt. When my fingers found her skin, skin that was silkier than her expensive dress, I groaned as I delved between her legs.

Rubbing against the crotch of her panties, I found slick heat, and I pulled back to rasp, "Baby, are you sure?"

"I'm sure," she whispered. "I need you."

I didn't want to argue—did I look like an idiot? But fuck.

"What brought this on?"

She arched onto tiptoe to try to kiss me again, but I stilled her by rubbing her clit, hard and fast, and then stopping my ministrations. She moaned and ground down against my fingers.

"Don't stop."

"I'll start again when you tell me what's going on," I breathed against her lips.

"Jen was..." She gulped, rocked her hips. "She..."

"What did she do, baby?"

"Made me think I'm not adventurous enough. That I should... start things more."

I blinked down at her. "Since when do you listen to *her* about *our* sex life?"

"I don't bore you?" she asked hesitantly.

"Baby, if you rocked my fucking world more than you did, you'd send me into a coma."

A startled laugh escaped her.

I started backing her toward the bed, not stopping until her ass was against it. When she tumbled down onto it, I loomed over her, dragging her skirts up, letting my fingers trail along her calves and thighs as I did so.

When I was done, I pressed my hands on either side of her head then rumbled, "You don't go to her for shit like that. You come to me."

She smiled at me as her hand went between her legs, and she started playing with her clit. "That's exactly what I did. I left Savannah, who's having a hair crisis, and Jen, who's bitching because her dress doesn't fit now, and I came to you."

She couldn't have said anything more likely to make me explode. Her words, her trust, combined with the way she was touching herself, set me on fucking fire.

I pressed myself against her then let our mouths do the talking.

As she explored me, I explored her. We ate at each other, devoured and tasted and savored, and when she was wriggling against me, her hips rocking back and forth like mad, I pulled back to rasp, "You are the sexiest woman on this fucking planet, Aoife."

Heat lit up in her eyes. "I love you, Finn."

"I fucking love you, baby," I whispered, then I groaned when she grabbed my dick and rubbed it against her slit.

"Show me you love me," she moaned. "Show me." Her pupils took up most of her irises, and I drowned in them as I slowly thrust into her.

And as I did, as we united, it felt like coming home but as if home had changed.

Had gotten better.

There was nothing between us now.

Nothing.

We had nothing holding us back, nothing keeping us in the past, nothing to stop us from heading forward into the future.

Her head tipped back, her gaze finally breaking free of mine, and I took advantage to maul her throat. To give her the hickey I wanted to see there all damn day.

As I made love to her, I branded her, then I fucked her mouth, giving her a taste of my roughness.

That wasn't for this time, maybe not the next, but we were walking back toward each other, toward a brighter tomorrow.

And that was when I pressed my forehead to hers and vowed:

"I, Finn O'Grady, take you, Aoife O'Grady, to be my wife. I promise to be true to you in good times and in bad, in sickness and in health. I will love you and honor you all the days of my life."

A shocked breath escaped her, and I felt her cunt clamp down on my dick, the beginnings of an orgasm stirring to life as she moaned, "I, Aoife O'Grady, take you, Finn O'Grady, to be my husband. I promise to be true to you in good times and in bad, in sickness and in health. I will love you and honor you all the days of my life."

And that was when the time for talking faded.

And I gloried in her pleasure, reveled in her orgasm, and found my own peace in her.

My love.
My woman.
My *wife*.

AELA: *How do you feel about becoming Cameron's godmother?*

Aoife: *Really?!*

Aela: *Really.*

Aoife: *I'd be honored.*

Aela: *You sure? I know we don't do the religion thing but I want him baptized.*

Aoife: *I understand. I wanted Jake baptized too.*

Aela: *You know what it means though, don't you?*

Aoife: *That I'll see them at the ceremony?*

Aela: *Yeah. How do you feel about that?*

Aoife: *I think I'm ready. Lena doesn't push things. Senior's not so bad now either.*

Aela: *You sure?*

Aoife: *For my godson, yes. I'm sure.*

Aela: *I don't want you to feel pressured.*

Aoife: *I don't. I don't have to say yes, Aela. But it's worth it. They're his grandparents, and they should be there. I don't have to talk to them or even look at them to play my part in the ceremony.*

Aela: *I'm so happy you feel that way. I really wanted you to be there for Cameron.*

Aoife: *I'm there for Shay too. You know that.*

Aela: *You're so maternal. I think I skipped that gene.*

Aoife: *That's a lie. You're an awesome mom.*

Aela: *Can I tell you something?*

Aoife: *Of course.*

Aela: *It's delicate.*

Aoife: *Go for it. I'm a big girl.*

Aela: *I forgot how difficult it is to have a newborn.*

Aoife: *Of course you did. Do you need some help?*

Aela: *I couldn't ask you to do that.*

Aoife: *You can. He's my godson. Who else should be there for both of you right now?*

Aela: *I just really want to have a shower.*

Aoife: *I know, sweetheart.*

Aela: *And I want to hear my favorite songs without crying.*

Aoife: *I can't help with that. But I can take over while you get showered, and I can even bring over food if you want.*

Aela: *I'm crying.*

Aela: *Why am I crying?*

Aoife: *Because you're tired and hormonal and YOU JUST GAVE BIRTH. Be kind to yourself, sweetheart.*

Aela: *It's so hard. And Declan's being awesome. He's there and doing stuff and trying to help and I just want to bite his head off.*

Aoife: *Well, he did this.*

Aela: *Yeah, it's totally his fault.*

Aoife: *Lol. I'll be over in an hour or so, okay?*

Aela: *Thank YOU <3 <3 <3*

Aoife: *Just take it easy until I get there. All right?*

Aela: *I will.*

Aela: *Aoife?*

Aoife: *Yep?*

Aela: *I already loved you but I'll love you even more if you bring your brownies with you.*

Aoife: *LOL. You got it. <3*

FIFTY-SIX

DECLAN

WHEN SEAMUS WALKED through the doors of the workshop, both black eyes were squinting as he immediately shook his head. "Mom won't like it here."

I frowned around the empty expanse. "What's not to like?"

"It's not right." He huffed under his breath. "Didn't you ask her for specs?"

"Of course I did." I shoved my fists onto my hips. "What's wrong with it?"

"Not enough light." He peered up at the ceiling. "She likes overhead illumination."

"I'll bust open the fucking ceiling then." I rolled my eyes. "Or buy her more lamps. You know how difficult it was to find this after the last two?"

"Telling ya, she won't like it, Dad."

I wasn't entirely sure what there wasn't to like considering the shopping list Aela had given me and which my crew had scoured the city to attain on her behalf. The fact she'd dropped the First Lady's commission hadn't changed her specs, God help me.

Either way, I'd bought the place now, and we'd have to reno it to fit her exacting standards.

Seeing as renting hadn't worked out, I was hoping that buying a place, gutting it, and shaping it to her specifications would move things along.

I already knew my woman was a pain in the ass, but this had taken a lot more effort than I'd expected, and Shay's immediate dismissal didn't put me in a better fucking mood.

She'd gone through two ateliers in the past six months, and I was running out of places to put her exacting ass.

Walking over to him, I chucked him on the chin so I could get a better glimpse at his eyes. "I let Brennan start teaching you how to fight because I didn't want you to be in a position where you couldn't defend yourself, Shay."

He jerked his head back and away from me. "I'm not going to let them talk smack about us."

I narrowed my eyes on him, wondering if it was that people were talking smack or if it was the fact Shay had a new brother and he was finding it hard to adjust. I knew that I'd hated it when Eoghan came along. Feeling displaced sucked balls.

"People always talk smack—"

"I don't get it," he rasped. "I don't get that they're terrified of us, of Grandda, but they talk this much shit about our family."

"Because terrified people do stupid stuff." I smiled at him. "Never heard of posturing? Bet your ass their fathers aren't talking smack about us.

"They're just dumb fucks, kid. I need you not to get into fights over this shit because it doesn't matter."

"I don't like it," was his stubborn retort.

"Since when did you defend Grandda, anyway? Thought you were still pissed over him not liking having to share restrooms with trans people."

He shrugged. "He's old."

"So?"

"We have to forgive old people and teach them to be better than they are. Anyway, it wasn't about that this time."

My lips curved despite the fact that nothing about this situation was a laughing matter. "What was it?"

Those two argued as often as Aela and I kissed. That was to say every time they clapped eyes on each other.

"He said the ballet was for girls again." He stuck up his chin. "We argued."

"Not sure you can teach an old dog like Da new tricks, Shay."

"We can try."

"You can," I agreed, "but just live your life how you want to. Don't let him stop you. That's the best way."

"Is that what you did?"

"No. It's what I should have done."

His gaze was measured as he took me in before he peered around the studio. "You need to get a skylight installed before you show Mom. She'll tell you this place isn't right otherwise."

I grumbled under my breath, "Such a pain in the ass."

He gave me a toothy grin. "I'll tell her you said that."

"You can," I retorted. "I'd tell her myself."

"No, you wouldn't. It would probably make her cry right now."

"Nah. Not your ma. Most women would cry, she'd just throw something at me."

His grin widened. "That's my mom," he declared, his pride clear.

Amused, I told him, "I got something for you."

"What?" he asked warily.

"There's an office. They're in there."

"What is it?"

"A gift."

"A gift?" His wariness tripled. "But I got into another fight..." Then he huffed. "Is this because of Cameron?

"Look, I get it. I'm an older brother now. I need to set a good example. But he's like three weeks old. I can't set a bad example when he can't sit up straight."

He had a point.

I cleared my throat. "This isn't because of Cameron. And it isn't about you getting into a fight. Your mom's going to punish you. I don't need to worry about that," I disregarded, stepping away from him and heading to the back office. "This is about you and the man you're going to become."

"You could tell her that it was self-defense," he argued, but I heard his footsteps and knew he was following me.

"Why would I do that?" I drawled. "It would be a lie."

The office was bare apart from a shitty desk and two chairs. On the desk were my gifts, and I took a seat in one of the chairs.

"You're not gonna be like me, are you, Shay? I commit a crime; I never do the time. That's not your path, is it?"

I knew he was about to answer, but then he saw the gifts and his eyes bugged. "Is that a gun?"

I nodded. "Know what a ghost gun is?"

"No." His brow furrowed as he dropped his school bag beside the seat and slumped in the chair. "What is it?"

"It means it has no registration ID. For all intents and purposes, it doesn't exist. To the government, anyway." I slipped the weapon across the desk. "Pick it up. See how it feels in your hands."

Eyes still wide, he did as I suggested, and because he knew how to wield a gun, I watched him go through the steps of checking whether it was loaded with bullets or not.

Even though I didn't want him to be comfortable with guns, I was proud of how he held it. That he knew what to do with it, but it remained alien to him.

At his age, I'd fired a gun too many times, and I didn't want that for him, but I knew from experience that you couldn't make a kid do dick. They made their own decisions and took their own path.

"You're giving me this?" he rumbled after a few minutes of gawking at it.

I didn't answer. "Look at the other stuff."

He blinked but picked up the Mont Blanc fountain pen. It had slivers of lacquer all over it, like a mosaic or a stained-glass window.

"Wow, that's heavy," he pointed out.

"Some parts are platinum; others are white gold." I shrugged. "It's limited edition."

He unscrewed the cap to reveal the nib. "I've never used a fountain pen before."

"First time for everything."

"It's mine?"

"It can be."

"It looks expensive."

My lips twitched. "It is. But the gun wasn't cheap either."

He gnawed on the inside of his cheek as he placed the pen down with more care than the gun. My heart leaped at the sight with hope.

When he picked up the ring next, he licked his lips. "This looks old."

"It is." I leaned forward and snatched it from his palm where he'd placed it. Rolling it around my fingers, I told him, "It's from Ancient Greece."

A shaky breath escaped him, and he proved himself to be mine and Aela's kid as he whispered, awe in his tone, "No way."

"Way. It's ancient gold, and the gemstone is—"

"Sapphire," he blurted out.

"Yeah. Apollo's symbol. They'd have worn a signet ring like this before they consulted the Oracle at Delphi."

He stared at me. "Wow."

I smiled. "See how the setting is in relief?"

Squinting at it, he nodded. "They're little flowers."

"Not flowers, leaves," I corrected. "From an olive tree."

"Whoa." He snagged it and raised it to his eyes to squint at. "That's so cool."

"I'm glad you think so," I told him as I crossed my legs at the ankle and sat back, watching him as he eyed the ring then picked up the pen, totally ignoring the gun.

I let him study them both, content to wait on him to speak, happy to just watch him.

After what Finn and Aoife had gone through... it had made me realize how fucking lucky I was. I mean, I'd known that already. But it was confirmation.

I'd spent the rest of Aela's pregnancy hovering over her like a mother fucking hen. I'd even *prayed* that we wouldn't lose our kid. That I'd get the chance to be there from the start this time.

Aela had done such a good job with Shay, and mostly, my influence was fucking that up. A part of me was terrified I'd do the same with Cameron, but I had to hope that she'd steer me on the right path.

I had to have faith.

"Why you giving me these, Dad?" Shay asked after a good ten minutes. His gaze darted to me and back again.

Did he know what it did to me when he called me that?

Dad.

I'd never thought about having kids before, despite knowing that in Da's eyes, it was our 'duty.' Yet, here I was, one sitting in front of me with blacker eyes than a panda, and one currently driving his mom crazy back home because he wouldn't sleep.

Reaching up, I rubbed my finger along my bottom lip and murmured, "Wanted to give you a choice. They're gifts but you don't have to accept them all."

He tilted his head to the side. "What do you mean?"

I reached for the gun. "They're paths."

"Huh?"

Twisting the weapon in my hand, I explained, "This is violence in the flesh. One click and someone's dead. One click, you've committed a crime that can get you put in jail. Everything changes when you press that trigger.

"You and I both know that I want you to be competent at shooting, but being able to do it doesn't mean you should. It just means that I'd like you to be able to defend yourself."

"I can't carry that until I'm eighteen," he pointed out.

"You never have to carry one, period," I retorted. "Your guards carry. That's plenty."

He sank back in his chair, and I knew I had his attention as I returned it to its earlier position on the desk and picked up the pen.

"The written word is a powerful tool, Shay. History is forged on it; laws are made with it. I figured that was worthy of a special pen."

I saw understanding glimmer to life in his eyes. "What about the ring?"

"What does an olive branch represent?"

"Peace," he replied.

Nodding, I told him, "You can go two ways, son. My way." The gun. "Or you can take a different path. The one you always intended on taking before you learned what I am and what I do."

He scowled at me. "I still want that. You know I do."

I didn't know if he knew it'd be close to impossible for him to get where he wanted when he was my son, when the O'Donnelly name was an albatross around his fucking neck in D.C., but I didn't say that.

I just said, "Sure, but every time you get into a fight, you're changing lanes. You're coming into my world, and you don't want that. These are your reminder." I gave him the pen and the ring. "You can use the pen at school and wear the ring. They're what'll keep you on the straight and narrow. That'll take you wherever you want to go." I studied the gun. "This will only get you deeper into shit and will take you away from your goals. It's up to you what you want, but you can't have all three gifts. You have to decide. *Now*."

Though he was scowling, I knew my kid's brain was faster than a whippet around a dog track. When he pocketed the pen and slipped on the ring, relief hit me hard enough to fucking wind me.

"You can keep the gun, Dad."

I smiled at him though I felt like goddamn crying. "I think that's the wise choice, son."

He pulled a face. "You really can't do anything about Mom?"

"I'll put in a good word for you. That's about as much as I can promise."

"I told you about the skylight," he commented.

"That's for her sake. This place is safe. *She'll* be safe working here. Cameron will probably have a nursery in this very room. You want them to be on secured grounds, don't you?"

Shame had his shoulders hunching. "Of course I do."

"If the skylight'll make her happy, then that's for the good, isn't it?"

"Sorry, Dad. You're right."

I got to my feet, and after he did, I leaned my arm on his shoulder. "I usually am. Just don't tell your mom that."

When he laughed, I smiled and squeezed him as I guided him out of the door and, hopefully, down a different path than the one he'd started to take.

"We all have choices in this life, Shay," I told him softly as we headed for the exit. "You're going to get hit with plenty of them soon enough.

"Drugs and pussy and all kinds of shit you shouldn't get involved in. Think about that future you want before you do anything dumb. One mistake and that's it. That future could be gone, *but* we won't be gone. No matter how hard you fuck up, your mom and I will be here. Okay?"

He peered up at me. "You mean that?"

"I do."

His smile was all O'Donnelly. "Thanks, Dad."

"No problem, son." I squeezed him again before I let him go to lock up the workshop. "Get into the car," I told him, even as I grabbed my cellphone and shot out a message to one of the contractors we used to get a goddamn skylight installed ASAP.

Who was pussywhipped around here? Not me, that was for fucking sure.

DECLAN: *You were right.*

    Finn: *Of course I was.*

    Finn: *About what?*

    Declan: *You're such an ass.*

    Finn: *I try. What was I right about this time?*

    Declan: *He didn't go for the gun.*

    Finn: *Oh. Good. I'm glad.*

    Declan: *You're not going to shove it in my face?*

    Finn: *No. I had a feeling he'd reject the gun, but you never know.*

    Declan: *No, you don't.*

    Finn: *He's a good kid, Dec. Adjusting to a new baby in the house is bound to be hard.*

    Declan: *I don't want him to be like us.*

    Finn: *He won't be.*

    Finn: *How's Cameron?*

    Declan: *Great.*

    Finn: *How's Seamus with him?*

    Declan: *Great.*

    Finn: *So maybe there's no reason he keeps getting into fights other than the fact he's surrounded by a bunch of jackasses at school?*

    Declan: *Yeah. That could be it.*

    Finn: *You know what it means that you're worrying about him?*

    Declan: *What?*

    Finn: *That you're an awesome dad.*

    Declan: *You think so?*

    Finn: *I know so.*

FIFTY-SEVEN

FINN

"GODDAMMIT," Aidan hissed as he plunked his ass down on an armchair in the living room.

"When's your next physio session?" I questioned, pressing the bottle of beer to my lips and swigging some down.

"Tomorrow." He grunted as he laid his leg out in front of him. "It's getting better. Today's just not a good day."

On the brink of answering, I arched a brow as the door opened and Conor swaggered in with a bottle of beer and his diamanté cat. "Where's Jake?"

"Why?"

"He likes the cat. I brought him the cat."

"To keep?"

Kid hesitated. "On loan." He peered around the living room. "I can't believe you're still staying in a hotel suite. It's a good thing you're a billionaire."

"Aoife likes it." That was all that mattered. It wasn't a permanent solution, but it was what she needed until I could find the right place for us. "And Jake's in bed." When he swiveled on his heel, I barked, "Conor, if you wake him up, I will shove this beer bottle where the sun doesn't shine. It took me three hours to get him down. *Three.*"

"We're dealing with a man on the edge," Aidan said with a laugh. "Don't mess with him, Kid."

Conor huffed as he dumped the cat by the door then strolled over to us. "He's always asleep when I visit."

"Stop by earlier, and don't pout." I shot him a withering glance.

"It was easier when you lived opposite me," he grumbled.

"Tough." I turned to Junior. "You sure your knee's getting better?"

"Oh, for sure. It's painful, but not like before the surgery."

"You don't want to shoot up?" Kid inquired.

"No, Conor, I don't want to shoot up," Aidan said on an impatient sigh.

"You sure? Finn and I will gladly sit on you again."

My lips curved as I raised my beer bottle to Kid. "Ain't that the truth."

He smirked, took a sip of beer, then asked, "Did Lodestar funnel that information to Savannah?"

Aidan angled himself toward Conor. "The bank account shit?"

Savannah had recently published an article that exposed the five banks where the Sparrows held accounts. Some CEOs and CFOs had resigned over the last couple days.

With no money, and fewer men in positions of power, the Sparrows were no longer just dying, they were on the brink of extinction.

As for our other problem—those *cheile* bastards—it had been all quiet on the Western Front.

"Yeah. The bank account shit," Conor confirmed. "Did Lodestar give her the data?"

"Of course. Why?"

Conor scratched his chin. "She's gone quiet on me."

Brennan and Declan sauntered in, Dec carrying a baby, Brennan two bottles of beer.

"Who's gone quiet on you?" Declan asked.

"Lodestar." He stared down at his own drink. "I'm starting to get worried."

"You know where she lives, right?" Brennan pointed out. "Just go visit."

His eyes rounded. "Go visit her?"

Declan snorted. "Con, she's with the Sinners, not the Romulans on Angel One."

"Whoa, someone's been watching *Star Trek*," Conor blurted out.

Dec shrugged. "Shay loves it. Cameron does too."

I smirked. "And you don't?"

His nose crinkled at the bridge. "I'd prefer an art documentary, but it keeps my kids happy. What the hell else am I supposed to do?"

Brennan shook his head. "You definitely don't take after the school of Da."

Dec stiffened and shot me a wary look—each of them did that whenever they mentioned their parents. Not Conor, though. Naturally.

"No, I fucking don't," Declan mumbled. "You think I'd treat my sons like he treated me?"

"Theoretically, and statistically, you should. Systemic abuse does that to a person," Conor pointed out.

"Yeah, well, I'm breaking the mold. And Aela would chop me up and store me in the freezer if I ever made my kids feel like they were pieces of shit."

For a second, the guys just looked at each other.

I knew what they were thinking—Lena hadn't done dick to stop Senior from making them feel like they were pieces of shit.

"You seen Ma recently?" Conor rasped.

A part of me tensed up, but they were my brothers and she was their mother. I'd absented myself from their lives, they hadn't, and I didn't expect them to. Aoife didn't either.

Both of us were just grateful we got to have our cake and eat it too.

Saturday night was ours. Sunday dinner was theirs.

I handled Senior on business, saw Lena every second Wednesday when she came into the city to visit with Jake, and other than that, I honored my wife's request that I keep them out of our lives.

I knew the brothers shot me looks, their shoulders stiff with tension, but I murmured, "I saw her on Wednesday. She's lost weight."

Kid started picking off the label on his beer. "A lot of it. Think she's off her meds again. Seen the state of her throat? She's back to scratching."

"I know she is," Brennan muttered. "Da's not much better."

Aidan drank some of his whiskey. "I'm not sure if we'll have much longer with them."

Brennan blinked. "Well, that's fucking depressing."

"Is it? They're both sick, Bren. Mentally and physically." He adjusted his seated position and grimaced, pain flicking over his features. "Maybe sending them to Florida would help."

Declan hooted. "Florida? Yeah, I can totally see them living it up in Boca Raton."

"Maybe they've got that seasonal depression shit." Aidan's tone was musing.

"Who does?" Eoghan demanded as he strolled into the living room.

"Your folks," I replied.

"Summer only just ended," Eoghan said, clearly confused by our conversation as he slumped on the sofa.

"Maybe they need more vitamin D," Junior retorted doggedly.

"They need their family around them," Brennan intoned, then he raised his hands. "I'm not saying they should get that, not saying they've earned the right, but that's their problem.

"Ma's met Cameron once. Aela's barely visiting and neither's Shay. Aoife, Jake, and Finn's places are dusty. The table's always half empty now.

"It's sad really. Of all the shit they did..." He shook his head. "Actually, it makes sense."

"What does?" Kid questioned.

"He raised us to adore our women, didn't he?" Brennan pointed out, earning nods from us all. "We would never cut ties for ourselves. That's not how shit works. But for them?" He laughed. "Funny how he reared us to be that way and that'll be his Kryptonite."

"You have a point," I mused softly, and like his words delivered them, we heard the soft laughter of our women.

Aoife's chuckle and Aela's bawdy snicker. Savannah's husky laugh, Inessa's soft giggle, and Camille's snort of amusement.

As they wandered into the room, they brought joy with them. Love. A levity that we'd all been lacking our whole lives.

They were our light at the end of a tunnel none of us had realized we were stuck in.

As Aoife settled beside me, perching her ass on the armrest of my armchair, a glass of wine in her hand, she shot me a smile that lit me up from the inside out.

Some might say that marriage had softened me.

But what 'they' didn't realize was... it had taken her love, our marriage, to make me stand up to the biggest, meanest motherfucker in the city.

Christ, on the East Coast.

Who was the pussy now?

CONOR: *Do you think I should?*

Finn: *Give me a clue. Should what?*

Conor: *Should visit Star.*

Finn: *Maybe preface messages with the entire question, Conor. We can save time that way.*

Conor: *Finn! I'm having a meltdown here.*

Finn: *Why?*

Conor: *She isn't talking to me.*

Finn: *Women do that. What did you do to piss her off?*

Conor: *Nothing.*

Finn: *It's never nothing. Did you forget her birthday?*

Conor: *No.*

Finn: *An anniversary?*

Conor: *Look, Star isn't a normal woman, Finn. Things like that don't make her mad.*

Finn: *Hahaha, excuse me while I die over here. ALL women are like that. I don't give a fuck what they say; they care about that shit. Put reminders on, set alarms, just never forget birthdays, anniversaries, or holidays.*

Conor: *You think I don't have a million reminders set for the family's birthdays? I know how to set a reminder, Finn.*

Finn: *So why didn't you do that this time?*

Conor: *Because I didn't forget anything! I gave her a damn gift recently. Anyway, she wouldn't stop talking to me over that. I even let her win our last game of Call of Duty.*

Finn: *How benevolent of you.*

Conor: *Shut up. Tell me what to do.*

Finn: *I don't see that there's any harm in visiting her.*

Conor: *What if I shouldn't?*

Finn: *What?*

Conor: *What if it's better if we never meet?*

Finn: *Conor, why would that be the best thing to happen? What's going on with you?*

Conor: *I'm fucked up, Finn.*

Finn: *No more than any of us. We all found someone, didn't we?*

Conor: *I'm worse than you.*

Finn: *Than Aidan? I doubt it. Do you skin people as well as electro-cute them?*

Conor: *No.*

Finn: *Well, then.*

Conor: *I'm wrong.*

Conor: *Something's not right in my head.*

Finn: *Okay, let's have some real talk here, Kid.*

Finn: *You are one of the best men I know.*

Finn: *You deserve love.*

Finn: *You deserve a future.*

Finn: *You are more than the sum of your past.*

Finn: *There is nothing wrong with you. Do you understand me?*

****TEN MINUTES LATER****

FINN: *Kid, don't go quiet on me now.*

Conor: *What if I don't deserve any of that?*

Finn: *You do.*

Conor: *What if you don't know the real me?*

Finn: *I know the real you, Conor. I know that behind all the BS, you've got a heart of gold. It might be tarnished, but that's life.*

Conor: *Gold doesn't tarnish.*

Finn: *Pedantic pain in my ass. But even though you are, you deserve to have whatever you want. Do you want Star?*

Conor: *I do.*

Finn: *Then you should definitely go to her.*

Finn: *Tell me what happens?*

Conor: *I will.*

Conor: *How's the house hunt going?*

Finn: *Fuck off.*

Conor: *Just thought I'd remind you that you ain't perfect.*

Finn: *Didn't need that reminder.*

Finn: *Look, you were the one who told me she's yours. So why the fuck are you dicking around? Get on with it, Kid.*

****FOUR DAYS LATER****

. . .

FINN: *Have you gone to see her yet?*

Conor: *I'm busy. I haven't had the chance.*

Finn: *Bullshit.*

Conor: *It isn't bullshit.*

Finn: *It is.*

Conor: *It isn't! Didn't you hear about those death threats Savannah received?*

Finn: *What? No!*

Conor: *It was bound to happen. She's pissed a lot of people off. Junior's going ape shit.*

Finn: *I'll call him. I get that you're busy, Con, but go to her. What do you have to lose?*

FIFTY-EIGHT

CONOR

A WEEK LATER

"WHERE THE HELL ARE YOU, LODESTAR?" I grumbled under my breath as I tried to send her another message.

I knew she'd been working on dismantling the Sparrows' massive funding network, and over the last few weeks, since Savannah's initial press release which exposed Lodestar's findings, bank accounts associated with the secret society had been handed over to the US Attorney.

But ever since our last video call when she'd opened her belated Christmas gift, she'd gone silent.

I'd scoured her usual hunting grounds, trying to see if I could find a trace of her, but she was quiet.

Stone-cold quiet.

She was a deadly weapon shaped like a female, but that didn't mean she was bulletproof.

If Savannah was getting death threats, maybe she was too.

Maybe she was already dead.

My fear meant that I'd been less productive than I should be.

The program that was running double speed to filter through the thousands of hours of recordings from across the Five Points had targeted conversations that I needed to listen to, but I'd been ignoring them.

My concern was for Lodestar.

We hadn't argued since before that video call, so I knew she wasn't mad at me. She'd even said she *liked* the gift, so it wasn't that.

All this was why I was making the drive to New Jersey.

Brennan and Declan were right.

She wasn't on Angel One.

She was in West Orange.

Just a drive away.

And Finn was right too.

I deserved *more*.

I deserved to have a future with the woman I wanted without my past fucking shit up for me.

Approaching another faction's territory wasn't a smart move, but where Star made me stupid, I wasn't smart. She did something to me, made my life easier somehow even though, case in point now, she made it harder too.

With her in my world, I worked harder and attained more. She kept me on my toes. Reminded me that you had to earn perfection.

She made me laugh; she got me mad.

She was my equal.

My balance.

Without her, everything was more difficult. Sleeping was harder. Eating was no fun.

Was this what love felt like?

It was inconvenient.

So far, I'd only experienced the good side. The bad hurt.

When I made it to West Orange, I knew I had two options.

I could go to the Satan's Sinners' MC clubhouse or I could go to Lily Lancaster's home.

After the clubhouse was bombed, the incident in which Star had gotten her injuries, she and Kati had moved in with Lily—one of the brothers' Old Ladies.

The clubhouse had been reconstructed, and the brothers had moved in back at the start of the year.

I knew she still lived with Lily so that Kati's sister could be nearby, but it was the daytime. It was likely she'd be at the compound.

There'd be more politics if I went there first though.

Deciding Lily Lancaster's house was the smart move, I pulled up her address in Google Maps and used the GPS to take me to her mansion.

Her father had been a Sparrow, and it seemed as if he and Da aspired to the same architectural tastes of overdone and gaudy because it was clearly an expensive property that stood out like a flashing lighthouse in the dark.

When I made it to the gates, my tricked out vintage Mini Clubman was scanned by the security systems, and then a voice sounded at the intercom.

"Who is this?"

"My name's Conor. I'd like to speak with Lodestar."

There was a hesitation, then a, "One moment, please."

It was more than a moment. It was *several.* But I didn't bitch about it, just waited, even as my phone suddenly lit up with a couple notifications.

Hoping it was Star, disappointment hit me when I saw it was from my program.

Three red alerts.

Slipping in an AirPod, I picked out the recordings that had triggered an alarm then frowned when I heard my father's voice.

"Wondered when you'd deign to pick up the fucking phone, Elizabeth. Didn't realize it would take nearly six goddamn months."

"I have more important things to be doing than speaking with mobsters," the woman sniped.

"So why did you decide to call me back?"

She hesitated a second. *"You heard that Eamonn Keegan is out?"*

"Old news. He's been sighted in New York though. Your husband's immigration policy really is as weak as they say it is."

That was when I had confirmation exactly which Elizabeth he was talking to.

The First Lady.

A hiss escaped her at the insult. *"Michael's gone missing."*

She'd only just found that out?

Confused, I waited for Da's reply.

It was a belligerent: *"And?"*

"What do you mean, 'And?'" she snarled. *"You're supposed to protect him."*

I arched a brow at that revelation.

"How the hell am I supposed to save him from cancer? If the bastard discharged himself to go and slit his wrists in private, well, he did the world a favor, didn't he?"

"You're a heartless bastard, Aidan," Elizabeth growled. *"You didn't have any men guarding him?"*

"Not my job."

"You made a deal."

Just when shit was starting to get interesting, I heard the crackle of the intercom, and I pulled my AirPod away from my ear to stop the recording.

"Who is this?"

"My name's Conor O'Donnelly."

"Of the Five Points' O'Donnellys?"

"Yes."

I arched a brow at the formal question, but for whatever reason, that had the gates opening.

As I started the engine, I drove down a manicured lane that was obsessively neat and found myself approaching the house where a slender woman was waiting in the driveway. Her blonde hair bobbed around her shoulders as she stepped over to my car once I'd parked.

"I'm Lily Lancaster," she greeted, leaning over to speak with me through the driver's window.

"Is there a reason I can't get out?" I questioned, gaze flickering over to the house. "Is she in there but doesn't want to see me?"

Lily blinked then wafted a dismissive hand. "No. My partner is very protective. If you go inside, it will start a whole argument about why you're here, and I have better things to be doing with him than soothing his ruffled ego."

"Your man's Link, isn't he?"

She didn't like that I knew that, but she nodded all the same. "He's got the flu right now, and he's a very bad patient. I don't need this to add to his stress."

Nose crinkling, I pulled back. "You might be contagious," I accused.

Her lips curved. "I did the smart thing and had the flu shot. He didn't."

Uneasy, I muttered, "Where's Star?"

"That's why I agreed to speak with you. I don't know. I was hoping you did. She mentions you a lot—"

"She left?" I ground out, interrupting her.

"She did." Lily frowned. "The only person who knows where she went is her foster daughter."

"Kati knows?"

"Well, we assume so. She's the only one who isn't worried."

"She left her behind?" At Lily's confirmation, a bad feeling spread throughout me. A little like blood poisoning, I could feel its necrotic crawl through my system. "Star would never do that."

"I'm afraid you'll find she did," Lily replied softly.

I cast her a look, saw her sympathetic expression, and gritted my teeth. "Did she give no clue about where she went?"

"No. But she's been acting strangely ever since she got her casts removed."

"That was months ago." At the beginning of the damn year!

Lily shrugged. "I know. It's the truth though."

I hadn't noticed much difference. Other than her being blood-thirstier in *Call of Duty* and her working longer hours, that is.

"Who's looking after Kati?"

"Her sister, Alessa, and her partner, Maverick."

Rubbing a hand over my face, I muttered, "She'd never leave Kati behind."

"But she did," Lily retorted, shivering as a nasty gust of wind swept her hair away from her neck.

I peered up at the sky, grimacing when I saw rain was coming. Either that or snow.

The weather had been acting weird. We'd had some snowfall a week ago so anything was possible... and they said climate change wasn't real. Snow in late September? It was barely fall.

"She wouldn't have left Kati behind without a good reason." I thought back to the last time I'd spoken with her and demanded, "When did she leave?"

"I'm not entirely sure. Star keeps peculiar hours. Kati was being bullied again," she offered with a grimace. "Star has an unusual way of dealing with things, and it was only when the principal demanded to speak with her that Alessa realized she'd left."

Unease made the hairs at the back of my neck stand on edge.

I rasped, "Kati didn't tell anyone she'd left?"

"No."

"Can I speak with her?"

Lily shook her head. "I don't think that would be appropriate."

My mouth tensed, but I nodded. Star wouldn't like it if I pumped her daughter for answers, either.

"Thank you for being so candid."

I wasn't sure why, but after a short study of my person, she sighed. "If it's any consolation, she left her rig behind."

Hope swelled inside me. "She did?"

Lily nodded.

If she'd left her computers behind then... "She'll be back."

"I didn't doubt she would be. I don't think Kati would be taking it so well if—" She broke off. "You mean... you thought she was going to hurt herself?"

"No, not that."

"You think she's in danger?"

Tension filled me as I murmured, "Yes, I think she is."

Her hand snatched out to grip a hold of my arm. "Will you try to find her?"

I gritted my teeth at her touch and grated out, "Oh, make no bones about it. I will."

A few minutes later, I left Lily behind, and though my temper was at war with my concern, as I rode away, I shoved my AirPod back into my ear.

I wasn't interested in whatever bullshit my father was involved in, but I knew I had to be.

On the ride home, I couldn't do anything to help locate Star, but this was something I *could* do.

Da's voice might sound collected, but I heard the throb of anger within it as he intoned, "*I made a deal with Michael, sure, but if he wanted guards, then he should have gotten his* cheile *friends to look after him. I'm not his nanny, Elizabeth.*"

"*You mean you don't know where he is?*"

Frowning at the question, I wondered why she was asking now. Michael had been dead for six months. I'd know. I was the one who'd delivered him to his maker.

Da had never mentioned Michael, his illness, death, and/or funeral, which left me thinking Ma hadn't told him what had gone down. Maybe he even thought the man was still alive?

All Da knew was that Aoife had found out about Ma killing her mom and that was why they didn't come around anymore.

Ma must have stepped in at some point though. Da wasn't the kind of man you said 'no' to. She must have stopped him from demanding Finn, Aoife, and Jake show up on Sundays.

Shoving that thought away, I had to ask myself if Da really didn't know Michael was dead yet.

This was confusing as fuck.

"I didn't say that I didn't know where Michael is, now did I? Funny how you're calling me. Someone whispered something in my ear recently about the pair of you.

"Imagine how surprised I was to find out you and Michael had a thing going. Wonder what the president would have to say about that..."

There was silence down the other end of the line. *"Do you, or do you not know where Michael is?"*

"Even funnier that this is the first time you've asked about him. His cancer's terminal," Da droned. *"Thought his little woman would care about that."*

"We had a falling out," Elizabeth bit off. *"He's supposed to be in a hospice, but there are no records of him—"* She hissed under her breath. *"Where is he, Aidan?"*

"Information like that comes at a price," Da taunted, leaving me wondering if someone had betrayed me. Had they told Da that I'd dealt with Michael? Or was this all BS?

Seeing as the man was fish food, there was no way my father could know his exact whereabouts, but when Elizabeth Davidson didn't bite, Da drawled, *"I'll be at Greenwood Cemetery at three. I'll meet you at my brother's grave."* He gave her directions on how to reach it. *"If you want answers, I'll see you there. And don't even think about bringing your guards along."*

"How am I supposed to get away from them?" she snapped.

"Not my problem. You want to know where lover boy is, you know where to find me."

I cast a look at the clock, and seeing that it was two-thirty, bit off, "Shit." Before I could call Aidan, though, I got another alert on my phone.

A flurry of static images popped up on my screen. I set them to shuffle on a loop so they played like a moving picture.

Star.

My brows rose at the sight of her in my apartment. A part of me was mad, another part wondered why she looked so fucking right in there.

As the images played, I saw her head to the only computer that wasn't connected to the internet and watched as she attached a thumb drive to one of the USB ports.

As she copied the hard drive, she grabbed something from the desk, picked up a pen, then started writing something on it.

She dropped the paper on my desk, took a photo, tapped her screen a few times, then tossed the note into the trash.

After, she retrieved the thumb drive then got to her feet where she pressed her hand to my chair, presenting me with a shot where she stood there, her eyes closed.

That hurt me more than anything she'd just done.

Her regret was real.

Raw.

Just like mine was.

She didn't have to do that.

She could have asked *me* for whatever it was she'd taken.

And as I stared at the photos, it was then that I saw the timestamp.

Thirty minutes ago.

But...

Four weeks earlier.

She'd delayed my system, fucking with it so that I received the security notification now.

Suddenly, I knew what it felt like to wait for the sky to fall down around my ears because my gut told me everything was turning full circle.

That was when my system went down. Even my phone restarted itself.

Fuck.

With time ticking away, I managed to connect a call with Aidan on my back up cell that I kept for emergencies.

The second he answered, I spat, "We have a problem."

DEAD TO ME: *Anyone around?*

Whistler: *Affirmative.*

Eagle Eyes: *Affirmative.*

Dead To Me: *Heard a rumor today. Wondered if you'd heard it too.*

Whistler: *Won't know until you tell us if it's the same rumor.*

Dead To Me: *Are you always so pedantic?*

Whistler: *Affirmative.*

Eagle Eyes: *Is the rumor about the First Lady?*

Dead To Me: *Yes. Seems like she's the target.*

Whistler: *I hadn't heard that until now. What's she done?*

Eagle Eyes: *Well, it's conjecture. They say she pissed off Dagda. Not sure how the First Lady got involved with the ECD... the state of this fucking country, I swear.*

Whistler: *How did she piss him off?*

Dead To Me: *They say that Dagda found out she was involved in his sister's death.*

Eagle Eyes: *I heard it was his brother's.*

Whistler: *He had a sister.*

Dead To Me: *You know this for sure? Is she dead?*

Whistler: *Affirmative. To both questions.*

Eagle Eyes: *Got a friend in Ireland who's close to the ECD. Apparently, it was the prime minister there who was the initial target because he didn't agree with the North and South uniting.*

Whistler: *That's changed?*

Eagle Eyes: *Seems like it. The UK's pissed at Davidson's stance on a unified Ireland, so it's muddied the political waters.*

Dead To Me: *I heard Dagda's in the country.*

Dead To Me: *I wonder if he's going to deal with the First Lady himself?*

Whistler: *She might not even be the target. This could all be one big witch hunt and we've just been sent in to kill our own kind.*

Eagle Eyes: *My source says otherwise. He heard that Dagda got some information at the beginning of the year about the First Lady, but he didn't believe it. Then he got proof. It's taken a month for him to sneak back into the US.*

Dead To Me: *What interests me the most is that I haven't been sent out for a long time but I know you have.*

Eagle Eyes: *So the US wants the First Lady dead?*

Dead To Me: *I think it's more likely they believe the risk to her safety is low. She's surrounded by Secret Service, don't forget. They don't fuck around.*

Eagle Eyes: *Wonder if he's as good as they say he is.*

Dead To Me: *I know someone who saw him in action.*

Whistler: *Who?*

Dead To Me: *A friend of mine.*

Whistler: *Friend of Dagda or foe?*

Dead To Me: *Definitely foe. He killed her mom.*

FIFTY-NINE

FINN

CALL IT FATE OR LUCK, but my realtor had dragged me across the river to Brooklyn for a supposedly 'once in a lifetime deal' when Aidan rang me.

Standing in a luxury condo in Park Slope, arguing with Eric about his stretching of my principal requirement, 'on the island,' I almost didn't answer, but when I let it ring, and then it disconnected, only for him to try again, I demanded, "What?"

"Finn, we're heading to Greenwood Cemetery."

I stepped away from Eric for some privacy. "Why?"

"Because Da's meeting with the First Lady there."

"So? Conor's toys," I amended for Eric's benefit, "will pick up on whatever's discussed."

"His system's down."

My brow furrowed as I twisted away, ignoring the palatial surroundings of the condo Eric wanted me to buy. "Was he hacked again?"

"No. He said something about a backlog of data, but he's not at his computers to fix it."

"Where the hell is he?"

"He headed to New Jersey. That Lodestar bitch has gone missing. He wanted to find her."

"I'm about five minutes away from Greenwood Cemetery. Want me to check things out?"

"Please. Traffic is crazy. ETA fifteen minutes."

I grunted. "I'll keep you in the loop."

"Thanks, bro. Conor says they're meeting at Paddy's grave."

A thought occurred to me. "What about her security detail?" I questioned with a frown.

"What about it?"

"The woman's got so many men guarding her, Junior, that she probably can't have a shit in private. The Secret Service isn't in the business of fucking around."

"I think that's dramatizing things," he grumbled.

"I don't. And I can't see her detail being okay with her meeting in a fucking graveyard in public." I scowled at my shoes. "This feels like a trap."

"Conor played it back to me. It's her, Finn. I think Da's going to hold what Paddy told him against her."

"Leverage?"

"Yeah."

"For what though?"

"For whatever he wants."

"You're the one who's supposed to be his heir, bro. Any clue what that is?" When he remained silent, I turned to stare out of the condo's bay windows and onto a park in the near distance. "What was the reason for her call?"

"She wanted to know where Michael was."

Eoghan's reply had Junior remarking, "She dug in deep enough to figure out that Michael isn't where Conor's hack says he is. That speaks of someone who cares."

Brennan agreed, "Da held his location over her head. He wants to talk to her, and he's willing to use whatever leverage he's got to get her out in the open."

"Why would he want that?" I demanded.

"Tell him what you heard, Eoghan," Dec inserted.

"According to a friend, the ECD have been targeting the First Lady for a while."

"The friend is a trustworthy source?" I queried.

"Definitely."

"She wanted their tagline in that dishware Aela was making," Dec argued. "She's a friend of the ECD."

"She's a friend of Michael," I countered. "Maybe Keegan blames her for Michelle's death? We know she was there that day."

"I tried to call Da," Junior inserted, "but there was no answer. I think he must have left his phone behind."

"What time's their meeting?" I asked.

"Three on the nose."

I stared down at my watch and grimaced. "Which way's the cemetery?" I demanded of Eric the second I cut the call.

He blinked. "It's just down that road there."

"I want you to find me something near Acuig Corp., Eric. I don't want to cross the river twice a day, do you hear me?" I sniped.

Aoife had just agreed to move out of the Victoria, but only if I vetted the properties first. I didn't have time to be pissing around on Eric's supposed 'once in a lifetime' deals.

"I hear you, Mr. O'Grady."

"You better," I intoned grimly, watching as he gulped and took a step away from me.

Smart man.

I headed out of the apartment, running down the stairs instead of using the elevator when it was taking too long to arrive.

When I was out on the road, I took off at a steady run. It was five to three, so I'd make it there faster if I didn't grab a cab and get stuck in more traffic.

As I ran, I had to admit that the neighborhood was nice. I thought Aoife would like it here, and the condo, while not to my taste in its current style, might be something she appreciated. Sure, I'd have to cross the river for work, but that wasn't much of a sacrifice if she liked it.

Eric would have been better off walking me around the neighborhood than showing me that fucking ugly condo.

When I made it into the cemetery, it took me a second to remember where Paddy was buried. But as I headed in that direction, I saw his crypt in the distance.

Surrounded by angels how it was, you'd have thought the Pope was buried within that tomb and not a mobster.

But the second I saw the crypt, I also saw a lone figure standing by the graveside. He had his back to the road, his head down, and because of the bright white of his hair gleaming in the low sun, I knew it was my father.

He'd been salt and pepper earlier in the year, but now all the darker tones had faded away.

I didn't know if it was because of the breakdown of the family, or if it was learning what had happened to Conor, or if it was the two combined, but Senior was a broken man now. It was clear to see in his stooped shoulders. His withered frame.

Was he sick?

I didn't know.

Lena hadn't told me the last time I'd seen her.

As I approached, I saw a woman standing close by. She was hovering, seeming to watch my father until she stepped out onto the scene.

I assumed it was Elizabeth Davidson, but how the hell she'd escaped her guards, I had no idea. It wasn't like the Secret Service were some two-bit security firm. To have given them the slip would trigger a bunch of protocols that made me wonder if her disappearance had hit the news.

Of course, Aidan was much the same. He had his own security detail as well, and I didn't think they were in the vicinity.

At least, I couldn't see them.

Whatever was going on here, Senior and Elizabeth wanted to keep it under the radar.

But why?

Surging forward with a burst of energy, I finally made it to Paddy's plot, and that was when I saw the woman jolt like she'd been stunned.

She screamed, collapsing like a paper doll into the grass.

I dropped to my knees the second I saw her go down, flinging myself onto the grass to make myself a smaller target.

Then there was a deep cry of pain.

Aidan.

Straining to see what was going on, I happened to see a flash far ahead in the distance.

What was that?

Light flickering against a scope?

Jesus.

Over a thousand yards away, it was only visible because I was scanning the scene.

That was when I truly registered what had happened.

Elizabeth slumped over the grave.

Aidan faced me, but on his front.

I didn't take a chance on the emergency services. Instead, I called in the medics who treated us for a price as I arranged for a car to come and collect us.

It was a Wednesday afternoon, and the place was quiet. But I didn't know if the sounds of sirens would be deafening me soon or not. It depended on whether someone had heard the shots and correctly interpreted what they were.

With that arranged, I crawled over to my father.

Uncertain if the shooter was still there, I rushed as fast as I could, but something I'd heard Eoghan say to him once felt very appropriate at that moment.

'You'll die an old decrepit bastard because only the good die young, Da.'

I knew Eoghan was right.

Aidan Sr. was too young to die.

Yet when I reached his side, and I saw the mess of his back, an uneasy sensation lodged in my gut. It didn't look good, if anything...

Jesus Christ, it was horrific.

I pressed my hand to his shoulder and rasped, "Aidan?"

He groaned. Long and low. Pained. Hurting.

I'd seen him felled by grief a lot this past year, and the sight of him down and injured, my old man, wicked and brash, taken out like he was prey, stirred my temper and triggered my fears like nothing else could.

Managing to shrug out of my coat, I balled it up and pressed it to his back where the bullet had done terrifying amounts of damage.

Turning him over as carefully as I could, I let his weight increase the pressure on my coat, praying that would stem the blood flow. He let out a hiss before, arms flailing, he screamed in agony.

"Da," I intoned grimly. "I need to stem the blood flow."

His voice was weak, a soft slur, as he muttered, "Finn?"

I watched his head flop to the side as he tried to find me, and I dropped down to look at him so he was more comfortable.

"It's me, Da. I got the medics coming in. Don't worry. We'll patch you up soon."

His eyelids fluttered, and for a second, he seemed to stop breathing.

I choked out, "Da? Wake up. It's not your time to die yet, old man."

A whisper of a smile ghosted around his lips and he said on an exhalation, "We always think that, son."

Tears pricked the backs of my eyes. "You still got plenty of Manhattan left to torment."

"Been a bad man, Finn," he whispered, breaking off a second to groan. "I deserve this end."

His pain hit me soul deep, so I whispered, "Come on, Da. You got this. Keep it together. You can't leave Lena. You can't—"

His hand snapped out at that, and he grabbed mine. "Knew I'd end this way. Second I saw her, I knew she'd be my death."

"Lena'd never hurt you," I argued.

His head wobbled like he was trying to shake it. "The ECD... they're poison. Worse than Sparrows. They're believers." Then he smiled, and his teeth were bright red, coated with blood that had me looking up at the road, trying to see if the ambulance I'd ordered had arrived. "I'd still do it though."

"Do what, Da?" I questioned.

"Snatch her. She was so beautiful, Finn," he said, his tone borderline dreamy. "I saw her walking down the stairs about to be announced for the ball, and I knew I couldn't let anyone else see her. All that red hair— I wanted that fire for myself."

"Did you know who she was?"

"I knew her father had a debutante at the ball, and the other women were all milk and water misses." He coughed, but this time it sounded weaker than before. "No passion in them. No fire. I had a feeling she was Cormac's, and I was right." His hand tightened on mine. "She did wrong, Finn. I know she did. But she won't—" He sucked in a shaky breath. "It'll be difficult without me."

I gnawed on the inside of my cheek. "Her boys will watch over her."

He nodded. "My boys are good." He squeezed my hand then cackled gruffly, "The apple fell far from the tree."

When he started coughing again, blood didn't just come up, it spewed out onto the grass.

Eyes averted, I heard the sounds of a vehicle and prayed it was the EMTs, but I recognized Junior's Range Rover.

Aidan's hand squeezed mine, hard enough to hurt, as he whispered, "At least it's not suicide. Could never..." He wheezed. "...die like that. The cathedral... that wasn't how I wanted to go. Thank you... for... saving us."

His words had me tensing. "You're not going anywhere." The way he was talking made me wonder if he was sick.

Blood spattered from between his lips as he ground out, "He gave me just enough time to suffer, but at least I get to say goodbye to you."

His eyelids drooped. "Got scared at the end. Ran like a pussy. But it's better this way."

Every muscle in my body tensed up at that. "You know who did this?" When he didn't answer, I almost shook him. "You knew a shooter was here?"

His hand clenched tightly around mine. "Remember, son, the ECD leaves no man behind, and they won't stop until they avenge their dead."

Casting a look at the cars, I pleaded with them to speed up. "I don't understand."

"Served myself on a platter to them. Lena would never..." He swallowed. "I broke her. I'm the reason she did what she did. The blame rests where it should. I broke up our family. She's paying the price now."

Lost for words, the sounds of doors being flung open drew my attention.

Screaming out a warning, I yelled, "There's a gunman. Active shooter," and watched them all drop to the ground.

Senior's hand squeezed mine again as I watched the others scramble toward me. "They're... here?"

The slurred words were barely understandable, but I squeezed his hand and rasped, "Yeah. They're here."

Eoghan reached us first, then Brennan and Declan. Junior appeared a second later.

Eoghan grabbed something from his pocket, a knife I saw a second later, then after rearranging Da and shoving my coat away, sliced down the back of Senior's. I watched as Brennan started helping, baring the open wounds to our gaze.

Declan grunted at the sight because the damage was extensive.

"Hollow-point bullet," Eoghan grated out, drawing something else from his pocket.

Duct tape.

"You carry that wherever you go?" I bit off.

"In my line of work, yeah."

Senior groaned as his youngest taped up his back then carefully turned him over to deal with his front.

"Where's—" He gulped. "—my boy?"

A wild look appeared in Eoghan's eyes as the tape started shifting against Aidan's blood-slick skin, and I closed mine a second, well aware that if the EMTs didn't get here soon, Aidan would bleed out.

I peered up at the road, praying I'd see Kid's Mini, and when I did, I rasped, "He's coming, Da. He's driving like a lunatic."

His smile lit his face up. "That's—" He sucked in a breath that sounded like a death rattle. "—my boy."

"Fuck," Junior ground out.

Eoghan, Junior, Declan, and Brennan worked hard to tape up the massive crater where the hollow point had done its damage.

I just held our father's hand, but as they worked, Senior told me, "Second you walked into my house, it was like seeing Frank again." He smiled. "I miss him, but I'll see him soon. Paddy's back. You won't be alone—"

"Shut up, Da," Brennan snapped. "You're not allowed to die."

My teeth clenched at that, and I bowed my head, trying not to fucking cry, but Christ, it was impossible.

My throat was thick with tears as I rasped, "He's right, Da. You're not allowed to die."

"Da..." Senior smiled again. That ghostly wisp of a smile. "Look after your mother until she comes to me."

And that was when his eyes closed.

He sucked in the longest breath imaginable before it rattled out, stuttering to a halt.

And I knew, *I knew*, that he was gone.

SIXTY

EOGHAN

I HEARD Conor's scream before he flung himself beside us.

Dead didn't mean dead. People died before surgery all the time. We just had to keep him alive.

We just had to.

Da wasn't allowed to die.

I started CPR, carefully pinching his nose as I pressed my mouth to Da's to breathe for him, as Conor snarled, "Let me help."

Brennan's voice sounded like it came from a distance as he muttered, "Eoghan's got it under control, Kid."

Conor didn't listen. His hands took over for me, letting me focus on getting oxygen to Da's brain.

"Where are the fucking medics?" Declan shrieked.

Finn spat, "They're incoming."

For another ten minutes, Conor and I worked. We didn't stop. We carried on, but when the ambulance finally showed up, I knew it was too late even though Conor was in denial.

When the EMTs rolled up, rushing toward us on the grass verge, Conor got in their way while I slumped back, watching as if I were outside the scene as my father was—

My cheeks ached with how hard I ground my teeth together, and it was quite by chance that I looked at Finn. That our eyes caught and held. That was what opened the gates to grief.

We stared at each other, both of us shaking our heads, trying to reason what had just happened.

Trying to understand.

Da couldn't be dead.

We'd just been bitching about him on the ride over the bridge. About how he liked to waste our fucking time.

But...

This was the opposite of that.

He was gone.

Fucking gone.

"He can't be dead," Conor howled, and when he went to punch the EMT who'd pronounced the time of death, Declan ran over to get in between the two men before it could escalate.

Brennan, on his knees, stared down at the blood-soaked patch of grass where our father had just laid, and he grated out, "It isn't possible."

A shaky breath escaped Aidan, and he whispered, "It *is* possible."

Most days, I hated Da. He'd screwed me over, had me beaten, but...

He wasn't allowed to die.

Finn shuffled over to my side, Brennan and Aidan too.

"Where are his guards?" Aidan rasped.

Finn bowed his head. "I don't know."

"Did you see it happen?" I asked, turning to him.

He kept his face angled down. "I saw them drop."

"And you were seen?"

He nodded. "Yeah."

I tried to keep my gaze veered away from where Da lay, but when Conor screamed again and punched Declan this time, I jumped to my feet and rushed over to them.

Declan and him began beating the shit out of each other, and I leaped into the fray, dragging them apart.

When Conor went for me, I stopped him by hugging him. Dragging him into me. Holding him fast in my arms.

When he sagged into me, I felt the tears that burned my eyes start to fall.

"I was too late."

His sob broke my heart, but I shook my head because the last thing Kid needed was to carry this burden. "You weren't too late. Da should never have come out here. He was exposed."

The words reminded me of the other day. When Inessa had bitched about the number of guards I had on her, and I'd chased her around the apartment again.

I could put a hundred guards on Inessa, but they couldn't stop one of my kind.

Conor hugged me tight, and I held him back just as fiercely, but I twisted him around, trying to figure out where the best vantage point would be from this position. All the while, I was aware that Da was there.

Right at my side.

Silent when he was never silent.

Still when he was never still.

Grief bubbled up inside me, but I dampened it down as I said, "Conor, I need you to not pick a fight with the EMTs."

"They gave up on him—"

"They didn't," I argued. Pulling back, I grabbed his face, forced him to look at me, and rasped, "You didn't see his wound. He was..." I closed my eyes. "He was a goner. I don't know how he survived as long as he did."

"Obstinacy," Declan whispered, drawing my attention to him.

I loosened one arm and grabbed him. We stood in a huddle. The three youngest O'Donnellys. Beside our da. United. Tied together. Bound, just like he always wanted for us.

For a second, none of us said a word, then Conor whispered, "What was his end game?"

"Blackmail." Declan swallowed. "What else?"

"Dumb fuck." I clenched my eyes closed. "How are we supposed to tell Ma?"

Our arms tightened around each other, but it was Conor who said, "Bren."

"This shouldn't be something we lay at his door," Declan argued.

The sounds of the ambulance doors closing and shutting drew my attention, and Conor's too. When he saw the EMTs walking toward the gravesite to check out the First Lady, he shrugged away from me and rushed over to their sides.

"Leave that bitch alone," he snarled. "She's the reason my father's dead."

"Go and stop him from getting into a fight, Declan," I ordered.

"Like that worked before."

"Is that the—" The EMT wobbled on his feet before he dropped to his knees. "That's the First Lady!"

I tuned them all out, ignored Conor and Declan's argument, and I stared at the terrain.

Finding a place I'd use, I returned to Finn's side. "Did you happen to see where the shot came from?"

"I saw a flash of light after I saw them go down." He got to his feet, slowly. Carefully. As if he'd aged in the last couple minutes—*I knew how he fucking felt.* "Over there." He pointed in the direction I'd picked out.

Taking off, I ignored Brennan when he called, "Where are you going?"

A couple seconds later, I heard heavy footsteps and knew from gait alone that Aidan was at my back.

While his knee was better after his surgery, and he could walk without a limp, his run was still more of a hobble than anything else.

As we wended our way through the gravestones and the tombs, I moved closer to where I'd have made my own sniper's nest.

There was no sign of any disturbance. No holes in the grass, no patches of dirt that were mussed, no indication of body weight that had crumpled the lawn. Nothing to prove someone had set up their kit here.

"Eoghan?" Aidan called out.

Gaze flicking over to him, I noticed that he was standing a few feet away from a grave.

Rushing over, I saw he'd found the nest. I turned to look at where my brothers were, the ambulance's lights flashing in the near distance, and I could see this was a perfect vantage spot.

On the ground, however, there was a pamphlet with a knife that cleaved it to the ground.

The phoenix fluttered in the wind.

"*Éire le chéile go deo,*" Aidan rumbled.

"The knife—" My hands itched to drag it out of the ground, but I left the key piece of evidence where it was.

"What is it?" he asked.

"It's a Fairbairn-Sykes fighting knife. They gave them to the SAS. They're a British military branch. Special Forces."

"Does it mean something?"

Fixated on the phoenix, much as he was, I rasped, "They're a calling card."

For a second, he didn't say anything, then he looked over at me. "I used to look forward to this day."

The ache started in my chest. "I did too. He wasn't an easy man."

"He sure as fuck wasn't. I never thought it would happen though. Not like this. Not—"

His words waned, but I got it.

The world was rid of one less psychopath today, but that psychopath left three grandchildren, six sons, and a wife behind.

I tightened my grip on his shoulder, not saying anything, just letting him know that I was there.

In the distance, I saw three helicopters approaching. ETA: 10 minutes.

The Secret Service had woken up to the fact that their protectee had gone missing.

About fucking time.

For the First Lady to have gotten away from her detail, someone high up had to have approved that. Which meant some heads were going to roll by the end of the day, and I didn't intend for ours to be among them.

The biggest murder investigation this country had seen since JFK's assassination was about to start, and the murderer didn't seem too concerned about being caught.

That didn't mean I wanted us to be embroiled in it, so I encouraged Aidan to start moving.

Aidan's gaze peered out into the distance, scanning the horizon for the helicopters much as I had.

As we raced over the grounds, I rasped, "We're going to take the ECD down, aren't we?"

His words were a vow. "We are."

SIXTY-ONE

AOIFE

I FROWNED when my phone lit up with a message at 15:04.

Unknown Sender: *Your mom can finally rest in peace now.*

Nausea bubbled up inside me. It went to war with the fear the message triggered.

Me: *Who is this?*

I didn't get an answer.

My dearest, darling Lena,

I'm pretty sure I know how today will end.

Is it bad that I'm hoping that it will be my last?

I received bad news, my love. The worst. I've been sick for a while, but the death I'm facing is a torture worse than anything I could put someone through.

Maybe that's fitting.

Maybe, after all I've done over the years, that's what I deserve, but I'm not a man who will take my fate lightly. I'm not averse to taking down my enemies as I go.

Eamonn Keegan called me a month ago, asking if a rumor he'd heard about the First Lady was the truth. I didn't have a clue what he was talking about. How could she have helped kill his sister? The man's a lunatic. But she was an out. If he discovered it was you who'd killed her, he wouldn't rest until you were dead.

This way, you're safe.

This way, he'll put me out of my misery. They never leave witnesses behind. I hope he hasn't gone soft in jail. This sickness... ALS... it's not something I want to endure. But I have to believe it's God's plan, and I have to believe this is too.

I love you, Lena.

With all the shit I've done, after all the moves I've pulled as the original filthy fecker, you've stood by my side when I made good decisions and bad.

I never imagined I'd get myself a helpmate when I met you. Never imagined you'd reign by my side like the true queen you are. But our days are done, my darling.

It's Junior's turn now.

Long live the Filthy King and let his star shine brighter than mine ever could.

Enjoy your life, live it to the fullest now you're free of me and the years of illness I had ahead, and know that I will always be waiting for you.

If it's in heaven or in hell, I'll protect you like I never did in life.

Yours forever and a day,
Aidan

To Be Continued In
FILTHY KING
(www.books2read.com/FilthyKing)

AUTHOR NOTE

Hello darlings,

How are you?

I cried. I cried so many times writing this book.

For Aoife, for Finn. For the family. For what should have been and for what could have been. And, love them or hate them, for Aidan Sr. and Lena.

I hope you're ready for FILTHY KING (www.books2read.com/FilthyKing).

I hope you're prepared.

Because I know I'm not.

Now...

The second FILTHY SECRET hits 200 reviews, I'll be dropping a bonus scene in my Diva reader group! You can join here to read it when it happens: www.facebook.com/groups/SerenaAkeroydsDivas

I know you're going to have questions. So, be sure to join my Spoiler room: www.facebook.com/groups/SerenaAkeroydsTeaAndSpoilers Room I'll be in there all release week and will be answering anything that's posted in there.

And I do have a release week giveaway going on here: https://kingsumo.com/g/te02w4/filthy-secret-release-day-event

With that being said, yes, you did come across some names and faces in FILTHY SECRET

These are the books they belong to:

Jen MacNeill (O'Donnelly) & Luciu Valentini - THE
    DON (www.books2read.com/ValentiniOne) &
    THE LADY (www.books2read.com/ValentiniTwo)
Eva Kingston & Martinez - INFILTRATED (*Coming
    soon*)

However, for Infiltrated, you'll have to join my mailing list if you're interested in knowing when and how Eva Kingston earned her notoriety. www.serenaakeroyd.com/Newsletter

Much love, and thank you for reading,

Serena

xoxo

THE CROSSOVER READING ORDER
WITH THE SINNERS & VALENTINIS

FILTHY
FILTHY SINNER
NYX
LINK
FILTHY RICH
SIN
STEEL
FILTHY DARK
CRUZ
MAVERICK
FILTHY SEX
HAWK
FILTHY HOT
STORM
THE DON
THE LADY
FILTHY SECRET
REX
RACHEL
FILTHY KING
FILTHY DISCIPLE
THE CONSIGLIERE

<u>THE ORACLE</u>
<u>LODESTAR</u>
<u>SILENCED</u>
<u>END GAME</u>
<u>FILTHY RICHER</u>

FREE BOOK!

Don't forget to grab your free e-Book!
Secrets & Lies is now free!

Meg's love life was missing a spark until she discovered her need to be dominated. When her fiancé shared the same kink, she thought all her birthdays had come at once, and then she came to learn their relationship was one big fat lie.

Gabe has loved Meg for years, watching her from afar, and always wishing he'd been the one to date her first and not his brother. When he has the chance to have Meg in his bed—even better, tied to it—it's an opportunity he can't refuse.

With disastrous consequences.

Can Gabe make Meg realize she's the one woman he's always wanted? But once secrets and lies have wormed their way into a relationship, is it impossible to establish the firm base of trust needed between lovers, and more importantly, between sub and Sir...?

This story features orgasm control in a BDSM setting.
Secrets & Lies is now free!

CONNECT WITH SERENA

For the latest updates, be sure to check out my website!
But if you'd like to hang out with me and get to know me better, then I'd love to see you in my Diva reader's group where you can find out all the gossip on new releases as and when they happen. You can join here: www.facebook.com/groups/SerenaAkeroydsDivas. Or you can always PM or email me. I love to hear from you guys: serenaakeroyd@gmail.com.

ABOUT THE AUTHOR

I'm a romance novelaholic and I won't touch a book unless I know there's a happy ending. This addiction is what made me craft stories that suit my voracious need for raunchy romance. I love twists and unexpected turns, and my novels all contain sexy guys, dark humor, and hot AF love scenes.

I write MF, menage, and reverse harem (also known as why choose romance,) in both contemporary and paranormal. Some of my stories are darker than others, but I can promise you one thing, you will always get the happy ending your heart needs!